the

REVOLUTIONARY'S
CONFESSION

George Grayson

INTRIGUE PRESS

For information, please contact Intrigue Press, P.O. Box 27553, Philadelphia, PA 19118, 215-753-1270

ISBN 1-890768-21-9

First Printing June, 2000

This book is a work of fiction. Names, characters, places and incidents are either the product of the author's imagination or are used fictitiously. Any resemblance to actual events or locales or persons, living or dead, is entirely coincidental. Although the author and publisher have made every effort to ensure the accuracy and completeness of information contained in this book, we assume no responsibility for errors, inaccuracies, omissions, or any inconsistency herein. Any slights of people, places or organizations are unintentional.

Library of Congress Card Number: 00-102628

10 9 8 7 6 5 4 3 2 1

To Mom and Dad, who taught me how to write and one or two other things as well. And special thanks to Sarah, Allie and Charlie for their patience, love and support.

If there is a revolution, there must be a revolutionary party.
Without a revolutionary party, it is impossible to lead the working class
and the broad masses of the people in defeating imperialism and its
running dogs.

The force at the core leading our cause forward is the
Chinese Communist Party.

—Chairman Mao Tse Tung
(Little Red Book)

PROLOGUE

I am getting older. I have spent so many years criticizing myself. Telling my story so many times, so many ways, always in a way that will satisfy the questioners. They are never satisfied. Each generation brings new questioners, yet always the same questions: Are you Counter-Revolutionary? Did you serve the Landlord Class? Have you reformed your thinking? Have you embraced Chairman Mao Thought? Are you on the Capitalist Road? Are you a Revisionist? A Running Dog? A Feudalist? An Intellectual? A Spy? Are you ready to confess your crimes? Your crimes against the People? Your crimes against the Party?

I have confessed. I still confess. The confessions grow tiresome. I've been forced to invent crimes just to keep fresh, just to keep my persecutors interested. Still, I have never confessed what I confess now: I am a true communist. Perhaps the only one left in China.

Gao asks, "Why do such a thing? Why write anything down? It is evidence. They will certainly find it and use it against you. Are you not concerned? At least for your family?"

I answer Gao with a shrug. "My family is gone. You know that. It is your own safety with which you are concerned. Is it not?"

Gao reddens. "I don't understand, Chen Hai, why you must take such risks."

He turns away. But his words take root. Gao is right of course. The risk is great, though somewhat vague. There is no way for anyone to really profit from what I have written. I have not given anything away, except the fact of my participation. My confession can only be used to punish me further.

Earlier today we dug in the frozen earth because we were hungry, because we were being punished for failing to meet the quota. I know that our Work Team delivered the required amount of sweet potato. But the cadres tell us now, three months after the harvest, that it wasn't enough. That five hundred Jin *of sweet potato failed to find the warehouse in Anqing. Our Work Team is being blamed; theft is suspected unless we may make amends. The cadres tell us that there is still sweet potato in the field, frozen into the ground. Indeed, they are right. Some unripened sweet potato, planted late and surprised by the frost can be found under the thin snow in the south field. We must recover this sweet potato to meet our quota or forfeit one half of our meager ration of rice and oil.*

The leader worked each row with a pick—the only pick for the whole team. We came along behind, scratching the hard earth away from the roots with our hands and pulling them out, one by one. Next to me Gao's fingers bled crimson into the dirt and snow. He ate a sweet potato while no one was watching. He chipped off a piece against a rock and let the freeze melt in his mouth. When the chip had softened, Gao chewed it slowly, ignoring the bitterness of the dirty skin, thankful for anything with some vitamin. Gao hid the mutilated potato in his shirt. He did not share. Gao's action says that he has turned a corner in his mind. That he now exists only for himself and only in the present. In this way Gao, I think, is the emblem for the Party. It too exists only for itself, for its own preservation. The People feed it, but it, in turn, does not nourish the People.

I do not want to become a shell like Gao. I want to preserve the core. I do so in my writing. My chicken scratches here in the margins are, indeed, another confession, but they comprise the story of my real life rather than the one I have crafted for the Party audience. Having this life on paper gives me comfort. It keeps my memories and secrets alive, keeps them from being erased or altered to fit some practical, temporary necessity. It is odd, but true: my secrets are more secure on paper than in my head. But such is the power of the Party to change things. Even our memories can be collectivized.

So despite the risks, and over Gao's objections, I have written it down so that I may look at the words from time to time and remember. I tell Gao that the words are for me and no one else. I am the writer and reader, the actor and audience. I do not want anyone else to read my words. They are a danger to others.

I say to Gao lying next to me, "You must burn these books if I am the first to go. Promise me that you will do so!"

Gao is silent. I think he may be sleeping. But then he turns to look at me in the darkness. His eyes are moist. "Chen Hai," he says—an old man's voice not yet fifty—"I can only promise you that I shall be the first to die."

1

December in Philadelphia

The brass plaque just to the left of the office door informed passersby that the occupant's name was Mr. Samuel Zhang. At the start of his career Sam had been delighted by the formality of that plaque. Seeing it, even if he was just coming back from the men's room, confirmed to him that he had arrived at a pinnacle denied to many. He had loved the firm for splurging on real brass for each of its two hundred associates. It spoke of their commitment to him and his career. They had picked Sam and a handful of others from a competitive field of shiny new law school graduates, and in order to reflect the integrity of that decision, they had etched his name right into the walls of their institution.

Now, several years later, Sam knew that the plaques were impermanent. His name was actually printed on clear adhesive tape that could be pulled off the underlying brass by anyone with unbitten nails. The brass would then be recycled for the next occupant. Such was life at a big law firm—far more transitory than the endless wood paneling and gray hair would suggest. And seeing the plaque these days, with the clear tape just beginning to curl and darken with dust at the edges, was a powerful reminder of his temporal place in the scheme of things, a reminder of the widening crack in his once-solid ambitions as a lawyer at Tew, Logan & Case.

Of course, the crack hadn't grown so wide on its own. It had been fed by a number of factors, most prominently the rapid deterioration of the institution's key man, Bob Silver, Sam's mentor and the reason he had come to Tew Logan in the first place.

Bob Silver had *once* been great, the firm's star rainmaker. Silver had personally interviewed Sam. On that day, Silver had first introduced himself simply as, "Bob, your new boss."

Sam had been taken aback by the tanned, pepper-haired man who held Sam's résumé and law school transcript before him. "Aren't you assuming that I will get this job?" he had asked. "Don't I have to pass muster with the six other partners I'm scheduled to speak with today?"

"Yes, you do," Silver replied. "And you will pass muster, as you say, if you simply do the following thing."

"What's that?"

"Pronounce the name of this venerable law firm correctly. The first name does not rhyme with *pew*. It just sounds like the number two. *Two*, Logan & Case." Silver's smile emboldened Sam.

"Well I appreciate that," Sam had responded, also smiling, "but then I should tell you that my name isn't pronounced *Zang*. The transliteration of the chinese *z-h* is a kind of *J* sound. Samuel *Jang*."

Bob Silver had found the exchange delightful, had roared with laughter, and over the next four and half years Sam was his personal property. Sam did all of Silver's work, often past midnight and over most weekends. In exchange, Silver shielded Sam from the wailing and gnashing of the other partners whose work didn't get done and recommended Sam's efforts at bonus time. It worked well—a symbiotic but not atypical relationship known simply in Philly law firms as the "rabbi system."

So Sam had been grateful for Bob Silver's coattails. Silver was a bit of an ass, but as a rabbi he was protective, even mothering at times. And best of all he was consistently retained to handle the most interesting corporate acquisitions and big-money venture capital deals in Philadelphia. He was considered a genius by clients because he could take any intricate deal structure and make it even more complex. And he was considered a power in the firm because the complexity of his deals generated huge fees. The more complicated Silver made the deal, the bigger the fee. The clients never figured it out, or if they did, they didn't care. They loved him and so did the Tew Logan partners who shared in every dollar he brought in.

Thus it was strange, Sam thought, that the man should let it crumble so. That he should allow his sometime quirkiness to overwhelm him, to grow to obsession.

Perhaps it was being around so much money. Or maybe it was his wife. Sam didn't know the reason, but Silver's behavior had grown increasingly bizarre over the last few months. Enough to add venom to the usual whispers that floated around the cafeteria and between the attorneys' offices and secretaries' desks.

The whispers about Silver had been around right from the start. Within his first week Sam had heard the sneers, the wicked little nickname, "Wanna-be WASP," that followed Silver down the hall. Sam didn't get it at first. Not until a wizened senior associate explained it to him, pointing out how Silver kept his gray hair slightly disheveled, as if he'd just come off the beach, and how he allowed his conservative suits to grow slightly tattered in the way of the bluebloods. Sam began to pick up some details himself. Silver never wore jewelry (unlike many of his partners who celebrated their elevation to partnership with a gold Rolex), and he cultivated old money friendships by joining the right clubs (often after years on a waiting list). He sent his increasingly estranged kids to schools that had served to distinguish Main Line lineage for generations; he advertised his oldest daughter's victories at the Devon Horse Show throughout the firm; and every summer he made a public point of sailing the toniest stretch of the Maine coast for precisely two weeks.

The firm's real WASPs thought nothing of it, but it drove the more orthodox Jewish partners crazy. They were his loudest critics for not acting like what he was: a Philadelphia Jew with a little bit of money. He was supposed to summer on the Jersey Shore—preferably Long Beach Island—not Maine. He was supposed to live north of the city, not west. He was supposed to drive a Mercedes, not a Range Rover. And most importantly, he was supposed to join *their* clubs and support *their* charities rather than the ones favored by those with numerals after their names—names truly etched into the walls of the old Philadelphia institutions.

Sam was from Chicago, not Philadelphia. In Chicago money talked and bloodlines concerned horses. Philadelphia attitudes were new to him. He was surprised that the walls separating cultures and religions were still maintained here though they crumbled elsewhere. He had to be taught that there was something forced, even slightly fraudulent about the emblems that marked Silver's outside life. And still, Sam thought, what does it matter? So what if Silver is reaching for something? Isn't everyone?

Or so he thought then. Silver had changed, his peculiarities and aggressions exaggerated to the point where even Sam, his greatest fan, found them unbearable. The worst of it was that the rabbi system trapped him now, inexorably hitching him to Silver for as long as he practiced law in Philadelphia.

And now, sitting here well past midnight on another Friday night, Sam was on the verge of quitting again. He'd contemplated his options a number of times—either responding to the endless calls from head-hunters seeking to place him at a lesser firm or just going home for a spell and living out of Dad's fridge.

It was so tempting. Just the idea of it cheered him up. But he couldn't do it. Not yet. Sam looked at the notecard tacked to the wall above the phone. He pulled the tack, flipped over the card. For the tenth time that day he read the inspirational message he had written there: *Finish the book. then you can quit!*

It was really the one thought that kept him going. The one thought that made the prospect of dealing with Silver's madness tolerable. Finish the book.

All he had to do really was polish it up a bit. The major work was done: two hundred pages saved on a little diskette. Just a touch of editing and he'd be ready to send it to the literary agents. Then, he knew, he was home free. It would sell. It was too good not to—a unique story with movie rights written all over it.

And when that first check came in, the fat advance on the royalties, then and only then would he march into Silver's office, thank him for teaching and mentoring him, and politely resign. There was no reason not to be polite. No reason to be insolent and angry because in all likelihood, Silver wouldn't even acknowledge Sam. He wouldn't even notice Sam's absence with his thinking so obviously and obsessively occupied elsewhere.

What Silver was thinking was, of course, the question on everyone's lips. He certainly wasn't thinking about his clients. Most of them he had ignored for months. And he wasn't thinking about his billings, because he hadn't sent out any bills. People knew he was thinking about women. His leering commentary made that obvious. And they knew he was thinking about money, because he kept referring to his pay-day being just around the corner. Sometimes the man's ambitions seemed to meld, as when he commented to Sam's secretary on a prospective hire for a summer position, "She's a hot number, Rose, and when my ship comes in, I'll buy ten just like her. Only without the Jersey accent."

Silver's obsessions had Rose calling the man *Gollum*, though never to his face. Sam would return to his office to find a bundle of telephone messages she left on his chair, each reading "Gollum called, Urgent" and spaced only minutes apart. Rose thought it funny, but Sam felt vaguely disturbed. Each message floated a picture in his mind of the twisted wraith from Tolkein's classic— gnawing bones in the darkness, speaking of "my precious." Except now the wraith wore Silver's face and hissed of Main Line mansions filled with models, private islands and yachting runs to Bermuda. All to be purchased upon the completion of his 'project.'

Sam wasn't working on this project. Neither he nor anyone else in the firm knew anything about it. Other partners—big partners like Nina Kracken, the firm chairman (she preferred the title to chairwoman or person), had even approached Sam to discover what occupied Silver's time. But Sam didn't have an answer. In the last weeks the only deal he had knowledge of was FeasCo. And while substantial, the FeasCo deal was not sufficiently complex to keep Silver in the office late at night poring over documents or away at vaguely defined client meetings. FeasCo was a straight-forward corporate acquisition, and as far as Sam knew he was doing most of the work himself. In fact, it was what had him here now on a Friday night with New Year's fast approaching.

FeasCo stood for the Far Eastern and Atlantic Shipping Company—a 150-year-old Philadelphia institution which bragged that it guaranteed every shipment the company had ever handled. Their TV ads showed divers bringing up a thousand crates of porcelain that went down in a 1926 ice storm and delivering the goods to a beaming Tiffany & Co. vice-president, seventy years late but entirely intact. It was a very solid guarantee, unique in the industry and Sam wished he'd never heard of it. It created a lot of extra work for him.

Because of this guarantee, and the fact that FeasCo had boasted of it since 1898, the company maintained on its books a contingent liability fund, a kind of reserve account, specifically for claims like Tiffany's. For every lost shipment over the years, FeasCo calculated an estimate of its value and the cost of its recovery. And there had been, Sam was loath to discover, a lot of lost shipments in the turbulent oceanic and political waters of the twentieth century. In fact the number of lost shipments was so large that ten large cardboard boxes were required just to house all the files. Ten large boxes which the boys from the mail room had dumped in Sam's office on Bob Silver's claim that the client insisted they be reviewed by Monday.

The client was not FeasCo. The client was a Hong Kong investment bank by the name of Jasmine Investments, Ltd. They had offered $350 million to buy FeasCo, all in cash. This was a rich bid, even by Hong Kong standards, and observers in the shipping industry commented that Jasmine must be very optimistic about a business that had seen very stiff, near fatal competition from air freight carriers. But Silver told Sam that Jasmine seemed very sophisticated and they had specifically requested that Tew Logan review the contingent liability fund. The Hong Kong Chinese were not going to buy FeasCo if it meant scouring the oceans for old ships filled with porcelain.

Silver instructed Sam that Jasmine was determined to make a decision on Monday about whether to go ahead with the deal. That meant that Sam was going to have read through the ten dusty boxes *and* produce a descriptive memo by then. It was only Friday; Sam had two days grace, but he was only on box number two.

He slumped in his chair, dispirited. The files in each box were in rough chronological order with a chunk, Sam noticed, of the 1930s missing. Silver had told him not to worry about the '30s yet, but to start with the most recent boxes and move backwards in time. Still, Sam had only made it through to the 1950s, and the Second World War with its thousands of lost ships loomed large ahead.

The vacuums of the night cleaning crew had been silent for about two hours, and the security guard had made his regular pass at midnight. Except for Silver, toiling down the hall on God-knows-what with the woman from Jasmine's San Francisco office, Sam was alone on the thirty-fourth floor.

"Finish the book," Sam mumbled to himself, pulling the file for 1950 from the box at his feet and letting his mind wander as it had all night to his earlier introduction to the woman from Jasmine. He had been quite startled by her, left stuttering by her aggressive bearing and stunning good looks. She had reminded Sam of his sister in those strange moments when he had caught sight of her randomly on the street or in the cafeteria at school and felt the quick pulse of attraction. An attraction that invariably passed when he saw who it was. The two women had in common a sort of Asian radiance—a graceful, airy way of carrying their beauty, self-aware rather than self-conscious, at ease with their place in the world and confident of their ability to move therein.

Silver had introduced her as Helen—no last name. Like Sam's sister, this Helen was forward. She looked men straight in the eye as if testing their strength in the face of her beauty. Sam failed Helen's test. He blushed and turned away from the clear eyes that probed his own. He stammered, "Nice to meet you," said he had better get back to work and watched with envy as Silver had touched her lightly on the elbow and invited her back to his corner office to "go over the numbers again."

That was just before noon, and as far as Sam knew Helen was still here, still in Silver's office, still going over the numbers and still, most certainly, way out of his league.

Sam sighed, checked his watch: 1:00 A.M. He opened the 1950 file and sneezed out a noseful of dust and mildew. Everything he'd looked at tonight had been produced on manual typewriters, much of it on carbon paper, and his fingertips were black from the old print and grime. Streaks of this mixture had gotten on his forehead and temples where he had tried to rub his headache away.

The top document in the 1950 file was dated both 1950 and 1938, causing Sam a moment's confusion. His eyes grew wide as he saw the title of the first report: LOSSES FROM THE SAN JUAN AND CRYSTAL PALACE.

"What the—"

Sam's heart skipped, his breath coming in gasps. Could it be true? The two names together, just like that? Simply coincidence?

Sixty years ago the *San Juan* and *Crystal Palace* were merchant ships running between the United States and China. And just three weeks ago Sam had heard of them for the first time, but not at Tew Logan, and not under circumstances remotely connected to the present acquisition of FeasCo.

Sam didn't believe in coincidence. The notion of coincidence—in the words of his favorite law school professor, Jason Behr—was the refuge of a lazy mind, a relief from the chore of digging for connections.

So what was the connection here? Sam couldn't begin to guess.

He had thought the story of the twin ships fictional, or at least highly embellished by the hallucinations of an old man. He had never believed that he would find corroboration, had never even sought it. And yet here it was, right in front him. The top document on this pile of crap told him, at minimum, that the ships were real. And if the ships were real, then what about the rest of the old man's story?

Sam kept reading.

Loss Report No. 1445   15 March 1938 / 22 March 1950

Vessels: San Juan, Crystal Palace - U.S. Registry
Account: Peabody, Noble & Co., Brokers, Shanghai, New York.
Description of Goods: 5,000 tons of Xi'an Marble, F.O.B. - Philadelphia.
Date of Loss: March 15, 1938
Circumstances of Loss:
March 15, 1938, Stevedores unloaded approximately 3,600 crates from San Juan and Crystal Palace. Crates were placed in clearance area of the Pennsport Marine Terminal, and duly inspected by customs officials. Representatives of Peabody, Noble & Co. presented warehousemen Kevin Shea and Eustace McCarry with identification specified in Bills of Lading. (Bills of Lading required only valid identification as local or mercantile agent of Peabody, Noble & Co.). Terminal service contractor loaded unknown number of trucks with specified cargo. Trucks bore the logo: "Schultz Overland Hauling - Scranton."
August 1, 1950, Oriental gentleman claiming to represent May-ling Soong, a/k/a Madame Chiang Kai-shek, and the Republic of China queried company

personnel at offices at 325 Chestnut regarding the destination of certain cargo shipped aboard the San Juan and Crystal Palace, March, 1938. Claimed that cargo was rare Chinese artifacts stolen from Chinese museums. Gentleman demanded shipping records and information which would help locate the final destination of shipments. When asked which shipment on either vessel he was interested in, the gentleman was unable to specify any contracting party, including Peabody Noble & Co., by name.

Gentleman was not informed that, except for steerage and personal effects, the size of the Peabody, Noble shipment of marble left no room for additional cargo. Gentleman was, however, informed that any shipments made on specified vessels were duly delivered in accordance with the applicable Bills of Lading and that further inquiries must be made in writing and addressed to the company's Vice-President and General Counsel, Dwight Zeeman.

August 2, 1950, Received unsolicited correspondence from U.S. Department of State requesting that any queries made by representatives of foreign governments be referred to them, particularly those concerning far-eastern nations.

August 5, 1950, Received formal demand from Consulate of the Republic of China for information on final destination of all shipments arriving Philadelphia aboard San Juan and Crystal Palace, March, 1938. Demand letter signed, Madame Chiang.

Estimated Cost of Replacement of Goods: Unknown

Estimated Salvage Costs: N/A

Amount Claimed by Loss Party: No formal claim against the company has been entered at this time.

Actions Taken: August 5 demand letter, together with photographic copy of our files, forwarded to Armond J. DuBois, U.S. Department of State. We have received no further correspondence from representatives of the Republic of China. Mr. DuBois stated in telephonic interview with Mr. Zeeman that Madame Chiang denies knowledge of the letter or the activities of any ROC agent claiming title to the cargo aboard the San Juan or Crystal Palace.

We have attempted to identify the Schultz Overland Hauling company, but have found no such entity of record in Scranton, elsewhere in Pennsylvania or the surrounding states. Peabody, Noble & Co. dissolved of record with the Department of State of New York, August 16, 1938.

Future Actions: No further action is planned at this time.

Sam read the audit report, stood up and read it again, just to make sure. He sat down heavily in his chair and rolled it back over the plastic mat. Wow! He could barely get his mind around it: the *San Juan* and *Crystal Palace* were real ships. As was their cargo.

Maybe from habit, maybe from a sense of duty, Sam picked up the phone and dialed Silver's four-digit extension seeking guidance. But he hung up abruptly before the first ring.

This conversation would require forethought. If the old man's tale was to be believed, Sam knew far more than he should. He knew that the mystery man mentioned in the dusty report, the fellow claiming to represent Madame Chiang, wasn't after the five thousand tons of Xian marble on the shipping manifest or, for that matter, precious artifacts stolen from Chinese museums. Sam also thought it unlikely that the visitor was from the Republic of China, the name given in 1949 to the island of Taiwan after Chiang Kai-shek fled there with his entire government. Chances were he was from the mainland, newly communist and marshaling its assets. The question was, did FeasCo or the State Department know all this too? And what about Jasmine Investments, Ltd?

Sam's mind was hitting on all cylinders; his imagination going just as fast on a parallel track. If Jasmine didn't know what was on those ships, Sam could use this opportunity to heat up a trail that had gone cold by 1950. He could pursue the secret revealed in the old man's life story. And he could do it alone, without competition, for no one in the world had the information that he had so recently come by. How could they, when the information was so personal to him?

Then again, what if Jasmine did have a clue?

Is this why we're willing to pay so much for a Philadelphia shipping company running on thin margins? If so, then Sam knew he must tread carefully. *Very* carefully.

So should he call Silver? He suspected that he had to if he wanted answers. And the only line of inquiry ran through Silver because Silver was the only person who could really tell him if Jasmine had an ulterior motive, even if he didn't know exactly what it was.

The only trick, thought Sam as he reached for the handset and suddenly felt a rush at the intrigue of it all, was not to give himself away. Not to Jasmine Investments. And not to Silver.

Silver answered on the first ring, "Yes?"

"Well," Sam started slowly, "I've got something here you should see. It was in those contingent liability boxes."

"Sam, it's one in the morning. Can it wait?"

"Am I on speakerphone?"

"Yes." Silver sounded irritated. But that was normal these days.

"Is the Jasmine representative still here, the one you introduced me to?"

"She's in the ladies room, Sam. What do you want?"

"Do you know if the Jasmine people looked at this stuff?"

"It's *our* job to do the due diligence. I would be surprised if anyone has been through those boxes in fifty years. Jasmine may be aware of one or two items, but they probably don't have a complete picture. One *big* reason for that is that we're still all waiting on your memo." Silver was a master at pointing the finger.

Sam realized he had to risk saying more if he wanted answers. "Have they ever mentioned any specific claims against the company?"

"I don't remember. Like what?"

Sam took a deep breath. "Well . . . for instance . . . and this is just one example, there is this unspecified claim about what might be a stolen shipment of marble that came in two ships from China in the '30s. Thing is—it wasn't marble. An ROC guy shows up later—"

"A what?" Silver interrupted.

"Republic of China, you know, Taiwan. Well, this guy shows up at FeasCo and says it wasn't marble, it was rare artifacts and they want them back."

"Which ships?"

"I believe they were called . . . hold on," Sam rustled some papers, pretending to look through the file. "They were called the *Crystal Palace* and the *San Juan*."

An odd period of silence.

"What kind of artifacts?" Silver's voice had dropped an octave.

"I don't know the details, I was just curious if, for instance . . ." Sam paused for a moment hoping the question sounded random and innocent, ". . . anyone from Jasmine ever mentioned those ships . . . or any others to you?"

☆ ☆ ☆

Bob Silver clicked the MUTE button so that he could hear Sam but Sam could not hear him. There was no one else in his big corner office just now, but he didn't want Sam to hear anything at all, not even his thoughts.

Silver walked to the file cabinets lining the wall beneath the panel of windows overlooking City Hall. He unlocked the cabinet in the middle and saw the three files neatly labeled 1937, 1938, 1939. Just as he left them.

He had deliberately kept these files from Sam, yet somehow the kid had unearthed the names of precisely the two ships he didn't want Sam or anyone else to know anything about. Too damn thorough for his own good, Silver thought, then cursed out loud.

A reflection in the window caused him to jump. Silver shut the cabinet and locked it before turning. It was the woman, back from the bathroom, studying him curiously. Christ, he couldn't let her know. Couldn't let her hear Sam's questions or see his own discomfiture or he would really be in the soup. Both he and Sam were supposed to be ignorant. Just two lawyers from whom, as all clients thought, the juicy details could be kept secret.

Sam was still on the line. He had to tell him something. Silver's mind raced for a solution.

"Hey, Sam?"

No response. "Dammit," Silver said and flicked the MUTE button. "Sam, you there?"

"Yeah . . ."

"Listen, I'm tired. I don't really understand what you're asking me."

"Let me explain . . ."

"No!" Silver said quickly, "Save it! Let's get a drink instead. You, me and the lovely Helen. Down at the Cherry Street Tavern."

"But what about all these boxes? The Monday deadline—"

"Forget it." Silver waved Helen over, hoping for her support, despite the rigorous agenda she had set for the weekend. Surprisingly, she played right along, crossing the room and leaning suggestively toward the phone.

"A drink sounds great! Come on, Sam. Buy a lady a drink."

"Well, all right, I'll meet you there after I— "

"Bullshit!" Silver shouted into the speakerphone, "I'm going to be in your office in five seconds and I expect to see you with your coat on and ready to leave. Understood?"

"Understood, just give me—"

Silver stabbed at the hang-up button, cutting Sam off. He stepped quickly around the great mahogany desk, helped Helen on with her coat, threw on his own. He led her down the hall, clutching her elbow until they reached the elevator bank.

"Hold on a sec," he said to her, moving back the way they came. "Forgot my wallet."

A moment later, Sam looked at him oddly as he entered the kid's small office cluttered with paper and boxes. Sam laughed at him.

"Orange ski gloves with a black cashmere coat?"

Silver grumbled, "It's the latest thing." He moved around the desk to look over Sam's shoulder. "Now what did you want to show me?"

"I thought you were in a rush?"

"Just show me!"

Sam nodded, pulled the 1950 file from beneath some other papers. "As you can see—"

Sam bent low over the document, looking to where he was pointing. Thus he didn't see Silver's orange glove in motion. He didn't see it pull the black Beretta from deep inside the cashmere coat, and he may have only felt the barrel for one curious second as it was pressed against the soft flesh behind the lobe of his right ear. Silver pulled the trigger without hesitation, just as the U.S. Army had taught him. The shot traced diagonally through Sam's brain killing everything it touched, and after a moment, when Sam's body stopped jerking, Silver calmly removed the powder-burned, bloodstained gloves Sam had found so goddam amusing and slid them over the kid's lifeless hands. He gently worked the right index finger through the trigger guard of the Beretta, careful not to touch any of the stains, then noted with satisfaction that the file Sam had shown him was absorbing blood, the old carbon copy disintegrating in the process.

Silver heard footsteps. Felt a rising panic. Could anything give him away? Did he look guilty?

Helen stopped dead in the doorway, her delicate face remarkably composed.

"What happened to him?" She asked in a low, rather abrupt tone.

"I don't really know. I was getting my wallet." Silver looked at her innocently and saw disbelief now cloud her pretty face. He instantly realized she could prove inconvenient, and just as the thought entered his mind, another brilliant idea followed.

"Helen, I think it might be easier for Jasmine Investments if you weren't here when the police came. Unless, of course, you want to be."

Helen looked at him crossly, but said nothing. Silver took her silence as assent, then moved quickly to the secretary's desk where he called the building's security guards and then the police. He then ushered Helen to the elevator bank where security was soon to arrive.

At this time of night, security amounted only to the guard in the lobby, and it took him less than a minute to travel the thirty-four floors. When the elevator door opened, Silver said, "Quick, this way," grabbed the startled guard by the arm and pulled him down the hall. Behind them, Helen took her cue, darted from behind the receptionist's desk and slipped into the elevator that the guard had just vacated. Silver knew that she could proceed unseen and unheard through the grand marble lobby and out the front of the building. And once she was out, she was anonymous. She probably wouldn't see anyone except the homeless man on the corner of Arch Street. And what was he going to say?

When the police arrived at Tew Logan eight minutes later, and after they had taped off the scene and made it their own, Silver gave a teary statement that Sam had been at the office at his request, and that it was his, Bob Silver's fault, that Sam had been so overworked the past few months. Amidst the flashbulbs and milling uniforms, Silver told them that, yes, Sam had sounded down, but not suicidal. He thought that Sam always thrived when things got most difficult. He didn't know about Sam's home life. He knew of no girlfriends, boyfriends or family. That night Sam had called him from down the hall to "show him something." He had heard the shot halfway there, near the conference room. He had run the rest of the way, but there was nothing he could do. He was sure Sam was dead. He couldn't remember if he touched the body. He thought it unlikely. He had called them from the secretary's desk. Why the secretary's desk? Because Sam's phone was covered in blood.

The police wrote everything down, told him that they would have follow-up questions tomorrow. They let him go.

Silver returned to his office. He had one more thing to do before he left for the night. Using his cell phone, Silver dialed the number for Jasmine Investments in Hong Kong. It was the middle of the business day there and the phone was answered in heavily accented English. Silver gave his name and the password he had been instructed to use.

After a series of audible clicks he heard a familiar voice.

"Listen," Silver said quickly to the man called Hu Zhong, "something happened between one of my lawyers here and Helen, the woman you sent to keep an eye on the deal. I don't know what's going on, maybe a romantic thing or something. But my associate, Sam Zhang, is dead. It looks like suicide but she was in there when it happened. I got her out of the building all right. But I don't know where she went from here. Just thought you ought to know."

The man thanked him and Silver hung up feeling satisfied. He could go home now.

His route to the elevator took him past Sam's office, now crowded with police, medical examiners and photographers. As he dodged around a short, swarthy detective he caught sight of the brass plaque announcing Mr. Samuel Zhang's name to the rest of the firm.

I guess they work as tombstones too, Silver thought, seeing himself suddenly surrounded by crypts full of dead and dying lawyers. It spooked him, and he stepped quickly onto the elevator when it came. Not me, he thought while descending toward the underground garage, I'm not going to die in my office. The doors opened and the momentary pang of mortality faded as he saw his new car waiting for him—his fire-red Range Rover which would take him home in style to the petite, once-blonde wife, who had undoubtedly left dinner in the oven and the lights on in the hall so he wouldn't stumble on the stairs.

2

Professor Jason Behr—"Behr" to all but his students—searched among the hundred or so faces comprising this year's Criminal Law class for one that appeared interested in answering his question. He could see that most of them were trying to hide themselves in the brightly lit lecture hall. As his glance passed over a row, heads dropped. Notes were suddenly jotted down, eyes averted. They didn't know that he wasn't interested in calling on anyone today. That he didn't want to hear them admit that they hadn't read the assigned case or give an answer that lamely repeated his question or came out sounding stupid and uninformed. What he sought was that one student who, after a month of silence, had come upon something in the material that struck home, that woke up something in that area of the heart or brain where the sense of justice lies.

He looked over the back rows. Nothing. He looked toward the middle and saw only the usual hand-raisers, the ones who just loved to hear themselves talk, no matter the subject. They would be thrilled to be called on, but he was sick of them—and so was everyone else. That left the front, where the cleverest and shyest students sat because the professors tended to look right over their heads when scanning the room. But all he saw was hair as the students bent their heads into their casebooks. He decided to answer the question concerning the meaning of "entrapment" himself.

But as he started speaking the students began noisily stuffing their notepads and casebooks into backpacks and putting on their winter coats. He figured he had about a minute before the bell rang (the clock hung behind him, and he usually had to guess where he was in the hour by the depth of the glaze over the students' eyes), so he ended his lecture in midsentence and yelled out his good-bye over the cacophony.

The departing students froze, remembering suddenly that he was going on sabbatical. Another professor would take them through the second half of the yearlong course and grade their exams.

Behr thanked them, more or less sincerely, for the spirited quality of their discussions all fall, and when he fell silent, the students dropped their bags and clapped vigorously. He always felt awkward when they did that. Mostly because they did it for *every* professor after *every* course, even the awful ones. He couldn't remember clapping during his law student days, and he suspected that the phenomenon was meant facetiously. Most likely the students were simply happy to be done with him and to be one step closer to the toil of lawyerdom for which they strove so eagerly.

Still, he smiled politely, feigned embarrassment, and hurried to make his exit. As ever, he wasn't quick enough; a couple of the hand-raisers caught him at the podium before he could get his notes stuffed into his briefcase. These people typically asked questions and made follow-up points designed to make them sound intelligent and engaging so he would remember them as such when it came time to write recommendation letters for judicial clerkships and other coveted posts. And, indeed, they were intelligent, their questions searching, their comments timely. But somehow he felt distant from them. He had hated the hand-raisers when he was a student, so why should he like them now?

Finally he freed himself and made the trek through the connected buildings of the University of Pennsylvania Law School complex to his office where Daphne had left a pile of pink phone message slips and other debris on his chair. It was her trick. He couldn't sit without moving the messages and other documents she had left there. And if he moved the pile to sit, physically touching it, he couldn't blame her for not receiving some vital message that lurked therein.

He placed the pile of messages on his desk, sat heavily and ran a tired hand through his brown hair. As he flipped through the morning's messages he chuckled. Daphne refused to organize his messages alphabetically, according to the time they came in or by any other conventional method. No, she ordered the pile according to the relative importance of the caller as she saw it. Thus, his daughter came first; his Mom second; then the publishers of his endless legal treatise, *Theories of Punishment*; then the dean (though he noticed that the new dean often slipped down the pile—maybe she didn't like him); then came fellow law professors; other UPenn faculty; callers Daphne had never heard of; and finally, at the very bottom, students in crisis.

Since Dan, his editor at Little, Brown made the top of the pile, and Behr had no progress to report, he flipped down to the unknowns. He discarded the first three automatically due to the toll-free call back numbers. "1-800" either meant a headhunter trying to place him at a law firm or a publisher trying to get him to assign their casebook for next year's class. That left only one unknown: Kristina Zhang, local number. Since his divorce, and since his inclusion in *Philadelphia Magazine*'s annual list of the city's most eligible bachelors, Behr had gotten a lot of calls from women he didn't know—more than he knew what to do with. But he mostly took the calls and returned the messages. After all, who knew what could happen, good or bad, to a handsome but increasingly lonely law professor not quite past his prime?

Kristina Zhang was not, however, looking for a date.

"Professor Behr, my brother Sam was a student of yours a few years ago." The woman's voice was young, but husky. Roughened, Behr guessed, from too many years of cigarettes.

"Sam Zhang! Sure, I remember Sam."

"Well, he . . . he always spoke highly of you, he . . . said that you had taught him how to think. I don't know what that means except that you were important to him. So we . . . my Dad and me . . . we would like it . . . we think Sam would have liked it . . . if you would say a few words at his funeral."

"Funeral?"

"Sam killed . . . Sam shot himself in the head . . . in his office." Behr could hear deep breaths, maybe controlled sobs between the words. It was sorrow, not cigarettes, that caught in her throat as she described the situation, how she had flown in from Amsterdam and her father from Chicago. How they were going to proceed with a burial in Philadelphia because of the circumstances, because Sam didn't have much connection with Chicago anymore, because Sam had really committed himself to Philly and the friends he made here. He heard in her tone resignation to the loss, stress in the hassle and, he suspected, incredulity.

Behr was stunned into silence. Kristina Zhang repeated her request and he finally stammered his assent, got the details. Yes, Old Pine Presbyterian Church, 400 block of Pine Street, two o'clock, Saturday, okay. She hung up. And only then did he realize, *tomorrow* was Saturday. What would he say to these people?

Behr rubbed his temples, closed his eyes. He could feel the swell coming.

Behr had seen plenty of death over the years, particularly in the early days of his career at the U.S. Attorney's office. This wasn't even his first student death—that had been a vehicular manslaughter in which a second-year Crim Pro student was struck on the Schuylkill Expressway while getting gas for his stranded Buick. But Behr never dealt well with death. Not when it was unexpected.

The sensation had first seized him when his father died, when the Cessna's engine quit thirty miles out over the Atlantic, and the man dropped into the water and out of his life. Behr had been at the airport—home from college—speaking with Dad on the radio, coordinating his fishspotting with the boats racing after a massive school of herring. He had heard his father curse once, say that he loved him, and give his position. And then it had struck the young Jason Behr—the overwhelming claustrophobia, the sudden, familiar, pressing waves that usually only hit him in tight spaces or crowds.

And it hit him again now. Overpowering him. The office clutter and the laden bookshelves and the questions crowding his mind—Sam Zhang? Suicide?

Behr bolted from the office, hurried down the marble steps and away from the law school complex. There was only one remedy for this: clear air. And to find it he drove five miles up Roosevelt Boulevard to Northeast Philadelphia Airport where Dad's old T-34 was hangared.

Even with the drive, it took only thirty minutes for him to check the weather, gas up, go through his preflight and get in the air, where he stayed at fifteen hundred feet until he was well west of Philadelphia and out over the well-groomed farms of Lancaster County. The flight began to work, to free his thinking. And while he went through the checklists, routines and mechanical tasks associated with even a simple low-altitude flight in good weather, he was able to condense the memories of what it was that had made Sam Zhang a special case, his favorite student, the one who made his shift in careers seem worthwhile.

Sam was in the first-year Criminal Law class, and for the first two months he didn't say a word. When Behr called on him, Sam either indicated that he was unprepared or asked that Behr pass on to the next student. He never once raised his hand to volunteer an answer or comment on the material.

But during one morning class, a particularly dead 8:30 A.M. class on the differences between "conspiracy" and certain "attempted" crimes, Mr. Zhang just came alive. He started arguing that charging people with a conspiracy to commit a crime, or an attempt to commit crime in many circumstances where the crime was still a long way from successful completion, was a cynical and ugly way for government to impose its will. It was thought-policing. If you couldn't charge people with actual misdeeds, you charged them with contemplating misdeeds, with thinking thoughts that the government didn't condone. If you trusted government to consistently do the right thing, then you had no problem with government policing the thoughts of its citizenry. You were happy that government had created a category of crime that put people in jail for just planning to hijack an armored car even if they were still far from actually doing it. If you trusted government, you were confident that they would not put people in jail for simply planning a public demonstration or just intending to post religious materials on a synagogue's web site.

Like a good lawyer, Sam had broken down the crime to its elements, and Behr could still picture Sam ticking them off on his fingers. One, an agreement between two or more people; two, to commit either an unlawful act, or a lawful act by unlawful means. Where was the crime? Sam had asked. Had anyone been hurt? All that had transpired was an agreement between two people to do something in the future. Maybe they were just boasting, or verbalizing desires or ambitions over beers. Unlike the crime of attempt, there was really no requirement that the conspirators have taken substantive steps toward the completion of the crime. All they had done was talk, and now they could be arrested and put in jail. Wasn't that, Sam asked, an awfully powerful tool to give to the good ol' boys at the Highway Patrol, the Wayne County Sheriff's Office, the Philadelphia Police or the political hacks at the Justice Department?

When challenged by some of the hand-raisers, Sam had vented a lot more and the ensuing, highly spirited debate had really woken up the class. For the rest of the semester and, indeed, in the four other courses Sam had attended over those three years, Behr had counted on Sam to challenge the suburban myopia of the typically affluent students. He could also count in Sam to inject passion and humor into any discussion. Sam had taught Behr as much about teaching as Behr had taught him about the law, and Behr had been sorry to see him graduate and leave the academic fold. He was even sorrier to see him dead.

So at ten thousand feet, with the jagged ridges of Pennsylvania coal country passing beneath his wings, Behr reified his memories of Sam Zhang into eulogy. And the next day— having arrived late at the grand neoclassical church on Pine Street—he told the small gathering how Sam's sense of history and perspective had taught him and many students a lesson about the application of law to everyday circumstances that they should carry with them for the rest of their careers. Behr told the congregation that Sam had been a rare kind of student and a rare kind of friend, and though he was deeply saddened, he knew that Sam would always be part of their world going forward.

Neither Behr nor the subsequent speaker, who appeared to be Sam's father, mentioned the method of Sam's departure, or for that matter, Tew, Logan & Case. While Sam's father talked, Behr looked over the other people in the nave. There were probably only twenty or so people in attendance, mostly Sam's age, and not more than four were Asian (counting the speaker). He had rather expected the endless family and white flowers typical at other Chinese funerals he had attended. He could understand that suicides typically generated low turnout. But the lack of family members perturbed him sufficiently that after the service and appropriate introductions, he raised the question with Sam's dad,

Dr. Harry Zhang.

"Sam has no other relatives in this country," came the response in an unexpectedly flat and pronounced Midwestern twang. "The boy's grandfather, my father, came over with my mother who died in childbirth while still on board ship. Sam's mother—my ex-wife—moved to California when the kids were very young and the last we heard she had moved back to China. His grandfather fell to cancer last year. His sister though . . ." the man indicated with a nod of his head, "is right over there."

Behr followed Dr. Zhang's nod over the pews and toward the pulpit where in the filtered light of stained glass stood a young woman in profile. She wore a long black dress cut in a Vietnamese *ao dai* style, tight and slit far up the right leg, her hair in a long pigtail worn over the shoulder and no jewelry that Behr could see. Her face was turned away, but in the way she carried herself, Behr sensed—even at a distance—a kind of comfortable elegance he had always found appealing. He mentioned to Dr. Zhang that she—Kristina—had called him and asked if perhaps he could be introduced in person.

The quality of the light, or perhaps the nature of the occasion in which core truths and priorities were being questioned, brought the aesthetic perfection of Kristina Zhang's features into sharp focus. As Behr moved down the aisle he found his heart racing at the sight of her. She had darker skin than her brother and stronger eyebrows, which exaggerated the enormity of her eyes. Large cheekbones made her face broader, giving her the ancient, exotic look of the steppe. She was at least six inches taller than her father, who stood only to Behr's shoulder, and Behr couldn't help notice the athletic, purposeful stance and movements of her body beneath the close-fitting dress.

After her father made a simple introduction, she held Behr's gaze for what seemed more than a minute before speaking.

"Thank you, Professor, I liked your eulogy," she said finally in a low, scratchy voice. "I think I can see some of what Sam saw in you."

Behr mumbled something, still captive to those bright, clear, questioning eyes.

"Yes, Professor, I think you'll do," she said. She handed Behr a card. "Please call the home number later today so that we can arrange to meet. I have a proposition for you. I hope you can accept." And she took her father by the arm and proceeded up the center aisle, past the wooden pews and out the large front doors of the church sanctuary.

Behr watched her go, then looked down and saw, with some surprise, that the card in his hand was one of Sam's business cards from Tew, Logan & Case. Sam's home number was listed just above the e-mail address.

3

It turned out that Sam's apartment was not far from his own federalist townhouse in Society Hill. Sam had lived in neighboring Wash West—so called because it lay to the west of Washington Square. It was an interesting, urbane neighborhood of coffeehouses, ethnic restaurants, record shops and used bookstores stretching from roughly Eighth Street to Broad and from South Street north to Market. Like Society Hill, the buildings were brick and dated from deep in the nineteenth century, but unlike Behr's tonier locale, Wash West was mostly peopled with renters. Artists and actors and waitresses; but also medical students, young lawyers and financial types who, after taking off their suits and professional veneer, wanted to feel young and alive in a way that only city life can offer.

After a detour to fetch, at Kristina's request, a bottle of Ketel One Vodka, a bottle of Schweppes tonic water and a lime, Behr made his way down Pine Street to the converted townhouse at No. 1239 where Sam's apartment occupied the third floor in stylish fashion with skylights, black leather furniture and the largest television Behr had ever seen.

"Sam's bachelor pad," Kristina said flatly with a short wave of her arm toward the fireplace and furry seat covers. She had changed from the funereal *ao dai* into a loose fitting T-shirt and baggy soccer shorts that revealed brown, athletic legs. Seeing her, Behr instantly felt old and regretted his choice of outfit. He looked too professorial in his tweedy sportcoat and brown loafers. Should he have dressed younger? Shown off the rugged Maine looks that had served so well in his collegiate days? He suddenly felt ridiculous even posing the questions. He was an accomplished attorney and lecturer, not a schoolboy, and Kristina Zhang was thinking about her brother and not the way Jason Behr had dressed himself today.

He handed over the brown paper bag with the vodka and fixings and followed Kristina to a slim kitchen where she mixed them each a drink. She polished hers off almost immediately, then made a second with substantially less tonic.

"I'm sorry if I seemed coy at the funeral," she began.

"That's all right."

"It's just that Dad's kinda sheltered. I want him to get over this as quickly as possible."

"Your dad is sheltered?" Behr had never heard a parent described that way.

"Yeah, I guess that's the word." Kristina shrugged and looked sadly toward the floor for a moment. She lifted her head suddenly and fixed her eyes on his. "Do you believe Sam killed himself?"

Behr hesitated a moment before answering, unsure that he could be delicate. "I was surprised when you told me how he . . . how he . . ." Behr reached for a euphemism, "how he ended his . . . Well, let's just say I was surprised. Sam didn't seem like that kind of guy. But," he continued, "I only saw him once after he graduated from Penn, and that was while he was studying for the bar. I really don't know anything about his life at Tew Logan, or anything else. We lost touch. Things could have been tough for him. Tew Logan is reputed to be a sweatshop, particularly for the kind of work he was doing. It wears people down."

"You're talking like a lawyer, hedging your response." Kristina said it sharply, then softened, "But maybe I should tell you more."

She mixed them each another—the vodka was incredibly smooth, even a little sweet—and she beckoned him into the living room and onto an uncomfortably hard, modernist couch. She sat across from him, leaning forward so that her hair, now freed from its earlier tight braid, fell straight down over bare arms and thighs.

"I don't think Sam could have done it. I realize that I've been out of the country for a while," she began. "Since college in fact. But Sam was my twin—I know him, and I know how we were raised. Sam really got into the whole Christian thing because of Baba, our grandfather. And Baba . . ." Kristina took a sip of the drink ". . . well, it turns out he wasn't really our grandfather, but that's another story, I guess. Anyway, he made us go to church; he made us study the Bible. Dad didn't give a shit about religion, but Sam and Baba became close and Sam obeyed his lessons."

Kristina stared intently at him with large, clear eyes, making him feel edgy and self-conscious. He wondered, what was that about Baba not really being their grandfather?

"So that's the first reason Sam didn't kill himself. The church wouldn't have allowed it," she continued. "Even more—Baba wouldn't have allowed it."

"I don't know that I follow you."

Kristina sighed, as if talking to a child. "Look, suicide is not an option for most Christians, least of all Catholics, Calvinists, Presbyterians and anyone else who feels that God gave you your life and it isn't up to you to take it away. The choice is for God to make. Baba really believed in that— he really believed in fate. You couldn't change fate, but you could make the best of it with self-discipline and clear priorities." She leaned back into the oversized chair and continued, "Sam wasn't exactly like Baba, he did things his own way a lot of the time. But underneath, he was Baba's son more than he was Dad's. Whenever a question came up about what he should do—he went to Baba."

"So his Baba didn't tell him to shoot himself in the head?" Behr said and immediately regretted the flip way it came out.

"No," Kristina responded softly. "Baba is dead. But that only means that if Sam had issues—big life issues—he would have asked: What would Baba say? And he knows . . . he knew . . . that Baba would have given him the lecture. Would have told him again about China, about Shanghai when the Japanese gunboats were shooting into the city from the river and people were being crushed under collapsing buildings and being burned alive. And he would have told him that pain and fear are a matter of perspective, and that he could use his imagination to gain the perspective that would make him feel better."

Behr nodded his head, understanding, realizing now that much of Sam's world view had in fact come from the experiences of the grandfather. He struggled off of the low couch and stepped over to the fireplace, then turned toward Kristina who was watching his movements with quick eyes. "I understand," he began in the soft voice and slow cadence he used for students upset about exam results, "that Sam was taught to view the world and his place in it a certain way. But people sometimes snap. Suicide is a decision people come to for a number of reasons—pain, depression, loneliness, hopelessness. Sam was a smart guy, but look around." Behr made a sweeping gesture over the room. "There is no evidence of another occupant here. Sam probably worked sixty, eighty, a hundred hours a week. And when he came home, he came home to an empty apartment. It may have overwhelmed him. Most young lawyers in big law firms just quit. But maybe he couldn't justify quitting to the ghost of his grandfather, maybe he only had one way out."

Kristina suddenly stood and began to pace. "No! I just don't see it." She was shaking her head, causing her black hair to fan out over her back and shoulders. She stopped pacing and sat down again, took a big sip from her drink. "You should also know," she continued, "that Sam and I stayed in touch, by e-mail mostly, but still . . . there was no indication in the e-mails, or when he called, that he was fundamentally unhappy. He complained about the partners and the hours, but he also said that he liked what he was doing. He would tell me about this and that company, weird things that were said in negotiations. How much money people had gotten when they sold the family business. And about that other stuff, about Sam being lonely, I think Sam liked being alone. Even when he was little, he could spend hours in his room playing with one toy, a car or something."

Kristina fell silent at the memory of the little boy playing in his room. Her lips pursed, her head dropped. And from beneath the hair that now fell over her face, Behr heard a single, long sniff.

He gave her some time. After a minute he lowered his head to see her face beneath the hair and asked, "So what would you like me to do?"

Kristina lifted her soft brown eyes to his and blinked once, slowly. "I want you to find out what happened. I want to rely on you for answers the way Sam did."

Behr took a deep breath. It had been a long time since anyone had asked him to be a hero. "Of course," he started, "I want to help you. Please know that. But I don't want you to get your hopes up. Look at me. I'm a law professor. I wear Harris tweed. What do you really think I can do?"

"Mr. Behr, I know something about you." Kristina raised a finger to prevent interruption. "I know that you have not always been a professor. I know that you worked for the Justice Department and I know that you have experience as an investigator. The newspaper accounts of that Pakistani banking thing are filled with quotes from you. Sam showed them to me once, years ago. He kept a little file."

"He did?"

"Yeah. He did. It meant something to Sam. He kept a record of your career. Your press clippings, your quotes."

"Well, mostly I said no comment," Behr quipped.

Kristina put on an annoyed face. "If you don't care to help, I have other resources."

Behr succumbed instantly. It was the pout, the same turn of mouth his daughter affected with stunning success over the past ten years. Behr found himself agreeing to help. Quite effusive really for someone without a clue where to begin.

Kristina excused herself for a moment, and Behr settled with his drink on the windowsill. He looked over Pine Street and the downtown skyline in the distance. It had been almost seven years since he had begun an investigation and the procedures weren't coming to him as automatically as they once did. As he sipped the vodka, he catalogued in his mind what he knew of the circumstances of Sam's death, most of which had come from the City & Region section of the *Philadelphia Inquirer*: One week ago Sam's body was discovered by a partner in the law firm. The partner had heard the shot. It was late on a weekend night. Or maybe just a Friday. The police determined that death was caused by a single, self-inflicted gunshot wound. The gun had been found in the victim's hand.

Not much to go on, thought Behr. But there were still plenty of nuances that could be fleshed out. Notably the whys and the hows. Why kill yourself at work? And, if so, why at that hour? Had he brought the gun from home that day? Had he brought it for that purpose of suicide or was he planning to shoot someone or something else? Did he always carry a gun?

The questions clicked through his head. Kristina came back, this time holding a beer.

"Do you know what Sam was working on when he . . . when it happened?" Behr asked her from his perch on the sill.

"No, not really. My last e-mail from Sam was about three weeks ago. It was really short. He only said something about how he was done with the cable TV company and was into shipping now. I never really paid that much attention to the details."

"Shipping, huh? Like UPS or Federal Express?"

"No, I think it was real ships. Boats. In the ocean."

Behr studied the apartment. He had never met a lawyer who didn't bring his work home with him, so he looked for a briefcase, litigation bag or carton of documents. There was nothing in the living room, or the kitchen. Kristina told him he could check the whole place, and he made his way into the bedroom where, next to a queen-size water bed, he found a small desk with a new looking laptop computer on it. He turned the machine on and fumbled with the touch pad (a poor substitute for the mouse), looking for recent documents. He didn't see much. Just one entry in the word processing program with the pathname:

c:\title.pge.

He called it up on the screen; his curiosity piqued as he read the only two lines on the page:

The Revolutionary's Confession
A Novel By Samuel Zhang

Sam a novelist? Well, Behr thought, why not? Many lawyers try to write; a fair number even succeed. Behr had also tried when he first began his career: a long-winded missive about an affair between a female law professor and a student that turns the law student into an adult and the professor into a schoolgirl. It sucked and he quit. But he had quit after at least a hundred pages of single-spaced text. Sam seemed to have quit after the title page. Unless, of course, he had saved the text of the novel somewhere else.

Behr scanned the area around the computer for disks, looking for anything with the words "novel," "book," or something similar. He found nothing—no disks at all. He called out to Kristina, who was rummaging in the kitchen, that he had found nothing related to Sam's job, but he had found something weird. Kristina came into the bedroom, bent over his shoulder to view the small screen. He could smell a light perfume—flowery, like jasmine tea. It was wonderful and alluring. He wanted to say so but quickly lost the thought as Kristina gasped sharply and clutched his shoulder.

"What?" he asked, startled by her reaction. "What is it? Does this mean something to you?"

Kristina turned, sat on the water bed, not answering.

"Come on, tell me, what is it? What's this *Revolutionary's Confession* anyway?"

4

With Kristina silent, Behr searched the computer's memory for anything similar, for any other written documents at all. Still he found nothing. The hard drive was clean.

Kristina, meanwhile, had neatly flipped herself off of the water bed and returned to the living room. He could hear the sound of doors opening and things being moved. He left Sam's bedroom to find her dragging from a closet in the front hall a large box, which turned out to contain old law books.

"Damn," she said, "what did he do with them?"

"With what?"

She looked at him, hands squared on her hips. "My grandfather's books, my real grandfather."

"Wait a minute! Explain that. What real grandfather?" Behr was surprised by how loud the question came out. His voice was fortified by the Dutch vodka, though he didn't feel drunk. He walked over to where Kristina was standing by the front hall closet, took her hand and gently guided her back to the living room.

"Look," he said gently now, still cradling her hand, "if I'm going to help—and I'm not sure that I can—you have to tell me everything.

And I'd like you to start from the beginning. Start with your grandfather."

Kristina nodded her assent, withdrew her hand from his. She began to talk. She told Behr about the man they had called Baba; how he had made a trip to China while she and Sam were in college; how he had brought some stuff back, though she had never seen it herself. Kristina told Behr as much as she knew about her family history. The real history. Not the one concocted years ago, the one her father had raised them to believe and to which he still ignorantly clung.

She told him that she was skipping some things, some of the personal anecdotes and suspicions she and Sam had entertained but were never able to confirm. But Behr got enough, or at least enough to conclude that the Zhang family story was weird and full of secrets. He had learned from his years in law enforcement that secrets usually hide or generate crimes. In any investigation, you dig first at the light soil, where it looks like people have tried to cover something up. Behr concluded that the Zhangs' story was the place to start, and that it could, just maybe, be integral to the investigation Kristina had commissioned him for.

And though he didn't know it, Professor Behr shared this conclusion with someone else—the man sitting in the white Econoline van parked three floors below. The man who, with his newly purchased microphone and oversized headphones, had picked up Kristina's monologue as it vibrated off the thin windowpanes fronting Pine.

☆ ☆ ☆

Bob Silver hung up the phone in his office and smacked his head twice into the back of his chair. It was like the prisoner's dilemma, he thought, just worse.

In the classic prisoner's dilemma, two crooks get questioned by the police in separate cells. If they both confess, they each get four years. If one crook confesses but the other doesn't, the confessor gets a deal and goes free while the nonconfessing crook gets seven years. If neither one of them confesses, they each get just one year.

So what do you do? Overall, the best result is achieved when both prisoners keep their mouths shut, limiting the aggregate jail time to two years. But in the mind of the individual prisoner, the best strategy is to confess like mad because the upside is complete freedom and the downside is four years, whereas silence yields an upside of one year and a downside of seven. Chances are then that both prisoners will confess with the result that each will spend four years in jail, eight in the aggregate—the worst total for the prisoners and the best for the police.

The question for Silver was like the question for the individual prisoner—do you trust the other guy to make a decision that benefits you both in the aggregate—or do you screw him so that you potentially benefit or at least limit your downside risk? Could screwing the client really save him?

Silver wandered down the hall for some grainy coffee from the machine, ignored his secretary's chatter and returned to his office, shutting the door behind him. True to the habit he developed in complex negotiations, he took out a legal pad and jotted down his options.

A. <u>Action</u>: Eliminate anyone with knowledge or potential knowledge of the ultimate target.

<u>Result</u>: No risk of retribution for leaking information. No need to share. Possibly fail in acquisition of ultimate target because critical information destroyed. Reaction of client?

B. <u>Action</u>: Follow the Zhang sister until her information yields fruit.

<u>Result:</u> Immense wealth, live like a pasha. Expose your deceit, incur wrath of the client for flying solo. Die.

The problem for Silver was that he couldn't really assess the downside risk of the first course of action. What would be the client's reaction if it turned out that the target of all their efforts was lost or inaccessible because of his fuck-up with the Zhang kid? They could get very upset and the downside might be the same as Plan B: they would kill him.

Silver's mind kept coming back to the woman in his office that night. Her cold, calm response to Sam's death confirmed what he had suspected from nearly day one: that Jasmine Investments was no ordinary investment house, that its employees were not just number-crunching bankers. Helen's reaction had not been that of a normal person. She had reacted like a soldier, like someone experienced with death, who analyzed its practical consequences before the horror registered—if the horror registered at all. No—there was something dark and determined about Helen and her employers. And seeing it confirmed for him that he was playing with fire—that the penalty for his employment of Lazlo, for his unauthorized research trips to FeasCo and the National Archives, for the murder of Samuel Zhang, could be death.

That had been Lazlo on the phone just now. The man had just given him key information. It was information the client didn't have because Lazlo was *his* man. Jasmine Investments didn't even know about him. Now Silver had the advantage; he was closer to the goal. But should he act?

Silver drummed his pen hard against the yellow legal pad. He ground his molars and regretted drinking that coffee; his thinking felt scattered and hurried because of it.

He tried to slow his breathing and his heart rate with it. Though he had turned off the office phone, he could still hear both lines ringing incessantly on his secretary's desk. She lied for him, told the clients he was in a meeting. Told his wife he was in a meeting. Told the police, a Detective Leone, "Yes. He *is* in today, just not available at the moment." The computer on the desk flashed an e-mail message sent to the partners on the Executive Committee. Christ, he had forgotten all about that meeting, where—undoubtedly—he would be called on the carpet. He had to tell them something good. Had to dig himself out of the hole and explain away the suicide of his associate. He had to find just the right words. But not now. Now he just had to get out.

Bob Silver grabbed his black cashmere coat and headed into the cold for a trip around Rittenhouse Square. A few blocks south on Eighteenth Street he passed near the familiar red door, felt the weakness, the stirring in his groin and decided a detour down Ranstead Street rather than aimless wandering was what a man really needed. A few moments later—and for the usual fee—his favorite gartered coed handed him a snifter of brandy before sucking him dry.

☆ ☆ ☆

Augustus Lazlo's van was too wide for American Street; he cursed violently at having to follow this guy on foot. He quickly pulled to the side of Spruce and slipped out of the vehicle, careful not to slam the door and draw attention. The cobblestones of the old alley were large and uneven and Lazlo was forced to watch his feet instead of the progress of the quarry who seemingly danced over the stones. Consequently, he almost missed seeing the guy enter a brick row house toward the middle of the block with a short, practiced turn of the key.

Lazlo studied the structure. Surveillance would clearly be a problem. If he couldn't get his van down the street it would be hard to train the microphone array on the house. He could do it from a small car, but a car would block the street and people would constantly be asking him to move. The house backed onto the gardens of the houses on Delancey, so he couldn't get to it that way. Shit, he thought, he would have to go in.

Going into the house was a problem, not because he was inexperienced in breaking and entering (a noted feature of his résumé), but because he worked alone. And if Lazlo was in the house, there would be no one tailing the guy when he went out.

Lazlo stepped closer to get a better view when the guy suddenly reappeared, this time in a leather flight jacket. Lazlo looked for cover, but there was nothing in the narrow street, no recessed doorways or thick trees to make him invisible. So he just kept moving, letting the guy see him, killing his anonymity. Lazlo's target had now fallen into step directly behind him; he could hear leather soles slapping on the cobblestones, gaining on him, forcing him forward. Finally they came to the corner. Lazlo was the first to exit, and he turned left on the chance that the guy would proceed to the shops and restaurants along Second Street. But after a few paces he heard the distinctive footsteps fading in the opposite direction, and Lazlo cursed loudly again. What to do?

He really had no choice. Since he risked being spotted if he continued the tail, now was the time to enter the house and find out about the lucky guy who'd spent the afternoon boozing with Kristina Zhang.

Lazlo retraced his way up American Street, pulling out the ring of master keys as he did so. His seasoned eye had previously noted that the front door bore the simple '70s-era lock of the Kwikset company and Lazlo flipped to the Kwikset master key just as he approached the door. As if he had lived there for twenty years, Lazlo inserted the key and pushed open the door. He even petted the enormous black and white cat who rubbed against his leg before he was even past the threshold.

Once inside Lazlo turned a quick eye over the cavernous living room that had housed the carriages of nineteenth century merchants, the medieval tapestries that lined three walls and the laundry, coats and books sprinkled over the simple furniture. It was interesting but not informative. So he looked around first for today's mail and found it in a small niche in the front hall. It was all addressed to Jason Behr or Professor Behr. Lazlo wrote "J. Behr" in a small notebook before continuing through the house in search of the answering machine. This he found in the kitchen, and he played the messages from a girl who instructed her dad that if he was there he should pick up immediately; someone named Ralph asking about a squash game; a fellow named Hank telling him that the new GPS was in and that he would go ahead and install it in the plane if he could find room on the instrument panel; and, finally, an insurance broker. Lazlo noted down all of these, including the broker and proceeded in search of a desk, or better yet, a computer.

He found both in a garret office on the third floor which opened onto a roof deck overlooking the city. Lazlo scrutinized all aspects of this room. He noted the diplomas on the wall from some Maine college he had never heard of and the University of Chicago Law School. He noted the framed letter granting Behr his appointment to the U.S. Attorney's Office for the Southern District of New York, the framed letter next to that granting Behr the Saul R. Golding Chair in Criminal Law at the University of Pennsylvania Law School, and the two framed pictures of Behr glad-handing former presidents—first Ronald Reagan, then George Bush.

The professor looked younger in these pictures, but not much younger. If anything, the guy was in better shape now, trimmer with more humor in his expression. The guy in the pictures, though good-looking in a square-jawed, Germanic kind of way, also looked grim. As if the weight of the world was on his shoulders and Bush was thanking him for carrying the load. Lazlo decided he didn't like that expression. Serious people were far more dangerous and unpredictable than flaky ones. They tended not to let go. He thought he might mention this to Silver.

Lazlo now turned his attention to the desk hidden beneath a mass of paper, books and file folders. He fished in the pile and found that it contained copies of criminal law cases, articles written by other law professors and newspaper accounts of some of the more horrific local crimes of the past few years, only one of which Lazlo could claim credit for.

The computer yielded some personal correspondence and a few hundred pages of something called *Theories of Punishment*. Lazlo managed one page before snorting derisively and switching off the machine.

So far this guy didn't appear too threatening to whatever Silver was doing. Jason Behr was a professor with hopeful ideals who lived alone and had a daughter somewhere. He had been in government but, more importantly, he wasn't now. So what was his story? Why was he involved? Good Samaritan? Were there really any John Waynes left in the world? Lazlo felt he needed some more personal information and was about to head to the bedroom for a peek in the nightstand when he heard the rattle of the front door key and the fast feet of the cat padding down the stairs to greet its master.

Lazlo swore sharply for the third time that day. He went for the sliding glass door, fumbled for a moment with the latch, then headed into the cold—out onto the roof deck with its commanding view of the Ben Franklin Bridge and unfortunate exposure to the wet chill whipping off the Delaware River. Slowly, quietly, he slid the door closed behind him, leaving the lock open, and turned his attention to the deck to look for suitable cover. A large object under a tarpaulin immediately caught his eye. He moved around behind it, squatted and cursed again as the full force of the winter wind struck his face and burned his eyes.

From his position he could see that the back of the professor's house dropped three flights to a brick patio that was completely surrounded by more brick walls and gardens. No exit there. On either side of the house stood other, similar sized houses. He could crawl over the roofs, but then what? They also had sheer, three-story drops. Getting off the roof therefore meant descending through a house, either Behr's or someone else's. But he didn't know who might be in those houses. If their owners spotted him and called the cops, he would have more significant problems than the professor.

He wanted to wait on Behr, but the wind and cold were getting to him. He peeked under the tarpaulin and saw that it concealed a decent-sized hot tub, drained for the season. A temporary solution, he thought, then pulled back half of the tarp and slipped into the molded plastic clamshell, curling himself into a fetal position at the bottom.

Shivering and cursing with his face pressed against the cold plastic, Lazlo waited for the sound of the front door, hoping the man had run out of cat food and needed to make a trip to the store. But he didn't hear the front door open or any other noise from the house except, perhaps, the hum of the television. The son of a bitch had probably camped down for the night.

Lazlo tried to warm himself; he rubbed his arms vigorously; he tried to imagine the warmth of this hot tub in summer. But he couldn't see himself in there. He could only picture Behr in the tub. Laughing, face turned to a yellow sun while lovely young law students climbed out of the broth to fetch more champagne. Lazlo found himself dwelling on the image—he couldn't shake it, and he began to hate Behr because of it.

5

January 4
William F. Ruddle
Under Secretary for International Affairs
Department of Treasury
1500 Pennsylvania Avenue, NW
Washington D.C. 20220

Dear Bill:

This letter serves notice of my resignation from the office of Deputy Assistant Secretary for Asia, the Americas and Africa. This resignation shall be effective from the date above written.

I realize that this letter may come as somewhat of a surprise, and I apologize for not giving you and the department better warning of my departure. Unfortunately, family matters make it impossible to give my current duties the concentration they deserve.

It has been an honor and pleasure to serve you and the American people, and I would like you, in particular, to know that I am leaving with a heavy heart. I know that our efforts to stabilize the present financial turmoil in Asia are not complete and require much additional attention. I only wish that I could participate further.

I cannot adequately express my appreciation to you for recommending me to this appointment except to say THANK YOU for the most interesting and fulfilling years of my professional career.

Good luck with everything!

Best Regards,
Michael Antonetti.

After reading Antonetti's letter twice through, Under Secretary Ruddle made two calls. First he tried Antonetti—who was unavailable. Then he called his boss, the secretary, knowing he would get through on the intercom.

"What's up, Bill?" Treasury Secretary Cyril M. Stephanos asked hurriedly.

"It's happening. Just like the NSC guys said it would!" Bill Ruddle blurted out the words forgetting for a moment to hide the grating South Boston accent the secretary so disliked.

"Bill, slow down, okay? Tell me who-what-when."

"Antonetti! It's Antonetti. He's gone. I got his letter in my hand. He cites family reasons, but I know it's bullshit. He never once mentioned his family when on the job. Listen to this." Ruddle read the text of Antonetti's letter over the phone.

Treasury Secretary Stephanos heard him out before responding: "Bill, you know as well as I do that people don't stay in any job that long in D.C. Their priorities change, they get better offers, their wives get better offers, whatever." He was starting to get annoyed. He wanted to get the news from a more rational source.

But Ruddle was heated: "No, not Antonetti. I send people all over the world for months at a time. Most of them complain, but not Antonetti. He ate up this job like it was candy. Someone got to him Cy— I know it, and I want an investigation. An investigation by *our* guys."

"Forget it," Stephanos said flatly. "We don't have the resources. If you want to find out why Antonetti quit, go ask him. Shit, man, he's *your* friend."

"I would if I could. But I don't know where he is." Ruddle exhaled loudly and Secretary Stephanos imagined that he could smell the corned beef the guy had for lunch. Ruddle continued, "I think you're making another mistake Cy. I can't say it plainer than that."

After hanging up on the secretary, Bill Ruddle rushed down the hall to confront Antonetti's assistant. She didn't tell him much. Apparently his resignation letter was the last thing he had given her that day. Then he had just put on his coat and left. He hadn't said where. Oddly, he hadn't said anything at all.

☆ ☆ ☆

Treasury Secretary Cy Stephanos had a few options and, counter to what he told Ruddle, numerous resources at his disposal. Under his direct jurisdiction he had the Secret Service, the Bureau of Alcohol, Tobacco and Firearms, Customs, the IRS and the Financial Crimes Enforcement Network. He decided, however, against involving any of these agencies directly. After his first year in office, he had created an interdepartmental task force whose stated mission was to oversee and coordinate the investigative activities of the Treasury Department and liaise with other branches of government. But in Stephanos' mind their true mission was to support and protect him and the integrity of his office in the political and financial arenas. He had wanted to call this elite group of agents the *Varangian Guard* after the Russian mercenaries who had shielded generations of Byzantine emperors that the Stephanos family looked upon as ancestors. He had, however, settled for the Vanguard after some of the less imaginative agents scoffed at the medievalism of the other name.

It was the Vanguard he called with the Antonetti resignation and the instruction to keep any resulting conclusions away from Ruddle, a loose cannon at best.

☆ ☆ ☆

Though he couldn't describe it as a good mood, Behr did feel purposeful, engaged, and more than a little spellbound by Kristina Zhang. Returning home along Pine Street, he had been so mesmerized by his thoughts of her and his possible lines of investigative pursuit that he had been almost struck by a slow moving van when he stepped into the street against the light. And even after he got home it took a minute to collect himself before he could prioritize the evening's tasks.

There were a handful of people he should call for general information. He should get hold of his buddies at Homicide to see if they were pursuing this at all. Then he should look up those of his students who had taken jobs at Tew Logan to get the scoop on Sam—who he worked for and what he was working on. He also shouldn't forget to follow up the suicide angle. No matter what Kristina said, suicide was always a possibility for an overworked lawyer. The Philadelphia Bar suffered at least a couple a year.

And then there was the question of the manuscript. Behr couldn't believe that Sam would have written a title page with nothing else. Maybe some budding novelists did that the way schoolgirls practiced writing their ideal married names in rolling script. But from what he could remember, Sam wasn't the dreamy schoolgirl type. No, Sam had probably written something and saved it to a disk. So where was the disk? Behr thought it might still be in Sam's office at Tew Logan. He would have to search the place, if only to rule out the possibility that it was there.

After a quick trip to the Super Fresh to get some kibble for the cat (his ex-wife's thoughtful legacy), Behr settled at the kitchen table to make some calls. As it was Saturday evening he found himself leaving messages. He had taken the law students' numbers from the Penn Alumni Directory. Detective Leone's number he had called up from memory. He also left a message for a woman he had recently met at a dinner party who specialized in the psychiatric treatment of certain types of professionals—mostly lawyers and options traders at the Philadelphia Stock Exchange. He wanted to ask her about suicide.

Now comfortable that he had put some of the wheels in motion, and not sure what to do from here—except break into Tew Logan—Behr considered the evening ahead. Having long ago exhausted the hospitality of his married friends (whom he had befriended when he was married himself), he had only a handful of options to amuse himself. These options (perhaps heading for South Street or the flashy new nightspots along Chestnut, a trip to the movies, or a nightflight over Atlantic City) he rejected *en masse* with an emphatic "nah," expressed loudly enough to wake the cat. This animal then followed him over to the wet bar where he poured half a glass of single-batch bourbon over a lone ice cube and flicked on the TV.

The twenty-four hour news channel was focused tonight, as it had been for months, on the two principal stories of the year—the President's libido and the continuing financial meltdown in Asia. A dead-serious news anchor noted that the Japanese had seen three major banks collapse and that more were on the brink.

Everyone thought the Asian economies had turned the corner until the Chinese suddenly entered the fray by floating their export trading currency, known officially as foreign exchange certificates (FEC) or, more simply, as the *yuan*. Floating the yuan had brought so much liquidity to the market, that currency traders and central government banks, including the US, had panicked and sold other Asian currencies, causing prices to plummet across the board.

No one was sure why the Chinese thought bringing the yuan to the international currency markets at this moment was a good idea. They had taken everyone by surprise. The yuan had been a highly restricted commodity.

As of a week ago, there was only one place in the world to get yuan, and that was from the Bank of China. By contrast, if you wanted yen, rupiah, won or any other currency in the world, you called your broker and placed an order.

Then, last Tuesday, without any real warning to the financial markets or treasury officials around the world, the Chinese Finance Minister announced that corporations earning yuan could now take their yuan home with them, and that the Bank of China and other mainland banks would be purchasing and selling yuan on the open markets. Markets in Chicago, London and Tokyo quickly made room for yuan denominated contracts and currency traders began speculating wildly. Money that had been tied up in yen and other Asian currencies was pulled out and placed in the yuan. The result was a deep plunge in the value of Asian currencies and the appreciation of the yuan.

Behr loved this stuff; he had no particular stake in the economic future of Asia and he watched the report with fascination. He loved thinking about the watery flow of money, and he still dreamed occasionally of another life as a free-wheeling currency trader with millions—billions at stake. He watched mesmerized as the images and sound bites flicked by. Treasury officials and central bankers from the EU, US and Asia—with sleepless eyes and dour faces—making speeches about the fundamentals, the soundness of their economies, the distortions caused by undue speculation. The show ended with a clip of the U.S. Treasury Secretary, the large and very bald Cyril Stephanos—a man Behr knew from personal experience to be dead right about ninety-eighty percent of the time—speculating that the Chinese had effectively prevented the three-year spread of Asian flu from infecting them by taking the offensive. Though knowing if that was their true intention was impossible to say because, Stephanos pointed out, the Chinese were not talking.

The hour turned, and deep concerns over international finance were suddenly replaced with burning questions regarding this year's Emmy nominations and the gross box office receipts of the Christmas season's blockbuster movies.

Behr listened to the simple chatter of the show's spokesmodel for a minute and rose to refill his whiskey. Crossing from the couch to the wet bar he noticed the cat mewing by the front door. He groaned. Early mewing, he had learned, called for a high level of strategic decision making. Letting the cat out now meant letting it in at some point too. And the cat usually wanted to come in at four in the morning. If not let in immediately, he would climb to the ledge outside Behr's second floor bedroom, scratch at the windowpane until Behr awoke in tremendous distemper and opened the window.

On the other hand, refusing to let the cat *out* would greatly agitate it. It would whine and moan by the front door for at least forty minutes. Then angry and disgusted at Behr's incivility, it would slink down to the basement and feast on extension cords and rubber bands. Once sated, the creature would creep silently up the stairs to settle on the Persian living room rug where it would spend the rest of the evening noisily throwing up hairballs. Long rubbery ones which, to Behr's horror, could not be effectively removed when wet. For two days he would be stepping around these stinky sausages until they were dry enough to be removed with a spatula and an entire role of paper towels.

With a few unkind thoughts directed toward his ex-wife, Behr decided to let the cat out. He opened the front door wide, made a servile bow. The cat haughtily raised its tail and crossed the threshold. Behr resisted, but was sorely tempted to kick that arrogant backside. He settled for slamming the door, hoping that would sufficiently convey his distaste. Now truly alone, he succeeded in pouring another drink without spilling, switched off the TV with the remote control and made his way to the second floor bathroom.

☆ ☆ ☆

On the roof Lazlo heard the slam of the front door and breathed a sigh of relief. Finally! The professor was gone. Stiff with cold, Lazlo wriggled out of the tub awkwardly. He replaced the tarp, then stepped to the sliding door and listened for any signs of occupancy.

Not a peep.

Lazlo slid back the door and slipped into the office. He listened again to the silence of the house, took a peek around the professor's office for anything he might have missed and then moved to the top of the steps—so far so good. He moved quickly down the steep eighteenth-century stairs, which creaked sharply with each footfall.

☆ ☆ ☆

Behr—just settled in the bathroom—heard the creak of the stairs and knew that it was no damn cat. Too enraged at the interruption for fright, Behr buckled his pants and threw open the door to the landing. The intruder, a stocky, Eastern-European looking man, was still half-way up the stairwell, not far away. The guy had a height advantage and knew it. He launched himself down the steps in a flying kick that caught Behr in the chest and sent him tumbling backwards through the doorway into the bedroom. The crack of Behr's head against the old oak floor stunned him, and he missed seeing the man approach.

Now the guy was right over him. Behr felt a knee land hard on his stomach. The blow pushed the air out of his lungs and bilious whiskey up into his throat. It hurt like hell. It also woke him up. And when the dark intruder reached to grab Behr by the neck to steady a punch to the face, Behr got hold of his wrist and pulled sharply forward, throwing the man off-balance.

He could move now, and with a wrestler's flip of the shoulders, Behr twisted himself out and over his attacker; he grabbed an arm. He yanked it back sharply, once, then twice, then again until he heard the crunch of a shoulder dislocating and an anguished cry.

Behr leaned into the hold, close to the man's ear. "What do you want?" He screamed at the ear, "Goddamn it, tell me or I'll pull this arm right off!"

"Go to hell!" the man breathed, and with a strength that caught Behr by surprise, suddenly pushed himself to his knees.

Before Behr knew it, the man had lurched sideways. He was standing now, and he tugged his limp arm from Behr's grasp.

Behr was thrown onto his back again by the man's sudden motion, and though he saw it coming, could not shield against the kick. It got him straight in the balls— Behr's hands went to his groin, he lost his balance, fell to his side.

His most sensitive nerve had been hit with a sledgehammer—he imagined Eastern European boots—and the memories of every previous injustice to the area ballooned to the surface: a baseball thrown by Dad, a lobster trap swinging from the winch, a kick from his ex-wife after the first custody hearing. Why, he wondered, why did they always have to get him in the balls?

Behr watched the man, awaiting the next blow but momentarily paralyzed against it. The man seemed confused. He was standing there, just looking down at Behr, rubbing his shoulder and occasionally cradling the limp arm that hung from it. Why didn't he act? Surely he had come here for something?

Now the man spoke. The accent was South Jersey. "Give me your wallet! Do it now, you miserable fuck, before I crush your skull!"

Behr saw the foot go back, and he curled to protect his groin. He felt it land in his ribs. Something cracked.

He wanted to tell the man that the wallet was by the front door; he started to say so, but he puked instead. He could feel the wet vomit slowly flowing under his face where it rested against the coarse wooden planks. It smelled of sweet bourbon and stomach acid. The pain in his crotch was overwhelming—a blackness in the center of his world, growing to consume him. His nervous system was short-circuited, his breathing irregular, his muscles not responding. He wanted to sleep, he wanted to throw up again, he wanted to drink water. But all he could manage was to remain conscious and curl himself tighter against the next kick.

The kick didn't come.

Behr opened his eyes and dared to look around. Had the guy moved around behind him? Behr lifted his head slightly, turning to look for feet and legs. He didn't see them—didn't see anything, just the room. And except for the spreading vomit on the floor, the room seemed unchanged. The small TV and VCR were in their place across from the big sleigh bed, the nightstands and closet doors appeared shut, as did the windows.

Using the door frame, Behr hoisted himself vertical, maintaining a wide stance. He stepped gingerly onto the landing and looked down the stairwell. He saw no one. He risked a step.

And then another. And then realized his mistake. He wasn't ready for the motion.

His body was rebelling—sending bolts of pain shooting from his crotch through his cracked ribs and up into his head. Behr lost his balance, teetered for one terrifying moment, then skidded head-first down the hard wooden steps. Now sprawled at the base, his torso wrapped in pain, Behr gasped for breath and looked again for the intruder. He could see from his position that the wallet he had left on the sideboard in the foyer was gone. The front door was wide open. He stretched his neck, trying to see out the front door. But he didn't see the swarthy little man. No—all he saw was the cat, peering in at him from the sidewalk. The damn thing appeared to be smiling.

6

"We're watching them right now and we're not the only ones," the man said into the palm-sized digital handset. "There is another vehicle approximately forty yards down the block which could easily be surveillance."

"What makes you think that?" responded the voice on the phone.

"It's a Bell Atlantic van, it hasn't moved for two hours, and no one has gotten in or out."

"They're union. Maybe the guy is sleeping?"

"Could be, but the kicker is the side window in the back. Bell Atlantic wouldn't spring for vans with extra windows. It's just something else that can break."

"Have you run the plate?"

"Yeah, the plate belongs to Bell Atlantic all right, but that doesn't mean anything. They coulda stolen the plate."

"Well, keep an eye on the van. But don't follow it if it separates from the Antonetti kids. They're the priority here, remember that."

"Yes, sir!" The man closed the handset on the beautiful little Qualcomm phone and resumed his observation of the pricey Chevy Chase school and its stylish tenants.

☆ ☆ ☆

Silver self-consciously ran a hand through his hair. He hadn't gotten it cut in some time and he felt suddenly shaggy and unkempt compared to the four other partners gathered around the massive walnut table that had cost them over forty-thousand dollars and a lot of argument. They, of course, were the model of lawyerly fashion chic. Directly across from him Murray sported a tight, custom-made monogrammed shirt fastened with gold cuff links in the shape of seven-irons. Next to Murray sat Beloit who never took off his jacket, even in summer, and was showing off a new pinstripe to go with his shiny manicure. One seat farther down, Adelman was fingering some kind of European purse for men, and next to him Jeremy Lake was vigorously masturbating his goatee. Since his divorce, Lake had gone through a textbook midlife crisis—or so he claimed despite the absence of visible evidence of crisis, or even mild discomfort on his part. He had acquired the obligatory Porsche (but with automatic transmission), a fashionable pied-à-terre on Rittenhouse Square, and—as Silver knew from his secretary's gossip pipeline—a nasty case of genital herpes. Silver could smell the guy's sweet musky cologne at a distance of three leather chairs and one broad table top, and he wrinkled his nose. This meeting was going to suck.

"Thank you, gentlemen, for being on time for once," Nina Kracken said as she marched into the conference room. She was fifteen minutes late for the meeting she had called herself. But that was the prerogative of the newly elected chairman of the firm and the highest billing partner in Tew Logan history.

"You're welcome, Nina," Lake said with a flirtatious lilt, pretending he wasn't as terrified as the rest of them of this five-foot demon in blonde.

"This is going to be a short meeting because I've got to be somewhere at nine." Nina Kracken sat quickly at the head of the table. "We all know why we're here. We can't have associates shooting themselves in their offices," she turned and glared at Silver with hard blue eyes, "can we, Bob?"

The other partners of the Executive Committee all looked at Silver, waiting for his explanation of the first suicide in Tew Logan history actually committed on the premises. Silver could hear their lips smacking. They knew that if he played this wrong, Kracken would drop him from the Executive Committee, and if she did that, he would sink—turn into just another low-level partner, scratching out a living.

He had to avoid her displeasure. He was already skating on thin ice. He had ignored his practice for months while pursuing the cargo of the *San Juan* and *Crystal Palace,* and he had alienated his partners in the process. Still, he didn't need to be completely obsequious yet. He still had leverage; some of the firm's biggest clients were his. They had initially come to Tew Logan instead of New York for *his* expertise, and they would just as soon go back to the New York law factories if he told them to. That was the ace he had always held over the bastards—the one card. And looking at them now, circling the table with shark-toothed grins at the smell of his blood, he thought it was probably time to play it.

"Nina," he began, eyes wide, hands folded in front of him as if in prayer, "I was sickened by Sam Zhang's suicide. Just sickened. Over the past two days I have thought of nothing else. I've come to the conclusion that I was the target of his bullet as much as he was. He meant for *me* to find him bleeding . . . meant for me to see pieces of his brain scattered all over the desk. More than anything, I think he meant for me to feel guilt and grief. And to question everything I do. He meant for *all* of us to question everything . . . everything that Tew Logan represents." Silver paused, making deliberate eye contact with each person in the room, allowing them to see the pain in eyes. "I worked the kid hard for four plus years. I should have seen the signs. I know . . . I know that I failed him. And by failing him I have failed everyone here." Silver now lowered his head, chin to chest, so that all could see the depth of his debasement, the personal horror driving his epiphany.

"We all know you're sorry, Bob," Jeremy Lake said, assuming Nina Kracken's sarcastic tone, "but now what? What are you going to do to keep associates from quitting and more importantly, our clients from questioning the way we practice law?"

Silver began, "Well, I—"

Lake cut him off. "Look, Bob, this thing made the papers. I've got clients calling me asking me what kind of outfit we're running here."

Silver looked right at Lake, wondering why Lake would be the first to be confrontational. Maybe the rumor was true after all, thought Silver. Maybe he was sleeping with Kracken. Whatever. It was time to drop the bomb.

"Since you ask, Jeremy, I'm going to resign. I am prepared to wind down my practice by the end of the fiscal quarter. At that time, I ask that the firm make arrangements to repurchase my partnership interest in accordance with our partnership agreement." Silver said this quietly, trying to sound sincere and committed to a drastic course of action. Again he made eye contact with all the key players, with Lake and Kracken and Murray.

Twenty seconds, he thought. If it takes them more than twenty seconds to respond, I've lost.

He had to wait less than ten before hearing the gamble pay off.

"Don't be an asshole, Bob!" It was Nina Kracken. "No one wants you to leave. You're worth too much to the firm. What Jeremy meant was, are you going to make a speech to the associates, or issue a statement over the e-mail or do some fucking thing to calm everyone down and keep their tongues from wagging?"

Silver suppressed a smile. "Nina, I appreciate your vote, as ever. But this incident has got me questioning my priorities. I don't know if what I've been doing every day is worth it. I sat in my office all day and asked myself: Is it worth the neglect that my family has suffered, that all our families have suffered? Is it worth the silent pain of our associates? You know, they work much harder than we ever did at that age. And is it worth the sacrifice of our outside interests? Let me tell you, I went home the other night, after the . . . well, after the police were done, and went around my study and saw all the things that used to interest me, that used to define me . . . books and paintings and music . . . I haven't touched those things in years."

Silver studied his audience. He could see jaw muscles tensing, hands fidgeting, brows tightening. Yes, they were worried now. Worried that he would really leave and take almost seven million in annual client billings with him. "I can't say that my decision is final, but I am ninety-nine percent of the way there. I will continue to practice law, but at a small firm, a corporate boutique that doesn't make such demands on my time or the life of its associates. I've got some prospects lined up. I just can't be a part of this anymore." Maybe he was laying it on a little thick, but this was fun. Adelman was visibly squirming—he had the most to lose since most of his time was spent litigating an antitrust case for a Silver client. And Kracken, wow, the pupils of her eyes had contracted to small hard dots. She looked fierce and menacing and Silver allowed himself the juicy memory of her—once, years ago—standing over him in a black leather bodysuit. He loved that image, but dismissed it quickly. He had work to do.

"So there it is. After twenty-five years, I think it is time to say good-bye."

"What are they going to pay you, Bob?" It was Jeremy Lake again, looking for ulterior motives and playing right into Silver's hand. What an idiot.

"Jerry, you must understand that a small outfit doesn't have nearly the overhead that we have. The rent is nominal; staff is very limited. Just think, no human resources department, no overnight word processing, no copy or mail room guys. If I keep even half my clients, I could double what I'm taking out of here."

Dead silence followed, and Silver knew better than to fill it. He had shot his wad, as the old soldiers used to say. Now it was time for the return volley.

Kracken was the first to jump in. "No one in this room is saying good-bye. You are going to stay, Bob, because this is who you are. You've only ever had one job, and that is as a lawyer at Tew Logan. But you also know that you've not been . . . how should I phrase this? Not all there lately. Frankly, none of us has a clue what you're working on. Maybe if you fill us in a little, maybe explain why you're not sending out your bills, then maybe we can find some room in the budget to increase your distribution by . . . let me think . . . a hundred and fifty thousand a year." Kracken spoke assuredly, expecting Silver to leap at the bait.

But Silver knew he was being lowballed, both because it was Kracken doing the lowballing and because he knew the budget as well as anyone. He wanted to hold out for more; wanted to hold out for an additional $250,000 to bring him an annual draw near a million like the New York boys had and enough to make the other partners at the table very angry. But he also knew that Kracken, in her beautiful fury, was right. He *had* been screwing around chasing after the ships, and now was not the time to push the envelope. Not while the cargo was still out there, not while Lazlo was following the sister, and Jasmine Investments was breathing down his neck. Now it was time to be a good boy. So he fed them bullshit about how complicated the FeasCo deal was getting, explained what a huge bill it would generate. Then with a smile just thin enough to convey his continuing heartbreak over the Zhang suicide, he accepted his additional one-fifty with modest thanks.

He thought he had played it pretty well. Still, there was hatred in the eyes of some of his partners. Jeremy Lake even began to question whether Silver was enough of a lawyer to command that kind of money until Kracken flashed him a look that shrank the little prick where he sat. There wasn't really need for discussion. There was nothing the other partners could do because Kracken had them by the balls. As a condition to her assuming chairmanship of the firm, she had demanded signed, but undated, resignation letters from each member of the Executive Committee. If any of them didn't play her way, they were off the team. Thus, despite their displeasure, debate ended, and the Executive Committee voted unanimously to increase Silver's allocation of the firm's profits to $810,000 per year, guaranteed.

Having gotten more than he ever expected from this meeting, Silver thought it time to hold out a conciliatory olive branch.

"Nina, about the Sam Zhang situation, I will do whatever you think is best for the firm. You know that I don't have your people instincts, and I don't know what would be the better gesture for the associates. If you think a speech would be a morale booster, I'll give one." Silver could see her softening, could see some of the gentleness returning to the muscles around the lips he had kissed so long ago. He decided to call it quits and stood up to effectively end the meeting.

Kracken stood too, not wanting to be out-positioned. "Good, I'll call a meeting of all the associates tomorrow. Only you and I need to be there. That . . ." Kracken gave Silver a curt nod, "should give you enough time to get a haircut."

Then, ignoring everyone else in the room she stomped out in her usual, tense posture, shoulders forward, head down. To Silver she always looked like a running back expecting to be tackled. He glanced over to where she had been sitting and noticed that her hands had left small, angelic palm prints in the high gloss of the boardroom table.

☆ ☆ ☆

Detective Leone wasn't available to see him on Sunday. So after the trip to the emergency room and a police mini-station on South Street, Jason Behr spent the day in bed catching up on his reading and watching network sports. The nurses had bound his torso and told him not to move around too much. Otherwise the rib wouldn't set. They had given him some codeine which made him dizzy and nauseous. Once he came down from that, he opted for scotch and consumed a pint before passing out.

By Monday the pain in his ribs had grown worse, though his groin felt significantly better and he was able to sit in the orange plastic chair in the Roundhouse without too much discomfort. He and Kristina had been waiting for Leone for almost an hour now, and he was just insisting on leaving Philadelphia Police Headquarters when the squat fellow finally appeared. Detective Tito Leone—sometimes just T—couldn't have been more than five-foot-four, and his forty-three years had been unkind to his features. His drinking buddies sometimes joked that all the hair on his head had migrated down to his back because there was more company there. They also made fun of his nose (large and pocked), his darkly Sicilian complexion, and his first name. The boys had been delighted to discover that Tito meant *giant* in Italian, and they roared when Leone had tried, quite seriously, to explain that his father had been a communist in the old country. That he, Tito Leone, had been christened such in honor of the great Yugoslav leader. The crowd joked, but they knew not to take their jibes too far. About once a year, Leone lost his temper, and they had all witnessed the harsh consequences of that.

Behr had warned the detective that he was bringing Sam Zhang's sister along. So when Leone walked in and saw the two, he replaced his normally ebullient humor with a stern, down-to-business expression that still couldn't hide his obvious delight in seeing a beautiful woman intrude upon the ugliness of a policeman's day.

"What can I do for you, Ms. Zhang?" Leone asked after shaking her hand and slapping Behr too forcefully on the shoulder.

"You could begin by telling me why there is no investigation under way of my brother's death, why I have to come to the police instead of the police coming to me, why I've been made to wait."

Leone cocked his head, took a deep breath, looked questioningly toward Behr.

"Ms. Zhang," he said slowly, "I realize this is distressing. This kind of thing doesn't happen every day. Maybe we should discuss this over a nice hot cup of coffee." Leone gestured toward the front door, but Kristina didn't budge.

"I've had plenty of coffee already, Detective, and I have other things to do today. I don't mean to be rude, but I think I deserve some answers."

Behr stayed silent. He also wanted to know the answers to Kristina's questions, and Leone, realizing that he wasn't going to get any support from Behr, beckoned them back to the orange chairs. Leone remained standing.

"You're right, Ms. Zhang, that we are not investigating this as a murder. But the homicide division *does* investigate all apparent suicides. Which means that I'm still asking questions. I've gotten a preliminary report from the Medical Examiner that I'm almost finished going through, and I have got some follow up questions for some of the lawyers around that firm. I gotta tell you though, it's a little weird, but so far it looks like suicide to me."

Behr thought he better speak up before Kristina erupted. "T . . . I mean Detective Leone, you said it looked a little weird. What's weird?" Behr was familiar with Leone's mind-set and knew to be concerned if Leone smelled something he couldn't reconcile.

"Well, I don't know if we should get into it here—"

"I can take it, Detective. Whatever you've got to say."

Leone gave her an appraising look. "Okay then, what's a little weird is that your brother was wearing a coat and gloves. We have no explanation except that the other guy on the thirty-fourth floor that night said it was cold and they don't always run the HVAC late at night."

"What's HVAC?"

"Heating, ventilation and air-conditioning," Behr chipped in.

"All right, what else?"

"That and the security guard in the lobby saying he saw four people leaving the building between midnight and about one A.M. when the incident took place. We have been able to identify three of those people as lawyers at Tew Logan, but the fourth we don't know. It could have been another lawyer or someone from the other offices in that building. The scrawl on the sign-out sheet isn't legible."

"Well, that simply involves the process of elimination; it shouldn't be too hard," she said flatly.

"It's harder than you think, Ms. Zhang." Behr could see Leone consciously staying patient. "There are thirty-four floors in the building. There are fifty to one hundred people assigned to each floor. In total, over twenty-five hundred people work in that building. And that's just tenants. I'm not even counting the cleaning staff, security guards, garage attendants, maintenance guys. Even if I talked to fifty people a day, it would take me over a month to interview all the tenants in that building."

"I think that you're making excuses. Frankly, I expected more." Kristina sniffed and began peppering Leone with more questions: "What was my brother working on? Who knew he was there at that time of night? Why has there been no organized search of his apartment? According to my dad, one of your officers spent all of twenty minutes in the apartment the next day. And where did my brother get a gun for Christ sakes? These are all the things you should be telling me!"

"We are following up all the leads we have." Leone protested, but found that he was talking to her back as she turned and marched out the door.

Leone turned to his old friend, clearly frustrated. "What's with her, Behr?"

"Well . . . you know how it is." Behr shrugged. "Let's get that coffee. She'll probably wait for me in the car."

The two men followed Kristina out the double doors and across the parking lot, headed for the aluminum snack truck on Eighth Street. A "grease pit on wheels" Leone called it. But that didn't keep him from eating most of his meals there. They took the steaming blue and gold paper cups to the edge of the parking lot where they could see Kristina sitting in Behr's car, a 1976 Porsche 914 that looked more like a squashed VW Beetle than a high performance vehicle.

"What's your interest in all this?" Leone asked Behr after loudly slurping the first sip. "I thought you had left this game."

"I'm not really in the game," Behr said, "it's just that Sam Zhang was a student of mine when I was starting out teaching. Actually he was one of the best students I ever had. He made learning the law into something special, so teaching law became something special too." Leone looked like he wasn't buying it. Behr figured the man would keep his thick black monobrow arched until he heard a motive that made sense to him.

"So Sam was my student," Behr continued, "and his sister asked me to help. You know I can't turn down a pretty lady in distress."

Leone grunted. "You're back in the game."

"I'm not! It's a one-time thing."

"Nah, you're back. She's pretty as sin—just your type as I recall. But you can't stay away from a good hunt." Leone gave him an odd look he couldn't read. "You're back because it's who you are. I don't make a habit of going around blowing sunshine up anybody's ass, but you were the best I ever worked with. You got your teeth into a case and you never let go. Not like those weirdos at the DA's or the wimpy little pukes we got at the U.S. Attorney's now.

"Believe me," Leone continued, looking up at him, "you got your teeth set in this one too, and you're not going to let go. And if you ask me, it's about time. All the professor crap is making you soft. Look at you. Corduroys for God's sake!"

"It's my uniform!"

"Yeah, right. Anyway, some of the boys down here will be real glad to see you back in action. And the FBI guys have been waiting for this for a while, I can tell you."

Behr felt himself blushing a little, flattered by Leone's certainty. The U.S. Attorney's office seemed like a hundred years ago. So much had happened since then, so much to jerk him from that prior identity. Still, it was good to hear that he was remembered—that his tenure in the somewhat unusual position he held was considered successful, though much of that success should be attributed to luck. Behr's position was unusual because he had to be both an investigator and a lawyer. Because his field, international financial crime, involved so much undercover work, often in foreign jurisdictions, the FBI couldn't even begin to investigate without a lawyer to guide them along. And Behr had become their guide, scheming and strategizing the course of their pursuits so well that one day—quite to his surprise—he found himself addressing a room full of FBI agents with respect to the biggest money-laundering stings ever devised and realized that he was in charge. That they were all looking to him for the next step not because he had the bureaucratic authority or the loudest voice or the biggest gun, but because he was calm and reasoned and knew exactly what that next step should be.

That case, Behr recalled, also introduced him to Leone. The FBI had brought Leone and some other Philadelphia police in on the money-laundering operation, because a lot of the money finding its way into the Bahraini branch of a large Pakistani bank was originating mysteriously in Philadelphia. "The Philly Connection" they had called it. That had been ten years ago, he realized with some astonishment. Ten years, almost to the day.

"Thanks, T, I mean it." It was nice of Leone to remember. Still, he didn't want to seem over excited. "But for now at least, let's take it one case at time. Fill me in."

Leone laughed, clapped him on the shoulder again; then he slurped some coffee through the cup's plastic lid before delivering the technical background he knew the former prosecutor could understand. Leone detailed the scene of the crime, noting that suicide was still, of course, a crime.

It had been a straight shot to the head, entering low, behind and slightly below the right ear, then exploding out the left temple. The gun, unregistered and untraceable due to the absence of serial numbers, was in the victim's right hand. They had confirmed that the victim was right-handed. As he told the sister earlier, the hands were gloved, which they found strange. Powder residue on the gloves and backsplash from the wound conformed to the anticipated pattern. The pattern and the fact that the powder matched traces in the weapon indicated that the gloves were worn by the actual shooter. This would present more of a cover up scenario except that the kid's coat was on too. And the coat was not put on the kid after the shot, because it was covered in blood and tissue from the exit wound. The splatter pattern was consistent with his wearing the coat when he got shot. So, if the kid was definitely wearing his coat when he got shot, it is not inconceivable that he was also wearing his gloves. And if he was wearing his gloves . . . case closed.

The problem with their analysis of people leaving the building was the security guard who was supposed to have seen four people leave. When the police arrived, the guard had already been called upstairs. As far as they could figure, a hot-shot lawyer named Silver had called the police and building security back to back. The guard left the front desk right away and went upstairs. They, the police, did not arrive till ten minutes later. That left a ten minute gap in which anyone could have left the building unobserved. So they potentially had more than one unidentified departure. In fact, they could have several more.

"So you see, Behr," Leone concluded, tilting the last sip of coffee directly over his mouth, "we've got a lot of information pointing toward suicide and some unanswered questions. And that's about it."

"Would it make a difference if I thought it wasn't a suicide?" Behr asked quietly.

Leone looked at his friend and opened his palm in a gesture indicating that Behr should proceed to tell what he knew.

"It's just a feeling really . . . I can't tell you anything concrete, like the kid was left handed or something." Behr shuffled his feet and looked toward Kristina in the Porsche. He decided not to tell Leone about *The Revolutionary's Confession* or Kristina's family history. He decided to ask questions rather than answer them. "T, when your guys did the crime scene, did they look at documents, see what the kid was working on, look at the computer, anything like that?"

A wind had arisen, funneling up Eighth Street and bearing an inverted wave of dust, grime and plastic wrappers before it. Leone turned from the oncoming cloud, flipped up the collar of his thigh-length brown leather coat before answering. "Funny you should mention that," he said over the wind. "The night of the shooting, we didn't remove anything but the corpse from the office, and then we sealed the scene. Standard procedure. We come back the next day to do an inventory and look around some more for a note or something which might set the kid off—you know the drill—a margin call from his broker, a "Dear John" from his lover . . . whatever. So we start scratching around, looking at documents, and all of a sudden it's like World War Three in there. Out of nowhere we got this guy Silver and some other stooge, stepping all over the evidence and yelling about client files, client confidentiality and proprietary information, whatever that means." Leone was getting animated, gesticulating wildly. "We go around the block with these guys, tell them that we got no interest in their client secrets, but that this is our scene now and they are facing obstruction of a police investigation, obstruction of justice and God-knows-what if they don't cool down. Well they start saying something else we don't understand and then, all of sudden, dead quiet. These guys just stopped talking. In midsentence—like someone threw a switch. I can't figure what's happening. They're still there in the doorway, but they're not moving, not talking. Then, one of the guys steps back and this fiery little number, a little past her prime maybe—"

Leone made the universal gesture conveying either outrageous expense or good looks, "This fiery little number just strides right in like she owns the joint. Well . . . it turns out she does own the joint. She's in charge of the whole firm. She says that we gentlemen are welcome to look at anything we want. That they will provide all the assistance they can. But that if we want to take any document off the premises, they have to review it first. Simple as can be. She leaves . . . Christ I'm getting wood just thinking about her . . . and Silver, all piss and vinegar a minute ago, now he looks scared, like he's going to pass out right there in the kid's office." Leone chuckled, grabbed the coffee cup from Behr's hand and took a sip.

"Where are you going with this?" He had to get Leone back on track and off his fixation on powerful women.

"Right. We look around, take an inventory of what's in the office and go home. We didn't really see any documents that made sense, so we didn't take them with us. The next day I'm exhausted, I'm watching the TV, I'm thinking about other things: the Phillies losing season, the Eagles' losing season, why a guy like me needs to know about yeast infections . . ." Leone was a fish that required a lot of play. Behr simply had to let him run out the line a little. " . . . the point of televised golf, and then I get a call from this kid just out of the Academy, Zapatero—his name means shoemaker, so we call him Shoeshine—and he's got a question. This is the question: Why does our inventory of the Zhang kid's office from the day after list *nine* cardboard boxes of documents when the crime scene photos clearly show ten?"

Leone shrugged, causing his brown leather coat to creak slightly and Behr to wonder if the man was actually wearing vinyl. "Good question, don't you think?"

"Good question," Behr answered. "What's the answer?"

"Don't know. I called this Bob Silver character this morning to ask him the same question. His little guard dog tells me he is in a meeting. So, around ten o'clock I go back over there. That's why I was late by the way." Leone waggled his head in some faint imitation of apology. "And you know what?"

"What?"

"Ten boxes."

"So you missed one. Big deal."

"We don't miss things like that. We have two guys each do a separate inventory and then compare, just for situations like this."

"Were the contents of box number ten tampered with?"

"We don't even know what the original contents of box number ten were, except that they were papers in file folders."

"So you may or may not have evidence of a crime, tampering with evidence, but no perpetrator and no discernable motive."

"That's about the size of it."

Behr reflected for a moment, looking at Kristina some fifty feet away and apparently fidgeting with the controls of his beloved car. What Leone had told him was indeed a little weird, a little suspicious, worthy of further investigation. But nothing he'd said was earth-shattering or even probative. And as Leone had indicated to Kristina, there was nothing which could flatly negate the preliminary conclusion of suicide. He said as much to Leone, who agreed. They also agreed that it was damn cold and they should head back.

"Where are you going from here?" Leone asked.

"I thought we would poke around Tew Logan a little. I might have an old student or two I could look up there."

"I got a better idea." Leone responded, pulling a small cellular phone from his pocket. He dialed a number from memory and smiled when he heard the voice at the other end. Behr could hear himself being described as not too old, late thirties, brownish hair, good-looking in a stupid, preppy sort of way.

Leone clicked the END button, shut off the power and jammed the phone back into his pants pocket. "You and your girlfriend there have an appointment with my nephew—he's been a lawyer at Tew Logan maybe two, three years now. His name is Mike, Mike Frattone. Just take the elevator to the thirtieth floor and ask for him, he'll help you out, but don't," Leone held up a warning finger, "get him in trouble. He's my sister's baby, and she'll take both of us down if something happens to him. *Capish?*"

"*Capisco!*" Behr affirmed, then watched Leone's curious form turn away and power itself through the parking lot and into the Roundhouse. Behr had always admired the man's intensity and realized, not for the first time, that he had lost much of his own in the years he had been out of law enforcement. When he turned back toward Kristina, he saw that she had gotten out of the car and was now leaning against the passenger door. Behr quickly crossed the tarmac between them and briefed her on Leone's statements. She didn't comment one way or the other but did ask what he had given away. Specifically had he told Leone about Sam's family history? Had he told Leone about *The Revolutionary's Confession*? About the books?

☆ ☆ ☆

A little way down Eighth Street, on the other side of a small pane of one-way glass, a voice answered Kristina's questions in a rough South Jersey whisper, "No Ms. Zhang, your boyfriend was a good little laddie. He didn't say anything about those items. Though I wish he had." Lazlo then tore off the headphones, dropped the mike in a box behind the front seat, gunned the van through the parking lot of Police Headquarters and up Seventh Street. He had to cut some corners if was going to catch the speedy little Porsche heading for the Vine Street Expressway.

7

Kristina was clearly impressed with Mike Frattone, and Behr felt the stirrings of envy at the kid's classic Mediterranean features. Capped with a full head of rich black hair, Michael F. Frattone's face held warm rich eyes, sensitive lips and a slightly flattened nose which spoke of past breaks and painful memories. Just the type of memories, thought Behr, that women love to discover over bottles of wine. The face was supported by an athletic build—he stood slightly above six feet—and he moved with the grace of a point guard setting up the three-point shot. He carried his suit well on his thin frame, though it showed a few threads and had a slightly worn shine.

Mike appeared within two minutes of their arrival on the thirtieth floor of Tew Logan. They were waiting in a reception area plush with couches, mahogany paneling and the latest business magazines. When they were offered coffee, Behr accepted what turned out to be a painfully bitter brew. He didn't have a chance to get rid of it, and as Mike guided them to the elevator and up to the thirty-fourth floor to see Sam's office he was stuck carrying the steaming cup with him.

The narrow elevator had a predictable effect on Behr's claustrophobia—his one publicly acknowledged weakness. He survived the trip up from the lobby by closing his eyes and steadying himself against the metal handrail. But on this short ascent, coffee and briefcase in hand, he couldn't hold on; he found himself shaking involuntarily, twitches just forceful enough to spill scalding coffee over his hand. Kristina and Frattone looked at him questioningly, but he didn't feel the need to explain. He hated Tew Logan already.

Mike led them from the elevator bank down a narrow, carpeted hall. "I'm not really sure if this is kosher," he said over his shoulder as they approached the yellow tape stretched across the doorway to Sam Zhang's cubbyhole.

Behr sought to reassure him. "Your uncle Tito said we were free to enter the crime scene. He said the police are basically done with it, and Kristina can pick up personal effects if she likes."

Mike turned around, walking backwards for a moment. "It's not the police I was worried about."

Sam Zhang's office wasn't very big, and Behr decided not to crowd Kristina while she looked around at those few items Sam had used to personalize the space. Behr waited in the hall and quietly asked questions of Sam's former secretary, whom Mike had introduced as Rose. Rose was a treasure trove of information, and Behr was enjoying her thick Scottish accent when he heard a deep, challenging voice echo behind him.

"Is there something I can help you with?"

Behr turned to find that the voice was that of a man standing uncomfortably close to him. Over six feet and pushing his mid-fifties the man was an inch taller and some fifteen years older than Behr. He had a look which seemed to demand respect or at least acknowledgment of his seniority. He didn't get either from Behr.

"I'm Jason Behr, I am here with Kristina Zhang to pick up her brother's personal effects. And you are?"

"Bob Silver. I worked with Sam quite a bit. I sit just down the hall."

The men shook hands, maintaining uneasy eye contact throughout. There seemed to be something moving behind Silver's eyes. Something quick and slippery. Something, Behr knew from experience, that had to be watched with the utmost care.

"I hate to be the bearer of bad news, and I know that she has come all the way from Amsterdam," Silver started, "but we . . . the firm that is . . . has a policy of not permitting people unaffiliated with the firm or specific clients to be present in attorney offices without that attorney being present."

"A sound policy," Behr allowed, "but under the circumstances I think it impossible that the attorney in question could be present."

Behr saw himself being assessed, looked up and down, categorized. He knew he couldn't seem too threatening, standing there in his corduroys and a shabby tweed sportcoat that was too small for his well-built frame. And Behr could see in the haughtiness that lit Silver's eyes that Silver did underestimate him—failed to imagine Behr as a danger.

But then, having overheard their exchange, Kristina came out, and Silver's whole expression changed. He became a different person, paler, older. He looked like he had seen a ghost, and Behr and Kristina and Rose and Frattone all watched the man visibly struggle to maintain the patina of a power lawyer.

Behr addressed Kristina. "Bob here was just telling me that you can't have your brother's things. Firm policy."

"I . . . I did not say that! That is a mischaracterization." Silver glared at Behr, then turned toward Kristina. "Ms. Zhang, I would like to say that . . . I want you to know . . . my heartfelt . . . you know . . . the resemblance is really quite remarkable."

Kristina turned her head slightly from Silver's open-mouthed stare. Behr could see she was troubled by the man's intensity. Silver stepped toward her, more composed. "But what I meant to say, mean to say, is that I can't tell you how sorry I am about all this . . . about your brother. I was here that night. I discovered the body. I worked very closely with Sam, we were colleagues. I feel that I have lost a friend."

"I thought that I had met all of Sam's friends at the funeral," Kristina said sharply.

Silver eyes widened, clearly not expecting a harsh tone to emanate from her delicate face. He stammered out something about his sense of guilt. How he blamed himself and how he thought others would blame him too. How he simply couldn't bear the eyes that would be turned in his direction if he had entered the church that day.

Silver caught Mike Frattone's bemused expression and gave him a cutting look.

"Mike, I am sure a young associate doesn't have time to be standing around."

"Actually Bob, I don't have much on my plate right now. Plenty of time to help a friend." Frattone folded his hands in front him with practiced catholic school innocence.

"Well then, I've got some work for you. You can wait in my office, I'll be done here in a minute," said Silver to Frattone, who shrugged, told Behr he was glad to meet him, told Kristina that she should call him anytime she needed anything at all, and then ambled down the hall.

Silver waited for Frattone to turn the corner before turning his attention to Behr and Kristina. "What we will do is have someone, maybe Rose here," he gestured to Sam's secretary whose expression was even more innocently insolent than Frattone's, "go through Sam's office and separate Sam's personal effects from the client-sensitive materials. She'll put it all in a box and send it to you. She will be supervised throughout by an attorney of course."

Behr could see that this was basically sensible. But he still wanted Kristina to get a shot at finding the disk if it was in there, and it took him only a second to turn Silver's argument around. "I can appreciate your being protective of your clients," Behr said, "but while you are being sensitive to their potential concerns, you are being highly insensitive to Kristina's *family* concerns. What if there are things in that small office that are highly private to Sam or the Zhang family? What if there are things that Sam wouldn't have wanted people to know about? A man's office, particularly if he spends the majority of his time there, becomes the repository for all kinds of things, personal financial information, correspondence. All kinds of things," Behr made a sweeping gesture with his hand that finished with his finger pointed at Silver's chest, "that you and your firm have no right to hold or even look at. Kristina will make the first cut at separating such personal items—"

"Mr. Behr that is impossible. Sam was working on transactions which involve a high degree of nonpublic information. Our clients would be horrified to learn that anyone not bound by the attorney-client privilege had access to such information."

"I'll make it easy for you then." Behr turned toward Rose. "Rose, could you take down the following." Behr waited for Rose to grab her steno pad. She looked up to show she was ready. "Rose, title the document: Confidentiality Agreement. First paragraph. This Confidentiality Agreement is made by and among Jason Behr, a resident of Pennsylvania, Kristina Zhang, a resident of the Netherlands, and Tew, Logan & Case, a Pennsylvania partnership." Behr turned to Silver, "You are a Pennsylvania partnership, right?"

"A limited liability partnership, actually. Under Pennsylvania law." Silver sounded slightly defeated. A confidentiality agreement took the wind out of any argument that could be made about confidentiality. Behr knew this and he also knew that without a good counter argument, Silver's only recourse was to be unreasonable and kick them out. And how would that make him look? Such an act would be the talk of the firm within minutes of its happening. Silver was already stuck with the reputation of having worked an associate to suicide. But now he would be known as the partner who worked an associate to death and then kicked his grieving sister out of the firm when she tried to pick up his stuff. No one would ever do his work again.

Yet still Silver resisted. He turned to Rose. "You can put that down, Rose." He pointed to her steno pad. "I will draft the confidentiality agreement myself. As it concerns matters involving the attorney-client privilege with respect to a number of clients, the agreement will, of course, have to be approved internally by our ethics committee as well as the senior legal officer of each client implicated. That may take some days, perhaps even—"

"Mr. Silver," Behr said in a slow, gravely cadence he hadn't used since his last cross-examination some ten years ago, "I feel that Ms. Zhang and I are wasting our time. It occurs to me that this is a unique situation in the history of your firm. Unique enough that the chairman of the firm should be handling all inquiries pertaining thereto. I believe your current chairman is actually a chairwoman, Nina Kracken. I've met her on a number of occasions, chiefly in her capacity as a Penn Law School trustee. I think that Nina would be very interested to hear how you are playing this and what it might cause me to say about Tew Logan to *every* class of Penn law students that ever sits before me again. She might not like it that you single-handedly made local recruiting impossible."

Silver regarded him with clenched teeth, his eyes just narrow slits. Behr was glad he had remembered Leone's story about Kracken— whom he had never met—and how she had silenced Silver simply by walking into the room. And now, in greatly similar circumstances, she had silenced the man just in the mention of her name. Whatever Kracken's authority over the lawyers in this firm, Behr rejoiced in it, for Bob Silver finally relented and allowed Behr to dictate the body of the agreement to Rose.

Of course Silver didn't give him an entirely free hand. He looked over Rose's shoulder, and interrupted Behr on several occasions, inserting points he thought were necessary including his right to inspect everything that Kristina or Behr removed from the office.

While Rose sat at the computer to type it all in, Behr, Silver and Kristina spent an awkward few minutes in the corridor. Silver was not prepared to let them into Sam's office until he had their original signatures on the document, and Behr and Kristina knew better than to push. Behr tried small talk, asking Silver how long he had been a partner. Seventeen years. What was his area of concentration? Mergers and acquisitions. Had the profession changed over the years? Yes, much more of a business now, much harder to make money. Silver responded to all the questions and asked some of his own. Behr was visiting at Penn? No. An associate professor? Full professor, really? Where had he gone to law school—Rutgers, Temple? (he intended a slight). Chicago? Good school. That's great.

Kristina stayed silent throughout this exchange, though Behr could see something working behind her eyes. Anger, frustration? He couldn't quite tell. Her expression didn't give much away, or he just couldn't read her yet. The thought saddened him, and he suddenly wished to understand all her expressions.

Presently Kristina stepped between the two men and over to Rose. She leaned over the divider between the secretary's desk and the hall. "Rose, I'm sorry, but are you almost done?"

"Just printing them out now, dearie!"

"Thank God. I don't think I can take another minute of these two." She leaned farther toward Rose and, just loudly enough to be intentionally overheard, whispered, "They're like a couple of talking penises, slapping away at each other, trying to settle which one is bigger."

Rose smiled broadly, despite the look on Silver's face. "Three hundred lawyers in this office, dear. Even the women grow 'em around here."

Suitably humbled, Behr and Silver did not argue over the version of the confidentiality agreement Rose laid out before them. She lined up three identical signature pages on the counter next to her desk and they took turns signing each one. Silver solemnly instructed Rose to make copies for the file, give each person an original and call him when they were about to leave so that he could abide by his duties in accordance with the agreement.

Rose yessed him and went off to make the copies while Behr and Kristina began their search of Sam's office. Behr made a conscious effort to remember the general outline of what he saw. The office was a nine-by-nine box, with a floor-to-ceiling window overlooking North Philadelphia, which appeared flat and, in a number of locations, burning. Most of the square footage was consumed by a large integrated bookshelf and desk unit that jutted out from the side wall at a ninety-degree angle. The position of the unit left little room for anything but the desk chair and boxes of documents.

The strange thing about the desk was that it was completely and incongruously clear. Every other surface in Sam's office was covered in piles of paper—some loose, some bound by rubber bands and clips or stuck in files. Behr rarely met lawyers with clear desks and generally distrusted those whose were. He thought it odd that Sam's desk should be clean, then realized, with a wave of sadness, that everything on the desk had likely been bloodied and removed by the police. He didn't mention this to Kristina. The dark stain on the thin grey carpet was enough of a reminder of her brother's fate.

The bookshelves were dominated by closing binders (hardbound collections of all the documents connected with a single deal), statutory collections of the Delaware Corporate Code, the Securities Acts, the Internal Revenue Code and various treatises on the ins and outs of leveraged buyouts, real estate acquisitions, equipment leasing, bank financings. The floor near the other walls was covered in stacked boxes of documents, and Behr saw that almost all the boxes had a small blue slip from the firm's records department with the same client billing number. This number he memorized.

While Behr perused the bookshelves, opening every book, Kristina navigated between the boxes and the desk to the computer resting on a back ledge in front of the window. Silver had expressly carved out computer files in the confidentiality agreement, arguing persuasively that any computer files on the firm's system properly belonged to the firm. Thus Kristina was barred from turning on the computer, but not from looking through the small boxes of 3M disks sitting on either side of the monitor. Each disk was labeled in Sam's difficult scrawl with a name and an eight digit number. She asked Behr about this and he guessed that the number was a client number and the name was that of the relevant transaction. Thus 147728.89 would identify a certain client, and the name CyberFax probably was the name of some transaction with the CyberFax company. Kristina grew frustrated to find that all the disks in each of the ten or so boxes she went through bore the same type of legend. All client-oriented. All the proprietary domain of Tew, Logan & Case.

Nothing appeared personal. Everything was business related, closed to their inspection and probably useless. Rotating carefully in the tight space, Kristina focused on the desk drawers and told Behr that she would begin assembling Sam's stuff. There wasn't much of it, as far as Behr could see. Kristina dug out a file listing real estate opportunities someplace in Maryland; mustard, duck sauce and soy sauce packages from Chinese restaurants; extra shoes and work-out clothes; a file of amusing e-mails and other items downloaded from the Internet. She put all these things, including the condiments in a box provided by Rose. When she was done with the drawers she went to the bookshelf. Most of the books had Tew Logan library tags on them. Those that didn't she put in the box. That was about it. Except for the pictures. She picked one up and was about to put it in the box when the tears started to flow.

Kristina lowered herself into the desk chair and wept openly. Tears streamed down soft cheeks. Behr tried to comfort her, and Rose too clucked from the doorway, "Let it all out dear. We all loved Sam—he's worth every tear."

Kristina waved them off, asked for some time. And while she held her face in her hands, her chest heaving, Behr took over packing the pictures. But not without looking at them first.

One was of the immediate family, taken maybe ten years ago. It showed a healthy and smiling middle-aged Asian man in garish ski clothes with his arms around a college-aged Sam wearing goggles on his forehead and Kristina, dressed, as now, entirely in black. Another photo showed an elderly man, also Asian, sitting comfortably in a large red armchair reading through small glasses perched on the very end of his nose. This must be the man they had grown up calling grandfather. Another was a browning black-and-white photo—yellowed at the edges—of an Asian family in front of a white clapboard house. The man was Harry Zhang, though much younger than in the other shots. Next to him, with her hands on the shoulders of a couple of chubby two-year-olds, stood a dead ringer for Kristina: gorgeous, tall and challenging. Her mother? Had Kristina ever mentioned her mother? Behr remembered hearing something about this woman—maybe at the funeral. But what?

Behr closed the box and placed it in the corridor. Kristina emerged too. She joined him in front of Rose's desk. Behr asked if she was all right. Kristina responded affirmatively. Rose coughed lightly. They turned to her and their eyes widened in unison when they saw what she was holding: an unlabeled computer disk.

"I didn't mention this earlier, what with that prick Silver giving you such a hard time, and it didn't seem like anyone's business. But Sam asked me to type in some corrections. It's his novel. Quite good really, all about China, except I don't know how it ends. He never gave me the rest."

Rose handed Kristina the disk, and just as she did so, Silver turned the corner. Kristina didn't have pockets in her stylish mourning clothes. Behr could see her trying to conceal the disk behind her back without drawing attention to the odd pose she was forced to assume.

"All done?" Silver asked. "Everything in the box here?"

Behr spoke up, gesturing, drawing Silver's eye away from Kristina. "Yep, that's it. Just some books and pictures; you're welcome to go through it."

While Silver squatted before the box of Sam's personal effects, Behr reached around Kristina, grabbed the disk and fumbled it into the inside pocket of his jacket. Silver caught the last part of Behr's movement, his head snapped around.

But Behr recovered, smoothly pulling out a thin case from the same pocket where the disk now lay.

"My card," said Behr, bending to hand one to Silver. "Give me a call if you find anything else that is not firm property. I can pick it up anytime."

Silver took the card and glanced at it suspiciously. Then he stood up with the box of Sam's effects. He thrust the box at Behr and let go, forcing Behr to catch and almost drop it.

"I hope that the next time we meet will be under better circumstances." Silver said. Clearly there would be no next time at Silver's invitation. The snake then turned toward Kristina, smiling voraciously and stepping close. Was he coming on to her? "Ms. Zhang, please accept my condolences about your brother and my apologies about the funeral. Please call me anytime. Anytime at all, just to talk if you wish. Rose will show you to the elevators now."

And with that Bob Silver abruptly and rather stiffly bowed, then turned on his heel and marched down the hall. Behr glanced at Kristina, saw her shiver, seemingly chilled and troubled by the man.

Rose came around the desk. "He's gone now," she said and placed a reassuring hand on Kristina's shoulder.

Kristina sighed and let the older woman guide them to the elevator bank.

The elevator appeared immediately. Behr held the door open with the outside button while Kristina thanked Rose profusely and Rose forced a hug on her.

"Sam would never have let me do that. So I'm getting it from you," she said, a tear forming in her eye.

Kristina stepped onto the elevator. Behr, with a deep breath, followed. They waved at Rose as the doors were closing. Suddenly Behr thrust his hand into the closing gap.

"Rose, wait! What client is number 103765?"

"Oh that, that's FeasCo. The two of them worked on almost nothing else the last few weeks."

☆   ☆   ☆

They arranged to meet late Monday at a diner in South Jersey. Lazlo liked meetings in South Jersey, particularly at night. No matter how suspicious, awkward or evil you looked, you were always anonymous in South Jersey.

Silver was late getting there. Lazlo watched with amusement from the window of the diner as Silver missed the entrance to the parking lot, bounced the Range Rover over the curb, across the narrow strip of lawn and into a spot which was barely wide enough for the car and probably too narrow for his ego. When Silver got out of his car, Lazlo was not able to see the man's face, and realized that this was intentional on Silver's part. Silver was wearing a big hat; he held his chin tucked low in his collar. He walked quickly through the parking lot, up the handicapped ramp and through the big chrome doors without once lifting his head. He looked around furtively before settling himself in the red vinyl booth and curtly greeting Lazlo.

"All right, what have you got?" Silver demanded immediately.

With his good arm, the one the professor had left in its socket, Lazlo pulled out a Walkman tape player and handed it to Silver. He had to laugh as Silver tried to get the headphones over his broad-brimmed hat. He stopped laughing when he saw the expression on Silver's face.

"Have you listened to this?" Silver asked in low whisper.

"Well, I heard it—listening is another matter," replied Lazlo noncommittally.

"Well, you don't know what you heard. So I'm going to give you an idea." Silver leaned forward, far over the edge of the white Formica table top decoratively sprinkled with little gold flecks. His face was less than a foot away and appeared to have recently been baked to a kind of orange color in a tanning machine. The man smelled of cheap perfume, and Lazlo speculated distastefully of how Silver had spent the hours prior to their meeting.

Of course most of what Silver told him, Lazlo already knew, having personally recorded the conversations between Behr and Kristina, the Monday morning meeting with Detective Leone, and the phone call made by Kristina from Sam's apartment earlier tonight. But Silver continued in his usual patronizing tone. It was a tone that Lazlo ignored only when it emanated from well-paying clients.

"What you don't know," said Silver, "is what's at stake. Even I don't know that. All I know is that it is worth a lot to the people who are paying me. Whatever it is, it came to Philly on two ships. And there is something written about those two ships on the disk. You heard Kristina Zhang's father say he didn't know anything about this book, this book that is on a floppy disk that somehow got out of our goddamn offices today."

Silver paused and turned his eyes out the window and once around the diner, looking for eavesdroppers. He directed his gaze on Lazlo and leaned forward even more. "We think the father is lying. We think he knows everything about these books and what they're worth to us."

"Who is we?" Lazlo asked, forced into a whisper by the proximity of Silver's face.

"We is you, me and my clients. That's all you need to know about we. What you *do* need to know are the next steps I want you to take."

Lazlo looked over Silver's smug orange face and didn't like what he saw. "You aren't giving me enough information. Without more information, I'm afraid my answer is no." Lazlo was surprised when Silver just smiled at this.

"I'll do better than that, Lazlo. You want information, I'll pay you to get it. Quite handsomely. First," Silver held up his index finger, "you will get that goddamn disk back. I don't care how you do it so long as nobody gets the idea that anybody is specifically after it. If you leave a trail, I won't pay you. It's that simple. Then, after you have placed the disk in my hand, you're on to step two. You go to Chicago."

"What's in Chicago?"

"According to my firm's computer records, Chicago, or more specifically Oak Park, Illinois, is the home of Kristina Zhang's daddy. You are going to question that old man in such a manner as to elicit the maximum possible cooperation. When you have secured that information and the confidentiality of that information, you will be rewarded with an additional cash payment of three hundred thousand dollars." Silver seemed to sneer a little when he said the number, and Lazlo recalled seeing that sneer on other people who were very impressed with the money they could throw around.

"I believe that figure exactly triples your usual fee." And with that Silver handed Lazlo a manilla envelope, which Lazlo found to contain a single printed page stating that Dr. Harry Zhang lived at 522 North Woodbine, Oak Park, Illinois.

8

With the disk burning a hole in his pocket, Behr still managed a few hours in his office while Kristina packed boxes of Sam's belongings and sent them home to Chicago. They agreed to meet for dinner at Sam's apartment. Behr promised to do the cooking.

Winter darkness had settled on Philadelphia, and though it was only eight, it felt like the middle of the night in the corner of Sam's bedroom where Kristina sat illuminated by the blue glow of the laptop's screen. As she inserted the disk into the drive, Behr leaned over her shoulder and thought about all that had conspired to bring its content before their eyes—all that Kristina had told him in the car after the scene at Tew Logan. The information was scant but curious. Whatever was on this disk was related to what her grandfather had brought back from China in 1988.

It turned out, of course, that the man wasn't her grandfather at all. He was their great-uncle, and he had greeted the kids with that astonishing news one summer night after Sam and Kristina had both graduated from college. Behr could only imagine their surprise. This man had lived with them all their lives, practically raised them after the sudden departure of their mother. They had affectionately called him

Baba and worshiped his keen-eyed sagacity and followed his commands and laughed with him until the laughter and smoke caught in his throat and they were all reduced to coughs and giggles. But that one night they didn't laugh. Their Baba had just come back from China and wore a look more serious than any they'd seen before. He made Sam and Kristina sit down, shut the door so their father couldn't overhear them. Then he told them what he had learned in China: that his brother, their real grandfather, was dead. He had died in 1976. The only traces left of him were the sad memories of an old friend in Shanghai, a man named Gao, and a box of moldy books that Gao had saved for many years and at great risk. This friend, Baba said, bent and emphysemic as he was, was likely dead now too. So all that really remained were the books, which Baba would keep in his office for a while.

They were told not to tell their father *anything*. Harry Zhang had grown up in suburban Chicago and Baba was his father. He had always thought so and was to think so for the rest of his life. Baba commanded Sam and Kristina to stay silent and so they did. Then, just over a year ago, Baba died, and precisely one month later Sam got a package from the old secretary in Baba's downtown Chicago office. The package had a note in it, not addressed to anyone in particular and written in Baba's hand. It stated that the enclosed contents had belonged Zhang Chen Hai, whose wish it was that they not be examined until after the twenty-fifth anniversary of his death and then only by members of his immediate family. The note was not signed.

Sam had written to Kristina about this package in an e-mail. He had asked her if she had ever seen its contents or heard anything more from Baba about the mystery (as they had referred to it) since that night in 1988. Sam mentioned the cryptic, unsigned note, and he mentioned the box—that it had red books in it, maybe a hundred small red books; and if you opened any one of these small red books, you would find that the margins around the printed text were closely filled with thousands upon thousands of handwritten Chinese characters. Sam said he was a little spooked by the whole thing, and then he ended the electronic missive with the statement, I guess I'll have to remember Chinese.

That was all Kristina knew. She never saw the package Sam had gotten from Chicago, never saw the books, and Sam had not mentioned them again.

But now they would find out more, and Behr hung close over Kristina's shoulder as she called up the document from the disk drive.

Classes struggle, some classes triumph, others are eliminated. Such is history.
Quotations from Chairman Mao Tse Tung

We have been in the mine since 1960. Sometimes we are sent to the fields, and when we are, I am happy to return to the mine. The day is more predictable here, even though I am an older man and the work is hard. I am content to contribute. Not like the others. They say that much of the product, the coal we dig, is sold to line the pockets of the Party Secretary and the brigade leaders. The complainers do not lie. I too can see that the Party leaders live well in our remote location. I can smell the meat and sweet cakes on their breath, see the shiny fat seeping from their skin. Even so, I know that most of the coal goes to the People, and thus my labor has purpose.

Gao likes to tease. He asks, "Could you not contribute more as the mathematics teacher you were in Anqing? Or as a deputy assistant finance minister? Is not your talent wasted here beneath the mountain?"

"No." I am patient even in the face of his mocking tone. Gao knows that we cannot go back to our former lives, our former identities. That we are confined in the miners' camp, and that we will die here unless we are moved to another facility or something drastic happens politically. Still, I answer him, if only to occupy the time.

"No, Gao, my talent is not wasted, for my presence here means that another able teacher has taken my place. Or that a new deputy assistant finance minister can perform the functions of his office with ease, without the burden of constant scrutiny and suspicion which made me so ineffective."

Behr's back began to protest his crouch over Kristina's shoulder, and he remembered that he had promised her a meal.

"I'm going to fix us some dinner."

Kristina didn't acknowledge. Behr repeated himself.

She looked up, brown eyes wide and curious, voice husky. "That would be great. I'm just going to—" she pointed to the screen.

"Keep reading," Behr suggested. Kristina nodded and turned back to the screen, and Behr made his way to the kitchen where he steamed some asparagus and ginger in the microwave and laid out the tuna steaks on some foil for broiling. After half an hour, he had the entire meal on the table and wine in the glasses. He gave a shout to this effect and waited for a few more minutes, sipping his wine, before wandering into the bedroom to check on her progress.

"What'd I miss?"

Kristina stared at the screen. "It's so sad," she said. "He's in jail—or some kind of work camp—and he has this friend, Gao, who he talks to. He's explaining his life to Gao; how he got into trouble at the Finance Ministry."

"Was he the Finance Minister?"

"No, assistant, deputy, something or other. And no one would trust him because he worked for the old regime."

"Pre-Communist?"

"Yes—"

"And he'd kept his job?"

Kristina look up from the screen. Behr saw that her eyes shimmered with moisture, maybe from empathy, or maybe just fatigue. "He talks about that! Apparently he was a Communist early on, from the '20s— even while he was working for the other side. He was spying on the Nationalists."

"So they rewarded him?"

"That, yes, and he was the only one at first who could do the math, who knew how look at and compute the statistics of the national economy when the Communists took power. But then he got hassled. His coworkers questioned his revolutionary credentials; they accused him of still being a spy and somehow beholden to the old regime. They branded him a counter-revolutionary."

"So what happened to him? Was he sent down?"

"I think so. That's where I am now. He's discussing his choices. One is to go this town, Anqing. It is a river town in a backward province called Anhui, but for some reason he doesn't have the travel papers to get there—Here, look."

I badly wanted to move. Anhui was to be a fresh start. In Anhui, a province without big cities, heavy industry, a major university, I—an educated man—would be something of an oddity. But I would be unknown, as would my history with the KMT.

Gao shakes his head, "People like you, Chen Hai, drag long tails behind them." He means that I trail a long past, a counter-revolutionary past.

"Yes," I answer, "but I thought that if I left the politics of Beijing, if I tucked this tail between my legs, no one would know or feel threatened by my past, however benign."

I grew desperate for a solution, a way out of Beijing and the barrage of criticism. But I was aware of only two options, two ways to escape. The first was physical. To move to Anqing—though without the necessary letters of introduction—and pray that I wasn't questioned along the way. But I didn't see how this was possible. Not on such a long journey. There was no way to stay in motion the entire way, as there was no direct route for me to follow. Not from Beijing to Anqing, or even Shanghai to Anqing, because the trains did not run all the way to Anqing. To reach Anqing, I would have to travel by boat up the Yangtze from Tongling, thus necessitating a stop in Tongling to make arrangements. And the only train to Tongling was out of Shanghai, and it ran infrequently. I must therefore stop for sometime in Shanghai. Each stop would expose me to questioning from the Public Security Bureau, and the absence of the official letters from the Ministry would force many awkward questions to be asked.

Then—as ever—there was the second option. Not a physical move as much as a philosophical one. That had been open to me for some time. A door open to the darkness, fraught with risks. Stepping through that door could make me a national hero— it could lead to elevation to the highest orders of the Communist Party. I could envision myself at breakfast with the Chairman, sharing a plate of Bao filled with sweet plum jelly and laughing with the young girls who served us tea. But this option could also brand me as the worst sort of traitor. Execution would be swift. And I would place everyone who had ever been close to me at risk. No matter where they were, even in America. Particularly in America.

I considered carefully, but eventually I decided not to step through the door. Not to reveal the secret I had carried with me for so long.

Disclosure might help me with the authorities, but disclosure, I thought, would be the ultimate counter-revolutionary act.

I was still a Communist, a true Communist, though that notion had been twisted of late. And despite all that had happened to me and all that was wrong with the Party, the revolution, I believed, had been for the best. So I believed, so I still believe, and were I to tell these petty officials what I knew of the events of 1938, the consequences would be disastrous. I would set the country back and turn Mao into another Emperor. No, I decided, best to stay quiet. Keep the country moving forward, and keep everybody safe. It was best for me to move to Anqing.

I see Gao's curious eyes burning in the darkness. "We are old men, Chen Hai."

"Yes, we are old."

"And 1937 was a very long time ago. So very long ago. Everything has changed. What could have happened then that matters to anyone now?"

"It matters."

"Will you not tell me?"

"I am sorry, old friend. But today is still too soon. As is tomorrow."

☆ ☆ ☆

Behr had finally gotten Kristina to the table where she picked at the tuna and left the asparagus untouched.

"How much of this do you think is true?" Behr asked.

Kristina twiddled the fork in her fingers. "I don't know . . . I'm tempted to think all of it is."

"So there is no 'novel' by Sam Zhang?"

"He . . . Sam was never that creative." The words seemed to pain her.

"So how good was his Chinese?" Behr continued "Good enough to translate all this?"

"It was better than mine." Kristina responded. "Baba always made Sam practice Chinese in the evening."

"Not you? Was he that old fashioned?"

Kristina responded softly, her eyes lowered, her head turned away. "No, it wasn't that. Baba made Sam study Chinese language, and he made me paint and draw Chinese characters, even if I didn't know what they meant." She seemed suddenly sad and tired and Behr felt an overwhelming compassion for her. He wanted to put his coat over her shoulders, hug her, kiss her on the forehead and tell her it would all be all right. But somehow he couldn't; perhaps he was still a little afraid of her. Or maybe he was afraid of something else.

Behr checked his watch, the pilot's watch his father had bequeathed him together with the plane, and saw the hands indicate the approach of midnight. He was tired too, and the pain in his ribs was beginning to flare and distract him. He rose to toss the dishes in the sink, then ushered Kristina into the bedroom. She did not protest when he shut off the computer and closed the lid.

"A tall whiskey for me and a soft bed for you. Doctor's orders. I'll be back first thing in the morning."

Kristina smiled faintly, thanked him and surprised him with a hug that lasted slightly longer and squeezed slightly harder than simple gratitude would typically permit. The pain in his ribs was now severe, but Behr was elated by the contact. He stroked her hair once, watched her lie down. Then he floated out the door, down three flights and onto Pine Street with the sweet breath of Kristina's thanks filling his spirit.

So it was that he didn't notice as he left that the front door to Sam's building was open. And he had no way to know, as he walked from that place in the cool damp along Pine, up Third and then right onto Delancey, that behind him a small blue flame was creeping along the old knob-and-tube wiring on the basement ceiling. And that just as he turned onto his own street, the flame darted up a hole in the kitchen cabinets to the first floor apartment, where it found some brittle shelf liner laid down thirty years ago and exploded to life.

9

Kristina dreamed of her bed in Amsterdam. It was her favorite thing in the city—an enormous four-poster covered in thick white blankets and deep down pillows. How the bed ever found its way to the fifth floor garret apartment she couldn't imagine. She had inherited the bed from the last occupant, and she would cede the bed to the next. She dreamed that it was morning, and the flat light from the North Sea was shining through the haze of dust and grime on the tall windows overlooking the canal water of the Prinsengracht. She dreamed of an arm reaching over her naked shoulders, a man's arm, strong and black with hair. But the hair was not hair at all. It felt like rubber.

Kristina's eyes opened suddenly, awakened by someone shaking her. She tasted smoke and began coughing violently. She saw the face of a monster, then realized it was a mask. A gas mask under a fireman's helmet. A fireman was shaking her. Telling her something. But she couldn't really separate his words from the harsh cadence of her own coughing. The coughs kept coming, tearing at her throat and echoing in her head. She couldn't stop. She wanted to know what was happening. She wanted to ask the fireman. But she couldn't stop coughing. She couldn't speak. She couldn't breathe. There was no air, only smoke—

thick white and yellow smoke. Choking her. Burning her eyes. She forced the intake of breath. She instantly felt sick to her stomach and retched.

She sensed herself lifted, tossed over the fireman's shoulder. The shoulder was digging into her gut. She felt sick again. She wanted to throw up. She wanted to sleep. Then she remembered. The disk. She wanted to get the disk! She tried to tell the guy: Put me down! Just for a second! But the words didn't come. She had to get free. She struggled and writhed, but the man just held her tighter. She tried pushing against him, against his broad shoulder; she wanted to get vertical, slip through his arms. He was too strong. The more she flailed, the tighter he squeezed. She just couldn't get the leverage between their bodies. Then she saw another route. She clawed at his belt, pulling herself farther over his shoulder. The sudden shift in weight sent them hurtling over. The fireman landed on his back; he lost his grip. Kristina was on her hands and crawled quickly toward the desk with the computer on it. She felt the leg of the desk; she pulled herself up. The smoke was thick here and she started gasping again. Maybe if she held her breath? Then the coughing would also stop. She tried. She held her mouth shut tight. She felt her lungs burning. She felt all the cells screaming for oxygen. She grabbed for the computer. Then came blackness.

☆ ☆ ☆

Detective Leone waived an admonishing finger at Behr. "You should have goddamn told me."

"About what? I thought it was completely unrelated. It still could be, for Christ's sake."

"Look, *I'll* tell you what's related and unrelated. That is a determination for *me* to make. Not you."

"Okay then, make it. Was the break-in at my place related to Sam's murder/suicide or not?"

"I don't know." Leone said softly, slightly chastened. "We're working on it. But the correlation is hard to miss, buddy. The Zhang kid's found dead. You get involved. Some guy breaks into your place and kicks you in the balls. Then this. The kid's place is torched. You've gotta think something is up."

"So you got the whole squad working on it, right?"

"No. But I'm not doing this alone. We got arson investigators from the fire department looking at the building. We got me and Shoeshine full-time for at least a few more days on the Zhang kid. And we got you, unofficially, so long as you promise to keep everyone fully informed."

"Hey, I reported the break-in and the attack to the duty officer at the mini-station on South Street. It's not like I kept any secrets."

"Silence is the same as lying." Leone was wagging his finger again, "Mama taught me."

As if to stress Leone's point, Behr stayed silent for a minute, thinking of the past few days. He questioned whether the guy in his apartment, the guy who had kicked his ribs could have anything to do with the strange death of a corporate lawyer. He still felt foggy about what was going on. After all, what did he really know up to this point? Sam was dead. Sam was working on some big transaction and he was also working on a book. Maybe not his own book, maybe a translation of the manuscript that had been pulled out of China. Sure, the story about the grandfather was weird. And the manuscript itself, what they had read of it, was fascinating. But not really informative. A dark thought suddenly occurred to him. He turned to Leone.

"Is there anything left of the place?"

"Nada."

"Shit." Behr couldn't believe it. He had not seen Kristina yet. Didn't know if she had saved the disk. She had been taken to nearby Pennsylvania Hospital to be treated for smoke inhalation and minor burns. Leone had come to Behr's house shortly after he had been to the scene. Leone had been called at home because one of the officers dispatched to the fire had noticed SAMUEL ZHANG, APT. 3A listed on the intercom and thought the coincidence worth mentioning. Leone had confirmed to Behr that Kristina was basically fine, but that she had been pulled out by the PFD just before the roof collapsed. Leone had described Kristina's dramatic exit from the building, slung over the shoulder of a firefighter, flames shooting out the window above them as they descended the ladder. Leone hadn't seen it himself. But everyone was talking.

"Let's go check on your lady." Leone made a move to the door.

"She's not *my* lady, Tito," Behr corrected.

"Yeah, but you want to her to be," Leone snorted, then led them out to the brown, standard issue Dodge he had left blocking American Street.

☆ ☆ ☆

"Where's my report?"

"We don't have anything on paper yet, sir."

"Well then *tell* me, have you found Antonetti?" The treasury secretary glared at the two agents standing stiffly on the blue carpet with its huge depiction of an eagle in flight.

"Not exactly," the agent on the left answered. "We have implemented constant surveillance of the Antonetti residence, the wife's activities and the school attended by the children. As yet, nothing seems out of the ordinary."

"Except for Antonetti's absence," Stephanos cut in.

"Except for that, sir."

"And do we have an explanation of that?"

"We overheard the wife telling one of the kid's teachers that her husband was away on business. In the Far East and that they might join him. She was concerned, sir, about what the children might miss if they were out of school for two weeks."

"Far East? Nothing specific, like Thailand, China, Bhutan?" Stephanos treated them to some sarcasm.

"No, Far East is all she said," the agent answered, deadpan.

"Is that it? Is that your report?"

"Yes, sir. I'm afraid we don't have much to go on."

"All right, get back to it then." Stephanos made a dismissive gesture with his hand.

"Sir? If I may, it would help if we knew the purpose of our mission here. It might make us more sensitive to any nuances." The second agent nodded his head vigorously in agreement.

Stephanos studied his two head-nodding treasury agents for a moment. It was necessary to keep information tight. He thought they had taken decent precautions in the past, but it was looking increasingly like Antonetti had turned. And Antonetti was near the top of the informational food chain. Stephanos hated to tell anyone anything at all. But he had to tell these guys something. Because, as they said, they had to be alert to nuance, and because they needed motivation. Motivation makes a man alert. And Stephanos wanted his agents as alert as starving coyotes are to the scratching of mice in the desert.

He decided to throw them some appetizers. The meal would come later. He triangled his fingertips and leaned back in the red leather chair, assuming a lecturing posture. "Michael Antonetti, as you know, worked under Bill Ruddle in International Affairs. Until his resignation last week, his job title was Deputy Assistant Secretary for Asia, the Americas and some other places." The agents were nodding again. They knew all this.

"What you don't know is that Antonetti was neck-deep in the current financial crisis. He was back and forth to these places every week, trying to sort out the mess. He's been our chief negotiator with every regime in Indonesia since Suharto, with the Koreans, the Thai—you name it. Everyone except the Japanese. We got someone else on them. But Antonetti wasn't just dealing with the money. What Antonetti was doing was carving out concessions in exchange for monetary assistance."

"Could we have an example, sir?"

"Example? I'll give you an example: NSA wanted to put a state of the art listening post in the mountains of Borneo—Suharto and Habibie stonewalled us for years—then Antonetti got us the listening post. There's more: the Thai military was protecting Burmese heroin producers in the northwestern mountains. Antonetti negotiated loans for the Thai central bank, and boom, some of the biggest opium warlords in the world land in L.A. in handcuffs. The Koreans were giving us a hard time on the commercial front, dumping electronics to carve out market share. Interestingly, the market share they were taking was from the Japanese. So we were getting shit from the Japanese about not protecting their goods from Korean competition. Imagine, gentlemen, the Japs of all people complaining about an uneven playing field! Anyway, Antonetti put the screws to some of the big Caebol—they're like the Japanese Keiretsu." Stephanos was about to explain but the agents nodded their understanding. "And the Koreans raised prices. So this guy, this *one* guy, Antonetti, was in the unique position of knowing the Far Eastern agenda of *every* branch of *every* department in our government. The DEA wants Burmese heroin, Antonetti gets it. The NSA and the CIA want intelligence gathering, Antonetti gets it. So that's Antonetti in a nutshell. He's got one of the most exciting jobs in the world. Then, without warning, he resigns. And if that ain't enough to scare the shit out of that idiot Ruddle, he disappears too. No one can find him, and he's got all this information in his head."

The treasury secretary had grown animated during his lecture, and a thin sheen of sweat was forming on his bald pate. The baldness caught the reflection of the sun coming through the windows of his massive corner office at 1500 Pennsylvania Avenue. The bright gleam of his scalp made Stephanos look biblical, visionary, as if God was trying to burst from his head. He knew he looked scary, but the agents, to their credit, stayed stiff and calm, processing the information they had just received. Stephanos admired their professionalism. This was why they had been chosen for the Vanguard in the first place.

"Sir, is there a particular sensitivity we should be aware of? Any current negotiations? Should we be especially alert to the agents of any particular country, or should we just see who shows up?"

Stephanos considered the question carefully. Telling them which country might give them too much information. What if one of them were caught? The fact that he was paying official attention would be known, and the suspected operatives would tunnel deeper, making their activities even harder to monitor. Then again, he thought, a hound must know the scent of its quarry or it'll just go barking into the trees.

"Boys, watch the Chinese. Every goddamn one of them. And be careful doing it."

The agents made their exit and Stephanos called up the quote screen on his computer and cursed. The Asian currencies were down again, except for the yuan. Once again, the yuan had managed to be the only Asian currency worth more today than it was yesterday. What were the Chinese playing at? And who was buying all this currency? Speculation alone couldn't account for it. And who else had the cash? Could the Chinese be secretly propping up their own currency, selling dollars and yen to buy yuan they had just printed? If so, why float it in the first place? Of course, it might not be the Chinese at all. They may have made a simple mistake, mistiming the market. And that would mean someone else was manipulating the markets. But who? The Europeans? What was their agenda? Stephanos felt two steps behind and didn't like it. He had spent his career well ahead of the next guy and grown wonderfully rich because of it. Now people were questioning his leadership and his wisdom. Saying that the former investment banker might be in over his head in the world of international politics. To hell with those people. He'd figure this out yet. He simply had to.

Stephanos reached for the phone and called in the next batch of agents. Unlike the last duo, these guys didn't have law enforcement experience. He had brought these guys with him from the brokerage arm of his investment bank because they knew money inside and out. And because they could be vicious. They had been traders and were now doing him a huge favor by taking million dollar pay-cuts to follow him into a new line of work. When they entered, Stephanos was amused at the outward difference from the last agents. Better suits, better hair, these guys didn't look government at all. They were perfect for the assignment..

"Gentlemen," Stephanos boomed in his best Wall Street camaraderie, "good to see you again!"

"Same to you."

"I got a little project for you, undercover sort of thing. You up for it?"

"You bet!" The three suited men said at once. This was what they had followed Stephanos for: the power and excitement that came with a badge.

Stephanos chuckled at their enthusiasm. "You're going to be doing something completely unfamiliar to you. You're going in as currency traders."

The three men shared Stephanos' laughter. They had been trading currencies since they were kids.

Once they settled down, Stephanos continued. "I'm going to split you up. Dick, you are going to Chicago. J.P., Hong Kong. And Gus, I'm going to start you in Philly in the currency options market and then move you to London. You are all once again employees of the esteemed firm of Rhine & Company. You will each be on the trading floor, concentrating on the Asians, particulary this new animal, the Chinese yuan. Basically I want you guys taking short positions. Sell yuan and see who is buying. If the buyer is a brokerage or another bank, try to dig the surface, talk to the traders, find out on whose behalf the buys are being made. What we got is someone buying up a lot of yuan, and we don't know who. Figure it out. You got me?"

The three men assented, followed up with questions about their individual assignments which were to start the next day. Gus asked, "So, how can you do this? You don't work for Rhine & Company anymore."

"Gentlemen, this isn't strictly kosher." Stephanos was comfortable telling them this. These guys were traders. Ethical dilemmas didn't concern them. They probably had more trouble picking out their ties than deciding between right and wrong. But he did feel he should warn them. "Squint is doing me a personal favor."

"Squint?" The men groaned. Squint, as he was universally known, had succeeded to the helm of the banking giant after Stephanos got picked for the treasury post. He got his nickname in the '70s when he was the first person on the trading floor to indicate a purchase of yen by pulling his eyes into an oriental squint. As tasteless as the gesture was (deutsche mark were indicated with a crooked finger under the nose meant to look like Hitler's mustache), it became universal in the pits, and Squint became famous in the small world of big money. He was also widely feared, a true bastard even to his closest friends. Thus Stephanos expected more groans with his parting words.

"And gentlemen," he said, eyebrows raised, "try not to lose any of Squint's money."

10

Behr stood by the doorway, listening to her breathe. Kristina was sleeping among the stuffed animals in his daughter's room and had been for almost ten hours. The painkillers were on time-release. He felt slightly foolish standing there in his faded boxer shorts and T-shirt, but he wasn't sure what to do with himself and hearing her slumber was gently comforting. In truth, he was accustomed to this hallway vigil. On his daughter's infrequent visits from California, when released from his ex-wife's jealous grip, Behr would often stand here, just as he was now, listening to the inhalations and exhalations of continued life, the vitality and strength of a loved one nearby.

Behr hadn't offered Kristina his bed. He didn't want the gesture to be misconstrued. Maybe that was a mistake, he thought. Gentlemanliness sometimes stood in the way of what you wanted most.

He suddenly felt embarrassed. He turned and stepped quietly down the hall to the bathroom for a shower. There his embarrassment worsened as he remembered that he was out of shampoo and had been using soap in his hair for weeks. When she got up and showered, he feared that he would appear to her just as he was, a boorish and lonely divorcé too far gone to deal with the niceties of civilized life. He stood immobilized in front of the glass door to the shower stall. Should he run out and get some shampoo? Maybe some conditioner? Bagels and fresh coffee for breakfast? It might make the place seem homey. She might like homey. But it would mean leaving her alone. And what if she woke up to an empty house and got scared? Surely she had experienced enough fright and uncertainty in the last few days.

Behr shook his head. He was being ridiculous. Just take the shower and get on with it.

When he emerged from the bathroom, clad only in a worn grey towel, Kristina was sitting cross-legged on his bed. She was still wearing last night's pajamas—his daughter's pajamas—only slightly too tight on Kristina's thin frame. The tightness of the pajama top over her breasts was incredibly alluring, but the familiarity of the fabric in another context was emotionally confusing. Behr had to focus his gaze elsewhere as they spoke.

"How do you feel?" he asked gently.

"I think I'm all right. My head is pounding but I can breathe," she answered, her voice rough. "By the way, thanks for letting me stay here."

"Hey, where else were you going to go?"

"You know, your daughter is a lucky girl. Lots of animals and toys."

"Well, guilt has a lot to do with it," Behr said slowly, still avoiding eye contact. He felt uncomfortable discussing his daughter, now almost twelve and probably still sound asleep in her bed in Palo Alto. "Every year, the animals get bigger and the toys come with more batteries. She probably sees right through me."

"She probably loves you dearly and misses you every day. Where is she, California?"

"Bay area."

"And why aren't you there too?"

"I don't know. Her mother doesn't want me there. She remarried. They're both software designers. Very dedicated, very driven. They had another kid about a year ago; she tells me they're building a new world for themselves. A new, more stable world for her and Maggie."

"So they've left the old world of Philadelphia behind?"

"Something like that." He wasn't very good with questions about the past, and especially not his family. He had grown to resent his ex-wife. He didn't know hate as an emotion. He had never really hated anyone. But his ex-wife generated the most intense dislike of which he was capable. A deeply selfish, controlling woman, she had forced his move out of the U.S. Attorney's Office because the job, she insisted, took up too much time. When he had landed the teaching job at Penn, she complained about moving out of New York. And after a year in Philadelphia, she announced that she was unhappy with the lifestyle afforded by his low professorial salary and suggested he approach the local law firms. But by this time, he had grown to enjoy teaching. In great part because of Sam Zhang, he had discovered a sense of personal mission that he'd never anticipated. So he decided to resist her nudging and told her to get used to it. Perhaps he had handled the situation indelicately. He could have massaged her a bit. Promised her the comfort that tenure and royalties from textbooks would bring. In truth, he couldn't fathom what she was complaining about. They weren't doing poorly. Philadelphia was comparatively cheap, Penn gave him well over a hundred grand a year, and she was starting to realize a very nice income, augmented with stock options, from her job at a New Jersey computer company. On top of that Behr's lighter workload eased her motherly burdens at home. It was Behr who got Maggie up and fed and to school most mornings. And he usually picked her up too, after which they would often do the shopping and household chores together. He and Maggie played house. They had fun with it, and Behr had thought that everyone was happy.

But one day the woman just announced that she was miserable and had been for some time. The marriage, she said, wasn't working out the way she wanted. She talked about her agenda, how it included a large suburban house and elite schools for Maggie. How it included foreign vacations and more fun than she thought Behr was going to provide. She told Behr that she didn't know him anymore. That he had become a *smaller* person. A typical academic with little, academic dreams. He certainly wasn't the dashing prosecutor she had married. A man who lunged at dragons and won every time. She didn't want to share his dreams, she said, and she certainly didn't want to live them. She was moving to California. She had already accepted a job there. A great job, one that would buy her everything she had ever dreamed of for her and Maggie.

Jolted and suddenly on the defensive, Behr had fought for custody. California courts didn't have jurisdiction yet, and Behr thought a Philadelphia court would give him the edge. Keep the girl in predicable, safe Philadelphia with a predictable, safe law professor at the region's best school. But the judge had gone the other way. Conservative old-world Philadelphia had ruled that the girl stays with her mother absent some sort of danger to her person. And Behr declined to appeal. The custody battle had been hard enough for Maggie. He didn't need to drag it out.

After a minute, Kristina brought him out of his angry memories. "I didn't get anything out of Sam's apartment. Not the disk, not the computer. Nothing at all."

Somehow, he had expected and been afraid of this. He looked over to Kristina to see if her expression would show the depth of her disappointment. She seemed sad, but at the same time, surprisingly strong.

"What now?" he asked.

"I was going to ask you the same thing."

Behr shrugged; momentarily stumped. Sam's manuscript was gone. Only last night a close reading of the *Confession* had been the next step, promising either to lead them to discover whatever was at the bottom of this thing, or revealing itself to be irrelevant. But with the *Confession* gone, likely melted in its plastic diskette, there wasn't much to go on. He felt stupid at not having printed out a copy. Sam had a printer sitting right next the laptop. They should, at the very least, have read more of it. Discovered the secret to which Chen Hai had been alluding, the one that could make him a hero or send him to his grave. God punishes the lazy, Behr thought, then remembered saying something similar to Sam's class years ago.

But in the midst of this self-recrimination, Behr remembered the source of the *Confession*. Those little books that Kristina had mentioned. The ones that this Baba character had dragged out of China. They hadn't found them in Sam's apartment, despite an exhaustive search yesterday. And they didn't appear in Sam's office at Tew Logan. They had to be somewhere else. But where? Hoping it would cheer her up, he excitedly mentioned the prospect of finding them to Kristina.

She didn't match his enthusiasm. "At this point," she said with a shrug, "you know as much as I do. And I don't know where else to look. I don't know what Sam did in this city, where he hung out. You probably know his friends better than I do. Most of them, I think, went to Penn."

Kristina's shrug caused the tight pajama top to ride up, revealing a thin, but soft midriff and the whiter curve beneath her breasts. Behr heard fatalism in her voice and realized with a suddenness of purpose that infects people when they are introduced to strong emotions, that he wanted—more than anything—for their investigation to continue.

"Hey," he said, "let's not give up yet! I've been down this road. Every investigation moves in steps . . . very many, very small steps. Not all of them forward. Now," Behr moved to sit next to her on the bed, his eyes locked firmly on hers, "let's think about places where people store things."

Kristina tilted her head towards him. "You mean, like train station lockers?"

"Well, more like locker rooms, self-storage warehouses . . . their cars."

"Sam had a car, last time I saw him."

"What kind of car?"

"A blue car!"

Behr laughed and felt his towel slipping, "Not a big help, Ms. Zhang. A *brand* of car might be useful. Chevy, Mazda, whatever."

"I'm sorry," Kristina shook her head, "I just didn't notice that. I've been out of the country so long, all these cars look foreign to me."

"All right, we'll shelve that." Behr could get the make and license from Leone later. Though finding the car on the streets of Philadelphia might take some time. He pulled up the towel, covering himself as much as he could and noticing that Kristina watched him as he did so. "What about other kinds of places? Did Sam belong to a gym, was he an athlete?"

"A gym? I couldn't really see Sam at a gym or even a health club. Not the spandex or steroids type. But I remember, he played a lot of squash through high school and college. I bet he kept up with it."

"Really? That's something, that narrows it down. There aren't that many squash courts in the city." He could only think of a couple dozen courts, most of them on university campuses. In Sam's apartment they could have answered these questions in five minutes. But the apartment was gone. No file cabinets full of bills, no locker keys or combinations written on the handle of a gym bag.

"Well this is a start anyway." Behr clapped his hands together. "Kristina, maybe you should call that guy at the law firm, the handsome kid. You know, what's-his-name."

"Michael?" she asked brightly.

"Call Michael, ask him where Sam played squash or find out if he played regularly with anyone at Tew Logan. In the meantime, I'll get on the horn with Leone and get a handle on the car situation." Behr pointed to a phone next to the bed and failed to avert his eyes as Kristina stretched to reach for it, showing off a narrow and silky midriff. He had to get out of this towel!

While she dealt with the Tew Logan receptionist, Behr threw on some pants and a shirt and headed downstairs to find his cellular. He discovered, as usual, that Leone wasn't available, but he did get Officer Zapatero who proudly told him that he had already undertaken the task of researching the make, model and plate number of the deceased's vehicle. This information he gave to Behr together with strict instructions that the car was not to be touched if Behr were to locate it before the police. The car, Zapatero warned in a voice just past puberty, might contain evidence crucial to the ongoing investigation. Behr complemented Officer Zapatero on his professionalism and quietly decided to ignore that bit about the evidence. Behr had been a federal prosecutor. He didn't need the Philadelphia Police telling him how to handle evidence.

He heard the shower start upstairs and guiltily remembered the empty shampoo bottle on the ledge. He wondered what Kristina's reaction would be. His ex-wife, for one, would have berated him for a week for such a transgression.

With Kristina in the shower and temporarily out of investigative tasks, Behr turned his attention to the cat. Some kibble in a bowl and two strokes on the head figured to be all the creature deserved for the day. He then made a pot of coffee, pulled the *New York Times* in its blue plastic bag off the front door and perused the headlines. Four of the President's former aides were suing the President and his legal defense fund for failure to cover legal fees incurred during three years of grand jury and congressional testimony. The European Union, led by the

French, had extended their ban of U.S. beef products to cover all U.S. meats including poultry, until an investigation determined the extent to which the Americans were hormonally or genetically making their livestock better than European models. And a feature article on modern Africa explored the fact that all ten of the civil wars burning on that continent could be traced to the artificial boundaries laid by the English, French and Belgian colonists of the last century. Behr read each of these stories, skipped bits about the Asian financial crisis (feeling that there was nothing new to learn there) and headed for the anemic sports section. He usually read the *Inquirer*'s once he got to his office because it was more extensive, and because on campus he could get it free. But he wasn't going to the law school today, so he had to make due with the *Times* and their usual emphasis on things that mattered only in New York.

The sports section put him in mind of school, and he realized with a happy sense of sloth that he didn't have to be in a classroom for a few more months. He wasn't teaching this semester, and the burden of preparing six lectures a week on the ins and outs of criminal law would fall to the visiting professor from NYU. Still, he thought, he should at least check in with his secretary, and peruse his messages and the growing pile of paper in his in-box. And he resolved to do so after they found Sam's car.

Behr never made it to his office that day. Kristina learned from Mike Frattone that Sam had been a member of the stuffy Philadelphia Athletic Club. After a sufficient quantity of coffee, they walked to the turn-of-the-century edifice on Sixteenth Street only to be greeted with hostility on the part of management. They told Behr and Kristina that it was club policy not to give out information on any of their members. "That is what is meant by a *private* club," the woman sniffed, though Kristina had explained the situation: that her brother was dead, that she just wanted whatever personal effects he may have left behind.

Behr tried to play the legal heavy. He warned that as the closest living relative to the deceased, Kristina now legally owned whatever items of Sam's the club may have in its possession. If they didn't turn the items over, they were, in effect, stealing them. But his arguments fell flat. Under thirty foot ceilings and surrounded by dark wood paneling, snoring businessmen and oil paintings of graceful horses and pinkish nudes, they were told to put their request in writing and then shown the door.

This unexpected rudeness was followed by an unexpected kindness. While recovering from their bewilderment on the sidewalk, a club member exited down the marble steps and approached them. He was a young, well-fed man in a tweedy jacket; he said that he had overheard the conversation and was frustrated by the club's belligerence. He apologized to each of them and stated that management was under some stress because of financial hard times. He also explained that their search would likely be fruitless. This was because the club had open lockers, just booths really, where the members change and hang up their clothes. If there was anything that a member wanted to leave at the club overnight, it was kept in a cardboard box in a secure room adjacent to the locker room. It worked like a cloak room, the man said, chuckling lightly, except it was box room. But very few of the members used the box room because access was restricted to the times when the attendant was available to retrieve boxes, and the attendant was approaching eighty and spent most of his time asleep in an unused sauna. The fellow doubted very much if a young member, a brother of the lady, would have kept anything there. Then, with a lascivious eye on Kristina, he invited them in for lunch. Behr declined for both of them. But he did so nicely.

"Strike one," Behr said as they wandered back to Twelfth and Pine to look for Sam's blue Volkswagen with an eye cast toward the darkening sky.

It started raining before they were even at Broad Street—a cold winter rain that struck their faces at an angle and forced their eyes into squints and their chins into their collars. They bought pocket umbrellas from a street vendor, but the gusts whipping around the grey stone blocks turned the umbrellas inside out and tore the fabric from the cheap aluminum spines. They threw the skeletons into one of the dumpsters that had appeared on Pine Street in front of the charred ruin that was Sam's building.

"This is awful!" Kristina shouted over the wind and suddenly heavy traffic.

"Nah!" Behr shouted back, smiling broadly—realizing that he was having fun, "this is what investigations are all about."

Kristina looked doubtful. "Now what?"

"Well, when a cat gets lost," Behr stepped towards her to be heard, "it starts walking in ever-widening circles until it finds something familiar. I don't want us to split up, what with all that has happened," Behr nodded toward the burned out apartment house, "so we'll walk together, starting down Pine. Then we'll head up Eleventh, then back along Spruce . . . you get the idea."

They walked in circles for a very wet hour, finally locating the car not a block from Behr's own house. It was a real city car. Dirty, dented, completely devoid of personal effects and parked nine blocks from its owner's apartment. Behr also noted the distinguishing mark of a Philadelphia car: it was missing almost half of its license plate. It was a strangely local crime. Small time crooks would bend back and cut off the part of a license plate with the registration sticker on it and then sell those stickers to dealers in North Philadelphia. Before Behr learned to garage his car, it had happened to him twice. Sam, apparently, had not opted for a garage. But in this scavenging climate, he had left nothing visible in the blue '86 Jetta for anyone to steal.

If the books were in the car, they were in the trunk, and Kristina suggested they call his detective friend to open it. But Behr quickly declined. If the books were really in the trunk, then Leone would have to take them back to the Roundhouse and process them as evidence. It would be a week before Behr and Kristina saw them again. And if they were competing with someone for information—that is, if the man in his apartment wasn't a burglar, and if the apartment fire wasn't an accident—they damn well couldn't afford to lose time to police procedure. Behr decided on an alternate strategy.

He returned from a quick trip to his house with a coat hanger, and after a few minutes of very publicly working it between the glass and the rubber, he hooked the cable that ran between the door handle and the button lock and yanked. The door opened; he had broken into the car. But it being Philadelphia, no one who saw them called the police.

He quickly found the trunk latch. From the rear of the car he heard a groan. He went back to find Kristina staring into emptiness. Nothing but the spare.

"Strike two," he said, and Kristina gave him a dirty look through the wet hair dangling in front of her eyes. "Let's get inside," he suggested.

Behr made them tea while Kristina petted the cat. The cat was thrilled. It sat in her lap purring loudly. She hadn't said much and Behr could see something like defeat clouding her features. He thought of some comforting words, and rejected them as too cheesy. He remembered some speeches his high school coaches had practiced on the team, speeches about keeping your eye on the ball and not letting setbacks make you forget who you were and what you were capable of. These were cheesy too. He couldn't think of anything particulary cheerful; he offered Kristina the shower to warm up.

"No thanks," she smiled. "By the way, I think I used up your shampoo. You should put it on the shopping list."

Behr smiled with her, enjoying her tact and enjoying the moment until suddenly Kristina leapt from her chair, displacing the cat which landed angry and hissing on the floor.

"Hey, give me your car keys!" she demanded.

"Uh, sure. What for?" Behr fished in his corduroys for the keys to the Porsche.

"For the box. From Sam's office. We never took it out of the trunk!"

Behr stood quickly too. They hurried to the garage to find the box exactly where they had left it. Behr's Porsche 914 was a mid-engine car, leaving a sizable storage area under the hood in addition to the rear trunk. They'd put the box in the front after leaving Tew Logan and then simply forgotten to bring it up to Sam's apartment. And a good thing it was. For if they had, it would have been destroyed together with everything else that was once Sam's.

Behr carried the box back to the house where they unloaded the contents onto the living room rug. There didn't seem to be much of interest. It would be tough finding a clue. Behr flipped through the legal tomes, looking for notes in the margin or message slips Sam may have used as bookmarks. He actually did find some of these, but the messages all seemed to be from Bob Silver, all written in the same neat hand, presumably Rose's. Many read "Bob Silver, Again!" Kristina meanwhile concentrated on the tray of knickknacks from the desk drawer. Pens, soy sauce, paper clips, saltines all ended up on the rug. When she was done with this, she began pulling the pictures from their stand-up frames, looking for things Sam may have tucked behind. And as she finished with each frame, she tossed its picture on the rug, close to Behr.

Behr lined up the photographs in front of him. There were six in all. The ski photo he remembered from that day at Tew Logan, as well as the old man in the chair and the black-and-white of the Zhang family in front of the old Chicago homestead. The other three he had glossed over earlier. One was of Sam on a boat, clutching a halyard. Another was of Sam with his arm around a blond girl in a Washington College sweatshirt. The last was of Kristina. Or at least it looked like Kristina from the back. She was bent slightly at the waist, applying paint to a huge mural. It looked like a Dutch still life from the 1600s, just much, much larger and with an almost photo-realistic quality.

"Is this you?" Behr handed her the photograph.

"Yep, that's me. Sam's only visit to Amsterdam. Maybe five years ago."

"Is that your painting? Is this what you do? It's fantastic!" Behr exclaimed.

"It's not all I do, but I look to the Dutch Baroque for inspiration. That one is called *Big Fruit*, I sold it to a collector in Palm Beach." Kristina said it matter-of-factly and handed the photograph back to Behr, who studied it again. The fruit was big all right. The high-gloss apple was almost as big as Kristina standing in the foreground.

"Do you know this girl?" Behr handed Kristina the photo with the blond.

"Nope."

"Did Sam ever discuss girlfriends?"

"He would have written about something steady. Just to prove he wasn't lonely, that he could get a girlfriend at all. No, I don't think this is anyone special." Kristina tossed the photograph back.

The name of the college seemed familiar, but he wasn't sure where it was. He climbed upstairs and turned on the computer. He ran the name through a search engine on the World Wide Web. This pointed him toward the college's own website which described it as one of the country's oldest schools. It was located in Chestertown, Maryland. On that state's Eastern Shore. And something about Maryland struck a chord. Behr ran back downstairs.

He immediately saw what he was looking for. It was right in Kristina's hand. "Give me that for sec!" And he grabbed the file away.

Yes, there it was, real estate listings for properties in Oxford, Maryland. Oxford was a town on the eastern shore of Chesapeake Bay—a kind of unofficial capital for the landed gentry and sailboat-crazy. All the listings were from the same broker: Jackson Properties. A number was listed at the bottom of each page.

"Call them," he said to Kristina. "Maybe they know this girl. Explain the situation."

Kristina got the portable from the kitchen and dialed the number. Behr listened in. A sweet, surprisingly southern voice answered.

"My name is Kristina Zhang. I'm looking for the agent who was working with my brother Sam, Samuel Zhang. Do you think you could look that up somehow?"

"Oh honey, I don't need to look that up. The agent was Barbara Cooper, but she ain't . . . I mean she *isn't* here right now. Maybe I can help you?"

"I was wondering, well you see, my brother . . . he had an accident. He died, and I live overseas and I don't know—"

"Well that's just terrible. Your brother was just a lovely person. So nice. I'm so, so sorry."

"Thank you, thank you very much. But you see, I came across this picture of him with someone. A woman. And I don't know who she is, and I think she may be from your area, and maybe if she was with him when he was looking at properties you might know her name and then I could tell her about what happened."

"Oh . . . I see." The woman said slowly, the treacle ebbing. "I don't recall anyone coming to the office with Sam. And I think I would remember, he was here every other weekend for almost a year."

"A year?"

"Oh yes, he was very particular."

"When was the last time you saw him at the office?"

"At the office?" The woman paused, her thinking audible in the clicking of her tongue, "Well, probably the last time was at closing."

"Closing? He bought something?"

"Oh didn't you know? It's a lovely little place, right on the water. Sailor's dream. Though it needed some work I can tell you now."

11

Jin Qing sat for a moment, distracted from the sadness emanating from distant Philadelphia. She stared through the window, watching the crows settle onto the outer walls of the Forbidden City, their black feet clutching the red brick in defiance of the strong winds that blew in from the Gobi. The winds carried with them the yellow desert sand that coated Beijing's great boulevards and squares and caught in the throats of its citizens. But the crows survived the wind and they survived the sand. They had even, she thought wryly, survived Chairman Mao. When he had moved the capital here, back from Nanjing, his officials had taken it upon themselves to kill all the birds in the city. An "antipest campaign" they had called it. But after they poisoned the birds, the insects thrived. Mosquitoes swarmed in Beijing's blistering summer heat, and even the ranking cadres and party members were not immune to the ravages of the encephalitis they carried.

Over the years the birds recovered. Tiananmen Square was now littered with pigeons, and the Forbidden City, adorned with its giant portrait of Mao, was attended exclusively by crows. Crows who, like the eunuchs in their day, jealously and viciously guarded the privileged turf surrounding the seat of power.

Jin Qing was suddenly disgusted by the sight and turned her own avian face from the window. Crows thrive in decay. And decay was everywhere she looked these days. In the government, in the party, even in her own ministry. The organs of state were becoming parodies of themselves. The discipline and visionary self-sacrifice which had defined the old order under Mao was giving way to infectious corruption and pettiness. All that remained in most corridors of the regime was the rhetoric of revolution. The underlying power that had created that rhetoric, or been born by it—the power of institutionalized Leninist zealotry—was being replaced by simple materialist greed. Greed which went unpunished, although only a few years ago it could have meant a sentence of death.

Her world, the Ministry of State Security, was still relatively pure. But as the principal intelligence and espionage arm of the government, its attention was turned outward. It focused on countering the threats to the system that came from abroad, from foreigners and from expatriate Chinese in Taiwan, Singapore and especially the United States. There was not much that her Ministry could do to cleanse the internal mechanisms of the country. That was the immediate job of the Ministry of *Public* Security and ultimately the job of the Central Committee of the Communist Party and its leaders. They were supposed to punish the provincial officials and company bosses who toured the fiefdoms in expensive cars, cellular telephones glued to their ears. They were supposed to ensure that satellite dishes trained on western media did not hide below the eaves of the people's houses. They were supposed to ensure that the best scientists worked on advancing China's technological weaponry, not developing cheaper production methods for American-owned toy factories. But they didn't. They were weakened. They were without strong leadership and without a real vision for the future. Not a Chinese future anyway.

Jin Qing's thoughts were intruded on by her secretary—a slight, androgynous creature who, she decided, was making a habit of sneaking up on her.

"What do you want?"

"Feng is here to see you. He has been waiting for some time. I believe you asked to see him at ten. Also, Hu Zhong just came in five minutes ago. You asked that I should inform you right away." The secretary stood partially bowed, his eyes on the floor before him. He did not want Jin Qing thinking he had seen anything on her desk.

"Show in Hu Zhong now. And say nothing to Feng. If he asks why he is kept waiting, say you do not know."

"I understand."

Hu Zhong was presently shown in and stood uncomfortably in the spot vacated by the secretary. Jin Qing bade him sit, and he did so tentatively on the edge of the wooden chair in front of her desk.

"Philadelphia, Hu Zhong. How could you let this happen?"

"Perhaps the agent has misinterpreted her orders, Minister?" Hu Zhong called her Minister as did most of her underlings. She was, in fact, only an Assistant Deputy Minister. But her command—the Foreign Affairs Bureau, which encompassed all the foreign intelligence operations of the People's Republic except those conducted directly by and for the military—gave her more authority than almost any other person of her rank in government. And her style of command gave her more authority than most of the top government ministers. Her own immediate superior, the Deputy Minister of Operations, and his boss, the Minister of State Security had never once, and would never dare question any decision she made.

"And how did the agent have the latitude to interpret anything? It was your operation. The blame lies with you."

"Yes, yes, Minister, the blame is all mine," Hu Zhong stammered. "I was merely trying to suggest a sequence of events."

"Correct me if I am wrong, Hu. There is quite a discrepancy in the two reports."

Hu Zhong nodded, saying nothing.

"Field agent Helen states that she overheard a conversation in which the subject, Samuel Zhang, admitted knowledge of the contents of the *Crystal Palace* and the *San Juan*. The very two ships we have been chasing."

"I recall seeing that in her report."

"And we know that he did not get that knowledge from his superior at the law firm, this . . . this—" Jin Qing paged through the report on her desk until she found the name "—this Robert Silver, because, in fact, you have consistently lied to Silver about the nature of what we seek."

"Correct."

"And we know that Samuel Zhang did not get that knowledge from the documents in his possession because we have been through those documents and know that they reference nothing but a fictional shipment of Xian marble."

She could see Hu Zhong was sweating, despite the cold draft that blew through the edges of the window. Jin Qing read from the report again.

"Field Agent Helen then attempted to lure Samuel Zhang from the law firm to elicit more information, but before she could do so, the boy was shot. Either by his own hand or, she suspects, by this lawyer . . ."

"Silver."

"Yes, Silver." Jin Qing now reached to a second pile of paper and lifted off the top document. She flipped to the second page. "Now your report, Hu Zhong, tells a very different story. You say that Helen acted on her own. That she was in Samuel Zhang's office when the shot was fired. That she had sexually confused the boy and that perhaps she had even fired the final shot herself."

"That is how it was reported to me, Madame Jin, by the lawyer Silver."

"What would be her motivation in killing the boy?"

"I have speculated about that in the report. If you recall, there on page four, I state—"

"Yes, I have it here." She made a show of slowly flipping the pages. "You contend that the agent considered Samuel Zhang's knowledge of the ships' contents to indicate a breach in security. As such, Samuel Zhang was a liability and under the standing directive of the Minister— that's me" She looked at Hu Zhong coldly over the top edge of her reading glasses. "She eliminated Sam Zhang before he could disseminate his information, taking care to leave no trace of herself behind."

"I think it a reasonable explanation, Minister. Perhaps the only reasonable explanation."

"Really? The standing directive was what, Hu Zhong? How did you explain it to the team in the field?"

"I gave orders that in this operation a breach of security must not be allowed to widen. Any compromised individuals were to be silenced. I understood that to be consistent with the Minister's directive." Hu

Zhong looked suddenly worried. "Should I rescind the order?"

"No! You shall not rescind it. But you shall amend it to what it should have been in the first place."

Hu Zhong looked confused and said he was unsure how the amendment should be worded. "Does the Minister have a suggestion?"

"I do," Jin Qing said softly, ominously. She wanted to explode at this man, berate him for his idiocy, maybe even punish him in front of the others. But such an act would do her no good. Such an act was not in keeping with the ancient teachings of Han Fei Tzu. She must show just enough anger to motivate him, but not enough to really frighten him into mistakes or disloyalty. She still needed Hu Zhong, at least for a little while. Even if he had grown dangerously erratic.

She had originally assigned Hu Zhong to the project with the hope that he would show the star qualities he had exhibited as a field officer. But the qualities she had so admired seemed absent now. He had spent too much time in America. He had grown sloppy and devious in his efforts to hide his errors. And Jin Qing was pretty sure he was hiding something now. Or, at minimum, skewing the evidence. She blamed Hu Zhong for this mess, not the girl. Hu Zhong knew they were probing Samuel Zhang for possible knowledge of the ships' cargo— Sam's father, after all, had been born on one of the ships. Hu Zhong also knew that Sam's firm had been retained in great part because Sam was an attorney there. Yet Hu Zhong had failed to properly instruct the field agents that the Zhangs were to be watched and above all, protected. And more fundamentally, he had also failed to pair the agent. Jin Qing had been in intelligence her entire adult life—an adult life which began in 1959 at the age of fourteen. And during that entire time, field agents operated in pairs. It was the basic unit of intelligence operations. Paired agents were the molecular building block of China's security apparatus. Pairing agents accomplished both an operational objective and a political one. The second agent was supposed to watch for basic mistakes, and, just as importantly, for a loss of political conviction. In this way, they had around-the-clock surveillance of their own personnel. The agents were instructed to report on each other, to notice increasing attachments to Western goods, foods, women, and to report on contacts that did not bear on a particular mission. Hu Zhong had failed to send a second agent to Philadelphia, and the consequences were grave. A good lead had abruptly ended with a bullet to the head. Dammit. It should have been Hu Zhong's head, she thought. Soon it would be.

"My first suggestion is that you clarify our objectives to the field agents." She spoke slowly, with staccato authority, as if talking to a child, "We are looking for information about the whereabouts of the cargo that left Shanghai aboard the *Crystal Palace* and the *San Juan*. Have them understand that knowledge of this information does not necessarily amount to a breach of security. Second," Jin Qing held up two fingers, "you shall make it absolutely clear to every agent in the United States that the Zhangs are to be protected until the level of their knowledge can be determined. If you have not done so already, you shall implement surveillance of the father, Harry Zhang, and the daughter, Kristina Zhang. The daughter moved to Amsterdam, though likely she is in America now. You must find her. The father is, as always, in Chicago."

If Hu Zhong was surprised by her familiarity with the Zhangs' whereabouts, he didn't show it. He simply acknowledged the order.

Jin Qing saw relief lighten his face. The stress lines in his forehead smoothed and some of the old arrogance again danced in his eyes. He thought he had gotten away with something. That she actually believed the totality of his report.

Of course, there were elements of truth in his assertions. But that played to his hand. Hu Zhong had anticipated her confusion, had guessed she would not know who to believe—him or his subordinate. So to appear credible, he admitted the smaller error, admitted to ambiguity in the orders he had given. And that way he shifted the blame to Field Agent Helen who, if Hu Zhong was to be believed, had killed a new source of valuable information or, just as preposterously, romanced the boy to death.

She looked at him now, hiding her disappointment, trying to appear unreadable as she dismissed him with a wave and watched him bow curtly before turning to exit. He practically ran through the double doors to the office. She waited two minutes for him to leave the floor, then carefully tore up his report. She swept the shreds into a bin that would be emptied later into the incinerator. Now she was ready for Feng.

She called her secretary on the intercom. Feng appeared almost immediately.

She was cheered by his appearance. He made quite a contrast to Hu Zhong. Whereas Hu Zhong was tall for a Chinese, and boringly handsome, the man before her now was stunted and dark. He had the wide cheekbones, stretched narrow eyes and rough brown complexion of a western Muslim, of a tough desert people who proudly traced their roots to the Mongol Khans. Feng reveled in the vicious savagery of his ancestry. And it was this savagery that comforted Jin Qing now, available, as it was, at her fingertips.

"I am sorry you had to wait. The reason you had to wait is because I had to see Hu Zhong, the gentleman you saw leave, before I knew what to tell you. I hope that you had the opportunity to study his face. Because he is your assignment. You are going to the United States. To the Americans you are a graduate engineering student named Kuang. But to every one else you are MID and you will, therefore, be met by agents of the Military Intelligence Department upon your arrival in New York. They are assisting you in the belief that you are *their* agent, not ours. Understand?"

Feng nodded once, meeting her eyes.

"Good. MID's New York office will assign you to Hu Zhong's team as an observer. Hu Zhong *must* think that you are MID. Act like a soldier. You should be able to tell if your cover is secure by Hu Zhong's manner. So long as he treats you dismissively, with arrogance and disdain, you are safe."

Jin Qing leaned far over her desk and lowered her voice to a whispered rasp. "You must understand that Hu Zhong is a traitor. An enemy to the People. He has lied to me. To my face in this office not five minutes before you entered. He is planning to grow rich from certain state secrets, and then defect."

She let the words penetrate Feng's thick skin, happy to see that they had their intended effect. She watched the man's eyes grow cold, almost black. She resumed.

"He must not be aware of your surveillance. It is not necessary that you know, minute to minute, what he is doing. Just so long as you know where he is. At all times. And at some time, I do not know precisely when, I shall contact you. When I do, I will simply instruct you to proceed. Your objective is to kill Hu Zhong. His death must be bloody and just public enough to get the attention of the media and thereby send a message to every field agent contemplating the lures of the West. Otherwise, I don't care how you do it. You are not to let anyone know this objective. Once you have completed your assignment, either I or MID will assist in your extraction. When you next appear before me, if you have been successful in all aspects of this operation and if you want it, you may take over Hu Zhong's position. That is a three-level advancement. Only one other person in the history of the Ministry has made that kind of leap. It was done in a similar manner."

Jin Qing did not elaborate that she had been the other person, that she too had advanced by assassinating her predecessor in office. There was no need, for the story of Jin Qing's career and her ruthless quest for the top was famous. It was also deeply—and very quietly—resented by the many agents, some ten and twenty years older than she, who had fallen in her wake.

"My instructions are then as follows . . ." Feng methodically repeated what Jin Qing had just told him. Jin Qing listened carefully, making sure the man got it right. When he was finished, she clarified a point or two and handed him a file detailing Hu Zhong's operations in the US. In contrast to her dismissive gesture toward Hu Zhong, she rose and guided Feng to the door, hooking her arm in his, allowing him to feel the special weight of the confidence she placed in him.

After she closed the inner door behind him, she stood still for a moment, her hand on the handle. Then she turned, and as she began to walk back to the desk, a movement in the window caught her eye. She looked. It was only the crows, now circling over the Hall of Supreme Harmony, vying for fallen crumbs dropped by tourists. They grew fat on these crumbs, both the crows and the tourists who fed them. Such was the population now of the Forbidden City. Crows and tourists. The seat of power for five hundred years of imperial rule dating from the Ming was now just a skeleton picked over by scavengers.

Jin Qing's stomach turned. She gripped the armrests, lowered herself slowly into the chair. She felt it again, the strange and increasingly familiar swirl of vertigo that had first struck her a week ago when she learned of Samuel Zhang's death. She saw a deep chasm opening between her feet, slowly widening until it stretched beyond her reach, and she was sent twisting silently, swiftly, irreversibly into the blackness.

Jin Qing closed her eyes against it. She forced herself to think of the job before her. Mostly this worked. The vertigo would abate when she was doing something to move her mission forward, or when she was setting things right, as when she sentenced Hu Zhong to death. Yet it returned, ineluctably, and for the first time in her professional life she doubted her ability to succeed. Strange that it should occur now. Just as she embarked on the biggest coup of her career, one that would finally establish China as a superpower on par with the United States and her as a contender for the Politburo.

And strange too that it should have arisen so suddenly and definitively, ignited only by word of Samuel Zhang. Certainly she had witnessed enough death, experienced enough pain to contain and control anything that circumstance might throw at her now. The Cultural Revolution alone had shown her more suffering than most people would face in a lifetime, perhaps a thousand lifetimes. Yet she had survived the Cultural Revolution, even thrived in the tumult and treachery without any of the crippling trepidation she felt now.

She tried to clear her head, making herself envision the future and plan the next few moves accordingly. She had already accomplished a great deal by sending Feng to America. She would soon be rid of Hu Zhong with his attendant liabilities. Then Feng could carry things forward until she assumed direct control. And direct control was what was called for now, even though she hadn't been in the field in years, and not to America since the 1960s. And there was the risk that she would be recognized—her face was known to intelligence services all over the world. Her presence might expose the mission. But if she didn't go? That was the greater risk. That in someone else's hands the mission would fail. No—she must go to America and see this through herself.

Jin Qing felt the vertigo recede; crystalline thoughts filled the void. She was focused now on the tasks ahead. Hu Zhong she had dealt with. But about the agent, Helen? She too still had her uses. She was generally disciplined and mature in her approach. And as the primary U.S. representative of the Ministry's front company, Jasmine Investments, she was responsible for a number of enormous financial and military espionage projects including the acquisition of the shipping company, FeasCo. That acquisition would have to go forward until Jin Qing could determine exactly what the company knew about the cargo's destination and all its records had been explored. The woman was also pretty and had been willing and unquestioning when instructed to exchange sex for information.

Still, she had been on location when the boy was killed. Whether she had anything to do with it or not, her punishment should be consistent with Hu Zhong's. It was, after all, in the writings of the sages: punishment only served the ruler if it was predictable, consistently applied and therefore appreciated by the society of subordinates governed thereby. The woman had blundered, she had not prevented Sam's death and not preserved the information he held. Her blunder would cost Hu Zhong his life. But should she be terminated as well?

Jin Qing never allowed command decisions to be influenced by emotion. In that too she was guided by the sages. Emotion distracted a leader and confused the troops. So said Han Fei Tzu and every strategist who ever advised a king. So she must question herself: Was she being emotional? It was a difficult question to answer. Could she even recognize true emotion anymore? She didn't really feel anything now except dizzy and perhaps angry. She thought, perhaps, that she should feel more—that even hard women would at least be sad, and common women absolutely distraught. But she was not like other women. And other women did not run the external intelligence operations of world powers.

No, she decided, she wasn't being emotional. If she terminated the woman, it was a matter of executing policy, of consistently punishing those who failed. It would be a calculated act, rather than an act of revenge. Even if vengeance was deserving. Even if Jin Qing got some satisfaction thereby. No, terminating the agent was the right thing to do, for if she didn't, her systemic authority was compromised and worse, Hu Zhong would know she had not believed him. For so long as Hu Zhong lived, he must think that he had Jin Qing's support. Otherwise he would wander. And he was too dangerous, had too much information, to be left on his own. He must think that Field Agent Helen was being punished, and punished severely with a sentence of death, solely on the strength of his report. That, thought Jin Qing, eyes darting in her head, is what he needed to think, and she would make Hu Zhong do the killing himself. It would be his last act as an employee of the People's Republic of China.

Jin Qing's mouth curled into a tight smile. She was satisfied with her resolve, could sense the chasm narrowing slightly. This was much better. She was at her best when moving forward. Sharklike. She hated distractions. And that's all this was and it would be taken care of. A mistake had been made. It had caused a setback. And the agents responsible would be called to account. She regretted the sentence passed on Helen. Helen was a good agent. But she had let her vigilance lapse, and Samuel Zhang was dead. It was a matter of law—Jin Qing's law—but law nevertheless and consistently applied. So she too must die, shortly before Hu Zhong—who was truly deserving of all that befell him.

Jin Qing's gut tightened, she felt a constriction in the muscles around her heart. Her smile faded. The woman's sentence left her cold. But for Hu Zhong's death she was suddenly eager. She wanted to taste his blood and spit it in his face. Hu Zhong hadn't pulled the trigger; Jin Qing didn't know who had. But the boy was Hu Zhong's to protect, and in that he had failed and attempted to pass off the blame. For that lapse, Feng would carry out the sentence. He would make it hurt. An eye for an eye as the Arabs said. Yes, thought Jin Qing, Hu Zhong would be made to pay. And then, maybe, she would feel something. Feel something as she once had for the boy she had helped name, her only son.

12

A van pulled off the curb—out behind them as he and Kristina left the garage. But Behr didn't think much of it until it too traced the four turns that brought them to the entrance ramp of northbound I-95. It was, of course, perfectly normal for a series of vehicles to negotiate to-gether—in funereal procession—the awkward route to the highway because there was only one way to get there along the colliding one-way streets the city planners had worked out with the community boards. Still, Behr thought, with all that's happened, best to be careful. And he kept watch in the rearview mirror as they sped up the ramp and into the stream of traffic.

He saw it was an older model, white and dirty and recognizable by the sagging frown of its bent front fender. It made the vehicle seem angry and aggressive and therefore easy to keep an eye on while bumping along the city streets. But once on the highway, Behr strug-gled. The low-riding Porsche didn't give him much of a view over the jostling crowd of long-haul semis and delivery vans that dominated this busy stretch. He only saw the frowning van occasionally as it shifted lanes behind him. And as it fell farther and farther back he began to doubt the necessity of his suspicions.

Kristina, meanwhile, was studying the scenery intently, and Behr began lecturing on the way that this elevated portion of I-95 followed the course of the industrial revolution in America. His daughter had once labeled this Lecture Number Fifty-Nine. It was one of his favorites, and the poor girl endured it every time they passed this way, which was only twice a year now.

Behr pointed a thumb back to where they had got on, in Queen Village. It was a community built by shipyard workers in the sixteen and seventeen hundreds. It was once stocked with Swedes; it predated William Penn. And now, he told Kristina, they were moving north, through Old City, Fishtown and the Northern Liberties, neighborhoods filled with eighteenth and nineteenth century factories that had churned out soap, sails, rope, gentlemen's hats, sewing needles and thousands of other everyday items for the growing nation and the world. Some of these factories had been turned into loft apartments, but most were now warehouses or simply abandoned. The factories were on their right, lining the Delaware. On their left, and Kristina had to lean over Behr to see, were thousands upon thousands of narrow row homes that had housed the factory workers; many of the homes built by the factory owners themselves and rented out at great profit.

He was about to launch into an explanation of the patriarchal system of factory communes when he suddenly glimpsed the van cut abruptly in front of a big truck, this time a Freightliner. Son of a bitch, Behr thought, he must be following us—trying to keep pace and forcing reckless moves to do it.

He didn't mention the van to Kristina, and he made no effort to lose it as they passed quickly over the next few miles. But he did lose enthusiasm for Lecture Number Fifty-Nine, and while he kept one eye on the slim rearview mirror, he happily let Kristina take the reigns of the conversation and describe her work and her reasons for moving to Amsterdam. Behr prompted her along from time to time with questions about her art, about the Dutch, about living in Europe. He asked (cleverly, he thought, for he didn't want to be too direct) if her boyfriend was Dutch.

"He is German," she replied, "but lives in Holland." She was looking out the window as she said this, at the twisted city of tubes that comprised a riverfront chemical factory. She missed the disappointment clouding Behr's face.

"Is he an artist too?" Behr asked after a second's pause, taking his eye off the rearview mirror and trying to hide his disappointment.

"Not really, he's more a professor, like you. Except he's also a dealer."

"Oh, a drug dealer. Very hip."

"No, Mr. Policeman, an *art* dealer. One of the biggest on the continent," Kristina scolded him.

"So he's a fat art dealer?"

"No, not fat." Kristina turned her attention to Behr, a thin smile forming at the margins. "The cocaine tends to keep him thin."

"Touché!" Behr threw back his head, laughing.

But the laughter was short-lived. In moving his head he had caught sight of the van again. Traffic had thinned after the Aramingo Avenue exit, and the mirrors showed the van prowling directly behind them in the far right lane. It was time for a decision. Behr downshifted to third, and the little Porsche accelerated quickly, bouncing through the ruts and potholes of the truckers' lanes.

Philadelphia was a tough town on drivers, particularly those who lacked aggression or horsepower. The outer lanes of a highway were used for passing, and the middle lane was left to the slow drivers who in fear and frustration were unable to exit the center lane groove as people zipped by on either side. So when Behr saw the van speed to catch up, he used this phenomenon to his advantage. He made his move. He punched a hole through the wall of cars in the middle lane, swerved into the fast lane, jammed the accelerator to the floor and left the van far behind.

"In a rush?" Kristina asked calmly.

"Just showing off," Behr said with a quick glance in the mirror. He saw that the van had now made it into the middle, but was falling farther behind as it looked for a gap in the fast lane.

Behr slowed, tapping the brakes lightly. He didn't want to lose the van yet; it wasn't part of the strategy. So he coasted a mile, watching it, giving it a chance. And after a minute, the van jumped into Behr's lane, angering the cars behind it into a fury of honks and flashing highbeams. Behr slowed further, some cars now passed him on the inside. The van closed the distance swiftly and after another mile was only a few car lengths behind them, shimmying violently at what must be top speed. "Now," Behr said under his breath, "let's see what this old car can do."

Behr again threw the Porsche into third and with a peek over his right shoulder, veered sharply in front of a blue sedan in the middle lane, a bus in the far right lane and up the exit ramp for Academy Road. He took the exit ramp at seventy miles per hour, and the small tires on the twenty-five year old car screamed on the turn over the bridge. But the car held the road, and when they came to the red light at Torresdale Avenue, he saw nothing but an eighteen-wheeler lumbering up the ramp behind them. An eighteen-wheeler and a large white sign with the posted speed limit of twenty-five. He turned to Kristina. He was smiling.

"I bet you can't wait to go flying with me."

Kristina wouldn't look at him. Both hands gripped the dashboard before her. "I was thinking a commercial flight might be available."

Behr chuckled and when the light went green he guided them gently up Academy Road through a neighborhood of neat brick row homes and individual lots that spoke volumes about the economic expansion of the '50s and the aspirations of the working classes. Of course he lectured her on everything he found interesting along the way.

After a couple of miles, the airport appeared on the left. Behr turned onto Red Lion Road, taking them past the 94th Aero Squadron Restaurant and down into the parking lot of the North Philadelphia Jet Center. North Philadelphia Airport had three long runways capable of handling the types of jets and large cargo aircraft that almost never landed there. Except for military airbases, it was the biggest, most underutilized airport in the northeast, and Behr loved it. He got hangar space at the Jet Center for nearly nothing; the only obligation being that he buy his fuel there. The mechanics were competent too and delighted to work on an antique like his T-34 Mentor.

The plane had been his father's. In fact it was the only thing specifically left to him in Dad's simple will. Rebecca, his sister, had asked for and gotten the house and he had gotten the plane. Not a bad deal, all things considered. The plane was worth more than the house and was in much better shape. But he hadn't told Rebecca that. He had simply flown it away after probate. The plane had been built for the

U.S. Navy by the Beech Aircraft Company in 1954. Intended as a trainer for young navy pilots, it was fast, agile and extremely tough. So tough that the navy still used a turbo-charged model for training, as did many governments around the world, including some, like the Argentines, who equipped it with guns and sent it into combat.

"This looks like something from a World War II movie," said Kristina once Behr lifted the hangar door.

"It's newer than that," he answered defensively. Kristina looked at him skeptically. "But not much," he admitted.

"Who sits in front?" She pointed toward the tandem cockpit with the fore and aft seats.

"I do, unless there is some objection."

"I guess I'll let you fly."

"Thanks."

"But I get to do the shooting!"

Behr pulled a laptop from his flight bag and dialed into the FAA's DUAT computer service. DUAT provided up-to-the-minute weather information and permitted him to file a flight plan on-line without having to talk to anyone. The weather page told him it was going to be clear all the way, with some broken clouds at twelve thousand feet. Pilots calling in had not reported any icing on their wings, but the winds aloft were quite strong, gusting to forty knots. This translated into a very bumpy ride.

On a subsequent screen—the flight plan page—Behr entered the call numbers for his plane, their destination, the estimated time of arrival, the amount of fuel he was carrying and various other items of interest to the FAA. They would be flying VFR, which stood for visual flight rules and meant that they could see where they were going. The alternative was IFR (Instrument Flight Rules) which meant that your whole flight, including your altitude, route and speed was directed by controllers on the ground. Behr didn't want that; VFR would be fine and give them greater flexibility. Filing a VFR flight plan just meant that the FAA checked to see if you got there in the time specified. If, within an hour after your ETA, you had not closed your flight plan either by phone, computer or over the radio, the FAA would start looking for you. Behr was not particularly concerned about not making it. But he filed a flight plan anyway. It was part of the game plan.

After folding the laptop away, Behr got the plane ready, pulling the chocks and pitot-tube cover. Kristina then helped push the plane out on the tarmac where Behr did a quick but thorough pre-flight. He lifted Kristina onto the wing and when she was situated in the cockpit, strapped her tightly into the shoulder harness and gave her the rundown on how to work the headset, the intercom, the radio and the stick and rudder, which controlled the plane's direction. He then hopped lightly into the front seat and lost himself for a few minutes in various systems checks and a pleasant nostalgia.

The front seat had always been Dad's, the one place in the world that was unequivocally his. Dad had made a living as a pilot. A poor living at that. But even after a day of flying, either in other peoples' planes or in the sea-battered Cessna he used for fish-spotting, he would come back to the cockpit of the T-34, with its oil-fragrant leather seat and gray battle-ready paint to consistently find a kind of simple peace that Behr only got whiffs of in his own airborne journeys.

Behr came back to earth. He started the plane. With the wind from the propeller whipping through the still-open cockpit, he finished the initial pre-flight, bumped up the throttle and steered noisily out to the taxiway.

"Are we going to leave this open the whole time?" Kristina asked over the intercom.

"You want it closed?"

"It's messing up my hair!"

Behr looked back and saw that Kristina's long black hair was, indeed, whipping around her head quite violently in the wash from the propeller.

"And I'm cold!"

He pointed to the shelf behind her head. "There's a jacket in the box," he yelled into the mouthpiece, then watched her struggle against the harness.

"You'll have to unstrap yourself first."

She did so, turned, and dug in the box for the jacket. When she pulled it out she began laughing. He could hear her over the headset. She had the intercom on.

"A varsity jacket, Professor Behr? Rockland Tigers? And football no less!"

"Why is that funny?"

"Were you the kicker?"

"I was a middle linebacker!"

"I don't think so."

"It was many years and thirty pounds ago."

"Thirty?"

"Maybe forty."

Kristina clicked off the intercom but he could still see her giggling as she wiggled into the old white-sleeved jacket and back into her harness.

"I can't get this buckled." Her voice was serious again.

"All right, I'll come back."

Behr unstrapped his own harness and climbed back onto the wing. He secured the big metal clasp, smiled at Kristina to show she was forgiven for mocking him, then closed the rear canopy over her head.

For some reason, he looked back, over the plane's squared tail and toward the parking lot. And what he saw made his heart jump. Son of a bitch, he thought. There it was. The van. Just sitting in the parking lot behind the chain-link fence where all the aviation buffs and weekend dads stood with their kids to watch the planes take off and land. Behr went cold. He knew the guy couldn't have made it to the Academy Road exit behind them. Christ, they had barely done it themselves! The driver of that van had to know, or at least guess, that the airport was their destination. But how?

It took a minute for Behr to realize that the necessary information had come from his own goddamn house. Whatever game they were playing was elevated now to another level, and Behr was damned glad for the little precautions he had taken.

Ground control told Behr that he was cleared for Runway 270. Behr acknowledged but told them that he would be switching frequency to talk to clearance control before takeoff. Behr dialed in the new frequency, then responded to the voice coming over the headset, "This is N-77 tango gulf papa, opening my flight plan."

☆ ☆ ☆

Augustus Lazlo was no pilot, but he had seen enough of military life to know a thing or two about airports. He knew, for instance, that every airport had at least three radio frequencies assigned to it, one for ground control, one for the tower, and one for flight clearances and contact with the FAA. Lazlo also kept aviation maps, mostly because they were the best maps around, and had dialed the radio frequencies for North Philadelphia into his scanner before he even left Behr's house that morning. It was no real trick, therefore, for him to sit there in the parking lot listening for Behr's voice. And it didn't take a great brain to note, as it squawked, everything Lazlo might need to know.

Lazlo had watched Behr standing on the wing. Then heard him talk to ground control. The sound of the man's voice coming over the scanner bothered Lazlo, made him self-consciously rub his arm, the same arm Behr had threatened to pull off that night. Lazlo grew angry at the memory. He had been bested, though only for a minute, by an amateur. It shouldn't have happened that way, but it had, and Lazlo still felt the pain. Now at least, the guy would show his colors, show what a lightweight he was. A lightweight who would tell him exactly where he was taking the lovely Kristina Zhang.

When he heard Behr's voice again, Lazlo smiled. "So you're switching to clearance control," he said out loud in the grubby van, "what a dumb fuck."

Lazlo turned the knob on the scanner in time to hear Behr give his call letters and open his flight plan. He bent closer. This was the key, would clearance control just tell him to go ahead, or would they confirm the plan? The scanner squawked again. Lazlo's smile broadened.

"Roger N-77 tango gulf papa, we have your flight plan, confirming visual flight rules, destination RKD, Rockland Maine, ETA fourteen hundred zulu time."

Destination Rockland, Maine. Wherever that was. Probably someplace rural where Behr thought the little honey would be safe from the likes of Lazlo. And maybe she would be. It was all up to Silver now. For this kind of money, Kristina Zhang was exactly as safe as Silver wanted her to be.

☆ ☆ ☆

Once they were level at one thousand feet, Behr banked sharply to the northeast. The steep turn gave him a clear view of the ground; he looked for the van. It had already moved! He could see it wheeling slowly out of the parking lot and back onto Red Lion Road, retracing the route to the city. He sighed in relief before clicking the intercom.

"How you doing back there?"

"The view is incredible! Look at all those little houses."

"Just wait until we're over the Chesapeake!"

Behr waited ten more minutes, taking them almost to the Jersey Shore before turning south for Maryland. As he did so he radioed Atlantic City clearance and canceled his flight plan. No, he told them, they would not be flying to Maine today.

13

Kristina could see that Behr enjoyed every second of the flight. After canceling the original flight plan over Atlantic City, Behr had veered the T-34 south by southwest, down over the brown mouth of the Delaware where the river widened into a bay feeding the Atlantic, over chemical works and hourglass cooling towers, over the flat expanse and brown winter fields of the Delmarva Peninsula, over the meandering headwaters of the Choptank River and on into the small airport at Easton.

Over this vista and throughout the flight, Kristina had basically been ignored. Aside from occasionally pointing out geographic or other landmarks on the ground, like the deep cut of the Delaware-Chesapeake Canal, or DuPont's corporate headquarters, Behr hadn't said a word to her. He was completely wrapped up in the glory of his task. And never once, though she had been expecting it the whole way, did he apologize for the bumpiness of the flight, the sudden drops or lurches of the plane as it was buffeted by vicious gusts and wind shifts. She would likely have had more communication from the pilot of a commercial flight.

Now they were on the ground, and Behr was fifty yards off busily negotiating hangar space with the base's manager while Kristina sat, still forgotten and quite trapped by the harness in the back seat. She was fighting with the straps when she was startled by his voice.

"Having some trouble with that?" he asked through a wide grin.

"Just get me out of here, will you?"

"Yes ma'am." Behr reached down from his place on the wing and pulled on the single lever which was supposed to release the entire mechanism. It stuck fast.

"Hold on a minute," Behr said and leaned over her to reach into the small storage space behind her head. He leaned so close that Kristina could smell his jacket leather mingled with the scent of apple. It was the soap he had showered with that morning. She had used it too.

Behr was now clutching a small canister of oil which he squirted onto the harness clasp. He tugged again and the mechanism gave. She felt his hands on her shoulders as he pulled aside the straps.

"Thank you," she said and accepted Behr's hand in getting out of the plane. She stood on the seat, stepped up to the canopy rail and jumped for the narrow edge of the wing where Behr caught her in an embrace that prevented her from tumbling. He stood her upright, their faces now only inches apart. Warm brown eyes searched hers. Finally he asked if she was all right.

Kristina didn't answer. She wanted to know why he was smiling like that, and found herself smiling too. Their proximity felt nice. His hold on her felt strong, and despite her earlier frustration at being ignored, she was comforted by that smell of apple and worn leather with its little bit of engine oil that clung to him now. In the low winter sun, she saw too how his afternoon beard poked from his chin and how the dry air aloft had chapped his lips. She liked his lips like that, they looked tender and exposed, and she thought she might like to kiss them someday. He had been good to her, he deserved at least one full kiss.

"You want me to gas her up?"

They both turned to the voice calling from the window of a small, noisy tanker truck which had just pulled up.

Now Kristina felt foolish, and she broke from Behr's casual embrace and clambered off the wing.

She left him with the plane, purposefully crossed the ramp to the Jet Center where, in a remarkably plush office she asked a secretary about getting maps, a rent-a-car, maybe a Coke. All three, she was told, were available right at the airport terminal, and while Behr dealt with the fuel truck, Kristina rented them a bright green Chevy Cavalier, consulted her new map of Talbot County, Maryland, and despaired.

Kristina had always considered herself a reasonably competent navigator, but this map was a mess. As far as she could tell, Talbot County was all waterfront. The coastline along the eastern side of Chesapeake Bay zigged in and out and around hundreds of small and large creeks, inlets and rivers. Each creek and river itself had creeks and inlets feeding it. Without very good directions, she decided, Sam's place would be impossible to find, even with the address the Realtor had given them.

Kristina asked the heavy girl at the rental agency for help with Sam's address.

"Oh, sure," she chirped, "that's out on Bailey's Neck, you can't miss it."

Kristina contemplated the girl's strange, low-in-the-throat, mostly southern accent and decided not to pursue further communication with this specimen. She returned instead to the secretary at the Jet Center who reiterated, "Bailey's Neck? That's just off the Oxford Road, you can't miss it."

Clearly these people had never left the area and couldn't imagine that anyone had. Kristina looked again at her map to trace the extent of the road to Oxford and after some minutes did, finally, notice branching off into the Tred Avon River a peninsula labeled Bailey's Neck. Her map didn't show that it had any roads.

Behr appeared beside her with their little bit of luggage. Kristina pushed past him into the driver's seat and guided the Cavalier out onto Route 322 where she found herself driving faster and braking harder than she otherwise might.

"You trying to make me sick; get back at me for the flight?" Behr asked.

"Maybe."

"Good luck."

She pursued the next five miles in jerks and starts but without a hint of nausea from Behr. In fact he'd been humming contentedly for some time. She gave up her effort and drove normally the rest of the way, down the Easton Parkway, right onto the Oxford Road, and after five or so miles right again onto Bailey's Neck. The address the Realtor had given them was down an unpaved stretch of mud and gravel off the Bailey's Neck Road, at the entrance to which stood a tree supporting about ten handpainted signs denoting the residents' various names. After a half-mile of ruts and potholes, they saw these signs reappearing, one by one, at the ends of individual driveways. They found Sam's driveway by the number. Sam had not nailed a "Zhang" sign to a tree, and Kristina somehow felt proud of him for that. It was the opposite of what their flashy dad would have done.

She turned the Cavalier onto a narrow track that ran beneath a cavern of tall red pine, the car moving smoothly over their carpet of soft brown needles. She nosed along slowly and quietly up to the house, her spirits sinking as it came into full view. It was a small, tired looking place—a one story structure with a gently pitched roof and graying clapboard siding, which was losing a battle to some green fungus rising from the ground. All the windows looked dark and their black screens were ripped and hanging in places, adding to the exterior shabbiness. She pulled up to the side of the house and saw that the screen door was hanging by its bottom hinge and slightly ajar. An open deck that ran down the side of the house and turned the corner around the front had weathered planks curling up in places and an outer rail that looked ready to collapse.

"What a dump!" Kristina exclaimed.

"What are you talking about? This is great!" Kristina turned in surprise, but Behr was already out of the car and bounding down the deck. She shut off the ignition and hurried after him.

She found him at the end of a dock that extended about thirty feet into a broad river. The dock itself looked new, and it matched a series of others sticking out of the tip of the peninsula like needles in a pincushion.

"See what I mean?" Behr asked with the same endearing smile that graced his face earlier on the wing of his plane.

Squinting, Kristina followed his gaze down the wide river into the great expanse of the Chesapeake Bay. The banks of the river were lined with more docks and stately homes that looked as if they had sat there proudly for two hundred years.

"Okay," she admitted, "I see what you mean." It was a gentle and wealthy scene, unlike other displays of money and privilege in its lack of ostentation or false modesty. Age, perhaps, had added an honest grace to the landscape. She could see why Sam had liked it, but not why he had chosen the dilapidated house behind them.

Then it occurred to her that they had no key to the place.

"Hey, how are we going to get in?" she asked Behr.

"Maybe it's open."

They walked around the exterior, turning doorknobs and pushing against windows. Everything was locked except the pitched doors to the basement. They both descended into a tiny room with two inches of cold, standing water that soaked their sneakers but found no interior access to the house. It was clear they would have to break in. It wasn't a crime, Behr reasoned, Kristina was a lawful heir who was simply administering Sam's estate. It was useful to have a lawyer around.

Behr scouted the perimeter again, finally deciding on window access through the bathroom. That way, he said, they could shut the bathroom door afterward to keep out the cold. Kristina helped him remove the window's outer screen, then watched him wrap his jacket around his arm, turn his head away and drive an elbow through a windowpane. He reached through, found the latch, got the lower sash partially open before it jammed.

"Damn," he said, then said it again as his six-foot frame caught in the narrow opening.

Kristina began laughing openly at Behr's wriggling efforts to get through.

"Fine, you go!" he muttered and extricated himself.

A moment later, and in one clean motion, Kristina had slunk through. And after a few seconds she unlocked the side door, admitting Behr and some much-needed air.

The house smelled damp and musty, but otherwise it was homey. The walls were lined in wood-veneer wainscoting and decorated with pictures of ducks and geese and dogs playing poker. The furniture was simple, campy stuff, though covered in a layer of dust and mildew. Some previous owner must have indulged a hunting and fishing fetish, for every surface was cluttered with displays of hand-tied flies, antique reels, goose calls and duck decoys that Sam—as far as Kristina knew— was simply not capable of purchasing himself.

Everything looked at least fifty years old. In fact, the only things that looked new, that looked like they had entered the house in the last half-century, were a natural-wood-finish desk placed in front of a huge picture window with views over the water and the computer with an oversized monitor sitting on top of that desk.

Kristina went to the computer immediately while Behr turned on some lights. Still standing, she found the power switch, waited for the messages from Compaq and Microsoft to flash by, then scrolled through the memory for evidence of Sam's efforts.

Frustratingly, like the laptop in Sam's apartment, the computer was clean. As far as she could see, nothing had been saved directly onto the hard drive.

Dispirited, Kristina pulled out the desk chair and went to sit down. Her leg bumped into something under the desk. Peeking underneath she saw a large cardboard box. She pulled it out and lifted the flaps.

"Behr!" Kristina let out a hoot. "Behr, I think we've got them. I think we have the books!"

Indeed the box was filled with small, six-inch books—the source of the *Confession*, the fruit of their efforts! Each book was wrapped in a bright red cover, adorned with a few Chinese characters and a small gold star. She picked one at random and opened it up to the frontispiece where she was greeted by a somber gray portrait of Chairman Mao Zedong protected by a page of thin rice paper. The portrait page itself was thick, laminated, permanent. In contrast, the red cover was cloth and quite worn, and the pages of text felt thin and brittle.

Whatever its condition, the book in Kristina's hand was the genuine article, the so-called Little Red Book, *Quotations from Chairman Mao ZeDong*. The publication that every Chinese schoolkid, worker and Party official had carried with them religiously during the Cultural Revolution. Kristina had never held a real one before. She had only seen the pictures that everyone else had—photographs of hundreds of thousands of blue-clad patriots eagerly waving their books in front of the giant portrait of Mao in Tiananmen Square; children with red armbands sitting in bare classrooms closely memorizing each quotation; cadres reading from the book to the peasants gathered before them knee-deep in a rice paddy, their pantlegs rolled up and cone-shaped bamboo hats perched far back on their heads. They were images of devotion, of obedience, of a disciplined culture so uniform and ubiquitous in its realm that it was unintelligible to most Americans.

Kristina flipped through the volume in her hand, increasingly amazed by what she saw. The top, side and bottom margins of each page were densely packed with handwritten characters. She picked a page at random and tried reading the scrawl. It was very tough going. The characters Baba had taught her coming back slowly. And though there were many she couldn't decipher, she got the gist. The author had written in columns down the right side of the page, then in the top and bottom margins, and finally on the left so that the characters bent in toward the binding.

"Can you translate this?" Behr asked from over her shoulder. Kristina traced down a column with her finger.

"It is now time for bed," she began, annunciating slowly, occasionally repeating and correcting herself, "They shut off our light bulb at ten every night. We collapse exhausted on the *kang*, all of us lined up in a row on the elevated wood platform. It is a cold night. I have only my thin quilt, and I am shivering. Gao whispers quietly and I agree. We huddle close, sharing our blankets. Sharing our warmth."

"Wow," Behr said, "you whipped that right off."

"I don't know," Kristina sighed. "This could take forever, I'm pretty rusty." She flipped through some of the other pages.

"There are whole pages I can't really make out, either because of the handwriting or what they say. I'm going to need some help."

"Well, I don't think you're going to find it here."

Kristina looked at Behr with a cockily arched eyebrow. "You can't read Chinese?"

"One of my few limitations, dear," Behr answered. "What I meant was that the Eastern Shore of Maryland is probably thin on Chinese translators."

"Oh, right."

"Well, do what you can. If you get stuck, I know a guy at UPenn who might help us."

Kristina felt in an instant trepidation, the memory of her narrow escape from the fire suddenly roaring back. "No way," she said, backing away from Behr and toward the desk, "No way do I want to go back to Philadelphia right now."

Behr must have seen her determination. "No need to go back just yet," he said soothingly. "We'll set up camp right here. You get started with the books, write everything down. And while you're doing that, I'll make the mission into town for supplies."

"Alone?"

"What's the matter?"

"Well . . . don't you think I should come along?" Kristina tried to hide the fear in her voice, to sound as certain as he. "After all," she continued, "I've seen the results of your shopping. We'll be washing our hair with Scotch."

"Look," he said, stepping toward her now, looking down into her eyes, "if you want to come along, I'd love the company." He tilted his head. "But," he continued, "there is nothing for you to be worried about here. Not even you knew Sam had bought this place. Your dad probably doesn't know about it either. So who else would know? Who would it even occur to that Sam had purchased property in rural Maryland? Huh? No one. This place was an escape for Sam, a place he could run to. And for that reason, I think we're safe here too."

His speech worked. Kristina felt secure again, comforted by his certainty, his smiles and even by the campy furniture and dusty wooden ducks that spoke of decades of escapism.

She let him go, but when he pulled out in the Cavalier, she also double locked the door behind him before returning to the desk and all the little red books in their box.

She laid them out neatly on the broad-plank floor before her. All the books appeared identical—same size, same cover, same portrait, same age. And each book was filled with the same close, tiny scrawl. They must go in some kind of order, she figured, and after perusing a few volumes found that the first handwritten character in each book was, in fact, a number. The Chinese today used both their traditional numbering and the western style, arabic numerals. But Chen Hai Zhang had used the ancient Chinese characters and numbered each book, ostensibly in sequence. She laid out the books again, this time in order. There were twenty-eight in all. Kristina groaned. As intriguing as this was, it would also take a long time to find any answers.

She left the books on the floor and went to the computer again, hoping that by chance she had missed something, that Sam had saved his translation and all she had to do was call it up from the hard drive. She flipped the power button, and after a moment she returned to the system's prepackaged word processing program. Nothing there.

Kristina stabbed at the mouse, ready to shut down the machine. But what was that? At the top of the START menu was something she hadn't noticed before, something called Corel WordPerfect. Another word-processing program? Kristina opened the application, then went into its file folders where she saw something that made her heart jump.

There they were, all in row. All of Sam's documents, all labeled by their chapter names: "Chapter 1," "Chapter 2," and so on.

Kristina clicked on "Chapter 1."

Her heart sank. A window popped up immediately with a "Cannot Open File" message. She tried the other chapters and each time, for each meticulously numbered chapter, the same window appeared. The files weren't on the system; Sam had only saved them to a removable disk. The disk, most likely, that had been destroyed in the fire.

"Dammit, Sam!" Now she would have to start at square one.

Kristina ran her hands over her face and tried to squeeze the mounting headache from her forehead. When that didn't work—it never did—she rose from the desk and wandered around the house in search of aspirin.

This was her first real look around the house, and she found that it contained a large master bedroom with one large bed and no other furniture. A second, much smaller bedroom was rendered impassable by an assortment of broken chairs, rolled rugs, standing lamps and boxes filled with even more dusty wooden decoys. Between the two, at the end of the short hallway with its sloping floor, was the small bathroom through which she had entered. Kristina was happy to see that Sam had kept it clean. There was even shampoo in the shower stall.

She found a bottle of Bayer with a 1980s expiration date, filled a pitcher with ice water and returned to the books. Kneeling on the hardwood floor, she began with book one to see if it corresponded to what they had read from the disk in Sam's apartment just before the fire. Sam's translation had, perhaps, been somewhat stylized, but the initial passage was basically what she and Behr had read before:

We have been in the mine since 1960. Sometimes we are sent to the fields, and when we are, I am happy to return to the mine. The day is more predictable here, even though I am an older man and the work is hard. I am content to contribute.

But hadn't Sam's translation actually started with a quotation from Mao? Kristina looked among the scrawled characters for what she remembered was something about the primacy of the Communist Party. It wasn't there. Was she missing something? She suddenly felt stupid as she realized what the book was she was holding: *Quotations from Chairman Mao*. She scanned down the first page and saw the relevant quotations printed under the chapter simply titled *The Communist Party*. So Sam had translated with reference to where the author was inserting his addenda. It was an interesting and clever device, even catchy. Clearly, Sam was contemplating commercial publication.

She moved back to the computer and typed a few of the more legible sentences on the screen. Then she stopped. What, she thought, was the best way to approach this? What was her purpose? Did she really need to recreate Sam's efforts, to create a publishable document? No—she just wanted answers about Sam and about the ghosts that were now haunting her family's past. So maybe she should just read what she could and not translate at all?

But somehow that struck her as wrong, lazy, even unfair. What if something happened? How would Behr or anyone pick up where she left off? Do the work, she decided, do the work now.

Kristina looked to the book before her, choosing, at least, to skip what they had already read in Sam's apartment. Finding where they had left off took her through the first book and one page into the second. To her surprise, the basic analysis and translation wasn't too hard. But deciphering the small characters was murder on the eyes. It brought back her headache, but she pressed on, fortifying herself occasionally with expired pharmaceuticals and a great deal of ice water as she typed in her grandfather's words.

I could not go on in Beijing. I packed everything I thought I would need in one steamer trunk and a shoulder bag, and I purchased a direct hard-seat ticket to Shanghai. It meant that I would be sitting upright on a wooden bench during the entire twenty-five hour journey. I was terrified that the ticket agents or railway officials would want to see travel documents. But no one asked me anything. They were far too busy. It seemed that thousands were boarding the Shanghai train. It was difficult to move on the platform. I hadn't wanted to pay for a porter and I was dragging my trunk behind me to a special luggage car when I felt a hand on my shoulder. I turned around nervously, preparing in mind an explanation for why I was traveling without letters of introduction from my former employer. But when I turned, it was not policeman or soldier that I saw, but my old friend and assistant Lin Ke. I had not seen him in years. Not since Shanghai before the Revolution. He had been in the Ministry; I was his boss for some time in the 1930s, before the Japanese invasion. And next to me, I suspected, he was perhaps the only other person still in the country with an inkling of the truth of those times. Though he couldn't know the details.

"Lin Ke!" I was quite delighted to see him. But Lin Ke was not smiling, and he made a gesture to indicate that I should not draw attention to ourselves. I lowered my voice, "Are you traveling to Shanghai too."

"No," Lin Ke said. "I came to the station hoping to find you. I heard that you were leaving."

I was surprised to hear that Lin Ke knew anything of me, let alone my daily movements. It had been over ten years since we last spoke and I had learned nothing of him in that time. I assumed that he left for Taiwan in 1949 with everyone else.

"You were always kind to me, Chen Hai," Lin Ke continued, "and I want to repay the favor while I can. I have come to warn you that you must be very careful."

"But I am moving to Anhui to get away from my troubles. I am leaving them here at the Ministry!"

"No, no, your troubles will follow you wherever you go." Lin Ke suddenly grabbed me by the elbow and leaned close. "They want to know, Chen Hai. About 1937. And they think you have the information. They are hoping you will lead them to it. That somehow you will slip, make a mistake. And when you do, they will be there, and they will learn from your error everything they need to know. Then, of course, you will become irrelevant to them. Disposable. Like so many others."

His words frightened me as I had not been before. At no time in my censure had anyone referred even obliquely to 1937. I was scared by this reference. But I was also concerned for Lin Ke. What an enormous risk he had taken! If they really suspected that I was involved, and if they were really monitoring me, they could have easily followed me here to the station. I glanced around us, but all I saw was the crush and swirl of passengers. I realized the wisdom of Lin Ke's choice in contacting me here. In the noise and crowds, it would be impossible for anyone to hear what we were saying or suggest that the encounter was anything but accidental.

"Why don't they just arrest me?" I asked, suspecting that he would know the answer. "Interrogate me with drugs and torture?"

"They are not confident, Chen Hai, that you would give them the correct answer. They prefer this method. With what's at stake, they want to eliminate the possibility of false leads or uncorrectable errors."

"Uncorrectable errors?"

"Death."

We were both silent for a moment, Lin Ke studying the faces of the milling crowd.

"Lin Ke, tell me, please, how do you know all this?"

Lin Ke bowed his head. He appeared embarrassed. "I cannot say. I must go now." He lifted his eyes to meet mine. "Please be careful."

I will never forget Lin Ke's intensity at that moment, or how, in two quick steps, he then vanished into the crowd. I was left standing there still holding up one end of the steamer trunk. The crowd streamed past; they cursed the obstruction in their path. The train's whistle broke me from my daze; I had to hurry. I checked the trunk with a porter and pushed my way through the press of bodies to a hard-seat car. It was completely full. All seats were taken, and even the aisles were crowded with people. I edged my way through until I found a small circle of aisle space toward the middle of the car. I went to put my bag in the luggage rack but discovered that someone was lying up there. He pushed my bag away roughly. Some of the other passengers squatted. I tried this too, but the lurch and yaw of the train made it too difficult for me. I kept tipping over, landing on my knees in the spit and filth accumulating on the floor. So I stood—for twenty-five hours—until the train pulled into Shanghai and I had to decide how to survive the layover without getting myself arrested.

Kristina typed the words into the computer, entranced by this rough vision of her ancestral home and the emotion of this man as he journeyed perilously therein. She was so caught up in the work that it took a moment to register the steady tapping sound behind her.

She stopped typing, and sat perfectly still. Listening. She wasn't imagining it. There it was, inconsistent, *tap . . . tap tap tap . . . tap tap—*

Not natural, she thought, and felt a tightness in her stomach. What could make that noise? It was too loud, too persistent for an insect or an animal. Too metallic.

Its source, Kristina knew, had to be human. But what? Who? Someone picking the locks? Working the windows? A surge of panic. My God, she thought, how did they find me here?

Her heart was racing now as she turned slowly in her chair, looking into the corners of the room and over the windows and the doors. Still seated, she could see the whole living room, but she couldn't see down the hall or into the kitchen or bedrooms. Kristina lifted herself from the chair an inch at time, desperate not to scrape the legs and give herself away.

She was standing now; she listened closely, but the noise had stopped. Christ, she thought, he was probably inside, waiting! She checked around for a weapon, a big knife, a baseball bat. Anything she could hit someone with. There was nothing in the room, the fishing rods were too light, the lamps too unwieldy. Kristina's eye landed now on the antique wooden mallards on the sideboard. She grabbed one by the neck and raised it shoulder high; she risked a few steps forward.

She stopped suddenly. There it was again! The tapping, the picking, persistent, intimidating.

What options did she have? She could wait for the intruder to come to her. Then hit him with a wooden duck. Or she could make a run for the door and get outside. That way, at least, she wouldn't be trapped in the house.

But what if he was outside, what if there was more than one? She might be running to her death. Frustration now joined the panic. She couldn't think straight. Her mind was turning like a square wheel. Was inside safer? She didn't know. But time was running out. After all, how long could it take someone to get into the house? To find the broken window in the bathroom and slide through as she had just a couple of hours before?

Kristina tightened her grip on the weapon. She *had* to take the offensive. The intruder would most likely come through the window, so all she had to do was position herself. Get him as he came through— hit him as hard she could with the wooden duck and then run for it. She knew she could run. She was in shape. And if she could outrun the stimulated men of Amsterdam, she could outrun this guy on the flat roads of eastern Maryland. She took a few more steps toward the middle of the room, then had to stop, her courage failing as she heard the noise much louder here, much closer. She felt herself shaking, felt her grip on the duck slipping with sweat.

Another sound now reached her ears. Tires on gravel.

Behr?

She didn't look back as she ran out the door. She was yelling to him. Yelling for him to turn around. But Behr seemed befuddled, just standing by the car with a bag of groceries.

"What the . . ."

"Someone is trying to get in!" Kristina ran around behind Behr. "We've got to get out of here."

"Hold on," Behr stood fast; he looked at her over the edge of the brown paper bag in his arms. "You sure? I didn't see anyone coming up."

"I heard him. He's picking the locks!" Kristina was now pushing at Behr, trying to get him in the car. He just wouldn't move. Instead he put the groceries on the ground. Took a step toward the house.

"Why don't you get in the car and lock the doors," he said without looking back. Kristina did as he said, angry with him for his bullishness. She reached around and locked the back doors, then watched him disappear around the back of the house.

God, she thought, what if he didn't return? This was really too much. Her fright was getting to her. She could feel herself shaking like she had in the hospital after the fire. The firemen had said that she was lucky to be alive. She was sure he was right. And if . . .

Kristina jumped at the tap on the window. Her head swivelled around and she grabbed for the mallard. It was only Behr, motioning to her. Kristina unlocked the door and got out. Behr put his hands on her shoulders.

"It's nothing," he said. "I've been all around and through the house. There is no one trying to break in."

"Well . . . what about the noise. I'm not making this up. I heard something." She was still shaking despite his calm demeanor.

"You did."

"And?"

"You heard the ice-maker."

Kristina's shoulders slumped as she suddenly recalled the two big pitchers of ice water she had consumed. Of course! The freezer had an automatic ice-machine. And the tapping was the sound of cubes falling into the empty tray.

"I'm sorry," Kristina said. She felt suddenly foolish but still angry with him for leaving her alone. "I shouldn't have gotten so frightened. I'll . . . I'll try to stay in control."

"Don't be silly! It's good to be vigilant." Behr sounded reassuring with no hint of mockery in his voice, and Kristina allowed herself to relax under the pressure of his hands now massaging her shoulders.

"But I've got to say," he continued, looking down at her right hand, "if it *had* been an intruder, you'd have been a sitting duck!"

Kristina hit Behr in the gut with the mallard—somewhat harder than she intended, then marched toward the house. He followed her with the bag of groceries, his gasps and laughter echoing through the woods.

14

"So you made it to Anqing without incident?"

"You know I did."

"But you have never said how. How did you avoid Public Security?"

"I slept on the street, in the clothes of a beggar."

"You had such clothes?"

"I turned my ordinary clothes inside out. The rough texture of the seams and some grease from the train doors made them look like rags."

Gao's eyes are closed; he lies on his back, his cigarette stub dead in his lips. He enjoys hearing about Anqing. He says he once fell in love there.

Anqing had once been a rich town, a river town with the beautiful Moving Wind Pagoda standing sentinel, commanding the narrowest crossing along the Yangtze. I tell Gao of this place where the green tea from the Huang and Dabei Mountains was loaded onto barges for the long trip east to Shanghai. I tell Gao of the school to which I'd been assigned—the red-tiled compound built by American missionaries in a valley of flowers— the students eager to learn, and of the joy I felt in encouraging their curiosity, however careful I had to be for many were *the offspring of Party officials. Gao wants to hear more of the town—of the sleek women there, but I speak instead of my growing fear of political retribution, of the averted eyes of my colleagues and the increasing number of self-criticism meetings we are all forced to attend. Even the students are encouraged to speak out against their teachers, to mark the ones with counter-revolutionary leanings. They are encouraged to speak out against me.*

For a time, I think I am safe; it is no worse for me than the others. Until one day at a special meeting attended by a Party Committee from the town, the headmaster, the only real Party member other than myself at the school, asked me if I had ever worked for the Guomingdang—for the hated government of Chiang Kai-shek. The question felt like a stab from a knife. I gasped; I was powerless to deny him. Clearly my file had finally found its way south from Beijing. And I was to be vilified before my peers once again.

Much as before, I tried to explain my role at the old Ministry of Finance. That I had, in fact, been a spy for the Communist Party. That I had been a Party member since the twenties, and that I had been rewarded for my service with a position in the new Ministry in Beijing after the glorious revolution.

As if rehearsed, the members of the Committee—sitting on their stage, suggested quickly that a spy is by nature a bad character, a man for sale who could be bought and bought again. A man so selfish as to serve two masters was counter-revolutionary, one with rightist tendencies. I was, they said, a candidate in need of corrective education. But in my case, work-study in the collective farm where the other teachers were sent, would prove sadly insufficient. My failings ran deeper. It would be best, under the circumstances, if I was given the chance to reform my thought in a special camp in the mountains. I was to depart in the morning.

So ended the meeting, atypically short, and with it ended my happiest year since the revolution. I scarcely knew what was happening. The next morning I was loaded with my steamer trunk into the back of a truck crowded with others. No one spoke, and after many painful hours of travel over the broken roads of Anhui, we arrived at the special camp. Even in the dark, the tall brick walls and guard towers told us immediately that this was not really a camp. It was a prison.

The prison was attached to a coal mine. And the prisoners were the miners. It was brutal, frightening work. I spent every day deep in the mountain simply waiting for it to collapse on top of me. After the first year, I and another fellow were assigned the job of checking and replacing the support beams. The previous two inspectors had been killed in an explosion. The other new inspector's name was Gao. We decided to work together, as our predecessors had. Gao had a background like mine. He was an educated man and over time we became very close friends. I can say now, that he is the best and last friend I am likely to have. We have worked together in the mine for twelve years now. We have spoken of so much. Of our childhoods, of our first loves, of the fate of our families and friends. We know each other as well as any two people can. But I have never told him everything. I have never told him what I did for the Finance Minister in 1937 when the Japanese began bombing Shanghai.

I look over to Gao's bunk, I see now that he has fallen asleep while I scribble and talk on and on. It is unfortunate for him, this is the part of the story he is always so interested in hearing. The part I don't tell.

Perhaps one day he shall know. But for now I am content to write.

The Japanese had bombed the city once before, in 1932, but not like this. In 1932, the Japanese were only trying to punish us. But in 1937, they wanted to conquer. And for the first time in my tenure at the Finance Ministry, I saw government officials begin to panic. Though the government capital was in Nanjing, five-hundred li to the northwest, many of its functions were carried out in Shanghai. The Finance Ministry was run from Shanghai because Shanghai was where the money was and where the ministers and assistant ministers lived. In some ways the Finance Ministry was an extension of the Bank of China, for the bank was controlled by T.V. Soong, and T.V. Soong was the richest man in China, some said the world. And it was he who kept the national government afloat. I knew, of course, that Soong didn't do it alone. That he needed assistance, particularly from the second richest man in China, Big-eared Tu.

Big-eared Tu—he seems like such an oddity now—a cartoon figure in the minds of today's children. They have seen the photographs, of course. He really did have big ears. They jutted from the sides of his head like mushrooms from a tree stump. But in those days, in Shanghai, there was nothing comic about Big-eared Tu. It was his city and he controlled everyone in it, including the foreigners. No one questioned him. He was the head of the Green Gang, the most powerful Triad in China. And, with the Japanese, the source for most of the world's heroin.

Once I heard a story whispered through the Ministry. H.H. Kung, the Finance Minister and his wife, Ai-ling, had invited some friends over for dinner. At the dinner, Ai-ling took Big-eared Tu aside and told him about the government's secret intention to raise the tax on silver. Consequently, the price of silver would drop precipitously. Clearly, she told him, he must sell his silver before the price dropped.

But Big-eared Tu was drunk that night and he misheard her. He did the opposite of what she'd recommended, began hoarding silver until Ai-ling's husband imposed the new silver tax. The price dropped, and Big-eared Tu lost a half-million U.S. dollars in a single day. He approached Ai-ling and Kung at their house that very evening; he asked to be reimbursed his losses. Ai-ling told Tu it was his own fault; she had warned him, spoken directly into those big ears of his. Was it her fault that they were full of liquor at the time? Tu left them on the veranda, and the next morning when the Kungs awoke, they found three No. 1 fancy coffins sitting on their front lawn, each labeled with the names of one of their children. By afternoon, less than twenty-four hours after Big-eared Tu had lost his money, he was given a special award by the Finance Ministry for five hundred thousand American dollars in appreciation of his dedicated service to the country over the years. I was not able to verify the whole story, but as the bureaucrat responsible for funding the special award to Big-eared Tu, actually cutting the check, I know that at least half of it is true.

Why do I remember that one story among so many? Did I find it amusing? Perhaps, yes. But it is a good story too because it says so well what was wrong then. How government was a private affair, a club where a small, violent and largely uneducated elite threw around millions while all about them people starved in the street.

It is funny for me, even now, here in my little cell at the foot of an Anhui mountain to think of those times, those names. So many of them connected. How can anyone today imagine the power wielded by a single family? T.V. Soong I have mentioned: immensely rich, Bank of

China chairman and the former Finance Minister who fell out of favor. But even out of favor he had influence because of his money and because of his sisters. T.V.'s successor, H.H. Kung, had married the oldest, Ai-ling, and Chiang Kai-shek, in turn and at the behest of the scheming Ai-ling, had married the youngest sister May-ling. The middle sister, Ching-ling, had married Sun Yat-sen, the father of the revolution, and after his death she became a kind of spiritual advisor to the nation.

The were all fascinating to observe and report on to my Party handlers, but my principal concern was observing T.V. Soong and H.H. Kung. T.V. Soong had, in the eyes of everyone in the know, been the last great hope for the Chinese economy. Soong was a financial genius and a hard disciplinarian. When Soong was Minister, we were not permitted to go out for lunch. We had to eat at our desks and were forbidden to speak socially to one another during the work day. Soong was equally disciplined with the nation's resources, and his strict discipline and sterling reputation made the western powers willing to lend to Chiang Kai-shek's gangster government. But Soong's discipline also got him into trouble with the spendthrift Chiang. And after one contentious argument over a $60,000 loan to purchase German warplanes that no one knew how to fly, Chiang struck Soong with his riding crop across the cheek. Soong did not hit him back. But he did resign immediately and was replaced a few hours later by H.H. Kung, who, it was said, knew as much about finance as the average twelve year old and did everything Chiang told him.

I knew about the riding crop because I saw the mark across Soong's face when he came to the office to gather his personal papers. And I duly reported the incident to the handlers at the Party safehouse in the French Concession as I did anything that spoke of change or weakness at the top.

My dedication in this treachery seemed obvious at the time. To me, to my way of thinking, the Party offered the only solution. The sustained hope for the future of China was with the Communist Party. Only the Party could harness the masses and bring us from the dark ages. And only the Party was willing to do it without the addicting, destructive participation of the West.

I was devoted to a theory, one to which I still subscribe, that China could only advance on her own terms, without the English and Ameri-

cans, Germans and French, even Russians whispering in her ear of guns and money. And though this theory was not unique, my job gave me a unique perspective on it, for it was my job to handle, move, account for the hard currency and bullion reserves of Chiang's regime. And from this position I saw how it was the West, or at least western bankers and industrialists, who determined the relative value of the Chinese economy. One day the western bankers might feel confident, and if on that day they valued the Chinese dollar as worth, for instance, five U.S. dollars, we were a rich country with good credit and bright prospects. But another day they might get nervous, set an exchange rate of ten Chinese to one U.S. Then we were deemed risky, capital flows ebbed, and at fifteen to one, loans were called and new investment halted.

The fluctuations were often rapid and steep, and they affected everyone. Each upward adjustment brought more peasants from the countryside to work in the factories, while a downward adjustment then threw thousands out of work and into the streets of the cities from Shanghai to Chunking.

I thought it the worst possible system for a country looking toward its future, and my young mind searched for alternatives. One day, in 1929, on a trip to Hunan to visit with the family of a girl who would later become my wife, I heard a speech by a leader of the Hunanese branch of the Communists. His name, I learned later, was Mao Zedong. Mao said to the crowd assembled there in Changsha's central square that we must learn that the value of a unit of currency was the value of a unit of labor. If it took a man an hour to build a chair, we could call that hour a dollar. That one dollar could be exchanged for the hour it took another man to build a table. In labor, therefore, a table and chair cost two human hours, which was equal to two dollars, and that was how value was measured in a communist system.

Mao's speech turned on the lights in my mind. Labor was the source of our wealth! Not gold, not silver, not the American dollar.

It was revolutionary. I was excited. I approached Mao at the podium, but was quickly pushed away by the people around him. I tried to tell them of my excitement, of my position and how well I knew the truth of Mao's words. They seemed not to listen, they were hostile. But then one man came forward. He did not tell me his name. He was very direct, he gave me a contact in Shanghai and warned that I was to be very careful. Because of Chiang, because of Big-eared Tu, Shanghai, he said, was the most dangerous place for a Communist in all of China, perhaps all the world. I must not tell anyone of my views except the contact. And from the contact I would receive my assignments.

Back home, despite the secrecy, I soon learned how things worked. The Party was hidden but active. It maintained liaisons with the labor unions and with members of the Comintern stationed there. The Comintern representatives were all western and I was suspicious at first. But I came to know them, and—except for the Russians—they seemed to agree that each phase of the revolution must proceed at its own pace in each nation. The Russians, of course, wanted to see another Russian Revolution. But how could we do that? How can you have a workers' revolution if all you have is peasants? The Russians never seemed to understand the point, but the others did. Especially one, an American. His name was Ambrose.

The Comintern representatives all had a cover story. Most of them masqueraded as journalists from small newspapers and magazines abroad. When I returned to Shanghai with my contact name, I was assigned two tasks. One, of course, was to collect information at the Ministry that might be useful to the Party. The second was to facilitate Comintern financing for the labor unions. Ambrose was the Comintern representative of the American Communist Party. I was told to meet him at a hotel.

We met often after that, Ambrose and I, sometimes every day. He was a caricature of a foreigner, without a single Chinese feature. He was tall, red haired and freckled. His nose was like the beak of a great bird; he stooped when he walked; he slouched when he sat. Though a Communist, his thinking was mostly independent; he often disobeyed orders from the Comintern leaders (who were all Russians anyway) and his own Party bosses in the United States. I could never understand his attitudes about this. I was concerned for him. I would ask if he did not fear reprisal. His consistent answer makes me smile even now:

"For what?" he would yell, "For doing the right thing?"

That was the story with Ambrose, he was always sure he was right.

☆ ☆ ☆

Kristina rubbed her eyes and checked her watch and was amazed to discover that it was past two in the morning. These few pages had taken her almost ten hours! She looked around and saw that Behr was asleep on the couch behind her. That, at least, solved the issue of only having one usable bedroom.

Stiffly, a hand on her lower back, Kristina made her way down the hall. She found the bed in the darkness, slipped under the covers and, despite their chill, was asleep within a few minutes and dreaming vivid pictures of Shanghai in the thirties. She saw crowded streets and well-dressed capitalists in chauffeured cars. She saw slinky women on the arms of men in dark night clubs and gangsters in black hats with Chinese eyes. She saw a young man in a vest and shirt sleeves illuminated by his desk lamp in a large government office. And she dreamed of him handing files to a sinister man with red hair who laughed each time he heard something he liked.

She woke with a start. What was that? What a noise! Kristina listened a moment to the cacophony before realizing what it was. She smiled, despite the hour. It was six A.M. and she had been awakened by the noisy conversation of Canada geese. There would be no more sleep this morning, she thought, and padded out to the living room where she found Behr already awake, drinking coffee. He was standing by the picture window with the view of the water.

"Look at them!" he said without turning, and Kristina walked over the cold floor to stand by his side.

"Wow," she said, "no wonder." The lawn running down to the dock was covered with hundreds of fat brown birds. They were all waddling about authoritatively, babbling away, their black beaks in constant motion. It had to be one of the funniest things she had ever seen.

Behr turned from the window and looked down at the pile of books, then at her. "Progress?" he asked.

Kristina shrugged lightly. She explained the basic problem: dense handwriting and a lack of painkillers.

"I have a solution," Behr offered, and a few minutes later, still wearing the clothes she slept in and with the box of Mao's *Quotations* in the trunk, they pulled into an Easton strip mall abutting a corn field. They headed for the ubiquitous big-box office supply store, to its bank of copy machines where they divided the books in half and went to work. The copiers were set to enlarge each page by the maximum 150%

and by 9:00, as the mall was filling up with shoppers, they had put together and stapled twenty-eight separate sheaves of the now easy-to-read, large-type *Revolutionary's Confession.*

Kristina nudged Behr in the ribs. "Let's get something to eat. Anything would be fine."

"Hold on a minute," he answered, "we have one more purchase."

"Can it wait?"

"We're here." Behr disappeared down an aisle and around the corner, leaving Kristina to guard the enormous pile of paper they had generated. When he returned he was awkwardly carrying a large box.

"What's that?"

"A fax machine. It is also a printer and copier."

"Of course."

Behr looked like a boy who had just given his grandmother a baseball glove for her birthday. "It will come in handy. Trust me."

Kristina shrugged, threw the copies they had made in with the box of books and lugged them out to the car. Behr joined her a few minutes later. "Still hungry?"

"Starving."

"I know a little place in town here. It's cute."

"Have you been in this town before yesterday?"

"Never," Behr said. "I just know things."

A short walk past gracious brick storefronts and a fine stone courthouse brought them to a busy little café where Behr pulled out a chair for Kristina. He ordered them coffee and something called the "King's Breakfast."

The rich food and coffee disappeared quickly, and under its influence Kristina relaxed. She felt herself getting silly, talking a bit much, laughing at all Behr's jokes. She realized it was the first time she had really laughed since hearing about Sam. But she didn't feel guilty. The laughter felt good. It was all right being here, being with this guy, Jason Behr, down here in this easy, uncomplicated place, slightly removed, as it was, in geography and attitude from the acceleration gripping the rest of the world. She felt confident too, like something was being accomplished. And once she was through with the translation, she was sure Behr would do the right thing with it— whatever that might be, whatever it entailed. He just seemed like that kind of guy. Calm, seemingly at ease, yet persevering. Probably quite dangerous in his own way.

So, she reasoned, she could take a minute to laugh. Behr was with her, and she was certain now that something would come of this. She would learn why Sam had been taken, and someone would be made to pay. And that thought—that someone could be held accountable, perhaps painfully—that thought alone was enough for her right now.

They finished their breakfast, headed back to the house in the Cavalier. Behr had been chatty in the cafe, but he was quiet during the ride, lost in his thoughts and open to being studied. She examined him with an aesthetically tuned eye. He wasn't exactly beautiful, but she liked what she saw in the strong northern jaw, the warm brown eyes flecked with color, a faintly irregular nose. She might paint him someday. Perhaps nude, she thought, then smiled as she turned her face to the window.

Tires crunched over gravel. Kristina got out.

"Looks like you're going through the window again." Behr motioned with his thumb. The side door to the house had locked itself when they left. They had forgotten to look for a key. Kristina skipped over to the window, but she was much less fluid going through a second time and she landed hard on the bathroom floor. Rubbing a sore shoulder she opened the door for Behr.

"I heard a thud," he said questioningly.

"I kind of fell."

"Head?"

"Shoulder."

"Ow."

"Yeah."

"Do you mind?" Behr took her hand, led her to the living room couch; he directed her to sit cross-legged. He sat close behind and pulled her coat down around her. He turned her face away and gently scooped her hair over the good shoulder. She felt his hands on her; strong hands massaging the injured shoulder, kneading away the pain. She heard him breathing in rhythm with his touch and felt its heat on her exposed neck. She arched slightly, letting herself fall back into his lap.

It really didn't take much thought. It was the natural motion. She reached up and pulled Behr's head down toward her. He too moved,

moved his hands beneath her head. He lifted, and he kissed her gently, then seemed to hesitate before Kristina pressed more firmly, seizing his embrace. Now he responded.

She pushed him away and got up from the sofa. She looked down at him in the clear morning light and saw bright, eager eyes.

"Yes," she answered to the question posed there. She reached down, taking his hand, and pulled him quietly to the bedroom.

☆ ☆ ☆

Blissful days. Behr wanted them to go forever. Even now, listening to her breathe, he felt a rapture, saw a world he had not imagined in a decade. The strained years of marriage and lazy encounters with some of the professors and older students at school had left him questioning his ability to feel. But now it came to him in a consuming flood. He had lain awake, occasionally stroking her baby-soft skin all night. With elegance and humor and passion, she had brought him back from a kind of death. And he hadn't even known he was dead. She had given him a wonderful gift, she had given him his vision and opened his heart. And for that he owed her everything.

He rose and began this day, as he did the last, by preparing a hot breakfast. And this breakfast, as the last, grew cold in the hours before she awoke. So he made a second one and greeted her with it in bed.

"What time is it?" she asked groggily.

"Getting on nine."

He watched her get out of bed, still naked, and marveled at the quality of her form. Even running to the bathroom she looked perfect. He brought the breakfast tray back to the kitchen and waited for her to emerge.

She greeted him with a kiss. "I like you, Behr," she said.

"I like you too," he responded, thinking he'd like her even better if she hadn't gotten dressed. I guess it's down to business, he thought. "So, how much do you think is left?"

"Well, it's hard to say," Kristina said after a bite of toast, "I've had to skip a bunch of the more illegible pages. But there's probably another fifteen books. So, another few days at least."

"You ready for some help?"

"I don't know. There is all this stuff about the Finance Ministry and the Japanese. It's full of technical jargon. I just don't know if I'm getting the translations right."

He had not seen the translation. He decided, finally, to ask the question, though he knew a positive answer could spell the end of this Maryland idyll forever. "How exact do you have to be? I mean, have you figured out what this is all about? If it explains anything at all about why your brother might have been killed?"

Kristina's face grew serious. She bit her bottom lip.

"Yes," she said, "at least partially. I've skimmed ahead." Then she rose from their breakfast and walked the length of the living room. "But I don't want to tell you just yet. Is that all right? I want to finish with all the books. Just in case there is more I need to know."

"I don't know if I understand."

"Look, it's big. Bigger than I imagined. What's in those books, the knowledge of what my grandfather did, people would kill for it. It's dangerous information to have in your head. And I don't know if I want you . . . if you should be walking around with it just yet."

"And you should?"

"It's too late for me."

"I don't get you. You just said it was big, it was important."

"Exactly."

"Exactly what?"

"This is something . . . if it is true that is, that would have real consequences . . . that we couldn't control. I keep thinking about Pandora's box. It's like that, I think."

"Will your translation of this thing answer the question of Sam's death?"

"Maybe. Maybe tell us why, but not who."

"Well . . . in my experience, why . . . the motive, leads you to who. So I think it important that you share your information so we can begin to—"

Kristina stamped her foot. "Look . . . I'm trying to tell you . . . I'm not sure. I'm not sure that I am up to this. It's so close to home. My brother, my grandfather . . . Baba. What if my dad gets dragged in? A few weeks ago I was in Amsterdam. My biggest worry was a clean coat of gesso. Now I don't know what's going on. I want to be able to go on with my life. How can I return if I'm dragging around these ghosts, this historical tail, as the man said? And what if more people get hurt? What if it's you?"

Behr heard her out, understanding every word and not agreeing with any of it. He didn't need to read the translation yet, but he also wasn't going to bury it. If even one murder had been committed because of the information contained therein, it had to be preserved, dissected and understood. It was that simple. *The Revolutionary's Confession* was evidence in a murder investigation, and if it also told them more, if something "big" was really at stake, then its value was, of course, priceless. It seemed so obvious to him, but he knew he would have to convince Kristina as well.

But Behr decided not to argue his case right now. It wasn't, as the judges say, ripe for judgment. Kristina was not done translating, and they were, after all, still having fun. No harm in sticking around a few more days and letting her come to the right conclusion. And how could he be angry with her? She had admitted to wanting to protect him.

Now Kristina changed the subject. "So . . . what about getting some help with the tricky parts?"

"Ah," Behr grinned, "that's why I got the fax machine. Observe."

Behr went to the machine he had set up yesterday with deliberate, painstaking attention to the instructions, and he pulled from it a single-page letter he had handwritten this morning. It was addressed to his weekly tennis partner, Professor J. Ely Faulkner, and it explained that the attached fax contained a number of pages from the autobiographical tale of a Chinese political prisoner. And while it couldn't be said where Behr had gotten the documents, Professor Faulkner should, with utmost discretion, read what he could and be available when they needed assistance with certain items in the translation.

"Faulkner is one of the top sinologists in the country. He also owes me some favors. He'll be delighted to get his hands on this, but he also can keep a secret. He won't share this without my say so. The question is, should I send it?"

"Is it secure?"

"Yeah, Faulkner's got the fax machine right in his office, and he keeps the office locked when he's not there. He's got relationships with a number of dissidents who fled after the Tiananmen incident in '89. He's pretty careful about security."

"Okay, but let's not send him too much. Just some of the technical stuff." Kristina went to the pile of copies they'd made and selected some pages she'd marked with red. These she handed to Behr who placed them with the letter on the fax. He looked up Faulkner's number in his address book, then keyed it in. He pushed the blue button, and the machine sucked the first page through. Behr turned to Kristina.

"My dear, we're all set. We have food, drink, a bunch of work and, of course, each other. In a few hours we'll call Faulkner and see what he makes of those chicken scratches. I, for one, couldn't be happier."

Kristina smiled at him. To his delight she reached toward him, wrapped her arms around his waist and pressed her cheek against his shoulder. Behr looked out over her head at the sun on the water. Two pleasure craft were making their way out into the Chesapeake Bay and a giant V of Canada geese traced the contours of the banks in their search for a peaceful spot. Behr knew he had found his. These next few days, he thought, might be some of the best of my life.

☆   ☆   ☆

On the receiving end of the fax line, in a small office in Williams Hall on the campus of the University of Pennsylvania, Sun Lee went about his duties as a teaching assistant to the famous Professor Faulkner. He had already put together Faulkner's teaching agenda for the day, graded some undergraduate papers and was now waiting for the multi-page fax to finish coming through so that he could put it on Faulkner's desk with his other mail. Since Faulkner didn't have a secretary, these duties fell to Sun Lee, who was happy, even eager, to do them. When the LCD window indicated that transmission was, indeed, complete, Sun Lee flipped the wad of paper upright, banged it against the table to even the edges and marched into Faulkner's office with it. As with Faulkner's mail and anything else marked "Confidential," Sun Lee made sure to read what was in his hands. He stopped in his tracks. The cover letter told him everything he needed to make a decision.

Sun Lee ran out of the office and down the hall where he quickly made a copy of the document, including the letter. When he returned to Faulkner's office, he sat down at the man's desk. He picked up the phone and dialed the number he had been instructed to memorize while still in China, while still applying to graduate school in America. The number had a Washington D.C. area code. He heard someone pick up and he asked, in English, if Cindy was home.

"There is no Cindy here."

"No Cindy? But she gave me this number, I have something for her," Sun Lee said, utilizing the coded instructions he had memorized with the phone number.

"I am sorry, you have the wrong number. Good-bye."

Sun Lee knew he had the right number and knew that he now had only two hours to get his package to the pre-arranged dead drop. There he would leave it and simply walk away. And at some time, someone whom he had never seen, or would ever see, would pick it up and deliver it to the Education Consul at the embassy in Washington. Everyone knew that the Education Consul was really an MSS officer who monitored Chinese student dissidents and gathered information. But Sun Lee was not perturbed by this. He had no affection for the dissidents. Why they would want change, why they would want China to look like America, like West Philadelphia, was a mystery to him. So Sun Lee knew he was doing the right thing.

The letter said that the papers in his hands were the story of a political prisoner. If that was true, he was sure that his government would want to see them before Professor Faulkner did. In fact, they would not want Faulkner to see them at all.

So Sun Lee threw the originals in the trash. Then he slid his copy into a large manila envelope, threw on his coat and headed east toward Thirtieth Street Station. There he would go to the news shop and slip the folder behind the display of automobile magazines. He was then to purchase something and leave immediately. After that, his job was done.

15

Jin Qing had Hu Zhong on the screen, his oily smile projecting almost too well over the satellite link from the Ministry's New York headquarters. She had resolved not to get angry with the man, to follow the prescriptions of the ancient teacher, Han Fei Tzu, in this matter. For as the teacher had told his one pupil, the great King Huan-hui, almost two thousand years ago: *The ruler must not reveal his desires, for if he reveals his desires his ministers will put on the mask that pleases him. He must not reveal his will, for if he does so his ministers will show a different face.*

For most of her career Jin Qing had followed the way of Han Fei Tzu. For what he said was as true today as it was then. And if she showed Hu Zhong her disgust with his bumbling, his unctuous flattery and platitudes, he would either run over to the Americans in fear or he would try to overcompensate for previous errors and probably cripple another mission. She must not get angry. She must simply be as the teacher described: *seeming to dwell nowhere at all, so empty no one can seek her out.* But even emptiness, she thought, is governed by certain immutable laws. Hu Zhong needed to be informed of the law, of her law, and the consequences of its transgression.

"Agent Hu, I must stress that the girl is not to be injured in any way. She is a government asset. Any injury to her will be visited five-fold upon the party causing the injury and upon you. Thus if her arm is scratched, you stand to lose yours. If she dies, we will punish members of your family to the fifth degree of relation. This is true for all members of the extraction team and shall be duly communicated to them. Is that clear?"

On the monitor she could see Hu Zhong stiffen and gray, his smile fade. "Perhaps," he said, "we should delay this mission. Leave the girl in place. Yes? For if we follow her, if we are patient, we will learn what she knows."

Jin Qing controlled the temper in her voice. She asked softly, "Are you questioning my order?"

"No Madam Jin! I was merely offering an alternative."

Jin felt a wave of hostility and loathing. What a small and retched man Hu Zhong had become. She wanted badly to accelerate the process she had put in place with Feng, but knew she couldn't. Not yet, not while Hu was still needed for the mission.

"As ever, I appreciate your suggestion, Agent Hu." The words almost made her choke. "But I am afraid the girl's information is insecure while still in her head. That is to say, if we know where the girl is, so may others. And we want to forestall the possibility of other parties gleaning her knowledge, such as it might be, before we do."

"I understand, Minister. A very clever strategy. You are most wise."

Jin Qing ignored the flattery. She would have been happy simply to hear the man acknowledge the order and carry it out. And be aware of the risks throughout.

"Is there anything else before I make preparations?" Hu Zhong asked.

"As a matter of fact, there is. When you go to the airport, there will be someone already aboard the Jasmine company plane. His operational name is Kuang. He is an engineer. He is also assigned to Military Intelligence. He will be assisting you in the extraction. Give him every courtesy. He will likely say little, but he has great operational experience. If he makes any suggestions, I strongly suggest you heed them."

"MID? On one of our operations? Forgive me, but isn't that out of the ordinary?"

"Yes, it is." Jin Qing didn't feel the need to elaborate. "Unless there is something else, Hu Zhong, I suggest you proceed."

"Yes, Minister."

Jin Qing touched a spot on the screen which terminated the transmission. She marched out of the communications room and turned down a drafty, tiled corridor to her office. She ignored her secretary's hello, shut the door behind her. She was in no mood for even basic pleasantries.

Why did it have to be so complicated? Why did each perceived advance in the quest seem to involve so many contingencies, so many opportunities for failure?

She wouldn't need Hu Zhong at all if she had more of the document. She was sure of that. But the fax to the University of Pennsylvania had been incomplete, only an excerpt from a document she could scarcely believe existed. To think, after all these years, that there was a written account, a memoir no less. It was almost too much to bear. The pages they received did not mention the author. But she knew it had to be Chen Hai Zhang. Who else could it be? Who else had they sent to the Anhui mines with a cellmate named Gao?

And why had Gao not informed her of this document? It was apparent that Gao was present during its creation, sitting there with Chen Hai while the man scribbled into the margins of Mao's *Quotations* of all things. Was not Gao under a sentence of death, was not every member of his family threatened lest he regularly inform on the man he'd been assigned to befriend? Clearly the friendship had become too deep. The informant became a conspirator, so that Chen Hai's secret remained hidden from her until a hint of its revelation suddenly and quite randomly appeared on a fax machine at the University of Pennsylvania.

And still she did not know. After all that had happened, all she had done in life to discover where Chen Hai had sent the cargo, she was still not in possession of it.

But she *was* closer. The passages before her, written in Chen Hai's own hand and delivered to her office in the random circumstance that her own daughter was unable to translate them, were in themselves useless. But they did provide a trail. A trail that began with the fax number printed at the top of the page—the sender's fax number—and the signature of Professor Jason Behr at the bottom of the cover letter. That was enough to tell her where Kristina was. And Kristina, poor girl, was now the key to her whole operation.

Jin Qing reached for the secure phone on her desk. She dialed a number in Beijing that linked her with the Military Intelligence Department, and they connected her with their field operations in San Francisco. San Francisco was MID's single biggest outpost outside Asia and the third most active in the world after Taiwan and Tokyo. It was almost exclusively devoted to the theft of technology from the Silicon Valley and to date they had been highly successful in their acquisition of chip and communications advancements. Their agents were mostly scientists and students attached to the region's myriad corporate and academic research facilities. MID scientists had even worked on the Star Wars initiative. But MID had also employed trained covert operatives. And now they had the services of her own Agent Feng, masquerading under the name Kuang and patiently awaiting the call she was now making.

The MID operators connected her with Feng on his encrypted cellular phone. She briefed him quickly, "You are going with Hu Zhong to the U.S. state of Maryland. Our officer in Washington received a communication from a field agent . . . a student really . . . providing the location of a woman named Kristina Zhang. The location was determined from a fax number, so we are not sure if the target is still at the location. The target is not to be harmed. Any injury, even mental, to Kristina Zhang will occasion the severest punishment. Is that understood?

"Yes," Feng grunted.

"Good. Hu Zhong, together with an agent named Helen and you, will lead a team that extracts the Zhang woman and brings her to a site in New York with which Hu Zhong is familiar. Hu Zhong has formulated a general plan. I want you to study that plan and correct the errors. When operational, you have one additional task. Hu Zhong must not know of it. The Zhang woman is concealing documents. Find them; they might be in the form of unbound documents, photocopies, or perhaps a number of editions of the *Quotations*."

"The *Quotations*?"

"Of Chairman Mao, of course, the Red Book. These materials are to be assembled and secured. And if you can keep them away from Hu Zhong, even better. Then, when the operation is complete—when Kristina is in the safe house—you shall carry out your original mission."

"Understood."

Jin Qing appreciated Feng's lack of conversation. He took instruction the way a computer takes code. And unless you erred in your programming, you could be confident of your results. "There is an additional nuance to your original mission."

"Oh?"

Jin Qing instructed Feng on the probable fate of Helen, Feng's assumption of Hu Zhong's command, and other matters including Jin Qing's own trip to the United States and the preparations that were required. Feng heard her through, and after he repeated her instructions verbatim she signed off, satisfied for the moment that one of her field agents was competent.

It was growing late. Jin Qing had a headache, and the western sun streaking through the grime on the window was making it worse. She closed the heavy red curtains and sat at her desk without turning on the lights. Her secretary came in and announced his departure. He wasn't surprised to find her in the dark, and he didn't ask after her health. She sat that way often, her vision uncluttered by the everyday objects and people around her. She sometimes wished that she could sit this way all day and be—as the teacher instructed—empty, still and idle. What had the great Han master said? *From your place of darkness observe the defects in others. See but do not appear to see; listen but do not seem to listen; know but do not let it be known that you know. When you perceive the trend of a man's words, do not change them, do not correct them, but examine them and compare them with his results.* Had she done all these things today? Had she seen the defects and guarded against them? Was there anything left undone? Had she given anything away?

Jin Qing went over every action and every conversation she'd had that day. She had operations running in Europe and Australia right now that demanded significant attention. And the zealots on the Korean peninsula had taken up most of the morning. Still, she was most concerned about Hu Zhong's mission. For if any of it went wrong, it could impact everything, and if it went right, she would know no greater victory.

She felt confident that she was doing what she could to locate the missing cargo. She knew how it had gotten to America—the records of the Far Eastern and Atlantic Shipping Company had told them that. Where it went after landing in Philadelphia was still a mystery, but Kristina Zhang should be able to tell them something, or at least set the parameters. And if Kristina couldn't, and her document couldn't, maybe the lawyer could. In retrospect, he, the lawyer had been more of a nuisance, more independent than she expected. He had behaved oddly for some time, and it was Hu Zhong's failing that he had not kept a closer eye on the man. Hu Zhong had not said it, perhaps not reached the conclusion himself, but Jin Qing was sure that the lawyer was responsible for the fire in Sam's apartment. Particularly since Hu Zhong's men had not set it themselves.

In the curtained darkness of her office Jin Qing considered the lawyer some more. Here was the error, she realized. She had not given him sufficient thought. Bob Silver had been hired, in great part, because of Sam (though Hu Zhong hadn't known that). But he had also been hired because they knew his character. They knew him to be hungry, a whore-monger and thief, and they prized those characteristics because they made him malleable. But keeping a thief in your house can be a dangerous thing. Especially when you have something valuable to protect. Jin Qing had not, she realized, adequately protected her operation from the lawyer. And worse, far worse, she had not adequately protected Sam and now Kristina. The lawyer, if it was him or someone hired by him, had almost killed Kristina with his ham-handedness. Thankfully, once Jin Qing had her in custody, that couldn't happen again. But she didn't have Kristina yet, and she had not assigned anyone to cover the lawyer to prevent his sudden appearance in this place, this Easton, Maryland, or somewhere else where he could cause harm.

So the real question was, what to do? It was a bit late for sudden shifts, for diverting resources to Philadelphia. Such a move would create a substantial risk of exposing her network. The movement of agents to new locales always tended to excite the FBI and generate a lot of unwanted surveillance. And she had learned the hard way that such surveillance could destroy operations years in gestation. It was really a tremendous risk.

Jin Qing pushed herself forcibly back from the great desk. She stood and turned to the window where she opened the heavy curtains to let in the sun, now too weak to annoy her as it sank below the massive curled eaves of the Forbidden City. A year ago, even a month ago, she wouldn't have taken the risk of exposing her field agents. But she was different then—more rational. She had not then known the pain of loss.

Looking upon the circling crows silhouetted against a dusty red sky, she could not recall a single instance in which she had allowed herself to regret the events of the past. Even in 1970, when she was recalled from America amidst the furor and uncertainty of the Cultural Revolution, even then—though her government, at a moment's notice, had forced her to abandon her American children—she had never allowed herself a single tear. Children are children, but the Party was her family. So she had been instructed, and so she had thought. But she couldn't make sense of such piety now, or the surging emotions that had come upon her so suddenly, so strongly after years in remission.

She was confused, adrift, unsure why she should feel so weakened. Sure, she had lost a son. But he was a son she had not raised, a son she had not seen since he was two. And though she had kept track of his progress, she had done so, she always thought, because the boy, in addition to being her son, was the grandson of Chen Hai Zhang. And it was the duty of her Ministry to observe the Zhangs, for their complicity had always been suspected. Perhaps it had been a mistake for her not to reassign the Zhangs to another jurisdiction or at least another agent. Observation of her own offspring had, over the years, likely muddled the lines. It was an operational error, her error. And now she was unable to summon the objectivity she needed. Everything seemed threatened, everything she had built in this Ministry and within herself. Still, she had to make a decision.

And as the city's crows celebrated the onset of darkness with a symphony of caws, Jin Qing decided to immediately move ten agents from New York to Philadelphia. They would watch Silver and stop him should he attempt to leave. That way, at least, she could buy Kristina a little safety. Was she being foolish? Taking unnecessary chances for a small reward? Risking the prosperity and security of a nation for the sake of one person? No—it was not foolish, Jin Qing reflected and marveled at the thought. It was what any parent would do.

☆ ☆ ☆

Jin Qing's movement of personnel to Philadelphia was, indeed, noticed by the FBI's counterespionage units who communicated the fact of their arrival via a joint task force on international financial security to members of Treasury Secretary Stephanos' elite Vanguard unit. Agents of the Vanguard now sat very straight in their chairs across from Stephanos in the large conference room adjoining the Secretary's office. Per his usual practice, Stephanos had seated them in a line entirely down one length of the table. And from his position in the center of the table opposite them, he grilled each of them in turn as to the results of their individual assignments. First, the agents assigned to watch Antonetti's home had reported nothing except the functionings of the usual household routine, minus Antonetti. But the second group of agents, the FBI liaison team, had reported the unexpected move of known Chinese covert operatives to Philadelphia.

Stephanos found this interesting.

"Do we know what they're doing in Philly?"

"Not really, sir," responded the FBI liaison, an extremely hirsute fellow named Dimitri.

"Come on, Philly isn't exactly a hotbed of Asian activity in this country. It isn't San Fran or New York. Do they have contacts there?"

"Actually there is a long history of a China/Philadelphia connection," chimed in the agent seated immediately to Dimitri's left.

"Oh?"

"Philadelphia's universities have been educating China's elite since the last century. In fact, Jiang Zemin's own son has an engineering degree from Drexel. Jiang is the Chairman of the Communist—"

"I know who Jiang Zemin is, Agent McKenna. I've had dinner with the man."

"Yes, sir, of course, sir. All I meant to say was that with Philly full of Chinese students, and Chinese students being the first advance of Chinese intelligence operations in this country, Philly is a natural base for them."

"That may be. But why rush in extra forces? Why risk our scrutiny?"

Dimitri fielded this one. "We're not exactly sure. They seem to be concentrated in the Center City district. They are billing themselves as a group of travel executives learning about Philly as a tourist destination. They have taken up residence in a hotel there, the Embassy Suites."

"Is that significant?"

"Well, the Embassy Suites is on the edge of the office district. It looks right into the windows of the three biggest Philly law firms. We're guessing that with that location, they are not interested in the students at Penn or Drexel or even in tourist activities, which are mostly on the other side of the city."

"Are they being watched?"

"Yes, sir, the FBI is maintaining round-the-clock surveillance."

"Thank you Dimitri, McKenna. Stay on top of this." Stephanos paused to scribble some notes on the pad before him. He scratched his bald pate with his pen, then pointed the pen at the agent next to McKenna, the first of his three investment bankers.

"Go."

"As you suspected," began Dick Felton, "there is tremendous activity in the pits on the yuan. I can't get up early enough to compete with these guys. Someone is buying. I've shorted the yuan on twelve different occasions in large block trades. Large enough that under ordinary circumstances, I would have attracted notice. People would have seen me selling and started selling too, without even asking why. So every time I sold yuan, even at discount, I expected to see the price drop, just in sympathy. But no go. I had a buyer on every occasion. And anyone piggybacking on my trades found a buyer too, a buyer who was willing to buy into a wave of selling pressure."

"Fascinating. So who's the buyer?"

"Don't know."

"Dick, the man on your left just told me the Chinese Ministry of State Security is flooding Philadelphia with agents, but he doesn't know why. You're telling me someone is artificially bolstering the value of the Chinese trading currency, but you don't know who. The point, gentlemen," Stephanos raised his voice in obvious displeasure and passed a slow, cold eye over the array of men before him, "is to generate answers, rather than accumulate questions."

"If it helps," inserted Gus Dolgin, who had been sent to the Philadelphia currency options exchange, "all the significant trades on the options I've been selling in Philly are being executed through a

Hong Kong investment bank that has a seat on the exchange. But I don't know who the ultimate buyer is."

"Let me guess who the bank is." The gravelly voice belonged to J.P. Wexler who had arrived late to the meeting from his stint in Hong Kong. "Jasmine Investments!"

Gus and Dick both turned to J.P. "Yeah," they said in unison.

Gus asked, "Who are they? I thought I knew all the players."

Stephanos cut in. "Jasmine is what we call an upstart. Five years ago they didn't exist. Now they are one of the biggest investment houses in Asia. The CIA has tried . . . and maybe Cummings here can tell us more about this—" Stephanos pointed toward the CIA liaison sitting at the far end of the table in partial shadow "—The CIA has tried to infiltrate Jasmine a few times and from what I understand, has been unsuccessful. Cummings, why don't you fill us in."

The man at the end of the table was the only sloucher in a room of straight spines. And in further contrast to the military buzz cuts of the Treasury and FBI agents and the slick styling atop the former investment bankers, Cummings's hair was unkempt and graying. He did not look up from his doodling when he talked. "The Secretary is correct. Our efforts with Jasmine have not borne fruit. And we're not sure why. Our agents, young Hong Kong broker types, are all still in place. But they have never initiated contact with us, and they have certainly not delivered any information. Moreover, they have repeatedly ignored our efforts at reestablishing communications within the agreed upon channels."

Gus leaned far over the table to address the CIA man at the end. "And what about Jasmine, who are they?"

Cummings didn't respond, so J.P. answered his longtime colleague. "I can tell you from my week in Hong Kong that Jasmine is *the* market maker there. They're into everything in a big way, securities, real estate, venture capital, you name it. Every time there is something going on, like a new office tower or oil exploration company being launched, they are either behind it or they got a piece of it. They're in the newspaper in three different columns every day."

Stephanos turned back to Cummings. "Does your agency have a working hypothesis you'd care to share?"

"We don't like to speculate, sir."

"Indulge me."

"Well . . . what we expect to find is that Jasmine Investments is some sort of front for the Chinese government."

"Would that be unusual?"

"No, the Chinese have a number of front companies which we have been able to trace through the chain of ownership to Beijing."

"But in this case you can't?"

"That is correct. Jasmine appears to be owned by legitimate members of the Hong Kong business community. Though none of them take an active role in day to day management."

"Which suggests?"

"That control of the company is somehow vested in Chinese operatives through other means."

"Which 'other means' cannot be determined at the present."

"Precisely."

Stephanos shook his head. He always felt like a dentist with the CIA guys, pulling teeth. "I'd like to request, Mr. Cummings, that you make another attempt to contact your people inside Jasmine. Tell them it is worth their while to talk to us. Whaddya say?"

"I would have to clear that with the director. "

"Of course." Stephanos gave Cummings a short nod of his head. But Cummings didn't move. Stephanos felt his anger rising. "No time like the present, Cummings."

Cummings looked up from his notepad, meeting Stephanos' eyes. Buried in that big bald head, they had a fierceness that must have frightened Cummings and prompted him to action. He gathered his pad and left without acknowledging the other people present. Stephanos watched him leave, then decided to take matters into his own hands. He hit the intercom on the speakerphone before him. His secretary answered.

"Audrey, see if you can get CIA Director Feynman on the line. Tell him it's me, tell him it's urgent."

The men in the conference room stayed largely silent while they listened to the CIA's hold music. Gus, ever the comedian, snapped his fingers to the orchestral version of the *Grease* soundtrack. Only Stephanos allowed himself a smile.

"Saint Cyril! Always a pleasure. What can I do for you?" The director's voice boomed from the speaker in the center of the table.

Stephanos raised his voice too, but more to be heard. "I've got you on the speaker. Present are members of the Vanguard, including members of the FBI. So don't say anything stupid." Feynman and he were old friends, but also competitors. Mostly for the affection of their Republican leader.

"I always say something stupid, Cy. You know that."

"Yes, I do. Let me get to the point. I understand you have some sources inside a certain Hong Kong entity named Jasmine Investments. I need those sources activated. Jasmine, either for its own account or on behalf of a client or multiple clients, is buying up all the Chinese currency it can handle. I need to know who and why and I need to know in forty-eight hours. Can you do it?"

"Take me off the speaker." The director's voice had suddenly lost its cordiality. Stephanos picked up the telephone handset.

"What's up?"

"Is this a secure line?"

"Of course, it's an extension of the lines to my office."

"All right, I'll tell you. But it goes no further. Understand."

"Understood."

"We recruited four native Hong Kong Chinese, recent university graduates, to take jobs at Jasmine. They never told us anything and we lost contact. Yesterday morning, all four of those men were found dead. They were bound, gagged, stripped naked, mutilated and then shot in the head. They were found together in a vacant luxury apartment in Kowloon. The coincidence of their simultaneous murder is too great for us to conclude anything but the obvious."

"Which is?"

"That we have a mole."

"Oh, Christ."

"Don't give anything away, Stephanos, act happy."

"That's great!" Stephanos smiled for the benefit of the other people in the room, who had all just become suspects.

"Look Stephanos, I'm telling you this because it sounds like we're running parallel operations. I want you to take extreme caution in what you're doing. I've seen the pictures of what was done in Hong Kong. I've been seeing the images in my head all day. They are extremely disturbing. Whoever we're up against here is playing for keeps."

"Who are we up against?"

"I think you can guess who the principal candidate is."

"Ministry of State Security?"

"Yes."

"Jin Qing?" Stephanos asked under his breath.

"Most likely."

"Shit."

"My feelings exactly. Watch your step my friend."

Stephanos put the receiver down. He tried to hide his trepidation from the other agents in the room. He had to, for any one of them might be the eyes and ears of Jin Qing.

16

Ambrose had taken a flat behind the famous music conservatory in the French Concession. I always enjoyed visiting Ambrose at that house, for day and night the students would practice. And their music, sometimes repetitive and untamed, but often clean and sincere, would drift over the rear lawn of the school and reach our ears through the open windows of the living room. Ambrose didn't feel as I did about the music, difficult fellow that he was. He particularly hated the string instruments and the vocalists, insisting they were tone deaf and not worthy of formal instruction.

Ambrose's problem—the source of my amusement—was that the school, though French taught, included courses in traditional Chinese forms such as Chinese opera. It was the operatic soloists that Ambrose hated so, and when they began to practice he would rise from his chair and insist that we leave the apartment immediately. I would laugh at him but inevitably agree to go to the nearby café where, he said, he could listen peaceably to the din of traffic and the chatter of street vendors.

One such a day, in the spring of 1937, the sopranos had once again chased us to the small metal stools of the sidewalk café. Ambrose was drinking some combination of gin and I my favorite black tea, when during our usual discussion of the Stalinist purges and the misdirection of the Party, an official-looking transport screeched to a halt in front of the café. Six large men burst from this van and, in a fury of overturned chairs and patrons, forced their way to our table.

Without warning they grabbed Ambrose roughly by the lapels, pulled him to his feet, twisted him around. They bent him over the table in front of me and handcuffed him in a crude manacle. I recognized the men as Big-eared Tu's. They were familiar here since Tu had won the title of Chief of Internal Security to the entire French Concession. I knew enough to stay silent; we were powerless against such men. I demanded no explanation from them. And none was given to me or to Ambrose as he was dragged off, knees scraping, to the van. I can still picture the vehicle then pulling from the curb, careening down the crowded Avenue Joffre with the same haste and self-importance with which it had arrived. Even today officials drive that way, racing about excitedly while in their ordinary duties they move so slowly.

I can remember being frightened. It was not supposed to be known that Ambrose was a Communist, let alone the official Comintern representative to the Shanghai branch of the Chinese Communist Party. And if Chiang's forces had been able to detect Ambrose's true purpose, then how secure was I?

As it turned out, I had no reason to fear for anyone but Ambrose. Ambrose did get a message to me a few days later, delivered by a fellow believer he had met in Big-eared Tu's cell. My position was secure. Ambrose had been given up by someone in Canton. Someone who, under pressure from Chiang's torturers, had stated that someone named Ambrose, with red hair, was the Comintern representative in Shanghai. Chiang, through Big-eared Tu, had acted fast. As far as Ambrose could tell from the line of questions put to him, they had not taken the time to follow him to ascertain his contacts here. They knew little, as yet, of the remaining Shanghai network, and he could certainly be trusted to stay silent.

My little informant left, and for a month I heard nothing from Ambrose until he suddenly, and at great risk to both of us, appeared at my door early one morning. It was well before sunrise. At first I treated him coldly (I still regret) for I felt his coming to my home a rash and impudent gesture. How dare he endanger us this way! What if he had been followed from the jail?

But Ambrose quelled my anger. He told me he was being forced to leave the country. That he was being escorted, at first light, from his flat to a ship now moored in the river. The ship was leaving later today for Australia. His expulsion was the best deal the American consul could get from Chiang who had wanted Ambrose tried as a spy.

I was shocked by this and also by his physical appearance, the loss of strength in his voice which now emitted from swollen and cracked lips in a halting sort of croak. He had been tortured, he said. Not hit or beaten so much as starved of food and sleep. He had been transferred, against the dictates of the French-Chinese Treaty, to a Chinese jail in the old part of the city. He had been kept awake with bright lights, loud noises and electric prods for almost a week. Thereafter, he had been starved. He was certain, as far as his memory could penetrate the delirium he had suffered, that he had kept his knowledge to himself. That I, together with the labor union officials and a hundred other covert plants, were still unknown to Chiang and the Green Gang thugs.

Ambrose wanted very much for us to stay in touch and I readily agreed. We had become close in his time here. He was, I realized with profound astonishment, the best friend I had outside my family. He was a confidant. My teacher and pupil.

We worked out a system by which Ambrose would take out advertisements in the classified sections of two major American newspapers. The newspapers, the New York Herald Tribune *and the* San Francisco Chronicle, *were available here, though they arrived about a week late. Each advertisement would be innocuous read alone. It would always concern the sale of a yellow farmhouse. But when read together with the other advertisement, under a simple alternating encryption code, it would reveal Ambrose's message. I was to do the same in the* North China Daily *and the* China Mail, *to which Ambrose would secure subscriptions.*

Thus arranged, Ambrose left my house as quickly and quietly as he had come in.

I never saw him again. Ambrose's departure left a great hole in both my personal and revolutionary life. The Comintern did not immediately replace Ambrose with another representative, and without

Ambrose, there was little for me to do as a covert Communist in Shanghai. Under Party orders, I kept with my work at the Ministry and occasionally reported goings on to my handlers at the safe house. However, I didn't have much to report that wasn't public knowledge. The Ministry had become a bit of a celebrity in town, with everyone watching the games H.H. Kung was playing with the nation's finances and the ongoing saga of T.V. Soong's turbulent relationships with his sisters and their powerful husbands. I could sense my handlers growing bored with my reports.

Some months later, and after daily searching, I saw my first ads for a yellow farmhouse in the American papers. I ran the encryption key through the ads. The first line, to my delight, said simply that Ambrose had arrived and was safe. But the second line began with a warning. "Do not admit frequent contact with me, or agreement with my principles. Disavow me. When my replacement comes, you must criticize me as rightist."

Bewildered, I searched the papers for weeks after that looking for more insight and took out ads asking for an explanation. Only once more before the Japanese invasion did I hear from Ambrose via the yellow farmhouse routine. He wrote that he had been purged. He had arrived in the United States to find that in his absence, a faction within the American Communist Party had fallen from favor for backing the wrong Russian horse. Stalin had elevated another faction to prominence, and Ambrose's affiliation, though dated by ten years, with the "Lovestoneites" was enough to strip him of all official titles and responsibilities. Ambrose finished his latest missive with the call to remember our conversations and to keep true to our shared vision and fate. I always have.

In the next weeks I remained concerned for Ambrose, but my concern for his fate was pushed aside by the Japanese.

Some said it was Chiang's fault. That it was an error in judgement to think he could direct the course of the war by taking the offensive and bringing the Japanese to the battlefield in the narrow streets of Shanghai. Some said it was the fault of Chiang's German advisor, General Alexander von Falkenhausen, who advocated guerilla tactics against the greatly superior armaments of the Japanese. I cannot say. I was not then in a position to judge.

I recall the city being circled by Chiang's army. They came down from the north where the Japanese had already conquered all of Manchuria and much of the countryside in the approaches to Beijing. I recall too, that no one knew who started the shooting on August 13, 1937, but we all thought the twelve thousand Japanese troops stationed in their section of the International Settlement would soon be overwhelmed by the eighty thousand Chinese. We all predicted an early victory, glory for the Chinese soldier.

But the Japanese fought hard, and they were quickly reinforced with aircraft and gunboats that hurled bombs and shells into the city from the air and from the Huangpo River. The Japanese were indiscriminate, and with the Chinese fighting in the streets, they shelled everything. No one was safe.

The horror of it first struck me one day as I was walking to the Ministry. I was almost to the front door when the building across the street simply exploded. The front wall blew into the street crushing everything and everyone beneath it. Twenty seconds earlier I had crossed that street. Just twenty seconds earlier. If I had stopped to greet an acquaintance or tie my shoe, I would have been one of the bodies barely visible amidst the blood and rubble. The building had been a department store and was filled with people rushing to accumulate as much as they could carry. Most of them died. We did what we could, but the building had fallen down upon them and we had no way to lift the shattered stone blocks and twisted girders. Emergency crews had trouble navigating the rubble in the street, and those we did pull out often died en route, the ambulances immobilized by more falling debris, bullets and the endless scatter of mutilated corpses.

In the middle of this the Ministry stayed firm. Most government workers were streaming to Nanjing, but Chiang wanted the Ministry officials to remain at their posts so as not to panic the bankers. So we continued to sit at our desks, to answer telephone calls and process monetary transactions while all around the carnage grew worse. From the high floors of the Ministry building, we saw the parks first turned into field hospitals, then graveyards as the mounting casualties overwhelmed the thinning ranks of medical personnel. Everywhere, in the Ministry, at home with all the doors and windows shut fast, the stench of putrefaction, of swollen corpses and detached and rotting limbs was with us. I could not grow used to it and would, at times, collapse in fits of retching. Many of my colleagues began deserting their positions, fleeing with their families to the northwest. But Chiang was not ready to admit defeat, though we could all see in the surrounding destruction that his army was beaten. Unofficial estimates put the Nationalist Army's death toll at 250,000. And that didn't include all those volunteer forces who had taken up arms in defense of their homes. With all the desertions there were not enough people to do the work of the Ministry, and I found myself spending weeks at time in the Ministry building, sleeping under my desk, scrounging for food.

A few weeks before Shanghai fell, in November 1937, I was summoned by intercom into the Finance Minister's office. I was not expecting to see the Minister himself, but when I opened the opaque doors, there he was, calmly sitting at his own secretary's desk and peering down his nose at something he was typing.

"Are you a patriot?" The Minister asked me this without looking up.

"Yes, sir, I am."

I did not lie, for I regarded myself as a patriot despite my liaison with the Communists.

Minister Kung then looked up from the typewriter. He stared intently at me for a few moments.

"I too am a patriot, Mr. Zhang," he said. "Please, come into my office." The Minister pulled his typing from the machine and led me into his enormous wood-paneled office.

"I've watched you," he continued from the position he had taken in front of the shattered remains of the high arched windows, "working tirelessly to keep our little operation afloat. I think that you are the person to whom I shall entrust a most delicate operation, if I may. I must warn you, however, that it may involve some risk. Some risk to your life."

I swallowed and nodded.

"Can I count on you?"

"Yes, sir. You can count on me." I said it as firmly as I could, though I fear I was barely whispering in his presence.

The man suddenly smiled. "Good! Very Good!" He strode purposefully across the grand office and sat heavily in a thick leather couch, his great weight causing it to wheeze. He bade me sit next to him. I could smell his cologne.

"Now, Mr. Zhang, let me tell you what you are going to do."

☆   ☆   ☆

Kristina nodded, but she was barely listening to Behr as he went through his agenda for the day. It sounded a lot like yesterday's. He was going to check on the plane, maybe fly around a little, pop into town for lunch. But she did hear him ask how it was going.

"I'm just editing a good part," she answered curtly.

"You going to finally let me read it?"

"I'll print out what I have. How's that?"

"That's all I need. I'll see you this afternoon." Kristina did not turn from the monitor to see him leave. She heard the door shut and made a mental note to print out her chapters. She grabbed the next of the little red books and flipped past the stern visage of the Chairman to the first page. She had skimmed this bit before. But she wanted to get it down right. This one book, of all twenty-eight, was critical, for it revealed what Chen Hai Zhang's story was all about.

☆   ☆   ☆

Minister Kung must have seen the doubt in my face. "I will show you," he said and pulled me off the couch and out his door.

Kung was a fat man. He waddled rather than walked, so that by the time we were through the main part of the office he was winded.

"I bet you have never seen this before," he breathed heavily. The Minister opened a door to what I had always thought a supply closet and stepped inside. Hesitantly I followed him in. I saw him unlock another door at the back of the closet. Behind that door was an elevator gate; the Minister heaved, and it rattled aside.

"Come, come," he said, "it is perfectly safe."

We entered the elevator and descended, the Minister operating the lever with surprising expertise. At the bottom, he again threw open the gate, and led me down a long concrete passage dimly lit by intermittent bulbs.

"We are under the street now."

Indeed, I could hear the rumble of activity above. I wondered if the concrete was strong enough to withstand the Japanese bombs, and asked the Minister the same. "We must hurry," was all he said.

At the end of the passage we were greeted by an enormous metal door. The Minister turned an electric switch next to this door. Almost imperceptibly, a distant bell rang on the other side. We waited nervously for a few moments, then heard bolts being moved. Another few moments and the door swung open. In the doorway stood an older man, dressed simply in traditional Chinese robes. Despite his age, he had a somewhat effeminate look about him, and when he turned and waved us forward I saw that he wore his hair in the long queue required of the Mandarins in the last century. I had not seen such a braid since childhood. Except for his beckoning gesture, he did not greet or acknowledge us in any way. Odd behavior, I thought, in the presence of the Minister. But the Minister did not seem to mind.

The old man led us down another passage to another metal door, in front which, at a small wooden desk, sat another man. He was much younger than the first, though similarly dressed and also carrying his hair in a long braid down his back. When we approached, this man rose from his desk and the old man shuffled off behind us. The younger Mandarin opened the second door with three separate keys, then led us through a series of empty rooms with gray painted walls and metal gates until he presented us to yet a third Mandarin seated at another small wooden desk. This third guard did not rise immediately, instead waiting until the second guard had returned through enough gates and rooms to be completely out of sight. I could not immediately understand what this guard's duties were. Whereas the other guards were each stationed before a large metal door, this guard seemed stranded in a bare room at the end of the line.

But presently the guard stood. He walked to the wall where a black telephone was hanging. He lifted the handset, mumbled something into the mounted speaker. We heard a great clanging and suddenly the rear wall began to open on invisible hinges. Indeed, this guard did have a door, only it was plastered and painted, hidden before us.

My surprise showed. The Minister was laughing, "You are like a child, Zhang! Really the technology is not so great."

But the surprise of the moving wall was nothing to what I felt next as we entered the chamber. For there, under a low roof, was the most awesome, unfathomable display of wealth I had ever beheld.

"Approximately five thousand tons, perhaps a bit more." The Minister slapped me on the back. I tried to do the math in my head, the amount was staggering.

"But . . . I thought we were nearly insolvent. That the war was eating up everything!"

"Oh, no. That is only what we tell Chiang, and what we have told him all along. Otherwise, I can assure you, this would have all belonged to Big-eared Tu long ago."

"Where did it come from? How have you kept this a secret?"

"Mostly, it is from the old imperial government. The Qing Dynasty, despite its lowly demise, was never poor. It was just poorly run. Its ministers, many of them eunuchs like the men who showed us here, didn't trust their emperors, and especially not the dowager Empress, any more than Soong and I trust Chiang Kai-shek. So they, as we, have lied and built walls to disguise the true wealth of the nation."

I was truly stunned by what Minister Kung was telling me. I could not imagine that years of famine, war and bloodshed might have been averted if only a Chinese government could have stood more firmly, bolstered by the power hidden in this room.

I grew angry and was about to vent my thoughts on the Minister, when it occurred to me that perhaps the eunuchs and finance ministers had been correct. There was wisdom in their actions. For shouldn't the wealth of this room be preserved for a government worthy of it? A government that wouldn't squander it? Certainly in the last hundred years, China had seen nothing but leaders too weak or too corrupt to take proper advantage of the wealth at their disposal. The weak were soon dominated by the corrupt, and the corrupt lined the pockets of their friends. The Minister was absolutely right. If Chiang knew about this room, it would be he and Big-eared Tu, Pockmarked Huang and their retinue of cronies who would profit thereby. It would not be the Chinese people. No—the peasants and the soldiers would continue struggling in their patriotism, as oblivious as ever to the slaps they received from above.

So I resolved to help the Minister. To do exactly as he commanded, with only one slight variation in his plan. And this slight variation would ensure, as the eunuchs and the finance ministers had long intended, that it was a good and just government that finally received the nation's inheritance. But I would determine if that government was worthy. And no one else. No one, that is, with the possible exception of Ambrose. The closest thing I had to an ideological twin.

I made up mind quickly, my vision finally clear of the opacity that seemed to have blurred my world for so long. I knew exactly what I had to do, and I laid out all the steps in my mind. It would be difficult, certainly. For on this end, I only had the help of the eunuchs. And on the other end? Well, I had to leave it for Ambrose to decide.

I turned to the Minister, who had been studying me intently, and asked if I could start immediately, given the immensity of the task.

"Of course, my boy," he responded, laughing. "Not only do I permit it, I demand it. These gentlemen," he gestured toward the eunuch, "will help you in any way they can. But forgive them if they seem a little sad. They have lost so much. First their jewels, and now their gold!"

The eunuch didn't acknowledge the jibe, but I could see his eyes turn cold as the Minister erupted in great chin-jiggling laughs. I watched them turn colder still as the Minister, still chuckling, ". . . first their jewels . . ." walked over to the nearest stack where, with fat little hands, he removed one large gold bar deeply imprinted, I saw, with the imperial seal of the Qing emperors.

"Five thousand tons of gold, Mr. Zhang," he said as he walked out the door still clutching the gold bar, "five thousand . . . more . . . or less."

☆   ☆   ☆

Kristina typed in the last lines, not quite able to get her mind around the figure. What did that add up to? It had to be a lot. The computer had a calculator function and she pulled that down. She knew that gold today cost somewhere near three hundred dollars per ounce. So a pound of gold, at sixteen ounces to the pound, would be worth $4,800, and a ton of gold . . .

"Shit," she said aloud. How many pounds in a ton? One thousand? Two thousand? She could never remember. But two thousand seemed more arcane and, therefore, more likely correct. So, two thousand times $4,800 and a ton of gold was worth $9,600,000. And multiply that by five thousand . . .

Kristina couldn't count that high. The computer's calculator showed her a forty-eight followed by nine zeros uninterrupted by commas. What did the computer have against commas? She wrote the number down on the back of an envelope and added the commas herself. Six zeros meant one million; seven zeros, ten million; eight zeros, one hundred million; nine zeros, one thousand million . . . no, one billion . . . Wow! Forty-eight billion. The gold her grandfather had seen in that room was worth forty-eight billion dollars today. So what had happened to it? She had to get back to work.

17

A cargo of five thousand tons was, in that day, too much for a ship on the Huangpo. I learned from the shipping brokers that only oil tankers could carry that much deadweight tonnage. I also learned that I would not find a junk, much less a tanker, amidst the press of people and merchandise fighting to leave the city before our imminent surrender to the Japanese. I called and visited every shipping company and broker listed in the Shanghai directory. I was offered space aboard ships in the nearby ports of Hangzhou and Ningbo. But, of course, the particular nature of my cargo didn't lend itself to overland freight. After a fruitless week of searching, I was ready to admit to the Minister that I was unable to find transportation.

I sought him out in person. First at the Ministry, where I discovered his office riddled with upward slanting bullet holes from the fighting in the street, then at his home, two miles away in a fashionable enclave within the French Concession. I found the Minister looking extremely displeased, preparing for his own departure, surrounded by overstuffed boxes and slippered servants scurrying about the house at his mercurial command.

He did not seem happy at my sudden appearance, and when I told him of the lack of ships, his face grew—all within a few seconds—very pale and then very red. He got up from the chair he was sitting in, and I prepared myself for the torrent of anger. But then, just as abruptly, he sat again. He began to say something, his fist raised in a gesture of authority. Then he dropped his head, merely saying, "No, no, no," in a soft, susurrant murmur—the sound of defeat.

The Minister's performance worried me. I was concerned that he would sack me on the spot. He would see the lack of ships as a lack of resourcefulness on my part and he would turn to somebody else for this assignment. I could not allow that. My plan, the plan I had formulated in amendment to the Minister's own, didn't permit others to get involved. I must keep this job to myself.

"Minister Kung," I said, "forgive me, but in my low station, I am perhaps unaware of certain resources. Resources of which you, perhaps, would know."

The Minister raised his head, fixing his eyes on mine. "Are you reading my mind, Zhang? Is that what you are doing?"

"No, sir, my abilities are quite limited in that area, I assure you. I merely thought . . . that perhaps—"

"I know what you thought; I was thinking it too. But it is a very dangerous course."

"Which course is that?"

"Why, Tu Yueh-sheng, Big-eared Tu! Were you not thinking of him too?"

"Only in vague terms." It was bad form to admit knowledge of the extent of Big-eared Tu's involvement in public affairs. The Minister accepted my discretion with an understanding nod.

"But what will I tell him?" he continued.

"Sir?"

"What will I tell Tu?"

"I don't follow you, sir."

"Are you being deliberately stupid?"

"Not deliberately, no."

The Minister now walked around me on the great, intricately patterned rug. He passed behind and closed the study door, and as he returned to his desk I noticed that he wasn't wearing shoes or socks. The Minister was barefoot! Somehow that struck me as odd.

The Minister resumed his seat. "Tu, as you are undoubtedly aware, controls the docks along the Huangpo River. He can ensure that a ship stays empty if we ask him. He can secure us two ships merely by telling the ships' captains, or the shipping company, that he has put a lien on their cargo for certain unspecified late payments. Tu does this regularly. The couriers never question it. They simply cannot afford to counter him. When he has made sure that the ships are empty, he will tell them he has another cargo that is ready to go and which will pay full price. That other cargo will be ours. But what, and this is the question I place to you again, do we tell our big-eared friend about the cargo? What do we tell him it is?"

"Why should we tell him anything?"

"Because, Zhang, he will be curious about our involvement; he will see the crates, and, more than anything, he will note the gross weight. Consider the question yourself: What does the Ministry have that weighs five thousand tons?"

"I see."

"I thought you might."

Seeing the normally ebullient Minister flustered this way, I realized the enormity of the risk we faced. If Big-eared Tu discovered the nature of the cargo, bad things, unimaginable things would certainly follow. If Tu were to appropriate the gold for himself he would instantly become the world's richest man. And with his ambition, he would use the leverage to wrest control of the government from Chiang (who, despite his flaws, did not have near the blood thirst of Big-eared Tu). Then, more than likely, Tu would strike a deal with the Japanese, dividing the country and the opium trade between them.

A second scenario, where Tu simply told Chiang about the existence of the gold was no more palatable, for Chiang would then appropriate the eunuch's vault and cement his place as leader by either cutting his own deal with the Japanese or gradually slipping the wealth into the pockets of his friends and family and the military when trouble brewed on the borders. With the extra wealth and armaments, Chiang might not defeat the Japanese, but he would easily crush the Communists now isolated in the western mountains. And the revolution I foresaw for my beaten and backward country would never come to pass. But no matter the scenario, whoever got the gold, both the Minister and I would be shot as traitors, quickly and without a trial.

The Minister intruded on my thoughts. "You must go to the man."

"Me?"

"Yes, you must find Big-eared Tu, preferably at night. Tonight, in fact, would be best. You must find him and tell him that I sent you. Bring him this." The Minister reached into a nearby desk. He removed an envelope and from my position I could see that the drawer was full of similarly sized, similarly stuffed envelopes. "Tell him that you were given this money by some Americans who want to see their cargo . . . their cargo of . . ."

"Marble?"

The Minister's face lit brightly. "Yes, yes. Marble. That is perfect! Something heavy, moderately valuable, but otherwise commonly exported and inconspicious. Brilliant my boy. Brilliant!"

The Minister was delighted. He reached into a box on the desk from which he removed a long, thin, very black cigar. He held it very delicately in his thick fingers. His nails, I saw, were well manicured, almost polished, and when he puckered his full red lips to admit the cigar, his face resembled that of an infant, eager and expectant, turning toward his mother's breast. Even today I can picture the man vividly as he was then.

And I remember too, quite distinctly, asking myself at that precise moment how it is that we allow such odd, misshapen, dissolute men to rise to positions of power. At the top, Chiang Kai-shek, our Nationalist leader, was small, leathery and entirely without teeth. A man who, despite an excellent marriage to a prominent family, spent his nights drug-addled and in the company of common whores and criminals. And one of those criminals, Big-eared Tu—who carried out vendettas with his own hand, often with the knife he was given as boy—had arguably more power than Chiang, because Chiang had to clear all his actions with Tu, and was, to a great degree, funded by Tu's opium profits when the banks and the Ministry ran (or pretended to run) dry. And who were these bankers and ministers? Ex-Finance Minister, now Bank of China Chairman Soong, immensely rich and connected by marriage to nearly everyone in power, was also a thief. His New York bank accounts were rumored to be filled with other people's money. And the new Finance Minister? That man sat before me now. He was not especially bright, ruthless or wanton. His effectiveness lay in being an infantile brat, one who had always gotten everything he wanted, including control of the nation's vaults. But that, I thought, is how it is with brats. They are never afraid of asking. And people will give them anything just to shut them up. I, for one, was risking my life for one.

That brat, my Minister, explained now what he wanted from me.

"You should be able to find the man at the Petrograd. It's a Russian nightclub in the International Settlement, just off the Bubbling Well Road. Every cabbie knows it. Tu owns a piece of it and likes to screw the dancers. He likes the tall, white Russians best. He hasn't slept with a Chinese girl in years . . ."

The Minister stopped. He looked suddenly tired and somewhat manic. All traces of his previous joy dissipated. "You don't need to know all this. You simply walk toward the man at his table against the wall on the right. Tell his handlers that you represent the Ministry. When they bring you to Tu, say that you have been approached by an American firm. Say that they have paid us some money to move their marble. That these are Americans we want to please because they also have arma- ments factories in California from which we can purchase supplies on credit. But only if they get their shipment of marble through. Then give him this envelope and the details of when the shipment is to travel."

I wrote down everything the Minister said. I did not want to get something wrong and have Tu somehow suspect our motives. The Minister continued, now lecturing with his finger in the air, "Tu will not agree to anything in front of his men. He doesn't do business that way. Tomorrow, however, if he agrees, he will contact you at the Ministry with his answer. If he doesn't agree, you will never hear from him. And we will not see the money again either."

"Does that money matter, with all we have in the eunuchs' vault?"

The Minister looked at me as if I was an idiot. "Of course it matters, Zhang. Every cent."

From his chair the Minister dismissed me. I heard a distant bell and one of the slippered servants materialized in the doorway. He guided me through the labyrinth, out of the house to the front garden. Though I had some hours to wait before my meeting with Tu, I walked quickly down the Avenue Joffre, up the Fujian Road and to the Minis- try's offices. There I descended again into the vaults where the eunuchs and I made arrangements to get the gold packed and to the docks. I informed the eunuchs of the general plan, and we decided to conceal the gold beneath slabs of marble laid at the top of each crate in case they were opened by Tu or customs officials. Getting the marble was easy. We simply had our men pull it from the floors and walls of the bombed-out buildings. No one questioned us. These days, everyone was a scavenger.

I watched the hours pass with a sense of trepidation. I did not know what to expect from Tu. The stories about the man were known to every foreigner and schoolchild. He was supposed to be without any moral underpinning. A man who would kill you where you stood if it suited him. He was a street orphan whose ability with a knife had secured him a position in the Green Gang before he was twelve. He then cut his path to the top, in part with the help of Chiang, and he had the connections and authority to move about the city unmolested and carry out his activities. Activities which included board chairmanships as well complete dominance of the vice-trades (though he was losing opium traffic to the Japanese). He was said to be a genius—clever, insightful, imaginative. Some argued that if it weren't for Tu's sage advice and support, Chiang would have lost power long ago. Tu traveled about the city with an entourage of bodyguards and women. He passed effortlessly through the borders erected by the French, British and even Japanese powers, and passed with equal ease between the boardrooms of the English trading houses, the carpeted shops of the Jewish merchants, the jazzy French cabarets, the Russian bordellos and the back alleys filled with bales of raw opium and young girls slated for shipment to San Francisco and London. Tu succeeded in all these venues, in part because those he dealt with, whether they be a beknighted chairman of the Shanghai Race Club, a government minister or a lowly brothel keeper by the docks, knew the stories. They knew that the man with big ears sometimes left the heads of his victims prominently displayed on posts as warnings to those who might cross him. They all feared that one of those heads might someday be theirs.

In three hours time, I was to meet Big-eared Tu. And I was to lie to him and attempt to pass the largest shipment of gold in Chinese history beneath his nose without him noticing.

I went home. I spent two hours with my new wife. A delightful interlude, I recall. We had not had, with the invasive Japanese and my work at the Ministry, much chance for intimacy in our short marriage. But her touch and warmth that evening also left me feeling small and guilty for the risks I was taking. I left our apartment and her concerned smile reminded me that I had really done the woman a disservice by marrying her. Though her family and mine had delighted in the union, her time in Shanghai had been nothing but hardship and war. And I was not such a great match really. A government bureaucrat. Indeed, a traitorous bureaucrat with a Communist Party membership card. What could I really offer her except disgrace with the possibility of a young death?

The sensation of guilt stayed with me that evening. And some time after I left the apartment, at approximately ten that evening, while showing my passport and Ministry identification for the second time that day at the French gates, I detected a hint of her perfume on my collar and resolved to do something for her. I had no idea then that it would mean our permanent separation.

My driver took us through the French Concession, pushed and honked through the crowd at the gates to the International Settlement and then bounced us between the craters and debris down the Nanjing Road to where it turned into Bubbling Well Road. We were almost to the end of the Settlement, with only China beyond the border, when the car turned right and then right again and pulled to a stop before a simple painted green door with a small sign above indicating the home of the Petrograd Club. Usually, a place like this would have been brightly lit, its doorway crowded with western and Chinese patrons scrambling to get in. But with lights extinguished to fool the bombers and the hazards of open exposure, everything was dark and seemingly abandoned.

I asked the driver to accompany me inside and wait by the door. Suddenly fearful, I also instructed him to proceed directly to the Minister's house in case something happened to me. I turned from him and the hat check girl, a large Russian woman in a dancer's leotard, inhaled deeply and descended some steps into the club. I immediately spotted Tu's crowd on the right side, exactly where Minister Kung said they would be. In fact, they were some of the only patrons in attendance that evening. And they were making quite a noise—clearly audible over the lovely black jazz singer standing in a spot of light on the stage.

I was completely ignored until I crossed an invisible boundary some twenty feet from the table. Immediately and in unison, three large men turned and moved menacingly toward me. I stammered that I was from the Finance Ministry, here to see Mr. Tu. I showed them my Ministry identification, and attempted to look innocent. Satisfied by either my credentials or harmless appearance, they yielded, whereupon I was taken to the man's table. At first, I couldn't see him. There were a number of people seated in the large round booth, many of them women. Beautiful women. Some of the most beautiful I had ever seen. Even today, when the cell mates play what if—what if we had roast pork over noodles, where the noodles have been fried in sesame and coriander—I describe these women with their yellow hair and enormous round eyes, their virtual nakedness and availability. I try to describe these women in minute detail to Gao and the other men in my cell; these men with coal dust imbedded in their skin, their cheeks hollow and teeth yellow, their eyes dulled by underground toil and complete acquiescence to the master apparatus, so that they may imagine what if . . . what if they could be touched, even for a moment, by exquisite grace.

I finally picked out Tu by the size of his ears. Otherwise I may not have noticed him at all. He was by far the smallest figure at the table. A thin man dominated by a large, closely shaven head, which in turn supported those great ears. His face was puffy and scarred, the nose flattened by childhood beatings. A droopy left eyelid and permanent grin lent him a sick and dangerous look which, when turned on me, froze me into silence.

"Speak, man. What do you want?" he yelled in a surprisingly high voice over the din.

It took me some time to gather my wits. I fumbled for the envelope in my pocket. I tried to hand it to him, but the table was too big to reach across. I gave it to a Russian girl at the end who passed it on.

"This is for you, Tu Yueh-sheng," I stuttered, using his given name. "It is from an American company. A company that makes guns."

"So what do they want from me? Do they want me to buy their guns? I have guns. I sell guns." Tu made a gesture pushing the envelope back the way it came.

"No, no . . . it is we, the government who wish to buy guns, big guns, sometime in the future. We want to keep these Americans happy. And

to keep them happy we need your help."

"Yes, I am always helping the government."

Tu laughed loudly and the table laughed with him, though many couldn't understand what he was saying. We were speaking in Shanghai dialect.

"We need to help them with a shipment of marble. They have lost their transport. They need two ships capable of carrying a total of five thousand deadweight tons. And they need them right away."

"And this," Tu said, opening the envelope and extracting a thick wad of British sterling notes, more than I had ever imagined, "is to get their ships for them?" Tu simulated spitting on the money. "It is not enough. I require twice this amount!"

I thought a moment, then took a chance. "You will get a second envelope when the shipment is aboard," I said with a note of fortitude that still surprises me. I was really gambling on the Minister's benefi- cence. But he did have a drawer full of these envelopes, didn't he? I prayed silently that they all contained the same thing. "I have been instructed that upon the marble being fully loaded and the ships' casting off, to remit the second envelope to you in person. It will contain the same amount. In British sterling."

Tu looked at me thoughtfully for a moment. His stare sent shivers through my spine. He was clearly sizing me up. Measuring me, I imagined, for a coffin. Then he spoke.

"Ordinarily," he said, "I do not make decisions late at night, while I'm at play. But I can tell you now that I will get you your ships. They will be ready tomorrow, and so must you be. One of my men will find you at the Ministry tomorrow morning and provide you with details. If you . . . sorry, the American clients require transport or stevedore services I can provide that as well. Though at an additional charge. Simply tell my agent tomorrow what is needed and he can make the arrangements and negotiate a price." Tu nodded and then turned his attention to the blond Russian who was making pouting noises. He caressed her cheek and whispered something to make her laugh. When he turned back, I thanked him profusely. On behalf of myself, the Americans and the Minister.

"Nonsense, Comrade Zhang," he said with a magnanimous wave of his hand.

How did the man know my name? And why did he address me as comrade?

"Anything I can do to help," he grinned, " after all, it is for the good of the Party, yes?"

18

Just on the other side of the great arc of the Bay Bridge, some fifteen miles across the Chesapeake from Annapolis, lie a series of strip malls and outlet shops welcoming the weekend visitor to the beautiful vistas and unspoiled colonial towns of Maryland's Eastern Shore. Along this stretch of Route 50, in front of the TigerMart at the Exxon station, a van, engine running, had stopped in such a way as to block access to the nearest line of pumps as well as to the front door of the store. On this, the first sunny weekend to provide a hint of spring, the gas station was loaded with travelers fleeing the confining doldrums of Washington and Baltimore. And many of these travelers could see that the source of the holdup, the source of the delay keeping them from their cottages and cozy B&Bs, was the grubby van blocking three pumps and the front door.

A genteel, middle class group, they did not make much noise at first. Then one or two patted their horns, hoping that a light, suggestive honking might get the van going. Finally from three cars back, an aggressive looking fellow sporting a baseball hat, a large mustache and wrinkled chinos, slammed the door of his Nissan Pathfinder behind him and marched purposefully toward the obstruction.

He strode past the darkened rear windows, caked with grime, and around the side rear panel. But when he got to the driver's window, all he could see was the backside of a large map of the state. He could not see the driver tucked behind it. Still, without a hint of hesitation, he knocked loudly on the dirty window. He was in full temper now, ready to face anybody, even the scumbag driver of a filth-encrusted van like this.

The map came down suddenly; two nervous eyes peered at him through the grime. These were not the eyes he had expected. The driver rolled the window down, and the mustachioed man made to speak. No sound came out.

"Can I help you?" asked a voice through the open window.

"Uh . . . uh . . . I was wondering . . ." he finally stammered, "if you were, you know, lost or something?"

"No, but you can help us find where we are going."

The man with the bushy mustache did just that. And he was quite friendly about it. He pointed the driver to the town and the side road and made sure the driver was additionally aware of certain landmarks which would make identification easier. He was thanked, twice, the window was rolled up, the van put in gear. It rolled slowly out of the gas station. The man watched it go, still slightly stunned.

She had been absolutely exquisite. Perhaps the most beautiful woman he had ever seen in person. And he hadn't even gotten her number. Oh well. She was probably attached. Most likely to one of those guys in the van. Still, he would have to look for her around town. Because he was staying near Easton too. Maybe he could teach her how to eat crabs. Maybe they could drink a few beers. The Japs drank beer, didn't they? Or maybe that was the Chinese. He could never tell the difference. Didn't matter. For her, he would drink sake or whatever she wanted. But he would definitely have to seek her out. And soon. It shouldn't be too hard, he thought. After all, how hard could it be to pick out a van full of Japanese in Easton, Maryland?

☆ ☆ ☆

Still rooted in the chair she had occupied for the last four days, Kristina took three chilling drinks from the pitcher of ice water and picked up the next book. She was coming into the homestretch now.

Only five books to go. She had cheated a little. Cut out some text and skipped some of the more gory stories from the writer's prison and coal mine days. They tended, she found, to make her sleep unsoundly and increase her nervousness when Behr was away.

And where was Behr anyway? He was supposed to be back by now, wasn't he? She looked over her shoulder at the clock on the microwave above the kitchen stove: two o'clock. He had been gone all morning too. Maybe he had gone flying, she thought. That always seemed to kill the day.

☆   ☆   ☆

I was as scared as I had ever been. I thought about Tu's parting comment for hours that night. Not sleeping. Not even for a minute. While my young wife snored lightly next to me in the small bed, I ran over his words again and again in my mind. A jumble of implications. Tu had called me by name and then invoked the good of the Party. Surely he had meant the ruling party, Chiang Kai-shek's Nationalist Party. Tu was certainly a public ally of the ruling party. And an avowed opponent of the left, the scattered bodies of Shanghai Communists and labor leaders a testament to his fanaticism.

Yet, the Nationalists didn't go about calling one another "Comrade." And Big-eared Tu had no reason to consider me his comrade let alone know me by name. I had heard myself introduced to Tu. When they brought me to the man's table, they simply introduced me as an assistant to Minister Kung. I know they did not give him my name.

So what could I say for certain? That Tu was the top hunter of Communists in Shanghai. That since 1927 he had made it his personal mission to provide the Nationalists (even in times of peace) with intelligence about the activities of the Chinese Communist Party and, when necessary, he went out of his way to kill its agents. Even foreign agents, as circumstance might demand. And Tu, who had no reason to know I even existed in the obscurity of the national bureaucracy, actually knew me by name. On sight. And he also knew that I was a party member. Though he didn't say which party.

But I knew that I only had one party membership. Though I worked for the Nationalist Party, I was not a member of their political organization. I didn't pay their dues or attend their meetings. But I did pay dues to the CCP. And I had been their spy for years in a city filled with spies.

Was it possible Tu really knew I was a CCP spy? And knowing that, was it possible that he would still arrange for the ships? And, more importantly, did he know what I really intended to do with those ships? Could Tu know what even Minister Kung didn't know about this operation?

I couldn't answer these questions. Not here, not lying in bed listening to the distant rumble of Japanese artillery and the gentle, sweet breath of my wife. I couldn't answer these questions, but I could take precautions. However drastic. I looked over at my wife, her clean, fresh profile oblivious to my distress, her smooth young skin unscarred by the worry and strife around us. I resolved to make her part of the master plan. To rescue her from the dual threats of the Japanese and, now, Big-eared Tu and his grinning innuendo. I resolved and acted immediately.

She didn't awaken at first. It took some shaking, some persuasion, some great hint of danger to get her out of bed. But by six in the morning I had her dressed and packed and ready to move. I pushed her into the Ministry car—the driver asleep in the back seat—and sent them both to where my brother lived in the carriage house behind our old family home in the southern farm district.

She had instructions to collect him, no matter the level of his resistance, and bring him to the Ministry. I would install them both in the Minister's office for now. That being, I thought, the last place that Tu would look for them.

Satisfied as to my family's immediate safety, I made my way on foot the three miles to the Ministry, past craters, field hospitals and the overused prostitutes of the old Chinese city. Halfway, I presented myself at the gates to the International Settlement and to the guards who jealously guarded them from simple Chinese like me. As Tu's guard had, not eight hours before, the gatekeepers accepted my Ministry identification and let me pass. From there I walked among the boarded shops and rubble, the homeless refugees of every nationality, until I arrived at the Ministry, where I descended the now familiar route to the underground vaults. The eunuchs did not seem happy at the news that the ships were available for loading. Perhaps they had secretly hoped

I would fail. And that their whole reason for existence—guarding the gold in perpetuity—would not come to an abrupt end with its departure. But they helped me anyway, duty-bound, I supposed, to obey the Minister. And after some time, they even adopted my sense of distress and hurry.

Following the plan we had developed over the past days, and trusting in Tu to deliver the ships, I followed the eunuchs with the first shipment on rails down a seemingly endless tunnel. I had no sense of direction underground, but the eunuchs assured me we were headed north.

And so we were. At the end of the tunnel was an enormous iron-bolted door. It took two men to open it. And on the other side of that was a second door, just as large and difficult to manipulate. When that second door creaked open on rusted hinges we immediately covered our eyes and noses against the strong glare and stench coming off the water. Suzhou Creek—in all its fetid glory—lay just three feet below. That the sun could actually reflect off such black water has always amazed me. And at times I still describe to Gao—when he grows restless—that image of the sun illuminating even the blackest, deadest places. But mostly he thinks I am a crazy man. He is long past the power of metaphor.

I entrusted the loading of the barges to the eunuchs and bargemen, and then hurried through the tunnels and iron doors and up the secret elevator to await details from Big-eared Tu. I arrived at my desk only minutes before Tu's man. A dark fellow, almost Mongol, and carrying, in the fashion of his ancestors, a large curved knife in his belt. The man didn't introduce himself; he just appeared in front of me on the deserted fifth floor and said in accented English, "Crystal Palace and San Juan."

"These are the names of ships?"

"Piers Fourteen and Fifteen."

"They are ready today?"

"If you are."

"Yes, we would like to begin loading. We will be bringing the shipment around on barges from a warehouse on Suzhou Creek. We will only require stevedoring help to unload the barges and load the ships. What will that cost?"

"American dollars or pound sterling? We will also accept the

franc."

"Yes, yes, but how much?"

"Eighty cents a ton. American."

I ran the calculation in my head. The whole shipment would cost over four thousand American dollars. Would the Minister pay that much? It seemed like an outrageous amount. Clearly we were being gouged. But it was worth it. We should pay anything to keep the gold from the clutches of the Japanese or worse, Tu and the Nationalist government. Time was the chief concern, I decided, not price. There was no need to haggle.

"Agreed," I said, *"provided that we can begin loading as soon as the first barge makes it to the piers."*

The man made a grunting sound, which I interpreted as assent, and then departed across the desolate office floor. I waited a little while longer at my desk hoping for the arrival of my family, nervously strumming my fingers on the reams of accumulating paper and watching the Japanese planes run their courses inland. I grew worried— something was delaying my wife and brother. But I couldn't wait any longer. I had to get to the Minister's house to collect the additional cash that would now be required.

Once again I proceeded on foot, making my way amidst the crush of refugees down the Nanjing Road and along a shortcut through an apartment complex to the gates of the French Concession. Unlike on previous days, the gates were clear of the usual mob. I was able to walk through without question. What was going on? I didn't have time to wonder.

I arrived at the Minister's house, surprised this time to find it quiet. Gone were the moving trucks and the scurrying servants loaded with boxes and household trinkets. From the outside, in fact, the house appeared vacant. I was instantly gripped with panic. If the Minister had finally fled with the rest of the government, how would I pay Tu? I couldn't even afford the stevedores much less Tu's bribe. I could feel the fear, a stinging bile, rising in my throat. I ran across the mangled front lawn to the house. At the front door I rang the bell and waited. In the past a butler had opened the door immediately. But this time the door remained closed. I rang again, pulling hard on the bell cord and listening to it echo through the house—the sound of empty rooms and *bare floors.*

After a few minutes, as I was reaching for the doorknob, I watched in amazement as the front door slowly opened, seemingly unguided by a human hand. I hesitated a moment before stepping through. But then I saw someone. Emerging from the dark divide, it was the hunched figure of an old man. He was so bent, like a sapling under wet snow, that he could not raise his head or lift his eyes to mine, though I could see he was trying. With his gaze fixed somewhere on my torso he informed me that the household was gone.

"Everyone? The Minister too?"

"Yes," he wheezed. "Everyone has departed. The Minister left early this morning after the announcement."

"The announcement?" I hadn't heard anything.

"The radio announcement. You must be the only man in Shanghai who doesn't know." The old man began cackling and coughing. "The Japanese, my boy, they announced that they have control of the city. A new curfew is in effect. Everyone must remain in their homes, except between eight and eleven in the morning. That is when they will allow us to shop for staples. You shouldn't be out. Unless you're one of them. Are you one of them?"

So that explained it. The Nanjing road was crowded because people were fleeing to Nanjing with the retreating Nationalist Army. And the gates to the French Concession were clear of Chinese because the Chinese population was moving west or subject to curfew. I was probably safe in moving about the International Settlement, but I had put my family at risk! I had sent my wife into Chinese—now Japanese— territory to collect my brother. And now they risked arrest just to follow my uninformed instructions. What a fool I had been!

The old man's head was still bowed before me.

"My name is Zhang," I said to his bowed head, "Did the Minister leave word for me?"

"Zhang? Is that your family name?"

"Yes, did the Minister leave word for me?"

"What is your given name?" Was the old man toying with me? I wanted to grab him by the shoulders and shake him.

"Chen Hai is my given name. Now, please, answer my question!"

"Zhang Chen Hai. Yes, the Minister left something. Follow me,

sir."

The old man turned. I opened the front door wider and followed him into the house. The rooms we passed through were completely bare except for the scatter of packing materials and empty boxes. The old man moved slowly, shuffling his feet over the red ceramic tiles. Eventually we came to the study, also bare save the large desk from which the Minister had pulled the money envelopes. I was curious that it had remained, then realized that it was too large to fit out the door. Most likely it had been assembled where it sat—custom-built around the Minister's corpulence.

The old man came to a stop. He reached under his robe and from some deep pocket removed a key. This key he handed to me.

"This is for you. This is what the Minister left. He specifically instructed me to give it to you here. Good-bye." The old man turned slowly. Shuffling back toward the door.

I called after him. "Is that all he said?"

The old man didn't say anything. But I could see his head nodding slightly.

"And what about you? Are you not going to flee with the Minister's household? Do you have somewhere to go?"

The old man stopped. Without turning around, his head bent to the floor, he answered simply, "I have been left," and then resumed his slow slide across the tiles.

I watched him disappear around the corner. I couldn't afford to concern myself with him. Just another tragedy. And I had my own agenda. I turned to the desk. The key must be for the top drawer, I thought. The money drawer.

I was right. The key opened the heavy oak drawer. Inside lay two envelopes and a handwritten letter addressed to me.

"Chen Hai," it began. I was surprised by this use of my given name. "The thinner envelope should cover the approximate price of loading the ships and any incidental costs you may incur. The thicker envelope is for you. I desire that it purchase a margin of safety for your family and, more importantly, your discretion. Though I don't really have doubts in that respect. When your task is complete, I expect you to resume your position in the Ministry in Nanjing. I look forward to seeing you then."

I examined the envelopes. The thinner did cover the cost of the Tu's dock hands, with a few dollars left over. And the thicker envelope, the one intended for me and my family, covered Tu's additional, extortionate demands. At least that problem was solved.

Running now, clutching the envelopes to my breast, I retraced my path out of the house, through the French Concession and against the tide of refugees along the Nanjing Road. When I got to the Ministry, I was swept with relief to see the Ministry car parked in front. My family had to be upstairs. I took the steps three at a time. But when I got to our floor, I saw no one—not among the workers' desks or in the Minister's own office where they had been instructed to wait. I made a complete circuit of the floor, and then each of the five floors below. I didn't see a soul, not until I reached the first floor.

And there I did see someone. It was my driver, lying in a pool of blood just to the side of the front door. I must have run right past him! Near the driver, some five feet away, was another body—its Japanese uniform soaked in blood. Had they shot each other? Had there been others? Had the Japanese captured my wife and brother?

I desperately made one last search of the building. This time calling out my brother's and wife's names on each floor. First floor, nothing. Second floor, equally quiet. Third floor, fourth floor, dead. Shattered furniture everywhere, a small shell must have exploded through the windows. I was back to the fifth floor, my yelling growing hoarse and panicked. I checked the Minister's office again and did a complete tour, looking under the desks and behind the torn curtains. Not a soul to be found. Where were they? I checked my watch and was alarmed at the time. My God! I still had to make sure the gold was loaded and ready for the docks. And I had to pay Tu's men, or they wouldn't do anything. Regretfully I gave up the search and hurried across the floor to the closet with the secret elevator.

The instant I yanked open the closet door, I heard a shot, felt a sharp sting in my arm.

I leapt back, stumbled over a chair and fell hard, hitting my head on a desk. I did not lose consciousness, but my vision blurred. I felt disoriented. Every instinct told me to run, but I couldn't remember in which direction. I waited for the second shot. The one that would turn me into a puddle of blood like the driver five floors below. But the shot didn't come.

Instead I heard, "Sorry, sorry. I am so sorry, Chen Hai."

My brother's voice. Fear turned quickly to anger. The stupid imp had shot me! My vision cleared and I saw my wife and him standing over me. The fourteen-year-old's face creased with worry and guilt.

"Help me up, you idiot, and get a bandage!"

They raised me gently to a sitting position. My brother tore off the sleeve of his jacket and used it as tourniquet to stem the bleeding from my upper arm. Thankfully the bullet had passed cleanly through, missing the bone and major blood vessels.

I ushered them back into the closet, and without explanation opened the rear door and pushed them into the elevator. Each of them had a suitcase which they had to hold over their heads in the tight space. We rode the elevator down and made our way through the iron doors, now unguarded while the eunuchs were busy loading the barges. I could see the questions in my brother's and wife's eyes. But they didn't ask and I didn't tell. I lead them through the tunnels, past thousands of crates, each containing a half-ton of gold and a covering slab of marble. The crates were piled everywhere, waiting to be loaded onto the carts which would roll on rails down the gentle slope toward the barges. The eunuchs had hired some coolies and a crane for loading, and when we emerged at the small wharf along Suzhou Creek, I could see that they had already loaded four barges full and were readying a fifth. At this rate, I realized, loading all the gold would take three days minimum. I could only hope that the Japanese didn't stop us mid-stream to investigate the nature of this supposedly American shipment.

I put my family aboard the first barge and we followed the creek around to where it emptied messily into the slow waters of the Huangpo. I saw our ships almost immediately. These were not the rusty hulks I had imagined. Tu had secured us two modern transoceanic cargo carriers. They would easily handle the weight of all that gold. But did they have room for passengers?

I found the small Mongol I had dealt with earlier at the Ministry in a shack on the end of Pier Fifteen. He was playing mah-jongg with a circle of ugly men. I handed him the envelope; he examined its contents for a moment, put it in his pocket and returned his attention to the game.

"The first barges are here, are you not going to begin loading?"

Tu's Mongol ignored me, his eyes fixed on the game. I repeated the question. The man held up a crooked finger in warning. I waited a moment longer, trying to decide whether to stay and pester him with my presence, when he suddenly raised a cupped hand high over his head then slapped his last tile down hard on the table. A mutter of curses went around the small crowd of men. The Mongol triumphantly gathered a pile of coins into his shirt and barked out a command I could not understand. The mah-jongg players all stood and exited the shack in an orderly line. The last was the Mongol. He nodded as he passed me, "Now we start."

And now I had one more task to accomplish.

I returned to the barges, mooring side by side under the cranes next to the San Juan. *I found a tarp and threw it over some crates to the rear. Then I ducked under the tarp myself and with a claw-hammer pried open one of the crates. It wasn't easy, I recall, and trying to lift the slab of marble took all my strength on the little leverage I could muster with the small hammer. I was able at last to remove four gold bars. These I placed in a duffel bag I had brought along for the purpose. Then I resealed the crate.*

After a few minutes I found my wife and brother on the pier. I led them up the ramp of the San Juan *and asked after the captain. We were directed to the second ship, the* Crystal Palace, *which we boarded, repeating the question to a crew member there. We were shown to an aft cabin, luxurious by shipboard standards, containing the captains of both ships. They too were gambling. Playing some sort of card game, a pile of American dollars and a bottle of liquor between them.*

"My name is Zhang, and I am responsible for this cargo."

The men looked up and introduced themselves in turn. I continued, "Here are the shipping papers you will need, including completed manifests and customs forms. I took the liberty of preparing bills of lading. Please sign them when the cargo is fully loaded. The cargo is marble. A specialty marble from Xian. It is very valuable."

The American captains seemed unimpressed. I realized that everyone must tell them how uniquely valuable their cargo was to them.

"I also have a favor to ask of you two." The captains looked at me curiously. "I would like you to provide safe passage to my wife and brother."

Both men shook their heads in unison. "We don't take passengers," the captain of the San Juan said firmly. "Company policy. Plus we don't have appropriate berthing for women."

"It's simply out of the question," the captain of the Crystal Palace confirmed.

I could see that the men were resolute. But I could not give in to company policy. "Perhaps this will help you change your minds," I said. I reached into the duffel bag I had dragged with me up the ramp. With pain flaring in my injured arm, I removed one gold bar and dropped it squarely on the pile of bills in the middle of the table. It landed heavily, upsetting the bottle and denting the dark wood. The captains studied its dull gleam silently, slightly awed, as did my brother. My wife looked at me questioningly. I simply shrugged and gestured for her to stay silent.

The captain of the San Juan spoke first, "This will buy some room on my ship."

"Also on mine," the other captain cut in.

"This is for both of you. I do not care which ship they travel on, so long as they are comfortable, arrive safely and remain unmolested by the crew. How you split this, that is up to you. I only suggest that you sell it in the United States. You will not get a good price for it here."

The men nodded their understanding, and we were shown to two small cabins joined by a bulkhead door on the starboard side. There I left my wife and brother.

I checked on them every few hours while I supervised the unloading of the crates from the barges sent around by the eunuchs. Big-eared Tu's men worked diligently, despite the onset of Japanese occupation. Oddly, they didn't seem to care. In their world, Tu was king, and the Japanese were just a distraction. But to me and the rest of the city they were more than a distraction. From the decks of the ships, I could look out on the water and the Japanese gunboats anchored every five hundred yards. A pattern repeated far upriver and down to where the Huangpo ran into the Yangtze and out to the East China Sea.

For the three days and nights it took to load all five thousand tons, I nervously watched these gunboats and the Japanese troops marching up and down the Bund. I pictured how it might end. How at any moment a squad would detach from its platoon, march the length of the pier and *discover the collected wealth of the world's most populous nation being quietly loaded onto two common cargo ships headed for America.*

On the second day, during the men's lunch hour, I crossed the Bund to execute that part of the plan that veered from the Minister's. I found the cable offices of the New York Herald Tribune *where I composed a lengthy coded message. I paid to have the message run as an advertisement every day for the next two months. I then did the same at the Shanghai bureau of the* San Francisco Chronicle. *Two months, I thought, should afford Ambrose sufficient opportunity to receive his instructions and make the appropriate arrangements. And if he didn't get the message? I couldn't imagine.*

With most of my tasks completed, I had little to do but watch the stevedores work and spend some last minutes with my wife. I must say, she was supportive throughout. And I will always wonder why she did not make more of fuss. For if she had insisted at that time that I accompany them to America, I would surely have done so. Would I not?

No, she did not complain; she stated her understanding, going so far as to say that in my position, she would do the same. Remain where my duty lay. Do my part to see the country through invasion and civil war, and then join them when things were more or less right again. I realize how hard this must have been for her. To be sent aboard ship to some unknown land with only a teenage boy to accompany her. And yet she hardly pouted. I thought I had married beauty and grace. But I had married strength as well. I loved her more than ever.

The third night passed, and on the morning of the fourth day the ships were fully loaded, everyone had their instructions and the captains wanted to sail with the first tide. As the Japanese were not yet at war with the Americans, the San Juan *and* Crystal Palace *were to be given safe passage down river. I gave my wife the three remaining gold bars. They were to be used to start their life in America. I gave my brother a sealed envelope with instructions for Ambrose. I described Ambrose—the height, the wild red hair and freckles, and told him to give the envelope to no one else, to destroy it before it fell into another's hands. My brother—he tried to look brave but I could see he was scared. I hugged him and told him that I was counting on him as a man. The poor fellow. He had no idea what was going on. No idea what the cargo was that so obsessed his older brother or why he had to leave now. But he had to do as I said, as I was proxy to our deceased father. That was simply how it was in those days. The young obeyed.*

The captains signaled their imminent departure. I hugged my wife, shook hands with my brother. We all had tears in our eyes. We all said that we would see each other soon, but underneath, we had doubts. Too much had happened to tear people apart. There had been so much death, so much random killing. There were was no way to plan anything in advance, especially not one's happiness.

I can say now that sending them to America saved their lives. What sort of lives, I do not know, for I never saw them again. But if they had fled to Nanjing with the rest of us, they would have likely shared the fate of so many other refugees. So many who, when the Japanese surrounded then conquered that city one month later, were shot and bayoneted, dumped into mass graves by the hundreds of thousands. My wife would have been gang-raped, her body used and discarded in an open ditch with the other women. My brother would have had his wrists tied with wire to prevent him struggling. Then, if early in the killing, he would have been shot. But toward the end, with the junior samurai turning their efforts into sport, he might have been buried alive, or beheaded in the single sweep of an ancestral sword. It is impossible to know, unpleasant to guess. The Japanese left no one alive who could possibly be a threat in the future.

I stood at the end of Pier Fourteen and watched the tugs pull the Crystal Palace, *then the* San Juan *into the river and guide them down the channel. I could see my wife and brother leaning against the rails watching me. We each stood rooted in our spots. None of us said anything. No one shouted or waved. We stood completely still, me on the pier, they on the ship. We watched the distance between us grow apart until the ships followed the bend in the river and disappeared from sight. I remained there for some time I recall. Finally waving and whispering a soft good-bye to all that had departed on those ships. My family, reduced now to a wife and brother. And the gold. The entire legacy of China's imperial past. Washed downriver and off to a new world where, I hoped, it would quietly disappear until the revolution was complete.*

19

Kristina typed in the last sentence slowly, then printed the page. This was as far as her work would go. Though there were still five books remaining, she found the tale of her grandfather's protracted death by cancer, treated only by Gao and sporadic injections of morphine from the miners' clinic, too heartbreaking for close translation.

And what had Baba said about Gao? That he too was sick, and that he had held onto the books until he was no longer certain he could do so. She couldn't imagine the risk the man had taken for his friend. In that system. She only hoped that Chen Hai had done right by him.

It was getting late in the day. Kristina had not seen Behr since he took off this morning, and she wondered what was keeping him. Perhaps, she thought hopefully, he had just stopped by the store for some dinner. She pushed herself back now from the desk and grabbed the pages off the printer.

She wandered into the kitchen, adding the afternoon's printout to the pile she'd kept hidden from Behr. She opened the fridge. Nothing but beer and cheese. She closed the door again and headed to the porch, then, after a few steps, out onto the dock.

It was cooler. The brief warmth, the hint of spring, that had marked their first few days was gone now. A semblance of winter had returned with a damp chill blowing off the river in front of the house. Kristina shivered. This weather, being away from the house and her work, it made her feel exposed, vulnerable.

Still, she let herself linger at the end of the dock, her eyes cast in the distance.

Another pier, she thought, another time. She tried to imagine Chen Hai standing in a similar position, looking out over the water, watching his family go, feeling his loss. She felt loss, too.

"Good-bye, Sam," she said suddenly before turning to the house, "I love you."

☆ ☆ ☆

Behr's eyes hurt, and his back was getting sore. It had been a long day in the plane; a long day of studying the instrument panel. He had flown on instruments most of the way, letting the voices on the ground vector him along the low line of the Blue Ridge Mountains, up through West Virginia and back east, over the interminable Maryland panhandle. Behr didn't mind instrument flying. There was a military uniformity to it that he simply enjoyed. On instruments, a routine circular flight from Easton, down to Norfolk, west to Charlottesville, then north and east again became a massive team effort, involving the pilot, the FAA and a host of personnel from various agencies on the ground. On this flight, Behr had talked to FAA employees, but he had also appeared on the radars and been controlled by the voices at Dover and Langley Air Force Bases and the Patuxent Naval Air Station. In these crowded skies, everyone spoke the same language and had the same goal. A basic goal really, following the flight plan without endangering the lives of the pilot, other people in the air or anyone on the ground. A simple flight became a mission. And the pilot, Behr, became the mission leader.

Thus Behr really didn't have to think about anything but following orders, within reason. And reason was guided by years of training and the rote memorization of emergency procedures and checklists. So when the guys at Patuxent had told him to vector east to a course of one hundred degrees to avoid unspecified military activity, he had done it, though doing so took him out of his way. And when Charlottesville control had told him to drop altitude to three thousand feet, he had obeyed them too, though the low altitude burned up much more fuel.

He hadn't questioned their orders because he understood that he didn't have complete information and they did. Dropping to three thousand feet could have meant avoiding a commercial jet coming into Washington National at ten thousand feet. Vectoring east over the mouth of the Chesapeake could have meant avoiding military jets on a training run, overflying an aircraft carrier or even avoiding an unfortunate tangle with a flock of parachutes. The reason didn't matter to him. For in such a team setting, he wasn't really in command. And sometimes that felt great.

It was in this mode, in this unreflective, mechanical frame of mind, that Behr now approached the brown gash of the Chesapeake Bay from the west. Seeing the brown water, suffused with the melt and sediment of a premature spring run off from the highlands of Pennsylvania, made him think of Kristina, viewing the same water from sea level.

Kristina had been a closed book lately. Passionate at times, but mostly distracted and uncommunicative. He could tell that she was completely involved in the translation, that it captivated her not only with its immediate relevance to Sam's death, but also as a story in its own right. What it was that Kristina found so absorbing, Behr didn't know. For she didn't tell him much, and she had not let him see any of the printouts she had squirreled away somewhere in the house.

"I don't let people see my paintings either before they're done," she had insisted. And Behr had not pushed. He knew she was close to finishing, and he would find out everything then. In the meantime he could fly the Eastern Seaboard and pretend to work on his own book, *Theories of Punishment*, and hope that they could remain anonymous a little while longer.

Behr hit the transmit button on the top of the stick and called in the termination of his flight plan. He would go VFR from here. He dropped down to one thousand feet and banked sharply right, pointing the nose of dear-old-Dad's T-34 down the line of the bay. Low to the water and southbound with the sun high overhead, Behr now felt like a fighter pilot or barnstormer from aviation's heyday.

He pushed the throttle and picked up speed, the overhauled three hundred horsepower engine pulling the plane at a sharp 180 knots. He climbed another thousand feet over the bump of the massive Bay

Bridge, then angled left, over the Miles River, in line for Runway 15 in Easton. But then, on an impulse, he broke off. He nudged the stick right, headed back over the bay, over Tighlman Island and south again. He found the mouth of the Tred Avon and followed its course. He could see the peninsula far ahead to his right, and though he couldn't quite make out Sam's house yet, he knew it was there. He would just buzz it once, maybe twice. Kristina said she liked his little bombing runs; it reassured her that he was close by.

So Behr dropped even lower. To three hundred, then two hundred, then one hundred feet over the water. He was level now with the tops of the trees on the right bank, and when he saw the extended point of Bailey's Neck, with its towering pines and select mansions, he broke right. A classic fighter's stunt. Perpendicular to the ground and smiling broadly, he shot across the point, looked down over the tip of the wing to see the familiar roof of the house nestled in the pine needles. And there too was the dock, and the driveway and—

What was that?

A car in the driveway?

No, some sort of van.

Was that really the driveway to the house? They weren't expecting anyone, and Kristina was adamantly against visitors. Who could have any business being at the house except he and Kristina?

He roared over, the scene now behind him—out of his view. He banked sharply to the left, pushing the throttle to full power so he didn't lose altitude so low over the ground. Coming around, he got a better view: the house dead ahead, the van with dark windows. A lone figure standing next to the van, smoking, looking up at him through dark lenses. Now gesturing, beckoning excitedly toward the house.

Another pass, another steep turn over the river.

He could see a number of people now. All similarly dressed in black clothes and dark glasses. They emerged in a hurried cluster from the house and quickly formed a rough circle. They were carrying something between them. A person! He could see arms and legs clutched, suspended within the circle.

Kristina?

He couldn't see a face. There was something over the person's head. But who else could it be?

They were taking Kristina! A dark, unfamiliar rage seized him. A rage driven by knowing that he was powerless to stop them, though he was only two hundred feet away.

He needed a plan; he needed time to think. But the black figures disappeared into the van. And the van was moving.

Behr banked the plane hard left, the sharp turn costing him fifty feet of altitude. Behr unlocked his gaze from the ground. He gasped. A stand of tall white pine swayed only a few feet ahead. Behr pulled back sharply on the stick, the T-34 began to stall; he pushed the throttle all the way, and finally the plane jumped. Behr held his breath as the topmost branches scraped the fuselage. He had missed disaster by inches.

Over the trees now, Behr turned to catch sight of the vehicle as it raced down the track for the Oxford Road, kicking up a wall of dust and gravel.

The road—that was the answer! A plan, however reckless. He noted the wind direction from the sway of the trees and realized it was feasible. He headed downwind, off the path of the van. He went about two thousand yards, spotted the streak of the black top and turned again, directly over the busy stretch between Easton and Oxford. Cars and trucks moved intermittently beneath him, driving fast, seventy miles an hour. This was going be dangerous as hell. But there was no other way.

Behr glanced quickly to his left; over the span of the wing he saw the wall of dust approaching fast. He had little space for this maneuver. And too little time.

The smooth road below him *was* fairly wide, a two-lane with some shoulder. But the telephone and electric lines crossed the road for every house, about every one to two hundred feet. He would have to hover just above their level, just above stall speed, then drop hard. If he missed, he'd tangle in the wires; the prop—turning at six thousand revolutions per minute—would shatter, and hot metal projectiles would slice in every direction. He would lose control. The plane would likely tumble end over end, over cars, over families, over houses. An ugly end, he knew.

But only if he missed.

Behr slowed to a near stall, and he lowered the landing gear and the flaps to full. The power lines passed beneath his wings, one line . . .

another line.

He had to do it soon, he couldn't overshoot.

He saw the hole. Now!

The throttle cut, the nose pushed down. He dropped, but it wasn't enough. The lines were at eye level, only a few feet ahead. Behr pushed hard on the stick; the plane responded and dove for the ground. The line passed over the propeller, Behr ducked inside the canopy. He heard a popping sound and felt a shudder as the line caught the tail and ripped off the poles. It must have severed, for he was still moving, the road rushing at him, cars swerving out of his way. Behr pulled back hard on the stick, stalling the wings and dropping him hard on the road. He had landed, but the plane was still moving. Over the roar of the engine he could hear the cars and trucks honking furiously. He only had a few hundred feet to go, and he just couldn't worry about them.

Behr jammed the throttle forward again and raced ahead. Bailey Neck Road was on his left, the van approaching at high speed, visible through the trees. It would be close. Behr had to get there first. If he could just block their access to the Oxford Road—

☆ ☆ ☆

The van and the plane were approaching each other at a combined speed of over one hundred miles per hour. The driver of the van saw the plane's course; recognition flashed in his eyes. He couldn't believe it. This was the pest who had been flying over them before. He turned to the woman in the passenger seat. She was as surprised as he.

"Helen, what do we do?"

"I don't know. Why don't you ask Hu Zhong."

The driver yelled to the back where the team leader braced himself against the side of the van. Hu Zhong heard the yell, then came forward to look for himself. Positioning himself between the two front seats and holding on tightly, he could see that a collision would be painful and highly unproductive. He came to a quick decision. Then gave his orders.

☆ ☆ ☆

Behr braked hard, almost standing on the pedals. He swivelled the plane left, pointed down the dirt track of Bailey's Neck Road. He waited for the impact—the van was only a hundred yards away, approaching fast. It could only be a matter of seconds now.

The road was blocked as far as Behr could tell. And the ditches made it impossible for the van to circumvent the stretch of his wings. So, he thought, they could ram him or they could stop.

He didn't know yet what he would do if they stopped. But he had come this far on improvisation; he had landed his plane on a busy public road, risking his life and his license, and he damned well wasn't going to give up now. Not without a fight.

At twenty yards the van stopped. It sat there a few moments, menacingly quiescent. Then started forward again, but far more slowly. Behr didn't understand this move; he was out of his depth.

Why did they keep coming when his plane was blocking their way?

At fifteen yards he saw the reason. Four armed men, two on each side, suddenly burst from behind the van. They fanned out, raised their weapons. The van was still rolling, the men marching alongside.

Behr was stunned. They were aiming their guns right at him!

But they didn't shoot; they just kept coming, weapons at their shoulders, sighted at his head.

Then at ten yards the barrage began. The hard plastic canopy, meant to withstand the occasional impact with birds, was not equipped for bullets and shattered in places as the shots struck home. Behr clawed at the shoulder harness and then dropped to the narrow floor; he heard the bullets tearing the aluminum skin of the plane. The rudder and aileron cables parted loudly, sounding like more gunshots. He knew it could only be matter of time before the wing tanks blew. He really had no choice; he had to move. Move or die.

From his crouch on the floor, blind to what lay before him, Behr gripped the throttle; he pushed forward. The plane strained against the brakes, then lurched forward as he released the pedals with his right hand. Behr was thrown into the seat with the rush of acceleration, then slammed into the instrument panel when the plane hit the van with a crunch.

He didn't waste a second. He hit the emergency release, shooting the entire canopy into the air. Standing quickly, finding his target, Behr raised the flare gun and fired. He saw the puzzled look in the man's eyes—Chinese eyes, only a few feet away—and their sudden pain as the flare exploded in their owner's belly.

Five more flares. Behr ducked quickly, loaded and stood again. He swiveled left, seeking the gunmen close by.

Where were they?

A volley of shots forced him down. Bullets came tearing into the cockpit, thudding into the seat, smacking the instruments, shattering their glass. Behr forced himself to look over the rim of the cockpit. The bullets were still coming at an angle, he tried to trace their trajectory. He couldn't see anyone.

There! A movement in the field. The rustle of the dead corn stalks had given one away. Behr raised the flare gun, fired. As he ducked, he heard a scream and smiled: Dad would have been proud of his boy's marksmanship.

Two down, two to go. The shooting continued. He heard rounds hitting the plane. But not around the cockpit. Between shots he heard yelling in Chinese. What were they saying? And what were they shooting at?

Christ, he realized, they were shooting the tanks! Waiting for a spark to blow the vapors that lingered in both wings. He stood a better chance if they were shooting at him!

It was time to move again.

In a single fluid motion, the flare gun gripped in his hand, Behr leapt from the cockpit and onto the left wing. Instantly he felt a sharp sting in his right shoulder, then another. The second shot spun him around. He lost his balance, saw the sky. Then he was falling. He felt himself hit the incline of the wing, then space, then ground.

The stink of spilled aviation fuel greeted his nostrils, and he felt his clothes soaking up liquid. But whether it was blood or gasoline, he couldn't tell.

The pain in his shoulder was now acute, debilitating, but Behr managed to scramble madly for the limited protection of the landing gear. He could still hear shooting, but it was more intermittent now. Maybe down to one gun.

Behr knew the fuel could ignite at any time. He was surprised that it hadn't. Just one spark, and he and the plane and the van would all go up in a quick and massive inferno. And still he didn't know where Kristina was. She might be clear, but she might also be in the van, its crumpled front end and shattered windshield all that was visible from where he lay.

Behr felt himself getting weak and risked a demoralizing look at his shoulder. Blood was everywhere, soaking his shirt and mixing with the viscid puddles of fuel and oil in the dirt and gravel of the road. He knew he couldn't last long in this position. He boiled it down to two choices: one, stay here under the wing and thereby risk bleeding to death or burning alive, or, two, emerge. Emerge and take his chances with the gunmen.

He couldn't decide. His thoughts were coming too slowly, bleeding through his shoulder along with everything else. He was drifting, and the question still lingered. What to do?

Was this, he wondered now, what was meant by a Hobson's Choice. A choice that is no choice at all. Or was he again embarrassing the ex-wife with his incorrect usage, his consistently poor word choice? "Antiphrasis" she had smugly called it.

The hated bitch, she appeared in his mind's eye, at the edge of his vision. Vision that was blurring in air that was getting harder to breathe. No oxygen, he thought, bad air.

A petulant voice in his head screamed: NOW! Move now! Behr momentarily closed his eyes, felt the approaching darkness, then summoned all he had. He lifted himself slowly, attempted to crawl. He screamed in pain and collapsed.

The wounded shoulder couldn't take his weight. He took a deep breath, then another, then dragged himself, pulling with his left arm, digging for grip in the rough gravel and edging toward the ditch.

The ditch would offer some cover, and with a grunt he managed to heave himself in.

Cold—it hit him—ice cold water at the bottom of the ditch. But somehow it revived him too. And he was suddenly alert; he sensed a change. What was it?

The shooting. That was it! The shooting had stopped. Behr raised his head over the edge of the ditch. But all he saw was the remains of the corn harvest. He would have to stand. On unsteady legs, it took all his strength. He managed to get himself up, expecting a bullet to come sailing at him at any time. He looked dizzily toward the van and saw nothing. Then looked toward the road.

There they were. He could see a woman running along the Oxford

Road, long black hair streaming behind. Kristina?

There was another group of black figures running ahead of her. Was Kristina chasing them?

He called to her, his voice a thin croak, barely audible even to him. He tried again, "Kristina!"

The woman stopped and swiveled. Behr saw something in her hands. A gun, tiny explosions of light sparked from its barrel. Bullets screamed past his ears. A second burst thudded into the ground in front of him. She couldn't get the range. But she didn't try again, instead turning and following the others. Behr lurched after them, but they were moving too quickly for him to catch up. He made it onto the Oxford Road where a few cars littered the margins, the occupants crouched in terror behind them or off in the trees.

Fifty yards ahead he could see Kristina's abductors. Could see them approach a minivan, claw open the side door, throw their bundle inside, drag out the driver and slam the butt of a rifle into her face, sending her sprawling and bloody onto the shoulder.

Behr stopped and tried to raise the flare gun. It was stupid to shoot. He might hit Kristina, or ignite the vehicle. But maybe . . . just maybe . . .

A hundred feet behind him, the plane's fuel tanks finally exploded.

A hot wave of dust and gravel threw Behr to the ground, super-heating the air, scalding his throat. He smelled hair burning and felt a rush of flame on his legs. He looked down in horror.

Roll, roll!

His mind screamed, and he forced himself over and over on the rough asphalt, over and over on the shattered bones of his shoulder. Heat. Indescribable heat in his wounds, and on his legs. Heat accelerating the onset of darkness. And just on the edge of that darkness, the periphery of consciousness, the sound of an engine, revving high, speeding Kristina away to some fate he now couldn't control.

"I failed," he said, bewildered. Then Behr closed his eyes.

☆ ☆ ☆

Hu Zhong pulled the minivan into a truck stop on Route 50, cruised slowly around the back side of the cinderblock and shifted to PARK. He turned around in his seat and glared at his team, now reduced by two members. Anger flared in his eyes and the remaining members cowered on the rear benches. All except for that Kuang fellow. He didn't seem scared at all. Just met his gaze calmly, expectantly, as if he was waiting for something he knew was going to happen. A cat sitting next to his empty milk bowl, Hu Zhong thought, then wondered who this Military Intelligence fellow, Kuang, really was. And why had Jin Qing put him on this mission?

"Is she still alive?" Hu Zhong demanded of his team.

"Yes, she is untouched. Breathing calmly, sir," Helen timidly answered, touching Kristina's gently heaving chest in reassurance.

"May I make a suggestion?"

The voice was Kuang's. A strange accent. Mongol but also tinted with the guttural tongue of the western Muslims. What was he doing here?

"What is your suggestion, MID Agent Kuang?"

"That we secure another vehicle. This one may already be compromised."

Hu Zhong thought a moment. The fellow was probably right. "As it is your suggestion, Agent Kuang, please proceed. We will wait here."

Kuang nodded his assent and slid open the side door to the minivan. Hu Zhong watched him in silence as the strange Mongol agent gracefully alit, re-secured the door and jogged from the van, around the corner and out of sight.

Hu Zhong then turned his gaze on the three remaining occupants. Helen, beautiful as ever, looked deeply flustered, even embarrassed by the encounter with the plane. The second agent, too, seemed to be retreating into his neck like some sort of tortoise, trying to be inconspicuous in a vehicle with four occupants. And the third occupant, her head covered with a hood, her hands and feet bound with thick layers of silver duct tape, she had some explaining to do.

He had planned this as an easy, flawless extraction. Now he was faced with attacking airplanes, explosions on a busy public road, a hijacked vehicle. They were supposed to be *covert* operatives. And this mess was almost the equivalent of an advertisement in the *New York Times*. Jin Qing would not be pleased.

He studied the tightly bound figure of Kristina Zhang. This woman knew something. Something that made her worth the effort. Jin Qing hadn't told him the connection. And indeed he had not been able to determine it on his own. But Helen had said that the brother, Sam, had known about the *Crystal Palace* and *San Juan*. And that—despite what the lawyer thought—what she overheard was more than passing knowledge. That the kid's tone indicated that he knew exactly what was on those ships. And if he knew that . . . did Jin Qing think the sister knew too?

She must. And Hu Zhong knew that if he could get the information from Kristina Zhang, *he* would be the hero, not Jin Qing.

Unless Jin Qing somehow claimed the victory first.

He could not let that happen! Hu Zhong struck a clenched fist against the steering wheel and stared out upon the weeds and debris of the truck stop parking lot. Jin Qing, he thought, had fettered him too often. And she bound him now as well. Kristina Zhang was not to be hurt, touched, or properly questioned until Jin Qing's arrival. So he had been instructed over the encrypted satellite phone. Jin Qing had reduced him to a lackey, an errand boy—a running dog who fetched and brought back to its master what the master demanded. In this case it was Kristina Zhang. And at great risk, it turned out.

No—this time Hu Zhong would be victorious. It would be he who paraded the recovery of the imperial gold before the Party's Central Committee at promotion time. And it would be he who vaulted to real Party status, over the head of Jin Qing and out of the evil corners she inhabited.

He had his own plans. He was nobody's dog. He was a decorated intelligence agent who was ready for a real leadership role. He would prove it, and he would do so with the vial waiting in the refrigerator in the Bronx safe house they had secured for the occasion. For with this vial—a potent mixture of scopolamine, synthetic adrenaline and psilocybin—he would get the truth from Kristina Zhang within three to four hours of its administration. And when Jin Qing arrived, he would already have the answers. Answers he could keep from Jin Qing until he was ready, answers he could keep because their source would be rendered suddenly unavailable.

Jin Qing would, of course, object to his methods, and then—oh yes—then he would have her. Because then he would inform her superiors that he had a tape of the Zhang woman's confession (as delivered to him) and that Jin Qing had stood in his way. Had, in fact, tried to keep the information as to the whereabouts of the fortune to herself. The implications would be obvious. And Jin Qing would no longer be trusted. Perhaps even disgraced.

Hu Zhong smiled broadly, his back to the agents in the van. His future lay gloriously before him, somewhere on the other side of this dirty Maryland parking lot. His future lay in the memory cells of Kristina Zhang—memory that would melt and come pouring out in a few hot hours of psychoneurotic babble. He knew with certainty that after the first injection, Kristina Zhang would have no choice but to tell all she knew. The scopolamine would encourage verity, and the synthetic adrenaline and psilocybin would combine to explode her inner ego, make her think that she was a god who explained the truth of the world to mere mortals.

Hu Zhong's visions of glory suddenly deflated, his heart leaped in his chest as the cab of a large truck turned the corner and came straight for the minivan. But when he saw the driver, he hooted with delight. It was Kuang! The dark little bastard had gotten them a truck—what the Americans called a semi. It would be ideally anonymous for the trip to New York. One truck among thousands, particularly in the Bronx.

In the Bronx—Hu Zhong smiled broadly at the thought—among the warehouses and abandoned shells, he would administer the drug. The drug that would finally tell him the location of the gold; the drug that would give him sole possession of the truth after it reduced Kristina Zhang's brain to a quivering jelly.

20

"You're not pissed?"

"Not really."

"But we have no idea where they are. They could be anywhere, anywhere in the country."

"It doesn't matter anymore. We don't need them."

"So you don't want me to follow up on this?"

Bob Silver smiled at Lazlo. He liked this fellow. Lazlo was so thorough, so diligent, he would have made a wonderful lawyer. Tew, Logan & Case could have used more like him.

But Lazlo didn't return his smile. "Are you cutting me out?" the man demanded suddenly, a dark suspicion clouding his already swarthy skin.

Silver looked around the diner, but nobody was looking at them. They were, as ever, anonymous in South Jersey, despite Lazlo's outburst. Silver tried to sound reassuring.

"Of course not, don't be silly. I simply meant—"

"The deal was Chicago. Three-hundred grand for the trip to Chicago. Now you don't want me there and you're telling me to drop the trail in Rockland where the professor never showed up with the girl.

That means you're busting the deal."

"It means no such thing. I admit, Chicago is off, Maine is off. But that doesn't mean I don't have work for you."

"The original price still stands."

"Of course."

Lazlo seemed to relax a little; he leaned back into the red vinyl cushion of the booth.

"What sort of work?"

"I'll get to that," Silver responded, then reached into his pants for two dollar bills which he threw crumpled onto the table. "Let's get out of here."

The men headed into the parking lot. Silver buttoned up his cashmere coat. It was cold here in Jersey; a strong wind was blowing up Route 70, whipping between the gas stations and billboards, kicking up fast-food wrappers and other trash that had accumulated since the last rain. The sky was darkening toward the west, toward Philadelphia, with the threat of an imminent storm.

Lazlo looked to the sky. "It's going to rain," he said flatly.

But Silver didn't move, didn't invite Lazlo to sit in the Range Rover even as the first drops hit their cheeks.

The heavy rain came quick. Lazlo looked unhappy, his normally greasy hair plastered even closer over his forehead.

But Bob Silver felt just fine.

"We have all the information we need from Ms. Zhang," he said. "Everything I wanted to know and more was on the disk you removed from the kid's apartment. In fact, I never even imagined how rich all this was. I was thinking on the scale of mice," Silver laughed, "and I should have been thinking about elephants. You get me? Elephants!"

Lazlo's eyes peered from beneath heavy, dripping eyebrows. "Look, I'm getting wet. Tell me what you want."

Silver reached into his coat, removed a thick envelope. "This," he said, patting it once, "is half of what I owe you."

Rain splattered over the manila, and Lazlo grabbed the envelope before it got it soaked. He tucked it under his shirt.

"The other half," Silver continued, "I will give you after you go to New York."

"Why there?"

"You're going to do a little research. I've put it all in a memo. You will find that memo in the envelope with your money."

"Research?"

"That's what I said."

Silver turned to his car. Lazlo's questions were growing tiresome, threatening to kill the high he'd been riding. He pushed a button on his key ring; he heard the doors unlock and stepped into the car. Lazlo made to follow him, but Silver waved him off. He opened the window and said to the man standing miserably in the rain, "You have everything you need, Lazlo. It's all in the memo. Good luck. I expect to hear from you soon, as soon as you have an answer."

Lazlo departed, and Bob Silver sat a for a few minutes in the parking lot with the engine running, letting the lukewarm air from the vents blow over his face.

He realized with some amusement that he didn't have anywhere to go right now. Nowhere they wouldn't see him and start tailing him again.

But sitting here was no good, so he pulled out, U-turned through a jug-handle, then headed back toward Philadelphia. Route 70 yielded to Route 38 and then to the Admiral Wilson Boulevard. Once on the Boulevard, Silver's gaze drifted off the road; he saw the Admiral's Lounge on his left, and without really thinking about it, he negotiated another U-turn.

Soon he was through the front door. He paid the cover charge, went through another door, and now he was with the other happy-hour customers. Single men mostly, truckers, construction types, assorted losers. They were grim, unsmiling men, silent and remote as they watched the energetic gyrations and simulated sexual frenzy of the two naked women on the stage before them. But Bob Silver's expression didn't match that of his new peers. He wiggled his knee, tapped his fingers on the table in rhythm to the cheesy disco blowing from the speakers. He felt strangely alive in this place. He thought the dancers might notice it too. Notice that one of the customers was special, a gentleman in a fine suit with plenty of money. A good-looking man who could take them out of here and fill their desires, if only he chose to.

A half-clad waitress now materialized at his side and asked if he needed a drink.

Silver turned from the show, studied the woman's full figure stuffed into its fish net. He noticed her weathered face and saw that once, not long ago, it might have been pretty.

"I would like some gin. Straight up in a tall, clean glass. The more gin," Silver grinned, and he reached around and patted her on the ass, "the bigger your tip."

The waitress made a face while she slapped away his hand. "Big spender, eh?" she mocked, then tottered away slowly on high heels toward the darkly lit bar.

☆ ☆ ☆

Kristina had heard those stories—or seen them in movies—in which the hostage identifies certain sounds that identify the landmarks along the road to captivity. The sound of tires over the metal roadway of a Harlem River bridge. The sound of an Oakland foghorn or a French train's whistle. The sensation of going uphill, or over water, or being buffeted by the wind. The smell of fetid canal water, freshly laid fertilizer, fir trees after the rain. In each case, the highly attuned captives were roughly aware of where they were being taken, or figured it out later, by observing all their senses. Kristina had always been impressed by this in the movies and thought that if anyone ever kidnapped her, she would do the same. Pay keen attention, then somehow guide the rescuers with her perfect recall of the sequence of motion and sound.

And yet, despite concerted effort, she simply had no idea where she was now or where they were headed. She knew, of course, that her captors were Chinese. Their language gave them away. And she knew that they had switched vehicles twice, and that whatever they were in now had a large and noisy engine. Probably some sort of truck. And that this truck was traveling over a highway because it moved steadily without stops for lights or other traffic.

But which highway? Going in which direction? She just didn't know. And that was part of the terror that began to consume her when she realized that Behr wouldn't be coming to the rescue again.

She had heard them say in high, gleeful tones that the pilot was on fire. The pilot that had attacked them with his plane. And under her hood, her face strapped with duct tape, Kristina had cried for this pilot who she knew could have only been Behr, buzzing the house to amuse her; then realizing, as he flew over, that she was being taken. And bravely—stupidly—he had tried to stop them, without ever realizing what was at stake. Without knowing what her captors were playing for and how determined they would be to get it.

She had erred miserably, fatally. The minute she read about Chen Hai's discovery of the underground chamber, she should have told Behr. So that he too could assess what they were up against. Instead, like a silly schoolgirl, or pretentious artist, she had shrouded her translation in secrecy. Why? Because that was how she—the artist—always did things, and up till now she had always thought that consistency made things right.

The truck slowed down. It lurched forward roughly, stopped momentarily, then lurched forward again. She felt a cool wet breeze on the exposed skin of her neck, hands and ankles. Heard the window being opened. A voice now. Speaking in English. "That'll be four ninety please. Thank you." A toll! They had gone through a toll. Knowing that had to be worth something, she thought.

Kristina tried not to dwell on her error. She tried to pay attention, like the heroic captives in the movies, tuning into all their senses. But it was futile to suppress the images of Behr that flickered on the hood before her eyes: Behr in aviator glasses, smiling broadly; Behr in the church after Sam's funeral, agreeing to meet her; then later, in Sam's apartment, pledging without hesitation to help her discover the truth of Sam's death. And how bizarre the truth had turned out to be. And at what a cost! First Sam—her twin. Now Behr. A man she was growing to love and lean on. A good man. A man who went out of his way to help. A man who would not flake at her touch, so unlike the artists and writers in her past.

She was sure now that she would not survive her captivity—that no one would be spared. And part of her didn't even care. Let these people have their gold, she thought, whoever they were. The damage was already done. They really couldn't hurt her much more than they had. And so what if they profited? What difference did it really make if they got rich? Even if they were evil. For when had great wealth ever been divorced from evil?

The truck slowed again. She could feel it decelerate, hear the gears winding down and the gush of the airbrakes. Now the breeze, the sooty exhaust, and again, "Thank you."

Another toll? It had only been fifteen minutes or so since the last one. Back-to-back tolls had to be rare, she thought. But maybe not. She didn't know the Northeast very well. Maybe there was a toll booth every hundred yards.

They moved slowly now, jerkily. The motion made her feel sick to her stomach. The stops and lurches and honking told her they were in traffic. Heavy, interminable traffic.

After what seemed like several, nauseating hours, the truck stopped. Many hands grabbed her from where she lay prone and dragged her down, out of the truck. Then she was being carried. She didn't struggle. Better to save her strength, she thought, for whatever else lay in store.

She heard arguing from where they had dropped her on the floor. A man and woman. Then several men and the woman. The woman saying they didn't have a choice. The men saying that it was against policy for two prisoners to share the space. The woman asked in Mandarin, "Then what do you propose?" And the men had no answer.

The hands gripped her again. But now only around the arms and shoulders. Her heels hit each step on the way down. She heard a key in a door, the creak of its opening. A few more steps. Then a second door. A few steps and then she was dropped. Her skull smacked against the hard floor, sending bolts of pain and light through her head.

She fought to stay alert. Not allowing the blackness to win. She heard a voice, a distant echo, asking in English, "Are you all right?"

But she couldn't answer. Not with the tape over her mouth. She felt hands, strong hands, sitting her up. She felt a wall behind her back. Now the hood was being removed, and she was blinded for minute when she tried to open her eyes to the glare of a single, bright bulb. Her vision returned and she saw a face. A nice face. Fatherly and concerned. But bruised in places and smeared with grime. The tape was pulled away gingerly, slowly from her cheeks, where it stung, and from around her head where it was stuck to her hair. She looked around the room. It was completely bare except for the light bulb and the man now working to unbind her feet. No furniture, no windows. Just the cold cement walls and floor. And a large metal door with a small air vent near the top.

"So," said the face, smiling lightly, "whaddya in for?"

"I . . . I don't know," Kristina answered half-truthfully, surprised by the familiarity.

The face laughed. "Well, that's all right. I can probably fill you in. On some of it anyway."

Kristina wasn't so sure. What could this guy know about her grandfather's story, about his duplicity in the 1930s?

"Okay, go ahead," she challenged softly.

"In a minute, my dear. There's no rush. After all, we haven't been formally introduced." The man took her limp right hand in his and shook gently. "My name is Michael, Michael Antonetti," he said. "Pleased to make your acquaintance, Ms. . . . ?"

☆ ☆ ☆

The pink message slip had gone unnoticed, wedged as it was between the leatherette vinyl cushion and the arm of Detective Leone's regulation issue police chair. When Leone found it, he was disturbed to notice that the time and date lines had been left blank. Couldn't anyone around here take a decent message for Christ's sake? And leave it on the desk?

Leone flipped open his address book and quickly punched in the number.

"Mr. Frattone's office," a languid voice answered on the first ring.

"Is he there please, it's his uncle Tito."

"I'm sorry Mr. Tito, he's not available right now." The woman had the rasp of a lifelong smoker. "Is there a message, or do you want his voice mail?"

"Can you tell me where he is? It's important that I talk to him."

"I can take a message, sir." The woman sounded bored. Leone didn't like that.

"Let me clarify: This is *Detective* Tito Leone of the Philadelphia Police Department. I wish to speak with my nephew, Michael Frattone, immediately. On police business. Any failure to answer to the best of your knowledge constitutes a willful obstruction of justice." That should get her! "I'm going to repeat the question. Can you tell me where he is?"

"All right, all right. He is in a meeting. Would like me to interrupt him? He is with some very big name partners."

"Do what you can, sweetheart."

Leone heard the click and void as he was put on hold, then he heard ringing.

"Conference room," came the short answer. Leone could tell from the echo that he was on a speakerphone.

"I'm looking for Michael Frattone. Is he there?"

"We're in a meeting here. He'll call you back." This guy sounded like a first-class prick.

"No, I need to talk to him now." Leone demanded, trying to sound just as unpleasant. It must have worked, for Mike came on the line a second later. The clarity indicated that he was using the handset.

"Hey, Uncle Tito, what's up?"

"You called *me* Mike. I'm returning the call."

"That was yesterd—no, two days ago."

"Yeah, I'm sorry about that."

"Look, I can't go into it now. I'll call you back when I'm out of this meeting. About twenty minutes. Okay?"

Leone assented. Twenty minutes became an hour, then an hour and a half. Finally the phone rang.

"Mike?"

"Yeah."

"What took you so long?"

"I was getting fired, Uncle Tito. These things take time."

"What?"

"That's kinda what I was calling you about the other day. Not getting fired so much as what I got fired for."

"What did you do, Michael? What did you do? And how am I going to explain this to your mother?"

"I, uh . . . how should I put this? I guess I hacked into the firm's computer system."

"Hacked? Aren't you linked up to it anyway?"

"Yeah, for the most part. But there are certain parts, certain files that are off-limits. Particularly to associates. Particularly the managing partner's files and databases."

"Would that be Nina Kracken?"

"You know her?"

"I had to interview her after the Sam Zhang incident. Quite a piece of work."

"Yet somehow attractive, don't you think?"

Leone declined to answer. "So you broke into her files. And for what purpose?"

"To find out why Bob Silver was fired."

"Silver was fired? Why didn't you tell me?"

"I tried. That's why I called."

"Shit. So I didn't call back and you went and committed computer crime."

"It's a gray area, Uncle Tito. Like you point out, I was tied into the system already. So do you want to know about Silver or do you want to lecture me?"

"What are you going to do with your life, Michael? Can you get another job?"

"Already got one. One of the firm's clients wants me to come in-house, starting next month. The salary is about the same and I get stock options and a key to the executive toilet. Now, do you want to hear about Silver or not?"

Leone sighed. Mike's mother, his sister, was sure to yell. And Leone would catch most of it. But if the kid had another job . . . ?

"All right, shoot," he said into the phone.

Leone was astounded by what his nephew told him. Even after a recent raise, Bob Silver had not billed a single hour of time to any of the firm's clients going back almost a year. Not only had he failed to service his personal clients and the traditional Tew, Logan & Case client base—mostly Philadelphia area companies that had been with the firm for a hundred years—but he had actively alienated them. He had ignored their phone calls, lied about the progress of his work, cratered transactions with which he couldn't be bothered and, according to complaints, been rude and dismissive throughout. So the clients had taken their legal problems elsewhere, costing the firm millions in lost revenue. But Silver had not been idle. He spent all his time working for some company called Jasmine Investments, and he had assigned associates to spend their time working for Jasmine as well, particularly Sam Zhang. He ran up huge computer research bills, running into the hundreds of thousands of dollars, and he even hired some private investigators. Yet in all this time, he had not charged Jasmine a dime. And he had paid for the research and outside investigators from the firm's coffers.

When recently confronted with this by the managing partner, Silver had grown defensive, then hostile. Ranting, he threatened to bring down the firm and ruin Nina Kracken's career, even her marriage. He vowed he would show them. And they had all waited for an explosion. But then he simply disappeared. He hadn't been to the office for over a week. No one knew where he was, including his wife, who thought he was on a business trip somewhere.

In his absence the partnership voted to terminate Silver immediately. In accordance with the partnership agreement, they bought out his partnership interest as per the stated formula, and applied the proceeds to some of the outstanding bills. They informed the clients that Silver was gone and some of them promised to come back to the firm. Others said that the damage was irreparable. The firm was now considering legal action. All of this was encapsulated in a confidential memo from Kracken to the Executive Committee. A memo which Mike Frattone had read on his computer screen, setting off silent alarms in the central computer room and getting him fired.

"Whaddya think? Pretty interesting, isn't it?"

Detective Leone certainly thought so. It made the death of Sam Zhang seem more suspicious than ever.

"So what now, Uncle Tito?"

"Now we find Bob Silver," Leone said calmly, as if it were an easy task. He really didn't know where to start.

☆ ☆ ☆

"So, where did you learn to fly, Mr. Behr?"

Behr hadn't realized anyone was in the room. He tried to turn his head to see where the voice was coming from, but the effort sent pain shooting through his shoulder and down his spine.

"You'll have to come around," he said as loudly as his dry throat would permit.

A figure walked into view; tall, athletic grown to middle-age, close-cropped blond hair. And wearing thick black shoes with a blue suit.

"FBI?" Behr asked.

"Special Agent Volkmer. I have a few questions for you, Professor.

I suggest you answer to the best of your ability."

"I know the drill, Agent Volkmer, I used to be an Assistant U.S. Attorney."

"We are aware of that. But that was a few years ago, wasn't it?"

Behr looked at his interrogator a little more closely. This was only the second human being he had seen since he woke up. The first, an elderly nurse, had answered his basic questions in a wonderfully pronounced Jamaican accent: he was in the Bethesda Naval Hospital; he had been treated for two gunshot wounds to the shoulder, a broken rib, and second degree burns over his legs. He was not to move and open the sutures. He was lucky to be alive; when they brought him in, she explained, he had almost no blood in his body. Any further questions could be answered by the doctor who would be along shortly.

But it was not the doctor who came next, it was this guy. An FBI agent. In the standard uniform, certainly, but more senior than might be expected. And his tone suggested a rank and hostility that didn't fit the situation, or Behr's history of government service.

"Can you tell me where Kristina Zhang is, Agent Volkmer?"

Volkmer frowned. "Why don't you first tell me what you know about the Chinese Ministry of State Security."

"Nothing at all."

"I find that hard to believe, Mr. Behr. You killed two of their agents with a flare gun. Would you mind telling me why?" The voice was authoritative; used to getting answers.

"Because they were kidnapping Kristina Zhang. Now where is she?"

"We don't know."

"Are you looking for her?"

"I'm not at liberty to discuss our operations with you at this time. What were you and Ms. Zhang doing on the Eastern Shore, Mr. Behr?"

"We were scouting film locations."

"Are you familiar with a document entitled *The Revolutionary's Confession*?"

"Are you?"

"We found this document, basically intact, inside a melted plastic bag in the freezer compartment of a house in Oxford, Maryland deeded to Samuel Zhang, recently deceased. We want to—"

"What do you mean, 'basically intact'?"

"The house was destroyed by fire at approximately the same time you were shooting flares into foreign intelligence operatives."

"Tell me more about these guys, Chinese Ministry of . . . what was it?"

"I'm afraid I'm not at liberty to—"

"Cut the shit, Agent Volkmer!" Behr's voice cracked. "We are on the same team here."

"That has yet to be determined."

"Well then I'm not saying another fucking word until I talk to your boss!"

"Don't be so hard on Volkmer, Behr. He *is* one of our best agents." The voice, eerily familiar, came from the doorway, just out of Behr's visual range.

"Who's that?"

"You don't remember me, buddy? I'm hurt."

A second figure joined Volkmer near the window, the great shoulders and bald head instantly recognizable. Stephanos! Now, of course, he was Treasury Secretary Stephanos, but then he was just Cy Stephanos, Wall Street icon. A man who moved markets with his purchases, a man who had offered Behr a job in his bank. "Any job you want Behr," he had said that night after they split a bottle of scotch in celebration of the indictments for money laundering handed down on several international bankers who were stung by Behr and his team, all posing as employees of Stephanos' institution. But that was a lifetime ago, and now the man was here in person.

God, Behr wondered, what had he gotten himself into?

"Cy, you're looking well."

"You're not."

"You know how it is."

"Actually I don't."

Stephanos stepped closer to the bed. "You landed your plane on a busy road, crashed into a van—stolen it turns out—and engaged in gun battle with agents of a foreign government. All this time, Behr, all this time I thought you turned me down for the easy life of an academic."

"I did."

"So . . . ?" Stephanos arced a thick black eyebrow.

"All right, Cy, I'll tell you."

Stephanos pulled a small metal chair up to the bed, gestured impatiently behind him. "Volkmer, why don't you take some notes?"

Behr told the story of his involvement with the Zhangs. He talked about Sam as a student; about Sam's strange death and Detective Leone's suspicions. And he talked about Kristina. How she had asked him to help. How they had been handed the *Confession* on a disk, only to have it disappear that same night after a fire consumed Sam's apartment building and almost killed Kristina. He talked about the strange behavior of Bob Silver, Sam's boss. And about the break-in—which he now thought connected—at his place and his fight with the intruder. He told Stephanos, with Agent Volkmer diligently scribbling away, how they had happened upon Sam's weekend getaway, and how, once there, they had discovered the box full of books, which Kristina translated without showing him any copy.

He detailed every painful maneuver of his battle with the agents in the van. And as he told the story, the images flashed in his mind, including the final one, Kristina hooded and bound, thrown into the minivan on the Oxford Road. How scared she must have been! And how devastated that he hadn't been there.

Stephanos turned to Volkmer. "So that's what the MSS is doing in Philly. They're watching that Silver guy."

Volkmer nodded. "I'll alert Arch Street. I think we put this Bob Silver in custody."

"Get on it."

Stephanos turned his gaze to the bed, looking Behr over. "You're a mess, Professor, but damned lucky to be alive."

"That's the second time I've heard that today."

"I don't think you understand."

"Huh?"

"What's at stake here. I don't know if I do myself. But here. . ." Stephanos propped a briefcase on the end of the bed and removed a thick sheaf of paper. "You've answered some of our questions, this should answer some of yours. It's a copy of what we pulled out of the Sam Zhang house. Damn interesting. You read that, and I'll check back in a couple of hours. I know you're injured and all, but I need you on my team. We've got a lot of work to do."

Stephanos walked out. Behr looked at the manuscript in his hands, *The Revolutionary's Confession* written in bold across the front page. The pain in his shoulders was getting worse, throbbing with his pulse around the perimeter of the holes the bullets had torn in his flesh. And he was aware too of the rising flame on his legs. A combination of heat and itch. He felt dizzy, causing the manuscript to swim before his eyes. He dropped it on his lap to steady it, then grimaced when he flipped over the cover page. The simple motion had sent lightening through his shoulder. How was he going to read this in two hours when he couldn't even hold it?

The anguish must have been visible, for Volkmer was smiling.

"Welcome to the Vanguard," laughed the man as he took the manuscript from Behr's weak grasp and began reading out loud.

21

The cell door banged shut. Antonetti sprawled on the cement before her, his face swollen and raw. He waved her off.

"There's nothing you can do. Just . . . just let me lie here a minute."

Ignoring his protests, Kristina helped him into a sitting position and wiped off some of the blood with her sleeves. This was the second time Antonetti had been pulled out in the space of a few hours, only to be hurled back violently. He had not discussed the incidents. And she had not pushed for information. But her trepidation was getting worse.

"What do they want from you?" she asked him after a few seconds of internal debate.

Antonetti did not respond at first. He seemed not to hear her, staring straight ahead, laboring for breath. Without meeting her eyes, he spoke: "They want me to tell them everything I know, everything I told you earlier, about the currency, the guaranties, the whole scheme."

"I don't understand. If it's their scheme, why don't you just tell them what they want to hear?"

"I can't. Not yet anyway."

"That's crazy. They're hurting you!"

"I know." Antonetti coughed harshly and paused.

"Look . . ." Antonetti's head lolled to one side, his one open eye fixed on her, "I'm not sure what they want from you. But all they want from me is confirmation that I know what they're up to, and some sort of assurance that I didn't tell anyone at Treasury or State. Once they have that, they don't need me anymore. In fact, they don't really need me now, but they're still unsettled by me. So once I tell them everything I know, everything I told you . . ." Antonetti drew a finger across his throat.

Kristina shuddered. "We're not going to survive this. This is what you're telling me?"

"*You* might."

"I'm different?"

"I think they need something from you, something to make their plan complete. I don't know what it is. I don't think I want to know. But my advice . . ."

The door suddenly swung open. A man stood in the opening, glaring down at them. He stepped aside momentarily and two younger men rushed into the room and grabbed Antonetti by both arms, standing him up and pinning him to the wall. Then the first man entered the cell.

He looked down at Kristina, smiled briefly, then kicked her hard in the ribs. Kristina heard a crack. She gasped for breath. The pain was incredible.

"Take him upstairs!" the man yelled in Chinese over his shoulder to the guards, who obligingly hauled Antonetti out the door.

The man switched to accented English. "Now, Ms. Zhang, I understand you have some information I want."

Every breath hurt. "Who are you?"

"My name is Hu Zhong, if you must know. And I am responsible for the death of your brother."

His admission hit her like another kick in the gut, only much harder. Sam's killer—standing right here, owning up to his crime as easily as ordering a cup of coffee. The cold son-of-a-bitch; he would get nothing from her!

"I can see that you are angry, Ms. Zhang. Your face is quite red!"

"I will not answer your questions."

Hu Zhong gave a snort. "I haven't asked you any questions."

Curled in a ball, clutching her ribs together, Kristina tried to read this man calling himself Hu Zhong. His easy manner, she realized, was pretense. Beads of sweat covered his brow, and his hands, when not clasped behind his back, shook jerkily. Greasy hair lay pasted to his scalp. His clothes were soiled and rank with cigarettes and constant wear.

Antonetti had told her about the organization this man represented, what their goal was. How the gold was to be the foundation for it all. And they didn't have it. The pressure must be getting to him. Maybe she could use that to keep him off-balance.

Appear defiant, Kristina thought to herself, stiffening her back. "If you're not going to ask me questions, I'm not sure what I can tell you. I'm not going to ask questions of myself. Asking questions is your job. Why should I do it for you?"

Unexpectedly, Hu Zhong laughed. "You don't have to do my job for me, Ms. Zhang," the man beamed as he held up a small vial of yellow tinted liquid and a large syringe. "This will!"

Kristina watched him, eyes wide. Was this some sort of truth drug? Could she fight it? Kristina felt the terror return, the abyss opening below. Drugs had never been good to her, not in college or in her early days in Amsterdam. It took days for her mind to recover its equilibrium, even after a simple joint. But this stuff . . . the color alone . . . a thousand bad trips in a bottle.

Hu Zhong pierced the top of the vial with the needle then slowly drew out half the liquid. He yelled something in Chinese. Two names. And instantly the goons who had dragged Antonetti away reappeared.

They moved quickly. Kristina fought their grasp. She kicked out, catching one in the jaw, and wriggled her arms from the clasp of the other.

Kristina managed to stand, she rushed for the open door only a few feet away. She had found her footing. If she could just get hold of the edge of the door.

A sudden weight propelled her forward and down. She collapsed in the doorway, one of the goons straddled on top of her, holding her arms to her side, pressing against the injured ribs. She screamed in pain and tried to writhe. But he held her tight. Dammit! How could he be so strong?

"Hold her against the wall!"

Kristina was lifted; she felt her back hit the rough cement. Knees were jammed sharply into her pelvis, forearms pressed into her shoulders. She saw Hu Zhong through a film of tears. He looked red and deranged; he was holding up his syringe, flicking out the pockets of air.

He put the empty vial in his shirt pocket. Her gaze shifted to his left hand, following its movement, the syringe now coming toward her.

Then his right fist caught her unaware. She saw it just before it landed on her jaw, twisting her head sharply around, splitting her lips.

"Enough silliness, Ms. Zhang! It is time to hear what you have to say."

She was reeling. She saw Hu Zhong standing close, could smell putrid breath steaming from an angry smile.

The needle seemed engorged, swelling in his hand, a large, nasty drop forming at the tip. And in that drop a mirror, wherein she saw her reflection, eyes wide, mouth streaming with blood. And she saw the sweaty back of one of the men holding her, and beyond that the open door and in that door . . . the face of a woman.

☆   ☆   ☆

His victim looked up suddenly and tried to turn her head toward the doorway. Hu Zhong turned too, following her gaze. What he saw made his whole body tremble.

"Jin Qing!" he said, bowing automatically at the waist. "We weren't expecting you till . . . we would have made preparations. Why are you early?"

"Why don't you give me the syringe, Hu Zhong!"

"But I was just about to—"

"I know what you were about to do. Let us say that I've come to assist you."

Hu Zhong paused. "Then you are not angry?"

Could it be true?

"Of course not. You successfully apprehended the girl under adverse circumstances and are using our latest chemical agents to determine what her brother knew, and what she knows now. Why should I be angry?"

Why? Because he had directly disobeyed her orders. Ordinarily, she would be furious.

But then Hu Zhong thought about what she had said. It was true; he *had* done all that. It had been difficult to get the girl. But in the end it was *his* leadership of the mission which made it successful. Perhaps, he thought, this would work out after all. Maybe he didn't need Jin Qing out of the way just yet. They could work together for now; get the information from the girl, and then . . .

Well, there was still much planning to do.

"Hu Zhong, why don't you give me the syringe and hold the girl's arm out so."

Jin Qing held her own arm out, hand beckoning. Hu Zhong dutifully placed the syringe in Jin Qing's open palm and grabbed Kristina's arm fast, glancing briefly at her terrified expression. Something about her face caught his attention . . . something . . . familiar . . .

Hu Zhong felt the prick in his neck, the thrust of heavy fluid entering his carotid artery. His face contorted. He swatted at Jin Qing's arm and felt it give way—the syringe clattered to the floor. He looked down and saw with horror that it was empty. She had injected the full dose! On a direct path to his brain.

In seconds, the drug went to work on his nerves, dilating his pupils, making the room grow increasingly concave, brightening the walls and faces into various shades of blue and purple.

Hu Zhong saw someone enter; it was the Kuang character. He too appeared lustrous, almost shimmering, as did his approaching fist. It was moving so slowly, Hu Zhong had to laugh.

The blow shattered his nose, sending a jolt of pain echoing through his head. Neon pain, flashing in the mind's eye. Ringing pain, with the bell high and constant. Hu Zhong struck back; he swung wildly at Kuang, but his fists met nothing but air.

He couldn't fight, he realized, not with the drug taking hold.

Another idea gripped him now. An alternative—escape the room, get control of the drug.

If he could just get some coffee . . . some alcohol, anything to bring him down. Even a glass of water, something cool, something familiar he could touch and taste. It was just upstairs, one flight away . . .

The doorway pulsed before him. The entrance to the womb, he thought, comfortably trimmed in red.

And suddenly he was looking up, his legs kicked out from under him. The light bulb overhead shot blue rings down to his face that made him feel warm, then cold, then warm again. He heard a deep rhythmic pounding, like a bass drum, and he looked around the room so he could ask the drummer to stop. But there was no drummer, just Jin Qing, Kuang, Kristina and the two men holding her. Kristina Zhang, yes—she looked so familiar somehow.

He heard a voice. Jin Qing's. High and abrasive and in rhythm with the drum. "Feng, you have your orders. Do with him as you wish."

Who was Feng? What was he going to do?

Hu Zhong raised his head to look at Jin Qing. To ask her. He saw her mouth moving, then he heard her voice, acoustically separated from the motion of her lips.

"You won't be hurt, Ms. Zhang, now that the rogue has been stopped. Come with me, and we'll give you something to eat. You must be famished."

Hu Zhong watched Jin Qing. Watched her reach out and gently separate Kristina from the guards, put her arm around Kristina's shoulders, caress the swollen cheek. Hu Zhong had never seen this tenderness in his superior officer. Jin Qing now swept the long hair from in front of Kristina's face and let it slowly slip over the back of her hand, over Kristina's shoulder.

How had he not noticed it before? Jin Qing—she was beautiful! The Assistant Deputy Minister was a beautiful woman, though sadly wilting. Had he been blinded—blinded by his own fear and hate? So much so that he could not see the flower that bloomed before him all these years?

Perhaps if he told her? Told her that it was love, only disguised as hate, that drove him for so long. Surely she would understand. Surely she would admit her own feelings toward him. And then . . . then they would be happy . . . together, and she would give him a glass of water.

Kristina Zhang said something. He couldn't tell what. He saw the lips part, lips that looked like Jin Qing's.

A figure approached, electric hair sizzling under the light. Kuang. Or Feng. He didn't know what to call him.

But he didn't have time for the man's distractions now. He was busy. Busy studying these beautiful women, seemingly made of glass. The curve of their eyebrows, the arc of their breasts. So lovely, standing there together. So lovely and clean. They almost looked like sisters.

☆ ☆ ☆

Jin Qing guided Kristina out and shut the door on the scene: Hu Zhong bubbling on the floor, hallucinating wildly, chattering about love and entirely oblivious to Feng standing over him with the long curved blade in his hand.

The image would always raise a smile.

Kristina walked ahead, between her and Hu Zhong's men, who stayed obediently silent—unfazed by the turn of events. They turned the corner as a group, climbed a short flight of stairs and were about to enter the kitchen when Kristina stopped in her tracks. Jin Qing followed her eyes to the corner of the kitchen where the body lay.

"I'm sorry you have to see that," Jin Qing said, touching Kristina's shoulder, "but in some ways it is good."

Kristina looked at her questioningly. "That woman, she was the one who pulled the trigger. She killed your brother. It was a grievous error. And one for which she was punished."

"I thought that other man, Hu Zhong, was responsible. He said so himself."

"Did he? Well, in many ways he *was* responsible. It was his operation. To my everlasting regret." Jin Qing moved to stand between Kristina and the corpse of Helen. "So you see, it was never our policy to hurt your brother. And it is not our policy or desire to hurt you now."

"Then let me go. And that poor man, Antonetti. He has a family waiting for him."

"We will. We will. But you must understand," Jin Qing led Kristina out of the kitchen into a small dining area where steaming boxes of take-out Chinese food dominated a small folding table, "that we can't release you until we've accomplished our objectives."

"Which are?"

"Oh, I think you know." Jin Qing gestured to the men who immediately fetched and set up two folding chairs on either side of the table. "In the meantime, I hope to make your stay as comfortable as the unfortunate location will permit."

Jin Qing ate well. She hadn't eaten anything since Beijing, twenty-two hours ago. And the greasy pan-fried noodles and dumplings she

continually piled on a paper plate weren't bad given the Bronx neighborhood, a place that gave a lot of credibility to her nation's anti-Ameri-
can propaganda. It was a rough place, she determined on her way from
the airport, but certainly better than some. The quest for anonymity
often drove them to the very bottom of society. To hovels and slums
swimming in waste water, nurturing anger and disease. She still took
medication for an Indonesian virus she caught in the '70s and could see
the track of the suppurating footworm that had been with her since her
first assignment in Cambodia.

"Eat," Jin Qing pushed a packet of chopsticks toward Kristina. "It
tastes better than it looks."

But Kristina shook her head, then looked away. Jin Qing shrugged.
She couldn't force the girl to eat, even when Kristina was a toddler.

Jin Qing ate the last dumpling in one bite and gestured for them to
leave. She showed Kristina to a room upstairs, a room with barred
windows and two single beds in opposite corners. Antonetti lay on one
of the beds, propped up on one elbow, reading *People* magazine. He
had a large plastic bracelet on his ankle.

Jin Qing clapped her hands, and she saw Kristina try to jerk away
as one of the guards grabbed her shin, shutting the clasp on another
plastic bracelet.

"I'm sorry, Ms. Zhang, but we will not be watching you very
closely," Jin Qing said. "In fact, you two have the second floor to
yourselves. So, just as a precaution, we are attaching these security
devices. If you cross the perimeter of the house, or certain interior
thresholds, an alarm will sound. And we will be very unhappy if it does."
Jin Qing raised an eyebrow.

Kristina's understanding showed in her face. She and Antonetti
were still prisoners. And the body downstairs should be a powerful
reminder to them of the will of their masters. Jin Qing had planted the
body deliberately along their route for two reasons. First, to show
Kristina that her brother's death had been avenged, to quell some of the
fire that might otherwise motivate her to act rashly. And second, to show
Kristina that death was routine for her captors, a factor in everything
they did. Its threat, therefore, could be very real.

She left Kristina without another word, not entirely happy with the
way things had worked out. It had been close with Hu Zhong. Feng

should have been more aware. She would talk to him about that and about losing the books and whatever copies existed. Even Feng was prone to errors, but forgetting the books, Chen Hai's own writing, in a burning vehicle on a public road was not what she had expected of him.

And now that the books were gone, Kristina held all the clues, forcing Jin Qing into the awkward position of ensuring that the girl told all she knew. But she wouldn't do it right now. First she would rest, just for a minute. It had been a long flight to America.

☆ ☆ ☆

"You want the magazine?"

"No, that's all right. You read it."

"It's the only news we'll have for a while."

"How long have you been here? I don't think you told me."

"About a month I reckon."

"I had no idea."

"Well, I think the worst of it is over. Now that the Hu Zhong character is out of the picture."

"You think they . . ."

"What I think is that this Jin Qing is pretty high up. One of the big muckety-mucks at State Security. And from what you say, Hu Zhong was not authorized to stab you with that needle."

"Thank God. He became a real mess. Almost immediately. Shaking and babbling. He said he loved us."

"I think the effects are permanent."

"Was it a truth drug?"

"During one of my sessions with the guy, he threatened me with it. Said it would make me want to say everything I know. That it would cook my brain, and the truth would drip like bacon fat."

"Quite an image!"

"I thought so, too."

"It's silly really."

"What do you mean?"

"The whole interrogation thing. Even if the woman hadn't interceded; if the guy had injected me, he could only have been disappointed."

"Why's that?"

"Well, I don't really know anything. Not like you do. Not all that stuff about the balance of power."

"Who knows what might be relevant?"

"Trust me, they would have been disappointed. If the location of the gold is what they're after, I don't know it. As far as I know, the trail ends in 1938 . . . with some guy named Ambrose."

"Ambrose?"

"Some American communist from the twenties, worked in Shanghai. The shipment was to be handled by him when it got to the States. Probably in 1938. Really, that's all I know. The guy's probably been dead for years."

"Interesting . . ."

One floor below Jin Qing thought so too, smiling broadly as she listened to Antonetti and Kristina on the small headset.

She had it now. A major lead. They were sure to have a file on an American Communist from the 1920s. And if her people didn't, the FBI certainly did. And she could always get those. In this case, the price would be worth it.

Jin Qing turned from the desk and reached for the satellite linkup in the small green backpack on the floor. She waited a moment as the unit booted up the encryption software—the latest from Silicon Valley—then punched in the number. She was told it would be a few minutes, but after less than one, the old familiar voice came on the line.

"Jin Qing, what a pleasant surprise."

"I have good news, Chairman!"

"Oh?"

"I think we can commence negotiations with the Japanese. Then the Koreas. It is only a matter of time now. We are finally on the path to recovering the gold."

Jin Qing heard laughter spill from the handset. The Chairman was pleased! And the good news had come from her lips. He would never forget that. Her career was secure, as was her daughter in the room upstairs. All this despite Hu Zhong's dangerous tactics. Thankfully he was out of the picture now. She hadn't needed him and his experimental drugs to get the information. Antonetti had done that for her. Antonetti could finally have his reward. He had played the role of the confidant beautifully.

22

Rocking on the porch of the white, wood-frame row house, the old man scribbled busily in a spiral-bound notebook. Behind him, behind the house with its neat backyard duly composted in preparation for spring, the great ridge of culm that dominated the rusty town of Shamokin came to its western terminus. Only now, some fifty years after the last bits of shale and other mine waste were thrown from the collieries, had vegetation begun to reclaim the ridge—birch trees mostly, with thin trunks and vibrant green leaves. They were the pioneers that managed to poke through the slag and allow Ambrose Bukowski the notion that the bitter hangover from the region's coal-mining days might finally recede.

Not that he wanted to forget the mines. Indeed, he was quite intent on remembering. For all around him the memories of his generation were dying, succumbing to black lung, cancer, alcohol and senility. Long ago the world's attention had wandered, and soon there would be no one left to tell the story of the tremendous human effort that dug millions of tons of anthracite from beneath the mountains of central Pennsylvania, mostly by hand and with devastating effects.

So every evening after he put his sister to bed, he would come out to the porch and begin to write. He wrote down scenes as they flashed through his head, following no particular structure or pattern. And when his hand got sore from holding the pen so tightly, he picked up the bottle of Four Roses whiskey he kept tucked under a corner of the blanket, sipped, gagged (as he had done all his life) and studied the lonely street in front of the house until the pain went away.

He would continue this way deep into the night, only stopping when the throbbing in his hand became too great or the whiskey turned his words into nonsense. Then he would step inside, slowly climb the stairs, tuck the blanket under his sister's chin and shuffle down to the room he had occupied with his brothers as a boy. Sometimes he would sleep.

He had repeated this pattern for the better part of a year and had now filled a box with scrawled-over legal pads that still needed to be put in some semblance of order and edited thoroughly. Editing would be essential, for he was beginning to think that in his senescence he may have told some of the stories more than once. And the volume of political rhetoric might be off-putting to these modern readers

This evening was warm for April in this corner of the common-wealth, and Ambrose was writing of his first day as a breaker boy. He had been thirteen years old and excited at the prospect of working a nine-hour day inside a coal breaker under the watchful eye of the stickman—a man who hit you with a stick if you did not separate slate and wood from the coal at the quick pace required by the Glen Burn Colliery. He had been thirteen years old and thrilled at the prospect of adult pay.

Ambrose described the breaker as he saw it then. From the outside, a huge wooden monster slanting off the side of the hill. From the inside, a tangle of girders, intermittently lit in squares by the windows cut not only for light but to prevent the wind from blowing the structure down. And through the girders fell the coal, sliding and bouncing through a series of chutes along which the breaker boys sat, methodically picking out the slag and dumping it on the conveyer.

The noise was incredible: hundreds of tons of coal in motion, steam engines, rail cars, cable pulleys, and the occasional scream when one of the boys got in their way. The entire time he was in the breaker, from his thirteenth year to the day he was old enough to enter the mines as a laborer, Ambrose had not said a word to anyone. There was no point, they couldn't have heard him anyway.

Ambrose tried to remember the name of the boy who had sat next to him at first, the boy who had fallen through the girders only weeks into the job.

It was getting difficult to bring up details like that. To his horror, he found that he couldn't even picture the kid's face, though it had once been very vivid to him. He reached for the bottle. He usually found that a jolt helped to loosen the memories locked away in the corners, though often it saddened him too. For the return of unexpected faces also recalled the tragedies that had befallen so many of them.

Still Ambrose sipped. And this time as he raised the Four Roses to his lips, he saw coming up the hill—filling the narrow street—a procession of headlights. Typically, traffic was thin in Shamokin this time of night, and four or five cars together was damn rare for Cameron Street. His time on the porch had taught him that.

And he was more surprised when all of the vehicles sloppily pulled up and over the curb in front of his house. He couldn't see inside them, the street light was too far away. But they didn't seem like local cars. They were clean, first of all. And mostly new. Except for the van. *That* had seen better days.

☆ ☆ ☆

"My friends call me Gus." Lazlo stuck out his hand and smiled briefly at the woman behind the desk. She did not return the smile. Or shake his hand.

"I'm sorry Mr. Lazlo, but we have no record matching that name."

"Is there any way you can check again? Maybe a cross index or something?"

The woman's demeanor grew forbidding. What was it, he wondered looking at her thin lips and colorless eyes, that made librarians and document clerks so damn mean?

"As I stated earlier, the files of the Communist Party of the United States of America are not open to the public. I'm sure you can appreciate our policy given recent history."

Recent?

"Miss Jenkins—"

"Ms."

"Ms. Jenkins, I wouldn't ask if it weren't important. My family has no other way to locate this man. And we have tried for years. All we know is that his name is Ambrose and that he was a member of the CPUSA in the late 1920s and '30s. Please . . . this fellow may be the only link we'll ever have to our granddad."

"I have told you that there is no one with the last name Ambrose registered with the Party during that period. That is all I can tell you. All I am permitted to tell you."

Lazlo felt the tightness in his neck and the pulse in his head that presaged certain fits of rage he was only now learning to control. Rage that always erupted whenever he was faced with institutional barriers and the drones who guarded them.

He simply had to get past this woman. If it meant breaking into the place, he would do it. If it meant burying that plaster bust of Lenin in her head, he would do that too. Anything to get to those file cabinets behind her desk. And wipe that sneer from her lips.

The thought struck like lightning. Lazlo swiveled to view the plaster likeness of Lenin and remembered Silver's memo. Of course! He had forgotten a key fact. It wasn't American records he was after, it was the international ones. He took a breath and got his venom under control.

"Would it help, Ms. Jenkins, if I told you that Ambrose worked for the Comintern in Shanghai during the relevant period?"

Ms. Jenkins frowned. "Comintern representation was, in fact, a matter of public record which we are permitted to disclose, unless we have on file a written request for confidentiality."

Clearly she couldn't bear the thought of actually helping him. But she sniffed and bore the humiliation. "Was this man the official representative of the Communist International in that location?" she asked, rising from her chair which scraped loudly against the worn linoleum floor.

She looked over her glasses at Lazlo for an answer.

"He was an American in Shanghai. I'm not really sure what the title was."

Ms. Jenkins gave out a derisive snort, muttered something that Lazlo didn't catch, then disappeared into the file cabinets on the fifth floor of the West 23rd Street building that served as the official headquarters of the Communist Party of the United States at the end of the twentieth century.

She left him standing there for almost half an hour. With no chair and nothing interesting to look at, he shuffled back and forth across the linoleum, kicking at the edges of the broken tiles, trying to knock them loose. With every pass he turned to the bust of Lenin, contemplating the man's legacy and the somber little Bolsheviks who still wanted to fight the man's battles—but nowadays from the relative safety of West 23rd Street. They were an odd bunch here in the headquarters building. No smiles, no bright colors. Baggy clothes. Ugly, serious people who made a pretense of seeming terribly busy. So busy they could barely find the time or energy to wave him vaguely toward the fifth floor records room where the pre-1950 files were kept.

Ms. Jenkins returned with a stack of files in her arms. She dropped them on the desk and separated them into two stacks.

"These files," she tapped the pile smartly with a pencil, "are year by year lists of Americans sent to the Comintern. And these files," she indicated with the pencil, "are year by year lists of all the Comintern representatives, not just American, in the Far East. The Far Eastern headquarters were located in Shanghai until 1933. Thus, all Far Eastern representatives were physically located in Shanghai until that time."

"Until '33, huh? Where would they have been in, say 1937?"

"I can't say."

"Still a secret?"

"No, the headquarters moved about between Australia, Tokyo and Hong Kong. All because of the political dangers at the time. For 1937, I imagine you would have to review all of the Far Eastern files."

Lazlo sighed; the files looked daunting. "I'm confused. Don't you just have Americans in China files?"

"If we do, Mr. Lazlo, they're not for public consumption." She spoke in a tone usually reserved for petulant children. "You will have to make do with these, the official, declassified records. The way it worked in those days was that each country's Communist Party sent a number of its people to the Communist International in Moscow. Pile one." She patted it. "The Comintern then sent these people around the world to act as its own agents. Pile two." She patted that. "The rule was that a Communist Party could not have a Comintern representative from its own country. Thus an American Communist could never be the

Comintern rep to the United States. Instead, that American might be sent to Argentina, or Spain or China to assist the nascent parties there achieve their goals. But when he was there, he was not American as such. Instead . . ."

Ms. Jenkins jiggled her shoulders and straightened her spine, brightening visibly, "He was the representative of the *world's* workers, an agent of the dialectic, bringing about international revolution."

"I see."

Ms. Jenkins raised an eyebrow. "I sincerely doubt that, Mr. Lazlo."

"Oh?"

Ms. Jenkins shook her head, indicating the hopelessness of Lazlo's predicament. He would not be saved when the revolution came. She pointed a thin hand toward the door.

"Turn left when you exit. The third doorway on the right leads to an empty office. You may use that until we close at four. I would appreciate your returning the files in the same impeccable order in which you found them. I will return from lunch precisely at two. If you have any questions, you can find me then." Lazlo checked his watch. It was only twelve. The woman's two hour siesta should give him plenty of time.

Ms. Jenkins pushed the files toward Lazlo, who clumsily clutched a pile under each arm and followed her out of the file room. On his way down the hall he heard her turn the lock in the file room door and he smiled broadly toward the empty corridor ahead of him. It was one of his favorite sounds—the sound of the heavy bolt on an old MacAllister Steel lock. When he was ready he would pick that lock. And he would do it in a matter of seconds.

☆   ☆   ☆

The hotel room was awful. Despite the cold mountain air and the truck noise from Route 61, Behr had left the window open to keep the stench of old cigarettes, mold and accumulated nastiness from suffocating him. Two days—off and on—he had rattled around here in the stink trying to find a comfortable way to sit. Two days just waiting for the old man to call and tell them to come around again.

The agents took turns waiting for the phone to ring. Each man got two hours in the room, while the others went around town asking questions and digging through county records. So far they hadn't found much.

Despite what they had read in Kristina's translation of the *Confession*, despite the fact that the man they had found living in this tired mountain town was the only real candidate for the Ambrose mentioned so prominently by Chen Hai Zhang, they were still empty-handed. For Ambrose Bukowski denied any memory of any contact with the Chinese at any time in his life.

It was a quite a letdown after all they had mobilized to find him.

They had left Washington by helicopter, Treasury Secretary Stephanos insisting that the cost and his personal attendance were justified in this instance. But the helicopter had developed rotor trouble near Reading, forcing them into shaky rental cars with bald tires that caused gasps and white knuckles on the still-frosty roads running into the mountains. But still they arrived in Shamokin with much hope, delighted that Ambrose Bukowski, the only Ambrose (first or last name) who had both been a member of the Communist Party in the period specified and served the Comintern, was still collecting Social Security.

They had pulled into town on Route 125, climbed the steep slope to Cameron Street, found the graceful Victorian row house with the slate mansard roof and four column front porch leaning over the sidewalk, and found a man sitting on that porch only a sip or two into the whiskey bottle at his feet. They had stepped eagerly, with Stephanos in the lead, up the three creaking steps to discover that the man answered to the name Ambrose Bukowski and did, indeed, have a minute to spare.

Stephanos and Behr, the agents on the porch and on the sidewalk, they had all grinned when they heard this. They had exchanged mental high fives and meaningful looks with one another, telling themselves that a great coup was about to pass. They had come all this way with relative ease, they had climbed into the mountains and into the past. And they ran smack into a brick wall.

A half-hour later they all watched as Ambrose Bukowski weakly held Stephanos' card up to the light, studied it a moment, and promised that he would certainly call them if he could remember anything. Anything at all about the old days. He was certainly sorry. But his mind just wasn't what it used to be. Bukowski had said all this pleasantly and without a hint of rancor. And Behr and Stephanos and the rest of the

Vanguard had no idea whether to believe the old man or not.

They retreated to a run-down hotel (the sign called it a motor inn) on the edge of the town where the valley narrowed, and discussed Bukowski in hushed voices. It was understandable, they agreed, that a man having attained the age of ninety-five might forget a thing or two. But was it really possible for a man to seem lucid and yet not recall the first half of his life?

It didn't seem likely to Behr. Not with the life Bukowski had led. They had done some research into this life, and it wasn't of a type that most men would forget. The man had personally witnessed some of the great movements and cataclysms of the twentieth century. He had worked in the coal mines, organized striking miners, joined the Communists and served the Comintern in Russia, Europe and China, all before he was thirty.

In the 1930s he had broken with the Communists, actually been expelled by them according to later testimony, kicked around coal country as a United Mine Worker's rep during the depression, then been recruited by Army Intelligence for his German and Russian language ability shortly before the Second World War. He had spent ten years in Washington as an intelligence analyst until he showed up on a list waved before the cameras by Senator Joseph McCarthy who claimed to have before him the names of ten godless communists who actually worked in the CIA.

Under oath Ambrose Bukowski did admit to having been a member of the Communist Party prior to 1937, but denied any affiliation thereafter. McCarthy's committee claimed not to believe him and questioned him *in camera* for over a week. They were never able to prosecute, but Bukowski did lose his job and his ability to get another one with ease. He returned to central Pennsylvania in the 1950s, worked in various capacities for the UMW and began receiving Social Security checks at his present Shamokin address in 1967.

Behr had been able to read all of this off the computer screen the FBI had installed in his hospital room. It had taken only a couple of days to dig out the records from the various databases, and once they had Bukowski's address they had mobilized instantly, dragging a heavily bandaged and medicated Behr with them.

And here—two unproductive days later—Behr sat inhaling the

odor of the hundreds of tired truck drivers, salesmen and adulterers who had inhabited this motel before him. Outside the room's one window, opaque with road grime and winter salt, a cold rain fell loudly into the puddles of the parking lot. The room too was cold, for the owner had turned off the heat prior to their arrival—when the place was empty— and now was unable to get the furnace started again. One of the Treasury agents had suggested burning some coal. The owner had laughed, but there was still no heat.

Behr rewound the tape recorder and listened to the conversation again. They had attempted to interview Bukowski three times now, and each time he had been pleasantly unresponsive—stating consistently that he had no present recollection of the old days, though sometimes things came back to him that he couldn't really place.

Behr sat forward on the bed, strumming his fingers on a stack of files.

There was something in the initial contact, in that first conversation with Ambrose, that bothered him. He had almost caught it then, the old cross-examiner in him hearing something inconsistent in the testimony of the witness. And maybe if he had been on the spot, doing the questioning himself, he would have followed up. But the FBI guys were asking the questions, with Stephanos taking the lead. And they hadn't caught it, the moment passed, and Behr's attention turned to other things.

Behr now pushed play on the small Olympus Pearlcorder and heard Stephanos' voice emanate from the small speaker:

"Ambrose Bukowski?"

Bukowski's answer was much fainter. "What can I do for you?"

"Is your name Ambrose Bukowski?"

"Last time I checked."

"My name is Cyril Stephanos. I'm with the Department of the Treasury. If you have a minute, I was wondering if we could ask you some questions?"

"All of you?"

"I know there are a lot of us, and I'm sorry about that. You see we work as a team and where one goes . . . well . . . we all have to go."

Behr heard a different voice, Agent Volkmer, in the background. "Why don't some of you wait in the cars." The sound of footsteps and doors slamming followed.

Stephanos again: "How long have you lived here, Mr. Bukowski?"

"All my life, Mr. . . . what was your name again?"

"Stephanos, sir, Cyril Stephanos."

"Sounds familiar. You from around here?"

"New York originally. You say all your life, sir. Have you ever lived somewhere else, in another country for instance."

A pause, the sound of creaking floor boards and shuffling feet. A cough or two. Behr recognized them as his own.

Bukowski: "I seem to recall that I have, but I'm not sure where. It was a long time ago."

Now Behr's voice, not as loud as Stephanos': "Are you presently being treated for any medical condition Mr. Bukowski? A cold, Alzheimer's, anything at all?"

"I take something for my heart. I didn't catch *your* name."

"Jason Behr, sir. I'm assisting the Treasury Department, but I don't work for the government."

An old man's cackle from Bukowski. "Well, good luck with that."

Stephanos, sounding irritated: "I realize it's late, Mr. Bukowski, and we're sorry to startle you like this, with all these people. We would like you to tell us about Chen Hai Zhang—"

"It could also be Zhang Chen Hai."

"Thank you, Mr. Behr, that's correct, Zhang is the family name, Chen Hai is the given name. We have reason to believe that you knew this man at one time. He claims to have known *you*."

A pause and again much creaking and shuffling. Behr recognized the sound of the old man's rocking chair and recalled the contemplative tilt of his head, edged in long wisps of reddish grey hair.

"I've known many people, but . . ."

"Take your time, Mr. Bukowski."

Behr fast-forwarded the tape. Bukowski *had* taken his time as well as few sips of whiskey before speaking again.

"I don't recall anyone goin' by that name. I'm sorry, gentlemen. But like I said, memory don't came back to me the way it used to."

Behr advanced the tape again, holding the button only halfway down so the voices blended into a high screech broken by occasional pauses where Behr stopped to see what was being said. Finally he found what he was looking for, near the end of that first interview. Bukowski's voice sounded tired now and ever so slightly slurred by the whiskey.

"So you see gentlemen, you can ask me all the questions you want. But I'm an old man, and I can't tell you much about it. I can't tell you about Communists, though the neighborhood children called me one. Or about the CIA. And I don't remember anything about any Chinese. But I have your card and the number at the motor inn—"

Behr pushed REWIND with his thumb and listened to that last part again. Then rewound and listened to the entire conversation again from the beginning.

Toward the end of the tape he was startled by the ringing of a phone. He picked up the hotel phone next to the bed, then realized that it was the FBI issue cell phone that was ringing. He fished it out of his coat where it hung on the back of the door.

A female voice asked Behr to hold for the Treasury Secretary. The man came on a few seconds later, "Behr, it's Cy Stephanos. Progress to report?"

Stephanos had returned to Washington almost immediately after the first contact with Bukowski.

"Cy, I think I got him, I . . ."

"Whaddya mean, the old man cracked? Told you everything and gave you directions?"

"Well . . . no, nothing like that. But I know now that he's lying."

"Lying! About what? He hasn't told us anything."

"About not remembering."

"All right, Mr. Prosecutor, let's hear it."

Behr paused to collect his argument and frame it for presentation to Stephanos. Then he began. "In that first interview, you started right off asking the old man about Chen Hai Zhang. Right?"

"As I recall."

"But not once did you refer to Zhang's national origin."

"So?"

"So, later in the conversation, at a point where Bukowski is summing up all the shit he doesn't remember, communism, the CIA, the Second World War, etcetera, he includes the Chinese. He specifically says he doesn't remember anything about the Chinese."

"What's your point?"

"My point is that we didn't tell him that Chen Hai Zhang was Chinese—"

"Come on! We were asking about China. I distinctly remember Garcia asking the man if he had been to China, knew any Chinese nationals, ate Chinese food . . ."

"After! That was after the critical part of the conversation. No, the words China and Chinese had not been iterated to that point. Bukowski made that connection himself. He said he didn't know anything about any Chinese. And the only Chinese person we had asked him about to that point was Chen Hai Zhang, *without* stating that he was Chinese."

"So the guy knows Zhang is a Chinese name. The same way I know Bukowski is Russian."

"Bukowski is not Russian, it's Polish. The 'owski' indicates a place name in Poland."

"Huh . . ."

"I think I should talk to him alone."

"That's not possible. First of all, you're not trained for this kind of—"

"I was a federal prosecutor. That more than qualifies me. And if the guy is deliberately lying, he is more likely to talk to me as a civilian than he is to representatives of the government that turned on him in 1952."

Stephanos paused, and Behr thought he could hear the man thinking. After a half a minute Stephanos assented. "All right, talk to Bukowski. But do it right, with a tape recorder and backup nearby."

"Backup? The man is ninety-five years old!"

"He can still pull a trigger, Behr. Don't be stupid. Just get Volkmer or Garcia to make the arrangements."

"Right, boss."

"And Behr, about that other thing . . ."

Behr held his breath; he had been reluctant to ask, too afraid of bad news.

"There's still no sign of her. We have been trying to track the Chinese agents at their usual haunts, but . . . well . . . they must be laying low. We haven't come up with anything."

Behr rose from the indented mattress. He headed for the open window and looked out upon the gritty road and its steady stream of small American-made cars and twenty- and thirty-year-old trucks that would likely not be replaced any time soon. Steep timbered hills rose on either side of the road, extending into ridges up to thirty miles long. These ridges—the eastern extent of the Appalachians—were the wrinkles on the Pennsylvania map. Low, tough, ancient mountains filled with the world's hardest coal. Billions of dollars worth of coal that no one had the inclination to dig for any more. The seams were just a little too deep, and oil was just a little too cheap to make the effort economical for anything more than strip-mining.

The place reminded him of some of the towns in Maine that his father had dragged him to as a kid. They were also Appalachian. And just as tough. But Maine had never had the boom times that this place did. And maybe that was a good thing.

Behr turned from the window. Stephanos was still talking. "Look, we got the FBI and the CIA on this. And the CIA isn't technically allowed to operate domestically. But they got a lot of ground to cover and—"

"I understand, Cy. And thanks. I'll go talk to Garcia now, then head over to the Bukowski place. I'll check in if I get anything."

Behr hung up quickly. He hadn't told Stephanos everything about his relationship with Kristina. It just wasn't in his nature to do so. But he supposed that his feelings were made obvious by his flailing rescue attempt along the Oxford Road. And Stephanos and his so-called Vanguard had showed the appropriate level of concern. They were treating Kristina as one of their own and her disappearance as a top priority.

The forced time in the motel only made it worse, he realized. As if he were sharing a prison cell with two guys named Longing and Worry who whined constantly in order to make their presence felt. It was odd in some way that he should feel this strongly about someone he had known for such a short period of time. And it was unlike anything he had experienced in the past.

The guilt was compounded now with a new thought—a fear really—that if he could feel so strongly so quickly this might be less than love. Maybe it was more of a rush, brought about by the thrill of the chase, the reawakening in the Behr psyche of the glory of being a part of world events. And like the rush from some new drug, his feelings for

Kristina might dissipate just as quickly when this was all over.

His two hours was up. Volkmer stood in the doorway and Behr pushed past him, heading into the drizzle, aiming for town and asking himself: where did Kristina really fit in? Was she just part of this ride?

He was saddened to admit that he didn't yet know. He knew he cared for her. And that he hadn't yet touched the bottom of these emotions. But could these emotions for her be separate from the other feelings kicking around in him? Or would the conclusion of this mission, in success or failure, also erase the tenderness he felt for the woman he still envisioned as he first saw her, illuminated by the stained glass of the Old Pine Street Church, her face soft and troubled and asking for help.

23

She was alone now and had been for some time. Antonetti had been escorted down the stairs, and from the sound of the front door and the cars outside, somewhere else. She missed his company. A nervous and high-strung man, he could still be very comforting, reassuring her that things would all work out and they would walk out of this strange episode perfectly intact and perhaps richer for the experience. She didn't know what, precisely, he meant by that. But he said it with such certainty, that she couldn't help but believe him.

She looked over to the bed he had occupied. He actually made it up each morning after waking. They had been given a choice of moldy books to occupy their time, and he had chosen Trollope—some 19th Century affair involving the replacement of a local bishop. He laughed out loud on occasion as he read it. A shrill, high laugh accompanied by exaggerated pointing and commentary. He was only halfway through, and the book lay open on the nightstand next to the electronic monitoring bracelet the guards had removed from his ankle before they took him away.

Kristina wandered over to his side of the room and picked up the unit. It was rather bulky and heavy, and she didn't know how it worked exactly. On a battery, she assumed. The blinking red LED indicated that Antonetti's was still operational.

Against his advice—"you'll just piss 'em off"—she had spent an afternoon trying to discover the internal thresholds that Jin Qing had told her about. It wasn't too hard. Their second-floor domain was small, and each time she approached one of the electronic barriers with her ankle, an alarm sounded downstairs and the guards came running. Antonetti had been right; they did get pretty touchy the second and third time around. But their anger hadn't scared her. Instead she found herself somewhat amused, perhaps by the small exercise of power.

She drifted through the doorway and toward the bathroom, absent-mindedly holding the ankle unit in her hand.

The house had been very quiet for several hours now. Usually she could hear the conversation of the guards and smell the smoke of the constant stream of cheap cigarettes they inhaled. But the air was clear now, and except for some occasional clanking from the kitchen she hadn't heard a word. Were they down to one guard? That seemed pretty relaxed for them. But it was worth finding out, and she had an idea how.

Kristina bent low, put Antonetti's ankle bracelet quietly on the wooden floor, slid it with quick flick of her wrist toward the open door of a large storage closet, and scurried back to her room.

Nothing. She sat on her bed amazed. No alarm, no angry guards. No Jin Qing telling her to stop playing games or her stay would not be so pleasant.

Kristina got off the bed. Poking her head out the door, she saw that the ankle unit hadn't missed; it had indeed slid over the electronic threshold of the storage room doorway. She knew the barrier was there, for she had previously set it off herself. So why had the alarm not sounded?

Kristina marched down the hall, stopping at the storage room, her gaze fixed on Antonetti's ankle unit which lay three feet beyond the doorway, the red light winking every three seconds. Didn't the light mean the thing was on? It had to. So the only explanation was that the electronic barriers, or force fields, or whatever they were had been shut off. If so, then she could just step—

The alarm was earsplitting, catching her just as she put one foot through the door and was bending to pick up the anklet. She heard footsteps from the hall below and then leaping up the stairway behind her. She wasn't alone after all and knew she wouldn't be able to get back to her room in time.

In one quick motion Kristina grabbed Antonetti's ankle unit and threw it down the hall and into her room where it landed on the rug without much noise. A second later the first guard turned the corner, then the second. This time they had their guns drawn.

The older guard, the ugly one, grabbed her shoulders and pinned her to the wall while the other made a quick check of the rest of the floor. He returned after a minute.

"All clear," he said in accented Mandarin. The guy was probably Cantonese.

The first guard pushed himself off Kristina and grunted in disgust. "This bitch is just testing us again."

"Let us lock her door then; at least until the Minister returns."

The ugly one nodded his assent.

Gripping her arms firmly, they guided Kristina back to her room; they shut the door. She heard the bolt slide home, and she lay back on her bed. Shit. Now she couldn't get to the bathroom. What a stupid thing to do.

But had it been? How could she have known that her unit would set off the alarm if Antonetti's hadn't? How could she have known that they had turned his off?

Another question flickered in her mind, and she tried to remember how it was that the guards had turned off Antonetti's device. She pictured them as they had come into the room earlier. They had told Antonetti to get dressed. To be sure to put on his shoes. Then they told him to lie back on the bed, and with some sort of key—it looked more like a wrench—they turned the lock on the plastic strap, and the unit fell loose. What else? Nothing. That was it—just one turn and the thing was off. They hadn't flicked any switches or turned any knobs. All they had done was unlock the clasp. And the clasp, she noted now, looking at her own, didn't have any wires running to the boxy part with the blinking light. It was just mechanical. It didn't turn anything on or off.

So how had they turned the thing off?

She picked up the unit from the rug and turned it in her hand. Other than the clasp, isolated on the thick strap, there didn't seem to be any moving parts. Nothing to turn or flick even if you wanted to. No switches or knobs. Nothing to adjust. What she assumed was the active part of the unit was simply a small beige hard plastic box about one inch high, two inches wide and three inches long, with that interminable light in the middle blinking in constant rhythm. Her unit had that same light. Also blinking every three seconds, though not in sync with Antonetti's. So if there was no switch—

Kristina returned the unit to the nightstand and paced over the turquoise shag carpet.

"I'm stupid," she said out loud, for she realized now that she had been framing the wrong question.

The question wasn't *how* the guards had turned the thing off, but *when*!

And as the answer dawned on her, the implications made her feel even dumber and infinitely more afraid.

They had been far more devious than they appeared—more devious and better prepared. Worse still, they'd had nothing to go on without Kristina.

And she had given it away—all away—without a fight. She had told them everything she knew without them even having to ask. She had been manipulated throughout.

Jin Qing, of course, had played her, let her think that the Ministry of State Security was close to reaching the prize, that Kristina was peripheral and would be released as soon as possible. Kristina had no reason to disbelieve what she'd been told, that she and Antonetti—her roommate in captivity—had already served their function, such as it was, and now need only wait while Jin Qing went about her business unmolested.

But the trick of it was that Kristina was not peripheral. She was *central* to their efforts because she had read the *Confession* and they had not. Somehow they had missed it in Maryland, and never had it before then. They weren't in Sam's apartment the night of fire. They didn't have the disk. But now they didn't need it.

Kristina's mind raced, the pieces beginning to click. Of course, she thought, they had gotten close without her—they'd known, at least, about the ships. Somehow they put together that the ships left Shanghai about the same time as the gold. And they had tracked those ships and discovered that they were owned by the Far Eastern and Atlantic Shipping Company and that they had docked in Philadelphia in 1938.

So, sixty years later, the Chinese agents landed in Philadelphia too, where, in all likelihood, they discovered that the trail had gone cold. And without knowing what else to do, or how to get to the appropriate records from FeasCo, they had decided to simply buy the company. They had retained Tew, Logan & Case to handle the transaction and—for whatever reason—her brother had been assigned to the deal. And somewhere in that process Sam had done something, or seen something, or said something, that had gotten him shot.

Antonetti had told her that the gold was the key to China's plan. While they could perhaps get away without it, success would be certain once they secured possession. For the gold would cement their international credibility and make their guaranties rock solid—guaranties that needed to be solid because the security of nations depended on it.

She had made Antonetti explain it twice. So she could understand what was so important that her brother could be so cavalierly eliminated in its pursuit. And Antonetti had obliged. Telling her quite proudly how he had divined the truth from a Philippine finance minister who had said more than he should have and been dropped out of a helicopter over Luzon as a result.

It was all the result of the currency crisis, he said, and the political upheaval that followed. Kristina hadn't understood the causes that well. Perhaps Antonetti hadn't either. All he said was that internationally there was a collective loss of faith in the economies of Asia. This loss of faith manifested itself in the devaluation of their various national currencies. And when investors and speculators began abandoning these currencies in favor of dollars and marks, Asia suddenly found itself poor and unable to pay its debts.

The West had tried to help. Antonetti led the negotiations that got the International Monetary Fund to provide massive loans and extend many of the old ones. Nevertheless, these favors were conditional. And one of the conditions was the fundamental restructuring of the cozy relationships that once made the Asian elite so rich, fat and happy. But it didn't really work out as the IMF planned, and Western investors continued to pull out, sending stock markets crashing and bankruptcies soaring.

Then came the white knight. And it wasn't the U.S.A.

No—this time the hero came in the form of a thin, older gentleman from the People's Republic of China. In quiet interviews held only with the top officials of each country, the man asked, "What if we were to guaranty the value of your currency? What if we, the PRC, publicly announced that the Thai baht and the Chinese yuan would be pegged at a two to one exchange rate?"

"How would that help," the leaders had asked, "when the world's currency is the dollar?"

The man had answered that the world's currency was not the dollar. It was, and always had been, gold. And gold would, in short time, be backing the yuan. The man had leaned close and whispered that the Central Committee of the Communist Party had approved the adoption of a gold standard for the yuan. Thus each yuan would be freely exchangeable at any office of the Bank of China for a fixed quantity of gold. And if their country agreed to certain concessions, their Thai bhat or Korean won or whatever it was would also be freely exchangeable for gold at any branch of the Bank of China. Their currencies would be secure against speculation, their institutions safe from the IMF, and their borders safe from the West.

So what was the concession?

Antonetti had grinned excitedly as he told her, delighted by the details of the diplomatic architecture. It was simple really.

The thin man from the PRC had told the Eastern leaders that if the Chinese were going to guaranty the value of their currencies, they were going to guaranty their security too. The participating nations would sign a treaty the Chinese had already drafted. A treaty not dissimilar to the one creating NATO. A treaty which would oblige the signatory nations to defend each other's borders, train each other's soldiers, share each other's technology and vote as a block in international bodies such as the United Nations. A treaty whose basic language and structure was non-negotiable if they wanted the economic security the Chinese were offering.

Antonetti learned that most of the countries that had been approached were interested but doubted the gold reserves of the PRC. Hadn't they lost their bullion in the revolution? Hadn't they based the value of the currency on the worth of a unit of labor in accordance with

Marxist/Maoist philosophy? Wasn't China poor in mineral resources?

The thin man had asked the Eastern leaders to keep their minds open. He would return with whatever proof they wanted. Then he asked them to hold the fact of their meeting in the strictest confidence. They agreed, and he bowed slightly, smiled and walked away.

The Philippine finance minister had been astounded by the visit, and when drunk and pressed by Antonetti as to why the Philippines were avoiding American economic assistance, he had blurted out the details. Antonetti had wanted to follow up with the man. But the next day he was dead. His body, Antonetti was told, had landed in the jungle.

Kristina didn't know what to make of Antonetti's story. It sounded so plausible at the time. And Antonetti had been so animated as he told it. But it didn't make sense to her that the Philippine finance minister should have been killed and Antonetti left alive to tell the story to the granddaughter of the man who stole the horde in the first place. Unless Antonetti had been left alive for a reason. Or unless Antonetti had killed the finance minister himself.

It was hard to know, and she thought she might be entertaining wildly unwarranted suspicious. But she knew, at least, that she couldn't trust the man. There was something about his stay in this mini-prison that was different from hers. And that difference was that he could have walked out of here at any time, because the electronic bracelet on his ankle wouldn't set off the alarms. It had never been active in the first place. Antonetti had known that, which is why he refused to approach the interior thresholds with Kristina. Because when the alarms hadn't gone off, she would have questioned him. And he would have had to come up with an explanation for not escaping—an explanation for why he had hung around and let her tell him about some old Communist named Ambrose instead of climbing out of the bathroom window and finding his way home to his wife and kids.

☆ ☆ ☆

In the far northwest corner of the Bronx, stretching between the affluent community of Riverdale and the working class Irish and immigrant neighborhoods of Woodlawn and Jerome Avenue, Van Cortland Park is home to old growth woodlands, a designer golf course, Dutch colonial architecture and the most active East and West Indian cricket leagues in North America. In warmer months, the park's vast playing fields are dotted with dark men in cleanly pressed white pants and sweater vests bowling, batting and dashing between the wickets. But for the strewn trash lining the perimeter, the city buses rumbling up the northern stretch of Broadway, the wail of sirens and other urban distractions, the scene was vaguely colonial, reminding Antonetti that this country was still actively being settled by people who brought as much to the mix as they took from it.

Still, he still didn't know why he was here and he was growing tired of waiting for an answer. Jin Qing had marched him from Broadway— where they parked—over a cinder track and the playing fields and then into the woods. At first they stuck to a well-worn path, occasionally stepping aside for skinny cross-country runners who bolted along dressed only in shorts and T-shirts despite the cold wind that blew off the hill.

But then they left the path, and with Jin Qing in the lead, they bushwhacked up a steep hill, climbed over massive granite ledges and arrived at the summit of a large hill with a commanding view of the park and cemetery to the east, and the projects and tangled streets of the Bronx and upper Manhattan to the south.

The scene on the summit startled him. He and Jin Qing were alone now, but Antonetti could see that this place was frequently inhabited. The great ledge and boulders at the crest of the hill had been painted over with graffiti, the letters as big as a man, the colors vibrant and reflecting the thin spring sun. Beer bottles, ashes, syringes, condoms and thousands of miniature zip-lock bags littered the cracks in the rocks and the small dirt clearings. Many of the perimeter trees also bore inscriptions, most as enigmatic as the writing on the rocks, though some just trumpeted simple messages of love.

Since Jin Qing was being uncommunicative, Antonetti walked a circuit along the treeline, examining some of the signatures and sniffing some of the baggies to see what the locals were ingesting in this cold, dramatic place. But he tired of this task after a few minutes and approached Jin Qing where she sat primly on the edge of a dark boulder.

"Okay, Madame Minister, you have my attention," he said, standing over her. "So what are we doing here?"

Jin Qing raised her eyes, briefly meeting his. "We are waiting for someone, Mr. Antonetti." Then she returned her attention to the view over the Bronx.

"Whoever it is better have the stock certificates!"

Jin Qing did not respond. Antonetti could feel the muscles tighten in his neck. He had done things their way. What the hell was going on here?

"Look," he shouted, "I've done everything you asked and more. I delivered the informants, I dropped out of the negotiations, negotiations that—by the way—would have set China back ten years. But no, I disappeared. And when that happened, the U.S. lost its advantage, just like I said it would. They lost their advantage because they lost me, and I know everyone. You know damn well that you couldn't have gotten this far without me."

Antonetti was pacing on the ledge in front of her now. He noticed a strange look on her face. It didn't look like fear exactly. But it was more than simple bemusement. Was it confusion? Could the great Jin Qing, the Tigress of the Ministry of State Security, the Dragon Lady herself, really be confused?

She was so damn inscrutable. So hard to read. It just made him madder.

"And the icing on the fucking cake," he continued, "is that I got everything out of the Zhang woman without you having to lift a finger. Faster than that nutcase, Hu Zhong, I can tell you that. And what was his story, huh? I thought he was going to kill me. Didn't he know what was going on? What our deal was? Getting beat up was not part of the bargain. But still I played along. Good little traitor. And have I seen anything yet? A single goddamn penny? Not a thing! I'm supposed to be in Hong Kong right now, living like Genghis Khan. But no, I'm standing in the Bronx, in some crackhead . . . "

Jin Qing's eyes flickered to something behind him and Antonetti wheeled around to see a man approaching, leaning into the slope of the ledges.

"You're late!" Jin Qing shouted to the man.

"My apologies, Minister."

Antonetti recognized the man as one of her goons. Feng she called him. Was this who they were waiting for? What could this guy bring to the equation? He certainly didn't look to be carrying what Antonetti was owed—the payoff that made it worthwhile for him to leave his country and increasingly estranged family for the debauchery of the Orient.

"What's this? We're out here—we're waiting for this guy?"

But Jin Qing was looking past Antonetti as Feng clambered over the rocks. When he was closer, she stood and addressed him in a low voice barely audible in the wind.

"Is everything in order for this evening?"

"All is in order. There was an incident with the girl, but nothing you need be—"

"Has she been harmed?"

"No, Minister, she is fine."

Antonetti followed this exchange and saw genuine concern on Jin Qing's face for the welfare of Kristina Zhang. He'd noticed this before, and he marveled at it now. Jin Qing didn't appear to care for anyone or anything. Her international reputation was one of heartlessness—perhaps the coldest, most ruthless spymaster in the arena. But she was also deemed fair. A woman who settled her debts as they came due. And that was why he had been willing to do business with her. There had been countless opportunities to sell out, but the promise of an earthly nirvana was attainable if *she* promised it and he came through with the goods. Or so he had thought. He was beginning to wonder. She was acting out of character, delaying his payday and now showing something approaching concern for the welfare of another human being. It just wasn't right.

Jin Qing turned to him now; she asked him politely for a few minutes with her assistant.

What could he do? He grunted his assent, then wandered to the crest of the hill. Directly down the slope to the west he could see where a deeply worn path emerged from the woods onto a low ledge scrawled over in Day-Glo orange and green, and he recalled their own approach from the north. They had fought their way through the brambles to get here. So why had they done that if there was a path right there? A well-trodden path leading directly up from the playing fields?

Antonetti wanted to put the question to Jin Qing. He turned around slowly on the narrow ridge of granite, carefully watching the placement of his feet. He looked up to find himself staring into the flat Mongol face of the agent named Feng.

Antonetti hadn't heard him approach; the man was only inches away. He smelled strongly of garlic. A movement at waist level caught Antonetti's eye, he looked down, but it was already too late. The point of the large flat blade had already pierced his abdomen.

☆ ☆ ☆

Jin Qing watched for a minute, fascinated by the simple, ancient brutality of Feng's act. Feng's people killed sheep the same way, gutting them alive and letting them bleed to death amidst much terror and bleating. True, Antonetti had not been hung by the feet first. He wasn't a sheep, and the viscera had not spilled from his body cavity in same neat arrangement as had he been. But the effect was the same. He had no chance of surviving his wound. And that suited her purposes for the moment. For Antonetti had become—what was the apt English expression? Oh yes, "a loose cannon on deck."

Even a week ago, she meant to keep her promise to him. And she certainly meant it when she said it. He was to get title to Jasmine Investments and its multimillion dollar portfolios. And some cash besides. But the man had ambitions. He would not have retired quietly. With all that money, he would have become a force in his own right, a powerful entity living right on her doorstep. A man whose intelligence and resourcefulness would not stay idle long. She didn't need that, and she didn't need him any longer. He had served his purpose well. All he had said was true.

Antonetti *had* given up the agents who infiltrated Jasmine before they could discover anything, then scuttled the negotiations between the Pacific Rim nations and the United States. And those negotiations would have made their own redundant because the U.S. was trying to do the same as they were, trying to exchange loan and currency guarantees for military security. Trying to keep America at the center of the world.

But there could only be one Middle Kingdom. And in a few days China would once again be worthy of the name. The world would revolve around her when the balance of power shifted, and the East created a security block stronger than NATO's. Stronger because China would be so much more dominant, and because the will of the master would be so cleanly defined.

Jin Qing watched Feng walk away from the body splayed out on the summit. He nodded to her and she understood. Antonetti was dead. It had taken but one thrust with the same knife that had dispatched Hu Zhong earlier. A second stab been not been necessary with either of them.

Feng approached, and she bade him follow. "Let's go," she said over the wind.

Feng followed her down the hill and into the woods where she eschewed the path again in case they encountered a jogger. He said something behind her which she could not hear.

"What's that?" she asked.

"I asked about the girl, Minister. What about the girl?"

"We'll take her with us."

"To Pennsylvania?"

"Yes. Why not? She may come in useful. And the company will be nice."

24

Jin Qing got two pieces of news via her cell phone as they crossed the George Washington Bridge into New Jersey. First was that their research had been confirmed by the mole with the FBI's own files. The only American communist named Ambrose with Comintern tenure was one Ambrose Bukowski of Shamokin, Pennsylvania. This made Jin Qing smile.

But the second item was more troublesome and erased her smile instantly. Now, despite the armor plating and bullet-proofed glass of the van, despite the quality of her handpicked team and their advance intelligence reports, she felt unsettled. The insecurity that gripped her from the time of Sam's death now shook her again. Just forcefully enough to shift her focus from the details of their mission.

There in the passenger seat, approaching the Palisades through the graceful cables and grand skeletal towers of her favorite American bridge, she felt again like a young mother. A young mother standing alone in the hall listening to her twins cry out against the demons only they could identify, demons that didn't include hunger, for the twins had been fed; or exhaustion, for they had slept all day; or illness, for they were otherwise the picture of perfect of health. On countless nights that young mother had stood wide-eyed and alone in the hallway of the simple split-level house, the thin carpet under her feet doing little against the penetrating Chicago chill. She had stood right outside Sam and Kristina's bedroom door and listened as one cried out, waking the other. And then she had fought to endure the endless heartbreaking wail that might go on for an hour or more.

"Can't you do something about that?" Harry had asked. The young doctor could never understand her attitude. He wanted her to run in and hold the twins every time they so much as murmured. Constant coddling was his preference—the American way.

But Jin Qing had resisted the advice of her putative husband, and had resisted her motherly instincts, too. *Her* children were going to be self-reliant, and if they needed comforting they would learn to comfort each other. They had to find reassurance in facing the dark together. And by the time she had been recalled, by the time the Ministry had decided that Harry and the old man they called Baba didn't know the final destination of the cargo on the *San Juan* and *Crystal Palace*, the twins were putting themselves back to sleep by cooing and singing to each other in the big crib they shared from day one. Jin Qing had done her job by them. The twins would look out for each other, and knowing that had made the task of deserting them so much more bearable.

Was it natural, she wondered as Feng guided the vehicle onto westward I-80, that she should feel this way? It might be. It made sense to feel as a mother now that the demons who had plagued her children again haunted the darkness around the edges. But it could also be a sign of some sort of decline. A malignant weakness and lack of resolve that manifested itself in the recurrence of sentiments not felt for thirty years.

It wasn't supposed to be like this, she thought. Forward momentum, carefully executed—that's what she was about. Insight and control were the principal tools she used to dominate. Yet here she was, engaged in the one of the most important field operations of her career, one which would define that career and her nation's future by its outcome, and she felt—what? Fright?

Could that be it? Was she scared? Certainly not for herself. She had never once feared for her life. But for her children? For Kristina riding in the back between the guards—perhaps, yes.

The demons were howling again. She sensed them creeping around the periphery. She sensed one in particular and resented his intrusion. She had to do something about that one. His specter was casting a shadow over her dreams. Happy dreams. Dreams in which she and Kristina were reconciled, drinking tea in a manicured Chinese garden—Kristina making jokes and Jin Qing laughing at them. Both women beautiful in their way, elegant and accomplished, steely and secure and made stronger still by the maternal bond which forever held them together.

It was an image she had so grown to cherish in the last weeks that she was reluctant now to get out of bed for fear the image would fade with the day. So far it hadn't. But the image was increasingly marred, darkened by the demon lurking behind.

Jin Qing's face apparently betrayed her thoughts. Feng was looking at her curiously. She had to fill him in on the calls she had received.

"That was Li in the U.N. bureau. He confirmed the name and the Pennsylvania locale with the mole. What we have conforms to the records in the FBI computer."

Feng nodded, turning his eyes back to the crowded highway. "And the second call?"

Jin Qing took a minute before answering. She looked out the passenger side window across gray lanes divided for express and local traffic. From their elevation the view was of rooftops, of flat warehouses and industrial parks and small houses near the factories. It was all so functional, so unaesthetic; New Jersey reminded her a lot of industrial China.

"And I heard the report from the agents we sent to Philadelphia."

She looked back at Feng. Saw that he was curious. She did not want to appear unduly concerned. It would be a sign of weakness—a point of leverage he could utilize. She turned back to the view of New Jersey and spoke in a voice too low to be heard in the back.

"They've lost contact. They're not sure how. Over the past days and again last night, the lawyer, Silver, eluded them. They don't know where. Apparently his car is gone too."

☆ ☆ ☆

The scene at the turnpike's King of Prussia Service Plaza was pretty grizzly, even to a veteran of ugly scenes like Tito Leone. The man at his feet had been shot at point blank range, evidently while urinating. Leone could see that for himself, but Captain C.J. Skolnik of the Pennsylvania State Police—Troop T—nevertheless felt the need to reenact the hypothesis.

"Corporal Wilfred, you be the victim. Pretend you're taking a piss." A uniformed corporal dutifully stood against one of the urinals lining the wall. While keeping his hands near his crotch and whistling, Captain Skolnik then strode over the tiles to the adjacent urinal, raised his right hand in imitation of a gun, pointed his index finger at a spot behind the corporal's left ear and said, "Bang." The corporal winced involuntarily, the ignoble death perhaps suddenly vivid to him.

Leone looked down at the actual victim where he lay on his side in a pool of blood and urine. Poor slob, thought Leone, he still had his dick in his hand. Of course, that in itself said a lot about the crime. It said that the victim was completely unaware of the gun when it was fired. And that was interesting to a mind like Leone's.

Most men Leone knew were pretty self-conscious in public bathrooms. They would likely keep a discreet eye on the other patrons. You never knew these days who might be sizing you up. The world was full of freaks and perverts and in view of this, most men obeyed the unwritten rules of bathroom etiquette. If possible, when choosing a urinal, you left as much space between you and the next guy as you could. And you anticipated the potential of more people coming. So, if you entered a bathroom with five urinals and the one guy was already pissing in urinal number one, you would go to number five. That way you maintained distance and left urinal number three for the next guy coming in.

All men instinctively knew this. And if you were alone in a bathroom like this, with—Leone counted—twenty urinals, it would be pretty damn peculiar for someone to choose the urinal directly next to yours. Of course, Leone thought, he was making the assumptions that the victim had been alone and that the shot came from close range. But the lack of witnesses and the powder burns on the victim's neck indicated these assumptions were safe—even without the post-mortem.

So what was the story? Leone knew that if he were pissing alone and a guy came up next to him, he would be pretty damn worried that the guy was queer or up to no good. He might not walk away, but he would definitely keep his eyes open. And any movement would likely make him flinch.

But the dead man hadn't flinched. The indications were that the guy had been complacent at the time of death, clutching himself, actively urinating—as evidenced by the streak on the wall—and facing forward. So not only was the victim unaware of the gun, chances were he also knew his killer.

Leone felt increasingly certain that his analysis was correct. It explained the evidence. But to Leone this was not the most interesting aspect of the case; it was not what caused him to stick around a crime scene thirty miles out of his jurisdiction.

As a Philadelphia homicide detective, Leone had certainly seen his share of dead bodies this year. But so far he had only seen two with identical wounds. And *that's* what was interesting. It was the point of entry that distinguished the wounds. In both cases the victim had been shot behind the left ear.

It was a pretty effective way of killing someone. The bullet passed through that vital brain stem area which controlled the body's functions. Not too many people knew that. In fact, most people, especially sui-cides, went for the temple and thereby risked coma without death. But in two cases, separated by only a few weeks and twenty miles, the shooter had aimed for the brain stem, and it was likely, in both these cases, that the shooter had a choice as to where to place the barrel of his gun.

Leone was about to comment on this to Captain Skolnik when the man's belt-radio squawked.

"I need a phone," Skolnik said quickly.

"There's a whole bank of them right out the door," Leone offered.

"Right."

Leone watched Skolnik move his massive bulk against the men's room door. The crime scene was a bit of a disgrace, he thought. There were people all over the place. But it probably didn't matter. The killer hadn't left a trace. He walked in, shot and left. He had probably touched nothing but the door. And—like Skolnik just now—he had probably done so with his shoulder.

Skolnik returned, appearing quite animated. "Usually these AFIS searches take hours," he said, referring to the Automated Fingerprint

Identification System recently installed by Lockheed Martin for the FBI, "but his one came back so fast because the print was on file with the Department of Defense."

Leone raised a questioning eyebrow.

"Our victim's name is Augustus Lazlo, honorable discharge United States Army, 1973. Got an address in Atlantic City. Name mean anything to you?"

Leone shook his head in honest denial. For in truth he did not know the name of the man he had seen standing with Bob Silver outside a South Jersey diner three days ago. But he didn't care to elaborate on this with Captain Skolnik. It would only complicate matters. He needed Skolnik to stay focused. So after denying knowledge of Lazlo, he bent the truth again.

"The reason I'm out here, Captain, is that I was following a man named Robert Silver. He drives a red, late model Range Rover 4.0, vanity plate reads M AND A. I don't know if he pulled in here because I blew a tire about five miles east and had to hitch with one of your guys. I heard the call on his radio." This much was true.

Leone continued gravely, "The thing about Silver is that he is a suspect in the murder of young Philadelphia lawyer a few weeks ago. The MO is the same. The victim—like this one—was shot behind the left ear. I think you should track this guy statewide. But be careful, he's some kind of sociopath. The kid he killed in Philly looked up to him like a father. Our information is that he's heading northwest. Toward Columbia County."

Leone watched Skolnik leap into action. There was nothing to mobilize a state trooper like the prospect of a murderer at large on his highways. He had basically told Skolnik the truth—only stretching the part about Silver being an official suspect in the death of Sam Zhang. His own captain had recently reviewed the file and ruled Zhang a suicide, then firmly instructed Leone to drop the matter and attend to his other cases. And with equally firm resolve Leone had ignored him, pursuing the case on his own time without backup or resources. But now that Captain Skolnik was sparked, Leone had the entire state police at his disposal. And chances were good that they would find Silver—or at least his car. Because outside of Philadelphia the instances of eighty-thousand dollar British four-wheel drives were pretty rare.

Even so, Leone had cause to be worried. Silver had slipped away from him and then crossed a major threshold in committing a daytime murder in a public facility. It showed the depth of his recklessness. He could certainly be considered dangerous now—and if what Behr had told him on the phone yesterday was true—highly motivated as well.

☆ ☆ ☆

Kristina didn't have time to consider the consequences.

The door was open. The guards had their hands full trying to push the van out of the mud. This was her one chance. They hadn't shackled her. It was their fuck-up, and it wouldn't happen again.

She leapt from the back of the van, passed airborne between the two guards manning the taillights, and hit the ground running. She headed straight into the woods up the side of the hill. It was a steep hill. The brush slowed her down, but it would slow them down too. She just had to keep moving.

Kristina heard the crash in the underbrush behind her. She heard Jin Qing yelling, and she knew then that they wouldn't fire on her. All she had to do was outrun them.

Outrun the smokers.

The terrain was steep and rough—slate outcroppings tripped her up and tore gashes in her legs every time she fell. Low shrubs whipped her bare arms and the cold began to penetrate her thin cotton dress. But still she scrambled and before long she was at a small summit.

She risked a look back and saw the young guard in the lead and the little Mongol close behind. They were coming fast, clawing at the hill. A quick glimpse of their faces told her all. She had embarrassed them in front of the boss, and they were really pissed. Though they might not shoot her, renewed captivity would be made to hurt.

Just out of their sight Kristina darted along the ridge for a minute to put some space between them, then veered off, descending through the thickest brush she could find. At the bottom she encountered a narrow stream and skidded down its steep bank like a skier. Her heart pounded so loudly in her chest that she didn't hear the guard who was catching up behind her until he was but twenty yards away. He yelled.

Kristina wheeled around, and she saw him at the top of the muddy bank. It was the young one—the one who always smiled suggestively.

He waved his gun, took one step—

He lost his footing, was tumbling down. Kristina leapt back to avoid being hit by the flailing man whose momentum carried him around and smacked his head hard on the boulder midstream.

He didn't move, and Kristina was already over the bank on the other side when she heard the guttural wheeze of the Mongol who had just emerged from the same bushes where his colleague had lost his footing.

"You are only making it harder for yourself!" he called to her in accented Mandarin.

Maybe she was, but Kristina didn't let up. She had found her stride now. It almost felt good running up the hill. The hundreds of miles she had put in along the canals in Amsterdam were finally paying off. Behind her she could still hear the rest of them. Hear them beating at the underbrush, cursing in Cantonese and another language she didn't recognize. But the curses grew ever distant, and the sound that now dominated her ears was the even pace of her footfall in rhythm with her breathing.

She was running like a deer— step . . . step . . . leap, step . . . step . . . leap—over fallen trees, along the natural contours of the hills. She used one hand to hold up the front of her thin dress, the other to sweep away the branches that whipped at her face. She didn't allow herself to slow down. She didn't dare rest, even when she couldn't hear the pursuit. Even after she abruptly changed direction over rocky ground that made tracking impossible and likely sent them careening down the wrong slope, she continued to run.

It must have been an hour—maybe longer—before she came to the top of a small rise and saw before her, nestled in a valley, a small town dominated by church spires and onion domes. The sight of it made her stop, and stopping allowed the fatigue to catch up with her. Suddenly she felt exhausted, sick to her stomach and, looking down at her body, saw that her dress was torn and her arms and legs bloody from the rocks and the brush.

The town beckoned.

Kristina approached cautiously, keeping an eye out for the van, for any Chinese faces. But there were none to be seen. The streets appeared safe.

But if it was safe for her, she suddenly realized, it was safe for them too. Kristina knew that she would be conspicuous. Her own Chinese face would stand out, particularly in its present condition. All Jin Qing would have to do was ask, and the townspeople would innocently give her away.

As would the police.

So safety required a phone call. And to do that she would have to find a phone.

From her perch halfway down the hill she could see that the town stretched along one main road that ran along the bottom of the valley. Directly below her, not fifty yards away and just slightly at the edge of the town, was a Sunoco station. And at the edge of that station was phone with blue Bell Atlantic sign. The phone was unfortunately placed; it was right next to the road. Anyone approaching—even if they didn't pull off—would be sure to see her. And would at least know that she was a stranger.

A panic was beginning to rise. Kristina studied the town some more but could not find what she was looking for. She did not see any more of the blue telephone signs, and she did not see any commercial establishments that appeared empty and likely to have a phone. In fact there were only three open enterprises that she could see. Two were bars—with a steady stream of inbound traffic this late in the afternoon—and one was a diner with large glass windows showing off a full complement of customers. That only left the Sunoco station, and looking back in its direction, she finally saw something that gave her a glimmer of hope.

Kristina flew down the hill and ran up the gravel embankment behind the station. She waited there a second, getting her breathing under control. Then she peeked around the corner of the cinder-block structure and saw that they were still there. Six cars, all waiting for the single pump of a rural full-service gas station.

It would take the attendant at least five minutes to fill up those cars, probably more. And that was plenty of time to make a call.

Kristina slipped around the corner, crept silently along the side wall and risked a quick glance toward the pumps.

It was better than she expected. The attendant—the only one she had seen from the hill—was busy under the hood of a red four-wheel-drive.

Without further hesitation Kristina turned the corner and calmly walked into the office where she saw a telephone sitting on a desk toward the back. She looked behind her once, but nobody was paying attention.

Kristina quickly picked up the phone and pulled it over to a dark corner out of sight from the road and the pumps.

In some ways she regretted what she was about to do, because it was quite unfair to get anyone else involved. But she really didn't have a choice, at least one that she could perceive right now. She was free, temporarily, very scared, and she had a phone. And with that phone she was going to dial the one phone number she could remember in this country. It was one that she had been dialing for years.

25

Over the years he had received many disturbing calls from her. Calls which told him she was quitting college, that she was living with an artist in a tenement on the lower east side of Manhattan, that she was moving to Amsterdam, that she didn't know when she might be in Chicago again, if ever.

But this call was different. This time she sounded scared. And the abrupt way she had hung up on the dimly heard command of a voice in the background gave her bizarre story credence and greatly inflamed his worry.

And the worst of it was that he couldn't do anything for her, except follow the instructions she had given him.

So after he scribbled a quick note to himself, Dr. Harry Zhang got the general number of the Philadelphia Police Department and asked for Detective Leone, Homicide Division.

It turned out that Detective Leone was not available, that no one knew when he might return, and Harry declined an offer to talk to another detective. Kristina had said he was not to trust anyone other than Leone, not the police and especially not the FBI. So Harry politely left a message, then called information for the number of the next person on Kristina's list. A young lawyer at Tew Logan—he seemed to recognize the name—a friend of Sam's?

Harry was informed by a secretary in sorrowful terms that Michael Frattone did not work at Tew Logan anymore but that she had a forwarding number. Harry called it, got the young lawyer on the line and after due explanation was given Detective Leone's new beeper number. A beeper, Frattone said, that his uncle had gotten last week for situations just like this.

Harry couldn't remember how long he waited for Leone to return the page. It seemed like hours—during which he paced the floors of his spacious suburban home feeling entirely powerless. Somehow, he knew, he had failed them, had let his kids drift away. And now one was dead and the other in danger. Baba had been right to condemn him and the American household he had created. Better to have kept Chinese standards, better to have reigned as a patriarch and imbued the kids with notions of filial piety than let them wander off and experiment with the new culture, quite unprotected and alone.

He heard the phone ring; he ran to pick it up.

It was Leone. Calling from a noisy place. Harry could hear voices and traffic in the background, and he wondered what he might be interrupting and how foolish he might sound to the detective who had interviewed him briefly the day after Sam's death.

But Leone didn't mock him or tell him not to worry. Instead Leone told him to make another call immediately. To talk to a fellow named Behr who was presently working with the Treasury Department and the FBI. He was given a number to dial.

Behr? Jason Behr? The all-American with the intelligent eyes? Didn't Kristina just mention that name? Didn't she say he was dead?

He asked Leone, who told him that no, Behr was alive, though quite beat up. As to Harry Zhang's second question, Leone couldn't speak. He didn't know of a mole in the FBI. But if Kristina said there was a mole, then he should be careful. Talk only to Behr and let him decide.

Leone hung-up. But Harry was still full of questions. What else could be done for his daughter? Why call Jason Behr? Should he have let Leone help further, gotten him to arrange an escort from the local police?

On this last point, Kristina had been emphatic. No police, she said, no locals. She had been so insistent, in fact, that she refused to tell her father where she was.

"Dad," she had cried, "that would only make me conspicuous, put me in more danger! These people can handle a small-town police force. They have a lot more firepower."

Harry contemplated ignoring her. She had not revealed her location, but he had Caller ID. He could find that area code, and with the help of the phone company, he could also find out the name of the town that corresponded with the three-digit exchange. And why shouldn't he? It wasn't as if Kristina was known for her judgement. She had always been slightly rash, particularly when it came to the police and other authority figures. So what could it hurt, really, to have the help of the local constables? At least *they* would be armed.

Still, she had been explicit. And that made it a tough call. Part of him just wanted to call this Jason Behr and hope for the best. But another part told him to do more.

Which begged the question, should he call the local police too? And should he do it first?

Harry Zhang looked at the wall clock. Almost half an hour had expired since Kristina called. And he still wasn't any further along to helping her.

He had to make this decision, and with his eyes still on the clock, he decided to get her whatever local protection he could. Then he would contact this Jason Behr. That made sense to him—bring all possible forces to bear. So Harry reached for the phone book and learned that 717 was in Central Pennsylvania. Then BellAtlantic told him that 874 was an exchange occurring most frequently near the town of Tamaqua, and they provided him with the phone number of the police station there. A young female voice answered.

"Hello," Harry began tentatively, not sure how to frame his request, "my name is Harry Zhang and I have reason to believe that my daughter Kristina is in some sort of trouble in your town—"

"You would have to talk one of the police officers about that, sir," the girl interrupted.

"Sure . . . fine, could you please connect me then."

"I'm sorry, but none of them are available right now. Could I get your name, a number? Someone will get back to you."

"Look, this is urgent. She is in trouble *right now*. I need to talk to one of your police officers. Can't you get them on a radio or something?"

"Ordinarily I could," the girl sounded oddly haughty, perhaps preoccupied, "but there was some shooting a little while ago at the Sunoco. I guess you haven't heard. But they'll be interviewing witnesses for the next few hours. When they're done, one of them will call you, sir. I promise."

Harry Zhang felt the blood drain from his face. What the girl told him could only mean that he had been too late. Something had happened. Something bad. All he could do now was call Jason Behr. And then he would make his way to Pennsylvania.

☆ ☆ ☆

"Fucking FBI," the old man growled after he knocked over the whiskey bottle he had left sitting open on the carpet.

"Now, now, why get yourself all worked up?" his younger sister reproached softly. "They don't know anything. They're fishing. That's why they keep coming here with their hats in their hands."

"They don't wear hats anymore. That's the only thing that's changed about 'em in fifty years."

His sister watched him for a moment as he took a towel from a drawer and threw it over the pungent whiskey stain.

"One of them sounded nice," she said when he resumed his seat at her bedside, "and what he said made sense to me."

"Which one was that?"

"The one talking Marxian theory. He hit pretty close to home, didn't he? Come on, admit it, brother! It was almost word for word what you've been saying all these years."

Bukowski turned his head slightly so that his sister could not see his eyes. She was right, of course. The guy had come close to the truth of the matter, at least as Bukowski saw it. He wasn't sure how the guy knew. Maybe because he was a professor and not a G-man. Maybe he had done some research, who knew? But the fact was that if the Chinese got their hands on the gold, the revolution was finally over. The last country on the planet with a chance of continuing the dialectic march from capitalism to communism would revert to pure capitalism. They would base their national wealth, their very sense of identity, on the value of their bullion rather than on the value of their workers. It was a fundamental shift, one much more profound than the department stores and giddy little stock markets that they had permitted so far.

Allowing the Chinese to discover the location of their ancient imperial gold would mean the death of communism worldwide. And Ambrose Bukowski didn't know if he could live with that thought. Even if true communism—the type he believed in, the type he and Chen Hai had fought for but not seen attempted since the late 1920s—was not being practiced in China today, it was, at least, the family bible kept in the drawer. It was the underlying faith of the nation to be drawn on when crises demanded it and available to future generations who might see more truth therein than their ancestors. Only the Chinese had the wherewithal to preserve it. The Cubans would fail with the death of Castro. The North Koreans as they grew ever hungrier. It was all up to the Chinese.

He had come close when Mao finally established his capital in Beijing in 1949—close to opening the channels of communication again, such as they were. The Comintern was gone, abolished by Stalin in a gesture of independence. But many of his old contacts were still alive. And he had taken some early steps, making some overtures on the American end to the large team of union men who had helped him hide the stash in the first place. But then he had gotten the letter. In the simple code they had worked out in the '30s, Chen Hai had effectively told him to sit tight and not contact him again. Above all, to stay true to the vision they had discussed so long ago.

He had done so unquestioningly and seen the wisdom of this course of action borne out by the dark, often bizarre history of the People's Republic. Not once since his receipt of Chen Hai's letter in the cool summer of 1951 had Bukowski been tempted to disclose the location of the gold to his government or to Mao's.

Until now that is. Until the professor told him that Chinese agents were hot on the trail of the gold and if they found it and used it to adopt a gold standard for the yuan, theoretical communism was as dead as Latin.

Bukowski looked down at his sister lying half-paralyzed on the bed and saw the affection and reproach in her eyes. She might be right. She usually was. She believed as he did and had taken care of him in the tough times following his censure and expulsion by the Party and later by the federal government. She had earned her voice. He should hear her out.

But not now. Her comments would certainly keep. And right now he wanted to be alone and think things through in a proper manner with some sweet whiskey on his beloved porch. Bukowski grabbed the depleted bottle off the floor and headed downstairs.

It was rude, he knew, because she was not done talking and could not follow him on those wasted legs. But he couldn't help being rude. Sometimes a man just needed time to think without the matronizing intrusion of a woman. Funny that women didn't understand that.

An hour later he was drunk. It didn't happen often. Mostly the liquor just made him sleepy, but now he could feel himself getting quite sloppy and emotional as he recalled the heroic effort of the forty guys he had used to haul the gold off the ships and into its new home.

A stroke of genius that had been. That and telling the guys it really was stolen marble they were hauling. Marble that belonged to the Lehigh Valley Railroad Company and which could be used to bargain for a better contract.

So what if he had lied to those men? So what if they were just in it for the thrill and prospect of better wages? They were still heroes. They deserved some recognition in all of this. If he was going to the tell the professor the location of the gold, he was going to make it conditional on the government giving some recognition to the men who had to carry it.

There was only one problem though. Only one problem with effecting his plan and making his sister happy. Of course, he thought, he *did* still have a rough idea, maybe the general outline and procedure. But sitting here in the dark three sheets to the wind, he couldn't quite remember how, exactly, a man might reach that pile of gold.

Sure, he'd mapped out the details on a notepad long ago and then hidden that notepad somewhere. But somehow he couldn't quite re-member that little hiding place either. Though maybe his sister did.

Yes—she had a knack for these things. Maybe she was still awake. He would just go up and ask her. And then, he thought, apologize for being rude.

Bukowski gripped the armrests of the rocker and slowly pushed himself up, hearing the rheumatic creak of his limbs and the floorboards beneath his feet.

"Damn board."

He'd hammered it down a bunch of times, but somehow it always got loose, always got louder and always woke up his sister when he stepped on it.

He was looking down at the offending floorboard, contemplating a quick repair. Consequently, he did not see the approach of the hand that grabbed his face and shoved him back into his rocker. And in the darkness of the mountain night he didn't see the face of the man who slid around behind him, got an arm around his neck and yanked him—feet dragging—into the house.

26

It was a rude awakening on this cool spring morning. They drove through a thin fog from the motel, past a long line at the McDonald's drive-thru window and a full parking lot at the Dunkin' Donuts. The night shift was departing Wal-Mart, and a procession of headlights marked the start of another day of strip-mining and ecological devastation for some sorry patch of the neighboring woodlands.

They were getting to know the rhythms of life here in Shamokin. The work day started early. Traffic was heaviest before 8:00 A.M. And so it was perfectly reasonable, Behr decided, to call on Ambrose Bukowski first thing and see if the man had come to any conclusions after their discussion yesterday. A discussion that Behr thought went pretty well.

"He's right on the fence," he had reported to Stephanos last night, "and I can see him leaning to my point of view. I think one more good talk in the morning, and we'll have some answers."

Behr, the prosecutor, was not usually prone to optimism when faced with a reluctant witness. But last evening he had seen his words hit home. He saw Bukowski's eyes narrow into a thin, concentrating squint and his head fall into a slow nod of understanding. Of course, there was no way for Bukowski to know that he was being played, and that his own political philosophy, as expressed to Chen Hai Zhang sixty years ago, was being thrown back at him. Bukowski couldn't know because Behr hadn't told him about Chen Hai's scribbled account of the old days, and that he, Jason Behr, had read every word of it (or as much as had been translated) with fascination.

"Better to just let him think I'm smart," Behr had said to Agent Garcia, "and that this is the conclusion smart people come to when they think of the fate of international communism."

Garcia, typically somber, agreed. They hadn't tried to push things with Ambrose last evening. Just plant the seeds and let them germinate overnight. By today, with luck, they would have something to harvest.

So this morning Behr and the big Mexican agent mounted the porch steps and knocked on the partially open front door in full anticipation that Ambrose Bukowski was up and ready to talk. That he was sitting on the couch with a strong cup of coffee and a detailed map directing them to the hidden location of the gold.

Such was their expectation, but that was not what they found.

They followed a trail of blood from the living room into the basement, down rickety unbanistered wooden stairs and over a packed dirt floor.

That was where they found him. Garcia's initial inspection indicated that the old man had been bound, stabbed once, then dragged into the basement. Then tortured. Presumably the stone foundation had masked his screams.

And there must have been screams, for short, thick roofing nails protruded from Bukowski's kneecaps and knuckles. And small slash wounds striped his bare legs and wrinkled buttocks. Still, that wasn't the worst of it. What sent Behr retching was the eyes. For the rest of his life, Behr knew, he would be haunted by those eyes. He would flinch that much more whenever an implement came near his own—would feel a dull ache deep in the optic nerve for fear that his eyes might someday join Bukowski's where they lay desiccating in the dirt of the basement, covered in grit and free from their sockets.

Garcia helped Behr up the stairs and into the living room.

"Come on, man," he implored, "get a grip on yourself, we got work to do! You have got to stay in control!"

Behr opened his mouth to speak but felt the bile rise in his throat. He gestured to Garcia to give him a minute. Garcia nodded, pulled out his phone, and over the pounding in his head, Behr could hear the agent's side of the call.

"The old man's dead, murdered, tortured first. Yeah . . . we have to presume the worst—

"No, sir, I don't know why the agents posted did not see anything. We just got here. We haven't talked to anyone—

"Yes sir, front and back. We'll be waiting."

Garcia hung up and that's when Behr first heard it. A scratching and mewing, like an animal, like a—

Garcia's voice drowned it out momentarily, "You take the front. I'll go around—"

"Shut up for a second and listen." Behr held up a finger and both men listened intently—hearing it clearly now: an intermittent cry, soft and rather high. A cat? Whatever it was, it was coming from upstairs.

They took the steps two at time and stopped on the landing to isolate the sound. Garcia drew his gun. Behr pointed to a door at the end of the hall. That was where the sound was coming from. They could even see the doorknob rattling slightly.

They tried to stay silent on the approach, but each footfall on the old wide-plank floor creaked louder than the last. They wouldn't gain the element of surprise. And it occurred to Behr that if Bukowski's killer was still present in the house, was still cowering with a victim in that room at the end of the hall, he had only to shoot Garcia to survive. For Behr was not armed, and backup was probably still a mile away.

What will I do? Behr asked himself. What will I do if Garcia goes down?

They moved slowly, coordinating each footstep to conceal that there were two of them. Ten steps. Then they reached the door. Garcia gestured to Behr to crouch low on one side of the door frame. Garcia took a position on the other side, then shouted:

"FBI! Come out with your hands where we can see them! Come peacefully and you will not be hurt!"

The mewing was more distinct now. But it wasn't a cat. There were words and Behr thought he could distinguish, "Ambrose . . . help . . . Ambrose."

Behr moved into position in front of the door. Garcia angrily waved him off.

"Wait for backup," he hissed. But Behr pushed anyway. The door opened inwardly but only a fraction. Something was blocking it. Each push by Behr elicited groans from the other side, and Behr, not knowing what to expect, was tentative at first. Finally he put his shoulder into it and something gave.

The men burst in.

She was lying on her stomach with her head toward them. Opening the door had slid her back along the floor, pushing up her nightshirt to reveal spindly legs almost bereft of muscle and covered in bed sores. Still she made that sound, the low pathetic cry of a wounded animal.

Slowly, so as not to frighten her, Behr and Garcia rolled the woman over. She had to be almost as old as Bukowski, and like the dead man downstairs she had traces of red in her otherwise white hair. They also noticed a strong smell and saw that a colostomy bag had torn loose at some point in her ordeal.

"Ma'am," Garcia said softly and slowly, "we are with the FBI. We had an appointment with Mr. Ambrose Bukowski. Can you tell us who you are and what happened here?"

They had to bend close to hear. "Brother? Where is my brother?" she asked.

Her faded blue eyes betrayed fear and worry. Behr and Garcia exchanged a glance, recognizing the same thought. They must only hint at the gruesomeness lying downstairs.

"I'm sorry," Behr said, "but your brother died last night. We think it may be murder. If there is—"

"Oh Lord! Are you sure—"

"Yes, ma'am, quite sure."

"Absolutely sure? He's pretty tough you know."

"Yes, ma'am. I'm sorry, but we are absolutely certain." Behr answered gently, then watched in quiet amazement as the old woman's whole body seemed to tense. Her jaw clenched, her neck tightened, her hands curled into little fists. Even the cloudiness in her eyes seemed to recede. She didn't look grieved. And she certainly wasn't happy. No, it was a different reaction entirely, and it suddenly occurred to Behr that she was angry. Very, very angry and probably quite prepared to talk.

Garcia began gently pressing his fingers against the woman's abdomen, checking for signs of internal bleeding. "You are in need of medical attention," he said, "did you fall, were you attacked?"

The old woman ignored Garcia's questions and probing hands. She turned her head slightly, fixing Behr in her gaze. "You're the one from last night," she began, "the professor."

"That's right, my name is Jason Behr."

"I'm Hilda. People here call me Hilly. You can tell your friend here that my legs don't work anymore, so you two are going to have to carry me. You put me in the bathtub, wash the shit off, and get me into my bed, and then I'll tell you want to know."

"We'd like to get you to a hospital . . ."

"There's time for hospitals later." Hilda's voice was still soft, but suddenly etched with authority. Behr and Garcia listened like children.

"You gentlemen have work to do. You have some gold to dig up and I think you'd better start soon."

Garcia almost fell over.

"Don't look so surprised young man. You came here today expecting Ambrose to tell you. But someone got to him first. So *I'll* tell you. Just get me off this goddamn floor and clean me up, and I will give you a map. A map that Ambrose drew himself when he was just as young and good looking as you are now. Maybe better looking because he was tall . . . and trim and he had all that red hair . . ."

The old woman's voice faded again. She turned her ahead away from Behr and Garcia kneeling at her side. But they still saw it. The single tear that collected in the corner of her eye and rolled thickly over her nose and down her cheek. Followed by another, and another.

☆ ☆ ☆

Stephanos had returned. They were gathered in a makeshift headquarters on the top floor of Shamokin's grand, turn-of-the-century public library building. Garcia was just ending his report.

"She is completely paralyzed from the waist down. Apparently she has been for a couple of years. That is why she was unable to open the door. What we've been told, and we have no reason to doubt her at this point, is that she was awakened by the sound of a creaky floor board on the porch. Apparently this is a nightly event that did not concern her.

But then there were unfamiliar noises, the sound of a scuffle. And then she heard the basement door and what she described as bumping and muffled screams. That was when she rolled out of bed and dragged herself down the hall into the small attic where Mr. Behr and I found her this morning. She had evidently been able to shut the door from the inside by pushing against it, but had been unable to lift herself high enough to reach the handle in order to open the door again and call for help. Mrs. Hilda Thorpe stated that Mr. Bukowski's attacker or attackers—she was unable to confirm a number—did not enter the second floor of the house and that she heard them leave approximately two hours after they arrived via the kitchen door to the alley."

The room was quiet for a minute as Stephanos and his Vanguard agents considered the ordeal of the woman who lay trapped in her house, paralyzed and listening to the torture of her ninety-five-year-old brother.

It was Stephanos who broke the silence.

"Garcia, what about this map? Is it useful?"

Garcia's stern face darkened slightly. "Yes and no, sir. We're having it analyzed now. What Mrs. Thorpe gave us was a hand-drawn map and some notes. The map might prove useful once we determine what it shows. You see, it doesn't have any names on it. There's a town, but it's just called TOWN. Hills and houses and mountains are similarly described and rendered with a simple drawing."

"And the notes?"

"The notes explain what to do once you have gotten to a certain point in the town. In essence, you have to locate the entrance to a certain mine, remove the cap—whatever that is—and proceed into the mine until you have reached the stables. Again that could be a term of art, though I'm not certain. The gold is apparently stored near these stables in the original shipping containers."

"So we're looking at local maps trying to match mountain towns with the one we got on the map?"

"Not just local maps, sir. In truth, this could be a map of any mining town in the world."

"That's just great. What else we got?"

The roomful of agents sat mute one second too long. Stephanos punched the top of the desk in front of him and reddened violently.

"Goddamn it, what else? Do I have to remind you gentlemen what's at stake here? We have Chinese agents on the loose in central goddamn Pennsylvania. We have a kidnap victim. And we have international currency markets going wild with the Chinese central bank and every fucking speculator on the planet buying yuan! Now is someone going to tell me what we are doing about this?" Stephanos' entire head grew increasingly crimson, veins stuck out where the muscles were flexed. It was a terrifying site. One that had gotten him far in the business world. "Let's start somewhere, how about with the Asian currency markets, is there any stability anywhere?"

Behr sat toward the back, simply listening. This was the government's job now. He would do what he could, but he was now out of his depth. Or so he had thought. Listening to the succession of reports made him realize that even the professionals were covering new ground. Three Wall Street types reported that the Asian situation was getting ugly. Traders and national treasuries with money to spend were pulling out of everything, especially Asian currencies, to bid up the yuan. As a result Asian and South American currencies were in a free fall with no one to bail them out. The U.S. Treasury had done what it could, but it couldn't risk sinking the dollar. The IMF had placed all its bets on Russia. And Japan and the European Union, the only other economies strong enough to combat the rise of the yuan, were paralyzed by political indecision. They were simply too scared to intervene.

When their report was done, a counter-espionage expert got up and told everyone how the FBI lost track of the Chinese agents, and that they were reduced to a house-to-house of the entire area in search of black hair and slanted eyes.

Another group was beginning a report on computer tracking and probability theory when a familiar voice with a flat Midwestern accent interrupted from somewhere behind Behr.

"What about the kidnap victim, huh? Kristina Zhang? Remember? What are you doing about her?"

Every head turned to see the new speaker. Behr recognized the man instantly. It was Harry Zhang—Sam and Kristina's dad. He looked awful. He had probably driven all night.

Behr rose, quickly stepped forward and introduced Harry to the assembly. He gave them a quick rundown of Kristina's predicament.

"So you see, gentlemen," Behr summed up, "Mr. Zhang here has more at stake than anyone. And I, for one, would also like to hear more of what we are doing for his daughter. She is—after all—the reason we have come as far we have."

Stephanos looked suitably embarrassed and glared at the FBI contingent as he made his way to the back of the room to give his condolences to Harry Zhang.

They talked briefly, with the immediate result that a separate team of FBI agents was dispatched from D.C. for the purpose of finding Kristina should she have continued to elude her Chinese captors. Harry admitted having his doubts, particularly the way her phone call had ended and the police reports of the shootout at Tamaqua—but he was insistent that more be done. So Stephanos obliged. This was one operation at which he was willing to throw resources.

Behr watched his old friend in action. Stephanos wasn't exactly the sympathetic type, but blunt decisiveness did give some comfort, and Kristina's dad seemed somewhat mollified. He'd gotten what he wanted—attention to the plight of his daughter—and was now content to join Behr on the sidelines as the black-suited agents went to work.

And go to work they did. Stephanos demanded speedier location of the mysterious town on Bukowksi's map, and soon satellite pictures with overlay maps began streaming in from the National Security Agency and National Weather Center. Garcia and Volkmer took charge of the search for the Chinese agents by coordinating their efforts with the Pennsylvania State Police who complained of already being in- volved in a statewide search for someone the media had dubbed the "Rest-Stop Killer." And Stephanos' deputies in Washington were told to do anything they could to shore up the yen before a continued slide destroyed the Japanese economy.

For one moment in fact, as Behr conferred with Harry in the corner, Stephanos' team seemed to be hitting on all cylinders, and Behr allowed himself a ray of hope.

But the next two telephone calls threw them all out of sync.

The first call was for Behr. A thin FBI man in an incongruously blue suit handed him a phone. It was Tito Leone.

"Behr, I been trying to track you down since yesterday. Where the fuck are you?"

"I'm in temporary headquarters in Shamokin. They moved us out of the motel."

"Well *tell* me next time. At least give a number. These FBI guys are cagey as hell."

"What's up, Tito?"

"Remember the lawyer, Bob Silver?"

"How could I forget a lizard like him?"

"I think we got him on murder one—"

"In custody?"

"Well that's the bad news. He's on the loose. Probably headed your way from what you told me. The state police are tracking him."

"I thought they were busy with the whaddyacallit . . . the rest-stop guy."

"Silver *is* the rest-stop guy! We have him on video. He killed a private detective that matches the description of the guy who kicked you in the ribs. Killed him in the bathroom of the King of Prussia Service Plaza."

"Jesus, the man's out of control. You have pictures of him killing the guy?"

"No, but we got pictures of the two of them arriving together in Silver's fancy little four-wheel-drive and Silver leaving all by his lonesome."

"Wow."

"Yeah, well that's what I said when I saw the MO."

"What about it?"

"Identical to Sam Zhang's. Bullet entered low in the skull, behind the left ear and exited high from the right, front temple. According to the medical examiner it is the head wound trajectory most likely to kill."

Behr paused, a feeling of grave certainty descending like a curtain. Whatever doubts still lingered about Sam's death instantly evaporated with Leone's description of the wound. In Behr's mind it was final: Silver killed Sam.

And now the man was roaming about central Pennsylvania after his second confirmed murder in quest of the same fortune they were and—Behr suddenly realized—with much the same information. Why? Because it was possible that Silver had that original disk, the disk with Sam's own translation of *The Revolutionary's Confession*. He could have retrieved it from Sam's apartment before he or his henchman set it on fire. And if that were true he would know all about Ambrose Bukowksi—

Behr hung up on Leone and quickly reconvened Stephanos, Garcia and Garcia's FBI contingent. He had to fill them in quickly. They had to watch their backs. It wasn't just the Chinese now. There was another player involved. It might just be one man. But he had killed twice so far in pursuit of this gold and would undoubtedly do so again.

Behr was in the middle of his explanation when Stephanos was called from the huddle to take another call. Behr and the agents stood silently and watched the great man's face turn from red to white.

"They've found Antonetti," Stephanos said flatly after he handed the phone back, "in a park in the Bronx. He was carved up like a Thanksgiving turkey. The NYPD couldn't ID him right away, but a beat reporter from the *Daily News* recognized his face. The murder of Deputy Assistant Treasury Secretary Antonetti is tomorrow's front page."

The implications were huge and obvious to everyone. Antonetti had been integral in Far Eastern negotiations. The news from Kristina, as relayed yesterday by Harry Zhang to Behr, was that Antonetti had turned. He'd been helping the Chinese with a scheme to stabilize Asian currencies in exchange for a Pacific security pact like NATO's.

The possibility of the Chinese scheme had been believed. But Antonetti's complicity therein was not. No one was ready to believe that America's top financial negotiator—a man with the one of the most exciting jobs in the world and a lovely family in the Maryland suburbs— was slumming with the PRC for simple profit.

But now they had to believe something. Antonetti's death meant one thing: that he wasn't necessary anymore to the people who killed him. And it didn't matter if he had turned or been tortured. Either way they had gotten to him. The American negotiating strategy was laid bare—and worse—the press was on top of it. Any mistakes would be instantly public and traceable to Stephanos and the present administration. If the Chinese got the gold now, the balance of powers would be tipped even further toward Asia. The U.S. would not only appear diminished by China's power; they would appear weak in having allowed it to happen.

It was a grim picture that the men considered in silence—a silence suddenly broken by the approach of Harry Zhang.

"What's going on?"

No one said anything for a minute. They all looked to Stephanos to answer. Finally, in a voice filled with determination and menace, Stephanos did.

"What's going on is that we are going to double the effort to find your daughter and this cache of gold. And we're going to do it before anyone else gets killed."

27

Oh, yes, he'd been angry when he entered the old man's house. Angry about yesterday. Angry about the wound. Angry that he'd had to use his gun.

Yesterday simply wasn't his fault. It was dumb luck, weird coincidence. It didn't mean his mind was any less fine, his actions any less controlled. He wasn't slipping, not him, not in the least. And he'd gotten out of there, right? He'd won the shoot-out, in a way. The Chinese didn't kill him, and he'd escaped from the gas station with but a single injury and his secrets intact.

So what if he didn't get the girl. He didn't need her. And so what if the Chinese now knew he was sniffing around the same part of the world they were. They didn't know where the gold was. And even if they had a general clue, they didn't have the information he had. Information that came right from the source, though only after he had scooped out the first eye with a spoon.

Bob Silver wound the bandage tighter around his arm and bent low over the mirror. The coke he'd scored off the hooker in Allentown had been a life-saver. It distracted him from the pain; it gave him life. He'd sniffed some right in Bukowski's home. And now he'd have a little more before he ditched the car.

He needed a boost for the walk. Fifteen miles was a long way for him under normal circumstances. But with a bullet in his arm, it would take all night.

☆ ☆ ☆

A rather heavyset, though still pretty woman from the NSA was the one to crack it. They had been greatly flustered in their attempts to locate the mysterious town on Ambrose Bukowski's map, though pull from Stephanos had the entire satellite imaging division working on it over the past twenty-four hours. And Stephanos, whose job it was to pay the bills for the secretive intelligence gathering agency, was furious that they had been unable to locate an entire town with well-defined features such as an east-west road running through a valley, a north-south road cresting the hills of that valley, a series of churches and a population— estimated by the town's size and typical population densities—of twenty-five hundred souls.

"What are we paying you for?" he had screamed at the cowering, sleep-deprived men and women in both the Washington headquarters and the Shamokin public library they had turned into a war room.

He hadn't gotten an answer for a number of hours, not until five in the morning when the helicopter landed. The woman had been flown in just to argue her conclusion to the secretary in person.

Behr and some of the agents joined him for the presentation.

"I know this sounds a little odd," she began after blowing her nose rather loudly in a flower-patterned handkerchief, "but it is the only possible explanation."

Stephanos gestured for her to get on with it.

"We have been working under a number of assumptions. Most notably, we have been assuming that whatever town we're looking for, particularly if it is located in this hemisphere—that is North and South America—"

"I'm aware of the division of hemispheres."

"Of course, sir. As I was saying, we have been assuming for locations in the Western Hemisphere that whatever town it is has probably grown since the map was created in the 1930s or at least stayed static."

"Sounds logical."

"Well, I began asking myself if it *was* so logical. Towns and geographies change. Particularly in mining areas. As you know, entire mountains can be leveled in pursuit of what is under them."

"So one of the mountains on the map disappeared. Is that what you discovered?"

"No, sir. It wasn't a mountain. It was the town itself!"

Stephanos snorted loudly. "I think I know why Richter didn't believe you," he said referring to the NSA Director who refused to endorse his own employee's conclusion but wanted Stephanos to hear it anyway.

"Yes, it sounds a little odd, but please, let me show you what I've got."

The woman's initial nervousness was gone. She appeared quite animated now, despite the doubt in all their faces, the early hour and apparent lack of sleep. She pushed past an astonished Stephanos toward a computer terminal resting on a foldout table. Within seconds she had dialed into the Washington mainframe and called up a copy of Ambrose's map that had been scanned in earlier. On the other side of the split screen she called up a color satellite picture. Two additional key strokes merged the images so that the map neatly overlaid the photograph.

Stephanos and Behr looked on wonderingly.

"All right, I see the mountains and the roads roughly where they should be," Behr commented from the corner, "but what about the town?"

"Well, that's my point—it's gone!"

Behr frowned. "I don't understand. There is a town in the satellite picture, but it's not the one from Bukowski's map. It's much smaller. There's only one church instead of ten. And only a handful of houses, compared to what we've got in the notes."

Behr's voice now rose an octave. "Did you read the man's handwritten notes? He describes the mine entrance as behind a row of three story houses. There are no row houses in the picture on the screen. Each house is surrounded by wide patches of lawn!"

The woman glanced up nervously from the computer screen, flustered by Behr's prosecutorial assault.

Stephanos put a restraining hand squarely on Behr's chest. "Hey, Mr. D.A., why don't you let the woman finish? Huh? She's come a long way."

But Behr would not be put off. It was late, Kristina had not been found, and he wanted immediate answers or a redirected search. He turned back to the plump woman at the computer with a slightly softer, though still pressing, tone.

"I'm sorry to be so insistent. But perhaps you can speed things along by telling us what . . . *exactly* . . . we are looking at and why."

"I'm sorry, I should have said right away," the woman said quickly. "What you are looking at is the town of Centralia. We have plat surveys from the 1950s showing a town matching Mr. Bukowski's description. Unfortunately the surveys are not in the computer database. But if you overlay those old surveys atop the satellite image and then match them to the map, you have an exact match."

"And where is this place," Stephanos bellowed, "Central America?"

"Oh no, sir." The woman looked suddenly perplexed. "I thought you knew. It's in Pennsylvania. Only about fifteen miles down the road."

☆ ☆ ☆

Like many Pennsylvania towns, Centralia was a casualty of the industrial revolution. When their convoy of black sedans, vans and bulldozers first drove into the place they were greeted by a bright yellow sign at the edge of town—PUBLIC ALERT: AREA SUBJECT TO MINE SUBSIDENCE AND TOXIC GAS EMISSIONS.

Behr was surprised by the sign that first morning, five days ago— surprised at the severity of its warning and the familiarity it assumed with conditions in the coal patch. After all, how many people really knew what "subsidence" meant or the danger it implied?

Still, dire as the sign's warning was, it now seemed inadequate. For the sign only hinted at why Centralia had changed since Bukowski drew his map in the late 1930s. The sign described the symptoms but not the disease. As a lawyer, Behr would have written it differently. He would have attempted full disclosure or some semblance thereof. Visitors needed to know the truth. They needed to know that Centralia was burning and had been since 1962.

It wasn't that the town itself was on fire. Buildings weren't in flame, there were still trees and well-kept lawns lining neatly laid sidewalks. Occasionally a car would speed through, halt at the antiquated STOP sign, and turn off for the next town.

But there was a lot of smoke. Enough so that after a few hours, no matter where you stood, it pounded into your head, burning your eyes and throat. The sulphur content combined with the high level of carbon monoxide made the smoke deadly. Signs of drowsiness were cause for concern. Carbon monoxide poisoning often snuck up on its prey; it might not be noticed until the victim passed out, and the molecules of the insidious gas finally crowded out all the oxygen in the bloodstream. By then it was often too late.

Such were their working conditions.

Some of the agents—including Behr—got away with wearing carbon monoxide detectors that beeped loudly when the level got too high. Others had to wear gas masks flown in by the army from their supply depot in Camp Hill. It all depended on where you were assigned—above or below. Either way, there were additional concerns. If you were above, you had to worry about sinkholes opening beneath your feet. And below the issues were simple too: smoke and heat. Massive, indescribable heat.

Locals just called it "The Fire." In the official reports of various government agencies it was termed the "Centralia Mine Fire."

It had started in a pile of trash heaped in an open pit. The pit had been dug as an isolated strip mine by the Birtley Coal Company in 1935, then abandoned and over time used as a dump. In 1962, something or someone ignited that trash and it burned hot. Hot enough to ignite a thin outcrop of the coal seam that Birtley had been scraping off all those years ago.

The seam that caught, known as the Buck Mountain seam, undulates under the mountains throughout the fifty-odd-mile stretch of the Western Middle Anthracite field. It is one of the deeper coal beds, surfacing only occasionally at the edge of mountain ridges or on the steeper anticlines. In some places the Buck Mountain seam is up to fifteen hundred feet deep, but in Centralia it runs near the surface before dipping beneath Locust Mountain to emerge again in the valley around

Brynsville.

The seam underlies all of Centralia, as do a number of others according to the studies Agent Garcia had ordered from the Bureau of Mines. The experts—old-time firefighters, geologists from Penn State, administrators from the Bureau of Mines—believed that only the Buck Mountain seam was presently burning beneath the ground. But they also warned that the layers of rock between the various coal seams had been so scarred and fractured by the excavation of both legal and bootleg mines and endless drainage tunnels, that there was no saying how the fire might have spread or in which direction. They all had theories of course, all of them different. But there was one aspect of the fire on which they all agreed. There was simply no way to put it out.

Attempts had been made of course—water and sand pumped in, ditches dug. But nothing proved effective. All that could be hoped for was that natural barriers, most notably the water table, would eventually contain the spread. Until then the fire would run its course, killing everything above it, deadening one hundred and forty acres and consuming more than twenty-four million tons of coal in the process.

Such was the final assessment by the Bureau of Mines in a 1980 report. And a few years—and few more containment efforts later—all the relevant agencies finally agreed that it was cheaper to buy out the remaining residents and move them elsewhere than to continue fighting a fire they couldn't see.

So those willing to move were moved, and their houses were demolished behind them, as were community buildings, churches and businesses. A few proud and stubborn people stayed. About 500 at first, most of whom gradually drifted away. Their houses were all that remained of Centralia—a few scattered houses accompanied by an onion-domed church up on the hill and a fire station down in the valley. It was an eerie sight, moving in its way. And Behr did not tire of contemplating Centralia from his perch in the FBI's churchyard camp. It was better than dwelling on the fate of Kristina.

Most of these mountain towns, he thought, the ones they had been through—Shamokin, Ashland, Pottsville, Tamaqua—they all looked similar, like slices from big city ghettos dropped incongruously in the middle of wooded valleys. They had a rough look, hard sidewalks, row houses crowded on top of one another, boarded-up stores and beer bottles lining the gutters. Centralia had once been this too. No better, no richer than any other place in the coal patch.

Now it looked like a park, not unlike one of those parks that are manufactured to resemble a scene from the distant past: an authentic Dutch homestead along the Hudson river, Lincoln's log cabin, a little house on the prairie or any colonial village between Salem and Williamsburg. In all these places the visitor was greeted with more space and greener lawns than the original inhabitants had.

But Centralia had those little extras that other parks don't. Like iron vent pipes billowing smoke and ash; a gray swath of dead baked trees a hundred yards wide stretching to the southwest; burnt cracks in the sidewalk and front yards that could open beneath your feet into a mammoth sinkhole that would serve as a new chimney for some part of the fire.

It made the place special, Behr thought. Full of metaphor and pathos. All those houses destroyed, perhaps a thousand in all. A thousand living rooms, a thousand porches, each with generations of memories. Perhaps not a great number when compared to the effects of war or hurricanes or floods. But those traumas happen suddenly. These people had warning. And yet even with that warning—thirty years worth—they had stayed in their little town until the combination of smoke, heat and a distant government forced them out. There were certainly lessons to be learned from Centralia. But Behr hadn't put them all together yet. A project for the future, he thought. Or one for a seminar class. Easier to let the students do the thinking.

It was coming toward sunset, almost time for Behr to shift his seat. It had been his habit over the past five days to come to this spot on the steps of the church on the hill and look out upon the town while the sun—when visible—sank into the western basin of the valley, and the slow procession of trucks crept from the site behind the Catholic cemetery where they had located a mine entrance roughly matching that featured in Bukowski's notes.

He could tell from the speed of the approaching vehicles that they had come up empty again. The team—the FBI agents, the mineralogist, the geologist, the two ancient mine guides culled from the bars of nearby Mt. Carmel—were beginning to treat their search less like a quest and more like a job.

The first couple of days no one had slept. No one had wanted to. Most of the team spent forty-eight hours in the mines, breathing through gas masks and shining their miners' lamps through the thick smoke crawling along the shafts. Stephanos had even stuck around, donning a mask through which he bellowed his orders and descending with the agents into the gloom. But when it became apparent that things were not going to be as easy as hoped, that they weren't simply going to uncap a sealed mine shaft and discover heaps of bullion illuminating the darkness, he had returned to Washington where Garcia briefed him by cell phone every few hours and endured an inevitable chewing out for lack of progress.

Behr, too, had joined the agents in their first foray into the mine. The descent was as terrifying as anything he had ever done, excluding his landing on the Oxford Road. He lasted exactly twenty minutes.

The first few tentative steps were not—as Behr expected—into a blistering inferno, but into a cold, damp chute that angled sharply downward. Everything was wet, the walls, the floor, their clothes, their hair. Ground water dripped down the walls, coloring them red with iron pulled from the rock above. It dripped off rotting support beams low over their heads. It ran between the rails down the floor of the shaft, seeping into their shoes, chilling their toes.

The water was always cold, always dirty. But it was also welcome. Because when the tunnel dried out after a few hundred yards, the smoke closed in. And the smoke was the worst trial of all. Worse even than the heat that surely followed.

At first, Behr managed to fight off his claustrophobia. As clammy and confining as the tunnel had been, he concentrated on keeping his eyes forward, focusing on the illumination of the floodlights carried by the agents ahead. He never looked back and only occasionally dared glance at the wet slate walls and the intermittent decaying timbers which were supposed to keep the mountain above them from collapsing, from settling ever so slightly inward and snuffing them out with a dim rumble that might not even be heard by people on the surface.

Behr desperately avoided thinking about the danger, telling himself that he was a little too old, a little too tough to be afraid of the dark. Wasn't he the guy, he remembered, who on a high school dare swam Rockland harbor in winter? And the guy who not so long ago crash-landed his plane and sustained gunshot wounds and burns that were just healing now?

He *was* that guy, he knew. But he was also the guy who had hated tight places since he was kid. And in that tunnel, beneath a million tons of rock, he had to admit that he was growing increasingly frightened and deeply disoriented.

Stupidly though, he had pressed on, following the lead agents deeper into the damp hole, lost in the sulphurous fumes and flinching from the heat that blasted as if from a furnace. At one point it was simply too much; he had gone too deep. And when his fears overwhelmed his curiosity, and the dark invaded against his determination, when he grew convinced that the gas mask was, in fact, suffocating him and that the heat of the fire would turn the rock above them into lava, he had torn the mask from his head and run blindly into the smoky black.

They found him unconscious fifty yards deeper into the mine. He'd struck his head on a timber and then succumbed to the fumes.

"Let the experts handle it," Harry Zhang suggested later after fixing his head and treating him for smoke inhalation. Behr understood what he really meant. It was a nice way of saying, "*You* can't handle it," which was certainly more accurate.

He was then relegated to topside duties, which boiled down to little but helplessly watching the FBI scour miles of underground tunnel for the gold and the surrounding woodlands for Kristina. Every now and then he talked to Leone, who had to return to Philadelphia, and the state police in Harrisburg who assured him that they would certainly find Bob Silver if he was still in Pennsylvania. He attended all the group meetings of FBI and treasury agents, helped organized their shifts and interview the locals, but since he was not in an official position, there really wasn't much for him to do, and his frustration mounted.

"Dammit Cy!" he had barked at Stephanos during their midday conference call. "The waiting will kill me before the smoke does. There's got to be something I can do. I think I should go back into the mine."

But Stephanos had been adamant. He wasn't going to risk another episode.

So Behr sat on the church steps. It was day five at the mine. Five days of only limited progress and no sign of Kristina or her captors. He tried to picture what she was going through. He tried to picture her face. Was she cooperating with them? Or was she being haughty and defiant and risking her—

Garcia's voice interrupted his thoughts. "Are you going to help me with this?"

The FBI man stood at the bottom of the stone staircase of the abandoned church and pointed to the trailer sitting in the high grass of the nearby churchyard. Behr understood the gesture. There was no need for Garcia to elaborate. It was time to call Stephanos.

But today, Garcia's trepidation was unwarranted—for today, Stephanos did not yell. Quite out of character, Stephanos seemed not to be listening at all as Garcia delivered his report.

" . . . we have now wired over a mile of tunnel with heat-resistant light fixtures. But the passageways we're finding don't seem to correspond with the maps. We're not sure why. It could be the bootleg holes. They're not easy to differentiate from the company's tunnels."

Garcia paused, waiting for Stephanos to erupt or at least comment. But they heard nothing from the secretary save a short grunt. So Garcia continued. "In addition, we're encountering collapsed tunnel, sir. Some of it where the fire burned through and took out the timbers. It takes a few hours each time to clear the debris and put in new supports. I would have to say that we're making progress, but we have no way of knowing how much or how far we have to go. But it is only a matter of time. As extensive as the network of tunnels is, sir, it is *finite* and we'll get through it eventually."

Stephanos finally spoke.

"It may already be too late."

Behr and Garcia exchanged a startled look. Their leader's voice sounded atypically weak.

"Come again," Behr said.

"I guess you haven't heard, guys. The Chinese Foreign Ministry held a press conference an hour ago, a joint press conference with the Philippine president and some members of his cabinet. They announced their withdrawal—that's both China and the Philippines—from AS-EAN and the formation of a new treaty organization to be called the Eastern Pacific Interdependence Compact, or EPIC for short. You should've seen the shit-eating grins on the Chinese delegation, even though it's just the Philippines they've signed up so far. We haven't seen the treaty yet, but from what we're hearing in the embassies, the Chinese have crafted an economic block like the EC's and a security block like NATO's. It's exactly what your friend Kristina said it would be. A package deal combining economic and military cooperation. They have to sign on for the whole package, and it's being offered to every country within a thousand miles of the Chinese border. Even India and Pakistan. Only the Filipinos have said yes so far. But no one has said no. And the way things are going with the currency markets, most of these countries seem receptive though dubious about the mechanism."

"What about our markets—how are they reacting?" Behr asked.

"As you might expect, they're tanking. Tanking further, I should say. Our exchanges were already closed when the news hit. But on Globex and Instinet and the other electronic exchanges, we're looking at October 1929. If the markets open tomorrow at the prices being quoted now, it would mean three thousand points on the Dow at the opening bell. And that's nothing compared to the hit our bonds are going take. It's bad news for the U.S. Treasury. I'm not going to be able to *give* a thirty-year note away."

"How can the Chinese do this without the gold?"

"I don't know, Behr. I'm sure that the Chinese don't have enough in their treasury right now to guaranty the obligations of all of East Asia. But they certainly have enough to cover the Philippines and thereby bring some legitimacy to the proposed structure. And Philippine markets, by the way, are going through the roof. They love the deal. Can you believe it? These are the same fucking people who called *us* imperialists."

Garcia and Behr thought they might be in for a lecture, but suddenly Stephanos cut it short. "Gentleman, it is high time for all of us to get back to work. You know what to do. I'll check in later. Around midnight. I don't think I'll be getting much sleep tonight."

Stephanos hung up. Garcia and Behr stared at the dead phone. Stephanos had said to get back to work, but what, exactly, was it that he wanted them to do?

After a few minutes it became clear that Behr and Garcia couldn't even agree on the priorities.

It made sense, of course, to get back in the mine. This was Garcia's preference—to find the gold, if it existed at all, and cut the Chinese off at the knees. But Behr thought it made more sense to divert all their resources to finding Kristina and the Chinese agents. Because with their testimony, or even just Kristina's, they could undermine the Chinese effort by simply disclosing that it rested on the collateral security of gold reserves that China didn't yet have. That the whole thing was based on five thousand tons of gold that hadn't seen Chinese soil in sixty years and was presumed lost.

The two men, joined now by Agent Volkmer, carried their argument from the trailer and back to the church with its commanding view of the valley and the setting sun. It was a good place to think. A good place to map out a strategy that might save the country from financial collapse and perhaps bring Kristina back to Behr and her father in one piece.

"I still think that Kristina's the priority," Behr insisted as they got to the top of the stairs.

Garcia shook his head. "I don't know, man. There's a lot of tunnel down there. I gotta make the effort."

"Listen." Behr turned to Garcia as they reached the top. He gently gripped the big agent's shoulders for emphasis. "This goes beyond my feelings for the woman. We . . . you, the government, you owe her. And moreover, you *need* her. If you put her on TV and let her tell her story, what do think the Japanese response is going to be, huh? I'll bet they're going to think twice about signing on to this EPIC thing."

"I still don't know," Garcia said after a moment.

Volkmer added, "Yeah, what's Stephanos going say?"

"He'll understand!" Behr fixed them each, in turn, with a good stare. "It's the logical choice. You go after the thing you *know* has to be around somewhere rather than the thing that just *might* be."

"I hear you Behr, it's just that . . . what is it?" Garcia turned to follow Behr's curious stare into the valley. Nothing seemed amiss. It all looked much as it had five minutes earlier, just a little darker.

Behr didn't answer.

"Come on, Behr, what are you looking at?" Garcia prodded, "You look like you've seen a UFO."

"Look over there." Behr pointed vaguely in the direction of the old Catholic cemetery near where the fire had started in '62. "Does anything seem strange to you?"

The agents looked down at the cemetery, at the great gray ditch full of dead trees and open fissures running from its southern boundary down the hill along Route 61, at the shuttered corner store. and a lone, brave man on a small lawn tractor. "No," said Garcia, "it looks like a normal day in Centralia."

"Except that it's not. Look directly at the cemetery, *that's* what's different."

Garcia peered closer. "You mean that we can see it at all!"

Behr turned back with a sharp look in his eyes. "Precisely. The vent pipe in that cemetery billows constantly. I've been looking at it for five days. From up here, depending on the wind, the view is usually obscured. But anthracite burns at a steady rate, and there is no reason for the vent to stop blowing unless the fire in that spot died or unless someone capped it."

Garcia looked thoughtful.

Volkmer looked angry. "Gentlemen, I can tell you right now that we didn't cap that vent today."

Behr looked between the two men. "So who did, my friends? Who capped that vent when the FBI wasn't looking?"

28

Since following the Americans to this strange town, they had been working at night. Biding their time each day in a discreet mountain camp until Feng told them that the same number of FBI and Treasury personnel had left the mine that day as had entered it. Then they would quietly descend through the woods, by a different path each time, until they emerged at the bootleg mine entrance they had discovered with the help of the man who dug it. He hadn't wanted to talk at first. But a sharp knife positioned beneath a fat chin helped him quickly admit the theft of coal from his erstwhile employer and the location of his crime.

The shaft of the bootleg mine was narrow—barely the width of a man, slippery and so steep and rough-hewn that any descent by foot or rope was simply impossible.

One of the younger agents, an epicene student originally conscripted for intelligence gathering at Cal Tech, devised a type of sled to which they were each, in turn, strapped with their equipment. This sled then skittered perilously down the incline before coming to rest on the tunnel floor one hundred feet below. The last man left on the surface would hoist the sled back, use it to cap the hole and then cover it with leaves and dirt before concealing himself where he was able.

Everything about the process required nerves of steel. From the clattering descent down the rough slope to the dark hunt through the tunnels.

But no one complained. No one dared, though Jin Qing could see the trepidation in the increasingly pale faces of her team. They just couldn't get used to it. Some got nervous being dropped in the hole. Others got spooked in the tunnels where the FBI shut down their lights at night. And everyone grew edgy when struck by the recurring heat and caustic smoke which had them clawing for their gas masks—masks that Feng had stolen right from the Americans' camp—and retreating up the tunnel until someone could assess the extent of the hazard ahead.

Still they pushed ahead, following a strategy devised by Jin Qing after close observation of the route taken by the FBI. There was no point, Jin Qing reasoned, in retracing the course of the FBI through the dark maze. Particularly since they stuck to the main tunnels and emerged empty-handed day after day. Better, she thought, to explore the drainage tunnels, the little bootleg shafts, the side tunnels which followed splits in the seam before they petered out. It was in these areas that things would have stayed hidden all these years. It seemed odd to her that the FBI kept pushing through the largest tunnels first, blindly insistent that bigger is better. Unless, of course, they knew something she didn't.

She had raised the issue with Feng.

"Do you think they have a map?" she asked.

Feng shrugged. "They act like people who know where they are going," he replied and pointed to the straight line of newly hung lightbulbs stretching into the darkness.

In the first days there had been doubt, both in her mind and in the faces of her team. Doubt about their direction and the feasibility of the mission, doubt which was born in reality but which had, nevertheless, easily dissipated tonight. For tonight was different.

Tonight they knew that the FBI team had no idea where they were going, even if they did have a map. Because the FBI's small army had pushed right by it. They had cleared a small cave-in, reinforced the timbers and strung their lights right past the fifty-foot depression from which Jin Qing had emerged to tell the small assembly of Chinese faces that she had found it. She had found her nation's lost gold.

☆ ☆ ☆

"Quickly now," Jin Qing whispered to the crew who seemed somewhat mystified by her lack of glee until they saw Jin Qing's discovery for themselves.

She could see how the Americans—in their typically sloppy manner—had missed it. They were still looking for neatly stacked twenty-eight-pound gold bars. But the gold didn't look like that anymore. By tucking it down a side tunnel against the edge of a coal-seam, Ambrose had put the gold directly in the path of the mine fire. And at some point in the last thirty years, the fire had indeed passed right through it, burning the wood crates, cracking the marble slabs and melting the gold into a great blackened mass that seeped deep into the fissures and holes left by the coal as it burned away.

It simply bore no resemblance to what the Americans were seeking. They were looking for something lustrous. But the grand wealth of imperial China was not golden any more. On its surface it was black, irregular, lumpy. Almost indistinguishable from the rock to which it had somehow fused in the intense heat of the fire.

Jin Qing had found it by luck when her flashlight fell and knocked loose a corner of its thick charcoal skin. Picking up the light revealed a dim glint of something other than the flinty shale and granite with which they had grown so familiar. And then the whole picture became instantly clear to her, so that she didn't know whether to laugh or cry, to celebrate or concede defeat and withdraw to the safe house in New York and call in her resignation.

The rest of the team, however, were unanimously disappointed when they were informed.

Even Kristina appeared sad despite her attempts to mask it with some unexplained jibe about her grandfather's revolution now, finally, being complete.

"What do you mean by that?" Jin Qing asked her.

Kristina only shrugged. The gesture annoyed Jin Qing to no end. The girl was really growing quite difficult, her escape attempts and insolent behavior diverting the team's attention from the mission ahead. And diversions where the last thing they needed. Speed was essential. Especially with the Americans hovering so very close.

Jin Qing turned away from Kristina to address the team she had circled around her. "We have two immediate tasks ahead. Because there is no way for us to excavate this mess underneath the Americans' noses, our first task is to conceal the gold without drawing attention to this little side tunnel. Second, as always, we must exit quietly without leaving even a hint we were here or where our attention was concentrated. Is that clear?"

Nods all around.

"Good. Now who has suggestions as to the concealment of the gold?"

☆ ☆ ☆

Silver could see them just ahead, gathered in a circle, their flashlights on the floor at their feet. At his own feet lay the guard whose head he had just knocked in. *His* slanted eyes would always stay shut, the lawyer thought. Then he giggled in spite of their proximity, in spite of the absolute need to stay silent.

Silver pushed himself farther into the small recess. It smelled like hay. And wooden gates made it feel like a stable, though a shallow one.

He hadn't heard what they were saying—they must be whispering—but their huddle was breaking up now. Some of the little spies were picking up rock and debris and hauling it down into some tunnel that lay just out of his sight. Another guy was walking slowly up the tunnel, back toward him, intently studying the ceiling.

Silver thought he might have to deal with this one, and in preparation he picked up the same rock with which he had felled the other guard. It was still sticky with blood.

But the Chinaman stopped, head still craned upwards. Apparently he had found what he was looking for. Silver watched the man reach into a shoulder bag and withdraw something like a towel which he stuffed into a hole Silver hadn't previously noticed in the roof of the tunnel. The man studied his work momentarily and then moved, eyes still glued to the ceiling. He passed Silver without a word, reached into his bag and removed another towel which he stuck up another hole twenty yards farther on.

The man's actions confirmed it. The Chinese had found it before the G-men had. Exactly as Silver hoped. And blocking the vents was a clever idea. This part of the tunnel would slowly fill with smoke, making it even harder for the chumps upstairs to see their way through, to see the gold. The only danger was that someone might question the lack of smoke coming from certain vents. But he discounted the danger. Who would notice that? Silver knew law enforcement types, they just weren't that smart or observant.

The vent blocker was safely past. Silver ventured farther from his hole. The group ahead wasn't so big after all. Kristina Zhang was there—still pretty tasty—and a handful of worker drones taking orders from a thin, sinewy woman with an air of command that brought on fantasies of Nina Kracken.

He first noticed her during the crazy shootout by the gas station. He had only stopped to fill up the ever-thirsty Range Rover and been surprised to see Kristina Zhang, of all people, making a phone call from the office. He had made an impetuous move, hoping she would give him some leverage, then been more surprised when Chinese agents spilled down the hill and from a nearby van.

The thin woman had gotten out of the van too and assumed immediate command, her every gesture calculated and efficient. Only once did she appear flustered during that episode, and it struck Silver as strange. Strange that a woman who showed zero emotion at the injuries Silver had caused to her own men should suddenly pale when he turned the gun on Kristina Zhang, an ostensible stranger—a prisoner to whom she owed nothing. Why should the woman care? Could the Zhang girl be that valuable?

Silver had been unable to pursue the question after one of the little fucks had put a bullet in his arm, forcing him to flee.

He had stayed ahead of them since then, even finding their little camp on the mountain as he wandered in search of a quiet spot for himself. And tonight he followed them here, a gut feeling telling him to stay close to these people, people whose moves he had learned to anticipate since the day they initially approached him in the guise of Jasmine Investments.

But watching the woman as she now directed the concealment efforts of her crew, Silver was reminded of what he had seen at the gas station, of the sudden concern which creased her poker face that day. She had given something away, something which Silver could place in his assets column. He would use that against her should it prove necessary.

For a quick second the woman raised her head; Silver could see her sharp features caught in the beam of a flashlight. She seemed to look right at him. Could she see him? Probably not, she was looking from light into darkness. But still he crept back into the recess without a sound. After all, he thought with a wry smile, the best lawyers should remain invisible to their clients.

☆ ☆ ☆

Jin Qing had learned to trust those instincts that told her danger was close. She felt it was time to move. She looked around the entrance to the side tunnel where the gold lay, now buried under rubble, and donned her gas mask against the thickening smoke.

Her team had done well. There was nothing to testify to their presence except the towels stuck high in the vents. And even if those were discovered, she had sent the men far down the tunnels in all directions so that no one vent gave away the locus of their interest.

She was confident that the gold would not be discovered by the Americans, but she still felt the strange foreboding. She looked into the darkness again where the tunnel descended deeper into the mountain and back toward the bootleg hole half a mile up the hill.

Something was there, she could sense it. The thin black hairs on her arms were electrified to its lurking presence. Was it the Americans? She wondered. Wouldn't they make much more noise?

A figure emerged from the darkness. Jin Qing drew her gun.

It was Lao Han, the student. Back from stuffing vents.

"Madam Jin," he said quickly. Why was the man out of breath? "Madam Jin, I have bad news."

"Proceed."

"Our entrance was open, the cover off. There was no sign of the guard and the Americans . . ."

The boy was gasping now. Jin Qing handed him a mask.

"What about the Americans?"

"The Americans are entering the mine again!"

"Through our opening?"

"No, through theirs. I saw them in the distance gathering at the entrance with lights. I ran back as soon as I saw!"

☆ ☆ ☆

Bob Silver was choking. The smoke in the tunnel had thickened much quicker than he'd anticipated. He figured he didn't have long here, that he better get out soon or he was going to die in this dark hole. And why stay? He knew now where the Chinese were digging, and he could always come back. Maybe even as an FBI agent. Who could tell with a gas mask on?

Silver crouched close to the floor sucking in the remaining fresh air. He would have to run back the way he came, following the route the Chinese had showed him. The bootleg shaft was some distance away—but if he ran?

Where were the Chinese? The problem suddenly occurred to him. He hadn't kept track of them all. Some had gone back up the tunnel, stuffing the vents. But had they returned?

It wasn't like him to forget. It must be the smoke. Distracting him. Throwing him off. If they were between him and the exit . . . then . . . then . . .

Silver's expression turned hard. Then they would just have to defend themselves, he thought. *He* was going to get out even if he had to go through them to do it. He had his gun. He had the rock, still matted with the blood and hair of the last guy who got in his way. It was they who should be worried. Watch your back, he said silently to his foes, you don't want to end up like Lazlo now? Or Ambrose Bukowski?

Silver touched the rock. Touched the gun in the pocket of his windbreaker. He felt secure again. He could leave now. It was time to make his move.

At the head of the side tunnel, he could just see the small group with their gas masks on. They seemed to be mobilizing. Putting things in backpacks. He would have to stay ahead of this group too. He might be able to take out one or two agents ahead of him, but he couldn't take them all on. Not in this state. Not with the smoke filling his lungs.

Then he remembered it. Oh yes! That would definitely help him now. Just when he needed it. A little coke. It would just take a second. And the Chinese weren't moving yet.

Silver reached into his wallet to remove the small triangle of folded magazine paper. He opened it delicately. Not much left.

The smoke was low now, only a foot or two off the floor of the tunnel. Silver put the packet of coke on the ground and kneeled over it. He rolled a dollar bill into a tight tube and lowered his face directly above the hard slate. In the dim light of the Chinese flashlights, the white cocaine made a vivid contrast against the wet black rock, the two extremes separated only by the glossy paper ripped from a magazine. A fashion magazine, he guessed. He could just make out the thin face and small breasts of an emaciated model peeking from beneath the snowy powder. She was pretty, he thought. And young. Just what he wanted. Just what he could buy for himself when he got out with the prize.

The footsteps startled him just as he finished. He hadn't heard the approach of those sneaky, slippered feet. But he heard them now. Saw them too. Passing right by his little alcove in the rock, trapping him.

His heart echoed in his chest, pounding with the drug, screaming for air. Could they hear it too? Could they hear his body rebel against the acrid smoke and bitter narcotic?

It was no use. He couldn't wait. Hesitation meant death.

He studied the feet coming down through the haze, passing inches before his nose. Big, small, slippers, slippers and . . . there . . . just what he needed . . . just in time . . .bright, white American sneakers.

Bob Silver drew his gun and leapt for those sneakers.

☆ ☆ ☆

Jin Qing caught the movement behind her. Saw a corner of the shadow as it detached itself from the wall of the tunnel and grabbed another shadow to form one. She couldn't distinguish the figures in the smoke. She raised her flashlight, but the beams reflected back harshly, blinding her momentarily. Who had been behind her. Just Feng, wasn't it?

No! Not just Feng. Feng was assigned to watch Kristina.

Kristina was back there too. Only a few feet away but indistinguishable in the fog. She heard a whisper. In Chinese. It was Feng telling her to shoot. To aim high.

Shoot at what, Feng? Who? She just couldn't see.

Jin Qing pressed herself against the wall. She shut off the flashlight as the shadow moved closer. Feng was backlighting the figure for her now. Not risking a shot himself without orders, lest he hit his boss and thereby jeopardize his career. Smart Feng, very smart.

Whoever it was, Jin Qing knew, he had gotten hold of Kristina. That much she could see. The outline of the two heads close together. The double body and the tangle of legs. The form was saying something now. Speaking in a sort of a croak. Speaking in English. A man's voice. Hoarse and insistent.

"I've got the girl!"

Jin Qing stayed silent.

"I've got the girl. Now let me through."

Again Jin Qing did not respond, and she made no move toward the approaching figure. She could see him more clearly now, could hear him coughing.

"You think I'm fucking kidding here. I'll pop her just like I did her brother."

The figure stopped. Jin Qing peered through the cloud, momentarily weakened by the man's words. It was the lawyer—it had to be—that odious lawyer, and *he* had killed Sam. It wasn't Helen after all.

Now she saw arms and elbows moving. And there was something about the shape of his head.

That was it—he had taken Kristina's mask! She heard her daughter gasp, heard the hacking cough as the thick sulphur burned into her young lungs. It wouldn't do to wait. The smoke was too thick. How long could Kristina last? Not more than a minute or two. And she certainly wouldn't make it out of the tunnel. Not as the man's captive; not without a mask.

Jin Qing wondered how far back Feng was; if he could see or if the light reflecting off the smoke was blinding him to the outlines ahead.

The figures moved closer. She had them in her sights. A few more feet and she could take him.

Just a few more feet and she could put a bullet right in the reptile's head.

Feng's voice, high and insistent, came to her through the smoke.

"Madam, you must not shoot! I take it back. The Americans, they will hear us if we shoot!"

Feng was correct, of course. She realized that right away. The Americans were probably halfway into the tunnel by now and pushing toward them. And while a gunshot might kill Kristina's captor, it would also kill any confusion the Americans had as to which tunnel to take. Jin Qing's location would be compromised as would the gold's.

It was a weighty consideration. A shot fired now would save her daughter.

But it would also mean the end of the mission.

29

Walls bulging in, the ceiling pressing lower, it almost looked like the tunnel was breathing or digesting him in the peristaltic waves of the esophagus. He could hear it too. Hear the rhythmic contractions as the tube tried to swallow him. Sucking him deeper into the mountain with a steady slurp.

Or was that just his heart he heard, the beats echoing against his eardrums inside the gas mask?

Harry Zhang was saying something to him now, shaking him by the shoulders.

"You all right? Try to think about something else. And for God's sake don't forget to breathe!"

Behr nodded, steadied himself on the doctor's arm. His head cleared a little and he realized that he *had* been holding his breath. He had almost passed out. Stephanos had been right to doubt him, and wise to send Harry along when Behr insisted on entering the mine.

Behr made it much farther than last time—almost a mile into the mountain to a crossroads where three tunnels shot out from this one spot and ran roughly parallel into the distance. All three had been explored by Garcia's team at one time, but not to their ends. And the geologist, the old miner and the two agents crouched over the map on the floor couldn't figure out to which of the three tnnels the above-ground vents belonged.

Stephanos was growing impatient with them, stamping his feet occasionally and giving off a slew of curses. To Behr he looked like a prize bull eyeing a cowardly matador. The man's irritation was understandable. Just two hours ago the secretary had been in D.C., but at the call from Garcia, he had scrambled into the helicopter and arrived at the head of the mine where he found his team gathering their equipment under a blaze of halogen. He greeted them in a foul temper for during the course of his flight north he learned that Thailand too had fallen sway to the Chinese pact. And with the Thais gone, the neighboring Burmese and Cambodians were soon to follow.

They were stumped now by the geography of the mine. The problem lay in the air shafts and vents which were indistinguishable from above but made all the difference when studying the old maps. This was because the air shafts were original to the mine and appeared on the maps. But the vents were bored later to let out the smoke and cool the tunnels before all the remaining coal dried into tinder. And while the airshafts had been dug straight down to provide air to the miners and drain flammable gasses, the vents were drilled at angles from convenient spots on the surface directly into the fire so that their pattern on the surface did not correspond to the course of the tunnels underground.

Of course, some correlation had to exist. And this is what they were looking for in the map laid out on the floor as Stephanos got increasingly irate and Behr desperately tried to think of anything but the weight of the mountain over his head, the crush of their bodies in the constricted space and the smoke growing slowly thicker around them.

Behr finally latched onto a thought to distract him; it ran to metaphor, and he addressed it to Harry Zhang who was getting increasingly edgy as well and might have use for a philosophical distraction.

"Think about this," he said, "think about the allegorical value of this scene. I bet Kristina could paint it—East meets West," Behr balled his fists and them brought them together slowly, "in a confrontation over wealth. Tremendous wealth. Wealth that will define who is to lead in the next century."

"Shut up, will you!"

It was Stephanos. He had a hand raised against Behr's continuing the lecture. But Behr would not be put off. A good thought bears mentioning. And, more importantly, talking kept down the nausea.

"Come on, Cyril, it's pretty amazing. Think about it."

Stephanos pretended to be busy watching the men with the map, but Harry Zhang appeared interested. So Behr continued.

"Think about this place, the battlefield where the ultimate confrontation is to take place. It's a smoldering ruin. An environmental disaster area. A sorry testament to our past and a dire portent of China's future. But it's not just any disaster area. No, it's a place that serves as a kind of pressure cooker too, superheating the showdown, but doing it slowly. Cooking it over the span of three decades until it's ready to explode.

"Admit it, buddy." Behr nudged Stephanos in the shoulder. "Admit that you see the symbolic value of this too."

The treasury secretary studied his old friend. "I'll admit nothing," he said through his mask after a short time, "except that the situation is indeed dire. Now," he held up a warning finger, "please, I'm asking you, don't make me sorry I brought you along."

Stephanos turned his back on them now, leaving Behr a view of the exposed back of the big man's head where the mask didn't reach.

Behr could see the tension there, the beads of sweat and the thick veins bursting from the bald pate. Behr felt instantly small, his concerns over one human life—Kristina's—suddenly minimized by the realization that the man before him had the weight of the world on his shoulders. Continents lined up for war, and his power to arrest the developing conflict no longer lay in high-level diplomacy or financial manipulation but somewhere at the bottom of a coal mine in Centralia, Pennsylvania.

Behr's heart went out to the man. And with it drained his claustrophobia. Somehow Behr was strengthening under the pressure, feeling more determined. He knew his goal was more complicated now. He had to undertake more than the rescue of Kristina—as much as that mattered to him. Nothing would be the same if they failed to stop the Chinese. A huge block would form in the East and the United States would be forever squeezed between it and Europe with financial ruin and war as an inevitable consequence.

Behr looked over the team in the mine to whom this mission was entrusted. There were seven of them total, with only four guns between the three FBI agents and Stephanos. It was up to them now—this small group assembled around the map at the tunnels' crossroad—to follow the trail of vents. A narrow lead, certainly, but as much as they were likely to get. So all they had to do was pick the right tunnel. Pick the right tunnel or—

"What if we split up?" Behr said from the back. "Send three people down one tunnel and two down each of the others?"

Stephanos turned around with an instant no. "Too dangerous, not enough firepower."

"Then let's call in more people! You've got thirty agents upstairs between FBI and Treasury."

Garcia shook his head.

"Everyone upstairs has been assigned—they're scouring the town and surrounding area. They've got miles to cover. Remember, we're the ones on the goose-chase here."

Behr hadn't expected opposition from Garcia. But another idea came quickly.

"Then what if we—"

It stopped him in midsentence. Behr looked to Stephanos and Garcia, who stood suddenly alert and dead still. Clearly they'd heard it too.

It was muffled certainly. And perhaps somewhat distant. But the sound was unmistakable to anyone who'd heard it before. An explosive crack. A gunshot resonating from the tunnel on the left, the smallest of the three.

In an instant they had four guns drawn, and the chain of lights down the side-tunnel switched on. Everyone crowded for the tunnel entrance. But Stephanos blocked them.

"Sorry, boys, but this is government personnel only. You," Stephanos pointed two fingers at the geologist and the old miner from Mt. Carmel, "head back to the surface and call in support, and you two," he pointed to Behr and Harry, "stay right here."

"Fuck that," Behr said fiercely, "I'm going!"

"Me, too," Harry Zhang echoed. "It's my daughter they have. And you have other priorities."

Stephanos looked the men over, sighed audibly into his gas mask, then relented.

"All right, just remember to stay back, and let these guys do their jobs. Understand?"

They mumbled an assent, and the party made its way into the entrance as quietly as the crushed rock beneath their feet would allow. But they were far from silent—they crunched with every footfall. In a whisper Stephanos ordered them out of their boots, and the men proceeded over the jagged surface in their socks, in great pain but deadly quiet.

They walked slowly and silently for some time. Every few yards they would stop to carefully examine their surroundings. It wasn't easy to gauge where they were or where someone might be hiding. Visibility was reduced, the smoke thicker than it had been at the crossroads. It was Behr who suddenly realized that it was in *this* tunnel where the vents must be blocked. He looked up and noticed—just a few yards ahead—a different shade of white offset against the coal smoke. It was hanging from the ceiling and as he pulled it out he saw it was a towel. A thick bath towel with Marriott Courtyard emblazoned across it.

He waved it in front of Stephanos.

"I see it; they steal towels too," said Stephanos without a laugh, then ordered the unblocking of every vent they passed.

Behr now expected to find more evidence, to feel like they were closing in. But he was disappointed for, excepting the towels in every vent and airshaft, they saw no trace of anyone's passage through this tunnel. No one but Garcia's team in the days before. No sign of something heavy being moved. No sign of sandwiches being eaten, wrappers or soda cans discarded. The Chinese, if they were here, had been careful. Maybe even covered their tracks. And in the numerous alcoves and side tunnels and seam excavations, Behr thought their team might just have passed them by. The Chinese could very well be running out the other end while Behr and Stephanos, Harry Zhang and three FBI agents suffocated slowly as they delved farther underground.

Behr felt the soreness returning to his ribs and shoulder where the wounds from Maryland had still not healed. Fatigue made the pain worse, he knew. And it seemed to be affecting Stephanos as well.

The big man was visibly slower. He seemed to have grown weak through the shoulders, his head was sagging. Stephanos was not a young man, after all, and his life had not been easy. Fit as he was, this hike and the pressure were taking their toll. Behr looked down and saw that the man's socks were stained dark with blood, likely cut against the sharp shale scattered beneath them. A quick glance showed Behr that his own feet were bloody too.

And still they walked, and stopped and examined each opening in the wall of the tunnel to see if it might lead to treasure or hide its seekers. Still they bled through their socks and weakened in the smoke which did grow thinner but not so fast that they could see more than a few feet ahead under the clouded string of lights or breathe without masks.

An hour must have passed before Stephanos finally called a halt and slumped against the wall. Harry Zhang rushed over to him, checking his pulse and as much of his eyes as were visible through the plastic lenses of the mask.

"He needs oxygen," Harry declared somewhat too loudly for Stephanos who shushed him with a stern finger.

"I'm not dead yet," the secretary whispered. "Just give me a second."

Everyone took the opportunity to rest, to massage their wounded feet and stretch their backs. For though the tunnel was just tall enough for a man to stand in, they had all walked in a crouch.

Garcia, dank with sweat, wet hair peeking from the edges of the mask, slipped down the wall next to Behr. The FBI man had suffered a gash in the bottom of his foot and was about to tear off a strip of cloth from his shirt to bind it when Behr stopped him.

Garcia looked up. "You're right," he whispered, "too much noise."

But Behr hadn't considered that. He was too busy studying the ground opposite Garcia. The tunnel widened there, forming a kind of shallow recess where someone long ago had built rough wooden rails, like a fence or a stall. And just visible on the edge of the recess was something that Behr knew none of them had dropped. But he had to ask the question anyway.

"Is that yours?" he asked of Garcia, pointing to the ground a few feet across from them.

Garcia studied the item and silently turned to Behr with a meaningful look.

The others had heard the question and looked into the recess too. Heads were shaking all around. It didn't belong to any of them. None of them had dropped a rolled dollar bill onto the tunnel floor.

☆ ☆ ☆

She could hear them crawling around up there, hear them coughing and sputtering and giving themselves away. If only she knew their numbers, their firepower. She wouldn't hesitate to fight them. Kill them where they sat.

She badly wanted to strike. She had the element of surprise. They had passed directly by the chute where they were hiding, the chute with the gold, and stopped slightly farther on. They wouldn't expect her to come from behind. With her aim and Feng's knife . . .

But the smoke was clearing in this part of the tunnel. If she were to hit them, she would have to do it soon while the visibility was still obscured. Otherwise the surprise was lost; they would see her coming and she would be dead. And in death she could accomplish nothing.

Feng gestured, trying to get her attention. They leaned toward each other, bent low over the corpse of the lawyer stretched between them.

"Madam Jin," he whispered so softly she could barely hear, "I think that we should abandon the gold for now."

What did he mean by that?

"Abandon it to the Americans?" she hissed. "Do you know what's at stake?"

"No, not entirely. But think, Madam Jin, the gold is hidden very well. They may never find it. But if they find us, especially now, they will surely know where it is!"

"So what do you propose?"

"That after they continue on, we run the way they came. We aim for their entrance."

"And if it is blocked? If the combined might of the Federal Bureau of Investigation is standing in front of that hole in the ground, then what?"

Feng lowered his eyes. "Then we die, Madam Jin, or we are captured. For which eventuality we, of course, have the capsules. Either way the Americans will not discover the location of the gold. It will be still be ours to extract when we are able."

Jin Qing did not respond for a moment. She could see where Feng was going. But how much had he really guessed? How much had she revealed with that shot in the tunnel above?

"Madam, we must decide soon! Is it the others you are worried about? Don't be. I checked that each one was supplied with a capsule before we departed this evening, as you instructed. I believe they are all willing to use it. If any are captured, one bite on the cyanide and the secret is safe."

Feng paused. Studying her closely. He seemed suddenly too keen. It wasn't like him to discuss strategy. What was he up to?

She couldn't see his hands—that made her nervous—and his eyes gave nothing away.

"There is only one problem," he continued. "*One* of us does not have the capsule. One who couldn't be trusted even if she did. She will give away the location to the Americans, yes? You must agree, Minister, her usefulness is at an end."

It was almost black at the bottom of the chute. A thin beam of light from the tunnel high above reflected off the walls, allowing her to see Feng's eyes boring into her. She saw that he had guessed it. Perhaps not all but enough to know that Jin Qing was ready to jeopardize the mission for Kristina's safety, that Jin Qing had done so already.

Now Feng was just making sure, asking her for permission to kill Kristina right here in front of her. Permission, which if not granted, would mean that Jin Qing was herself compromised and had to be eliminated.

She couldn't fault the man for baiting the trap this way. It was the right thing for Feng to do. Clearly, she had trained him well, and he had learned by her example that one must question those superiors who got in the way of the nation's interest. And do it slyly so they might not know it was being done.

Jin Qing admired the irony: here was her own tactic being successfully used against her for the first time in her career. She was being questioned by an underling, and it was the most dangerous one she knew.

Jin Qing looked over to the outline of Kristina in the darkness. She'd been quiet since the incident above, and strangely compliant, not arguing when they turned back and headed into the chute. Kristina could easily cry out now and give their position away. But she held her tongue. It could just be the paralysis of fright, but Jin Qing thought it might be something else, something akin to gratitude for killing the man who had caused Kristina such pain, who had murdered Sam so coldly just two months before.

Jin Qing was increasingly impressed by her daughter, proud of her strength and determination, her intellectual gifts. She was striking to look at too, and even now, with all she had been put through, she held herself well, not once showing a sign of weakness to her captors.

So would it help if Kristina knew? Before it was too late?

Jin Qing had considered telling her a thousand times—simply stepping forward and saying, I am your mother, the one who left you and Sam playing on the kitchen floor that day. Can you forgive me, daughter? Can you understand that I was forced to abandon you when the order was given by my superiors in Beijing? And that while I was under orders, it was still my choice to obey? And that I would give anything now to have chosen the other way—to have your childhood back?

She hadn't done it. She hadn't confronted Kristina or even hinted at the knowledge. It wasn't for lack of nerve, she thought, rather it was a considered conclusion as to the best course. For Kristina was a strong woman, in part, because she was confident of who she was. She had grown up without a mother and taught herself how to survive that way. Kristina had built defenses and mechanisms for interacting with the world that might all be destroyed if Jin Qing rocked the foundation. Silence was the one gift she could give her daughter now.

That and killing Feng.

Jin Qing's eyes flickered over to where the Mongol sat; she reached behind her, but Feng anticipated the move.

His knife was drawn even as she found the handle of the gun; he slashed at her, stretching far over Silver's body to do so.

The blade cut deeply into her forearm, then slid over her chest. But Jin Qing was delighted.

Feng's was a bad move, a combat error, for it put him far off-balance.

She grabbed at Feng's wrist with both hands—blood spurted from her wounds, but she kept her hold and used the leverage of the dead lawyer's body. And as she pulled him forward over the corpse she gracefully pivoted around behind him, released her hold, drew the gun and fired directly into the back of the man's dark skull. Feng died instantly, and with him the dream of a new China.

☆ ☆ ☆

They surrendered without a fight. Six people emerged from the tunnel one hundred feet behind them with their hands raised.

On Garcia's orders no one approached them before they had all lined up facing the wall. Then slowly—Garcia in the lead and guns sighted through the smoke—the agents made their way down the tunnel toward the six.

Despite the occlusion, they could see that two of the figures were women. One of them quite small and bleeding heavily from a wound in her arm and less so from the chest. The other figure, Behr knew, was Kristina. He would recognize her body anywhere, even in a coal mine. Behr's heart flooded with love and relief. She appeared unharmed.

"Son of bitch!" Stephanos exclaimed as they grew close., "They're wearing our masks."

It was true. Behr laughed out loud as he saw that each of the six was wearing a U.S. Army standard issue gas mask identical to his own.

"Some chutzpah, don't you think?" Stephanos said, addressing the question to him. Behr only smiled and made his way directly to Kristina, Harry Zhang close on his heels.

It felt good to hold her again. Better than he had ever imagined. She hugged him tightly and then gave a little cry as she noticed her father standing behind him.

Through the mask, amidst the fumes, they filled each other in. Behr noticed the older woman watching intently but forgot all about it when Garcia poked his head out of the chute.

"Hey, I think you all should see this!"

Kristina stayed in the tunnel with her father while Behr and Stephanos followed Garcia down the chute where the coal seam had burned out. When they got to the bottom they immediately focused on the two bodies, one on top of the other, a Chinese national and Bob Silver, still recognizable despite the absence of half his face.

But Garcia was not interested in the bodies, he was pointing at something else.

"Over here, gentlemen."

They followed the man into a narrow passageway filled with boulders, old timbers and rubble. They found him squatting in a far corner; he was shining his light directly on the ground, a spot that seemed oddly smooth compared to the jagged shale that had marked their passage thus far.

Garcia drew his gun out by the barrel, looked up smiling, then smashed the grip into the floor before him. It left a dent. A very deep dent.

They were congratulating Garcia as they emerged from the chute, clapping him on the back. The nature of their discovery obvious to everyone in the tunnel.

A harsh voice, authoritative and strangely plaintive, now cut through their revelry. "That gold is the property of the People's Republic of China, which hereby states its claim. You have no right to it."

Kristina filled them in. "Her name is Jin Qing. She's the leader."

Stephanos eyed the woman, his head tilted back. "So you say, sister. But that gold is on U.S. soil. Pretty deep in U.S. soil, I must say."

"We demand its return!"

"You can demand all you want—"

"This will be addressed at the *highest* levels. I'm sure that you would not want to risk—"

"Do whatever you want, Ms. Qing. I'm pretty high-level, Secretary of the Treasury, but you can complain to the President. Even sue us if you want."

"That is precisely what we will do."

This threat came from a thin Chinese at the end whose hands were still pressed against the wall as Garcia patted him down. "I have studied your laws. You have no right to detain property that belongs to another. We can sue you for . . . *conversion* you call it. And we will win."

Jin Qing now took up the argument, "If you are, as you so often boast, a nation of laws, then you will be forced to deal with our claim. And the due process of your laws, when all is said and done, will deliver us our gold. Even if it takes time. We can wait. Certainly until you are out of office, Mr. Secretary. In the meantime, we can still collateralize what is here in the mine."

Now Stephanos did appear worried. The basic sense of their words registered on his face. It *was* their gold after all. Or it had been all those years ago. And even if the form of their government had changed, it was a government that was acknowledged as the legitimate successor to the previous regimes. As far as the United States was concerned, the present government in China was officially recognized and had standing to sue in a U.S. court. He turned to Behr.

"What about it, counselor? Can they state a claim?"

Behr stepped forward, assuming the grave, judicial expression he once used on juries. "Conversion—to the best of my recollection—would be the right action to plead. Conversion basically means that someone has taken something in your possession and converted it into their own."

"We didn't take that gold," Stephanos protested.

Behr turned to him. "Well, Mr. Secretary, an action in conversion also may lie against someone who has merely *detained* property against the wishes of the original owner or possessor. So on a purely academic level . . . there is an argument to be made that there has been a conversion."

"Be sure that we will press that claim—"

"However," Behr held up his palm against Jin Qing's interruption, "in order to make your claim you have to plead it correctly in your suit. And in order to properly plead a case in conversion in the courts of Pennsylvania, which have jurisdiction *in rem* as they say, you must adequately *identify* the property you claim as your own."

Stephanos leaned toward him.

"My understanding," Behr continued, the growing smile invisible beneath the gas mask, "is that the gold lost by China, if any, was cast in standard twenty-eight-pound gold bars which each bore the imperial seal of the Qing Dynasty. I haven't seen any gold bars like that in here. But if you can find any such bars in this mine, you will certainly be able to state a claim in the Court of Common Pleas for which relief can be granted."

It was Stephanos' turn to laugh. The big man tore off his gas mask and boomed loudly. He marched over to Behr, clapping him firmly on the shoulder.

"You know, Behr, sometimes it *is* useful to have a lawyer around."

☆ ☆ ☆

It was over. In her own mind, at least, she conceded defeat.

She flicked at the edge of the capsule with her tongue. She had snuck it into her mouth before their surrender. She had ordered the others not to. There was really nothing left that their suicides might hide. But she was different. She had years of operational information in her head and only a vague claim on diplomatic immunity. She would only get out of the United States with a fight, or some kind of swap. But after this defeat, her own people might not want her back. Might not be willing to exchange for an agent without a future.

And she didn't particularly want to go back. There was nothing in Beijing for her now except disgrace . . . perhaps a trial. There was no going home, that was certain.

But she did want to keep her secrets. And the risk that they might be dislodged by American interrogation had her thinking about the cyanide pill nestled in her cheek. She could do it right now. While they were chanting points of law. They wouldn't even notice till she pitched to the floor.

The tunnel was clear of smoke. They were all taking off their gas masks. She didn't want to do that. But now one of the Americans was unstrapping it for her. Pulling it from her head, gently tugging the loose hairs from where they had tangled in the clasps.

Should she do it now?

Jin Qing let herself slide down the wall of the tunnel. She sat in a small heap, clutching the tourniquet around her arm, her side against the wall, her knees pressed against her chest.

She only looked up once.

He was staring directly at her. She dropped her eyes again, but it was no use. He had seen.

"Jenny?"

Harry Zhang hadn't lost that flat, Midwestern voice she remembered. "Jenny is that you?"

She smiled thinly but did not speak.

"Who's that, Dad?"

Jin Qing watched Harry hesitate for a moment. Watched him think all the thoughts she had gone through with respect to their daughter. She watched him draw a different conclusion.

"Jesus, honey, I don't know how to tell you except that . . . this woman here . . . Jenny we called her . . . well, Kristina, she's your mother."

Kristina Zhang stood stunned. Jin Qing saw her daughter's incomprehension, wanted to reach out to her, comfort her, but somehow she didn't dare.

There hadn't been a reaction yet. No joy or revulsion had registered. Only shock. Jin Qing looked to her daughter's troubled face. She could see herself reflected in Kristina's eyes, a pathetic figure, thin and huddled on the floor. She saw Kristina abruptly turn her gaze to her still-gaping father and then move over to another man. The one who argued law. He was a handsome one with intelligent eyes, the one Jin Qing had heard about—with the plane, the professor. She approved of him now. She could see his devotion to Kristina as well as his strength, though pride, she thought, will one day get in his way. Still, Kristina should keep her hold on this man.

If only Jin Qing could advise her.

The professor was gesturing now, pointing ever so slightly with a lifted chin in her direction. Kristina's eyes questioned. But the professor gestured again. This time tilting his head for emphasis.

It took a moment. Then Kristina took a step. Then another. And soon Jin Qing beheld the vision of her daughter standing over her, looking down through a tangle of dirty hair. She saw the trepidation in her eyes, saw them soften. She watched as the girl slowly bent to kneel directly before her. Jin Qing looked into Kristina's eyes, but did not see what she feared most. She saw no hate in those eyes, only questions.

Now she felt her shame. She felt the weight of her failure as a mother pressing down unbearably. She lowered her head and tried to push further into the wall. She wanted to be smaller, for no one to notice. She wanted to bite down hard and have all this pain just go away.

She sensed a movement and looked up to see Kristina reaching out to gently place a warm hand on hers.

Jin Qing cradled the capsule between her teeth. She did not deserve her daughter's forgiveness, she knew. But she did not deserve death's either. And death was the easy choice.

Jin Qing turned her head away. She made her choice. And spit the capsule onto the floor of the mine.